Age of the Dryad

Book Two of the Dark Oak Chronicles

Jacob Sannox

Cover by Tarzian Book Design

Maps © Arkolina – www.arkolina.com from original artwork conceived by the author and illustrated by Arkolina.

Typeset by Polgarus Studio – www.polgarusstudio.com

For Sam Batson.
You changed my life.

Age of the Dryad is the second book of The Dark Oak Chronicles. If you haven't read the first book, Dark Oak, I'd recommend that you do before you get started on Age of the Dryad, as it's a continuing story.

Jacob Sannox

Acknowledgements

Thank you to all my first readers.
Sami, Anna (who also has to put up with the entire process), Ben
(who has read this book more times than me) and my parents, whose
comments are always invaluable!

THE OLD CONTINENT

THE SOUTH CONTINENT

The Butterfly Isle

Halflight
Hold

Elaris • Narra

Brookmouth

Long Isle

MAIN
ISLE

Princefall

THE ISLES

Chapter One

The Butterfly Isle

The Dryads were stalking her, mostly unseen, but sometimes appearing as silent sentinels who predicted her path and appeared ahead of her. For the most part, Rowan paid them no heed, but when her mood was low or the day's toil wore her down, she would rail at them and set about them with her fists. Of course, she did the Dryads no harm, and when she realized they would not attack her in turn, Rowan used beating them as catharsis, ignoring the ragged mess she made of her hands.

Days had passed since the ship's crew had been killed and her youngest son, Declan, taken beneath the waves by a Naiad before her eyes, and she had set out alone in one of the ship's boats. She had struggled with the oars until she finally drew close to land. Rowan had trudged, bereft, up a stony beach of the Butterfly Isle, and up on to the cliffs of the unfamiliar island. She kept the crashing sea, now far below, to her right, and the dense forest to her left as she walked, hoping to circle round the coast and find some port where she would beg for aid before setting out on the far longer journey in search of her eldest son, Callum, whom she had left on the Old Continent at Oystercatcher Bay when he refused to leave his father, Morrick.

The first of the Dryads had appeared to her as she stepped into the woods to pass water. Rowan froze, seeing only two ominous human shapes ahead of her in the darkness. She had managed to call out to them, but they merely exchanged a glance and she watched, mouth agape, as they both stepped backward, seeming to disappear into the trunks of trees.

She decided she could wait a little longer before urinating, and walked on.

After that, the Dryads were Rowan's constant companions. She felt their presence, even when she could not see or hear them. She tried to speak to them many times, but they would give her no answer, sometimes sending her flying into a fury. They were human-shaped, shedding a skin of bark when first they formed from tree trunks or dropped from branches overhead, revealing what resembled a body of polished wood that seemed to mould itself into their chosen forms before Rowan's eyes; imitating clothing, weaponry and, last of all, facial features, or, at least, carved versions of them. Vines or leaves grew from their scalps like hair, and she had seen them thrust out roots from their hands, extending their fingers, to wrap around fallen trees and haul them out of her path. They helped in other ways, once fending off a wolf pack and sometimes bringing her berries or nuts, but only after she was weary from searching for sustenance. Much of the time, they were nowhere to be seen.

When twilight came each day, and the sun sank into the distant ocean, Rowan would sit with her back against a tree and scan the horizon for lights until her eyelids grew heavy and sleep took her. When she woke in the night to the sound of wolves howling or a storm picking up, she would pull her cloak about her and take comfort in the certain knowledge that the silent Dryads were watching her. She could not be sure, but Rowan felt these strange creatures would not let her come to any harm. Nevertheless, her skin prickled at the thought of their sinister, emotionless faces, for she could not discern their intentions or their motives.

Day after day she trailed through the woods, until one morning, perhaps an hour after waking, she came upon a small cottage set back from the cliff edge, nestled in a nook of the treeline. A plume of smoke rose from the chimney.

Rowan broke into a run, her eyes threatening tears of relief. She rounded the south side of the cottage, which was devoid of windows, and, as she did so, she skirted round the low stone walls of a square pen that contained several grunting pigs. Rowan slowed as she approached the cottage door, but she had been spotted, and the door swung inward before she reached it.

'Hold it right there,' said the woman who now blocked the way into the cottage. Rowan skittered to a halt, both hands held up to placate the woman.

'Thank the Forest!' she said, but her words were incomprehensible as she began to weep. The woman in the doorway scowled at her and poked her head out to look around. Rowan collapsed towards her and, probably on instinct, the woman took her in an embrace. The whole of Rowan's body heaved as she sobbed, and the woman held her tight.

'Are you hurt? What's happened?' said the woman. It was no use though. Rowan could not calm herself enough to speak clearly.

The woman sighed and continued to look around, but saw nothing to concern her. Reluctantly, she ushered Rowan inside, turning away from the door as she did so.

'Don't take on so. I . . . ' but the woman's words were cut short, and she let go of Rowan, who wheeled away as she was released.

A living root curled itself about the woman's neck and hurled her backwards off her feet. Rowan shrieked and groped to catch the woman, but she was not fast enough.

When Rowan turned she saw that the woman was being carried away from the cottage. She was clawing at a root that wound tightly around her neck and held her aloft, even as it drew back towards the Dryad who had thrust it out from its open palm, an extension of its body. Aside from the root, the Dryad did not move at all and was barely perceptible as alive. It said nothing, and it made no sound.

The Dryad paused only to look the struggling, wide-eyed woman up and down, like a fisherman examining his catch, then it turned to look Rowan directly in the eye and wrenched the woman sideways, hurling her over the cliff edge. She made no sound as she fell, her neck already broken by the violent motion.

Rowan screamed and dropped to her knees, sobbing. The Dryad creaked as it walked silently towards her, but Rowan paid it no heed, knowing there was nothing she could do to fend off the creature. She had no need of fear, though, as it walked past her and ducked into the cottage.

A few seconds later, Rowan jumped as the sound of splintering wood and smashing furniture spilled from the doorway. She checked over her shoulder to see if the Dryad was coming, then, satisfied that it was busy with its destruction, she ran to the cliff. Rowan crawled to the edge and peered over. The ocean beat against the high cliffs in a fury of water and foam, but there was no sign of the woman's fallen form. She could not have survived, Rowan knew, and she turned her back on the sea to wait for the Dryad to emerge. After all, there was nowhere to run. A last cascade of shattered wood and broken pots flew out of the door, and then the Dryad appeared back outside. It looked at Rowan, nodded once and marched towards the trees.

'Why?' she screamed after it, and it stopped moving. It began to turn its head slowly towards her without adjusting its neck until the angle looked quite unnatural. When it spoke, its mouth opening looked like the splitting of a bent branch, green fronds hanging over the shallow cavity.

'Dark Oak commands it,' the Dryad croaked, and its whole form shook as though the effort of speaking had been traumatic.

'Who is Dark Oak?' she demanded. 'That woman didn't do anything to deserve death!' was all she could think of to say. 'Why do you haunt my footsteps? What are you?'

The Dryad turned its body towards her, and it looked down at the ground as though trying to remember something for a moment, then met her gaze as it spoke again as though repeating something learnt by rote.

'There will be no comfort. No solace. No home. No company. No relief. No respite.' It creaked, rocking its head in an eerie fashion from side to side, never breaking eye contact.

'There will be no escape,' it said, and with that, the Dryad turned and disappeared into the trees.

Rowan could not manage a reply. She watched the creature disappear.

She sat by the cliff edge while she recovered her breath and her heart rate slowed, her hair whipping in the wind. Rowan once more looked down into the tumultuous ocean and scoured the base of the cliffs for the woman, but she could see nothing. The sea had claimed the corpse.

It took some time for Rowan to find the energy and inclination to dust herself off and resume her journey, but eventually anger replaced the sadness, fear and self-pity. The killing had been an injustice, after all. Whatever unknown grudge these Dryads had against her, the woman had played no part in it, and now she was dead. Rowan seethed as she picked her way through the debris strewn outside the cottage. As she passed the pen, her mind turned to practical considerations, and she pondered whether the Dryads would allow her to slaughter the pigs for food.

The interior of the cottage was in ruins, the furniture reduced to splinters, and the remains of a stew dripped down one of the walls. Rowan saw a cradle in the corner in the room, long disused but perfectly made-up, and the sight of it made her light-headed, as she remembered that of her daughter, Bracken, whom she had drowned in the Whiteflow to save her sons. She braced herself against a wall, leaning against it as she took in the details of the dead woman's life.

Rowan found her strength once more and set about searching the cottage for anything of use, disgusted with herself for scavenging and thereby profiting from the woman's death. But she had to survive if she was to be reunited with Callum, and so she searched on, gathering up some articles of clothing, a few implements and a sharp knife. Rowan was making her way out when she found a crude necklace amongst the rubble on the floor, and this she fastened around her neck to bear with her the memory of the nameless lady who had lost her life simply for taking Rowan in an embrace.

Rowan pulled the door to the cottage shut as she left and let loose the pigs from their pen, as it was clear that the woman had lived alone. She could not bear the thought of spilling their blood after the morning's slaughter, and there was no sense in letting the animals starve to death.

She returned to the cliff edge and sat with her legs dangling over the drop, leaning back on her hands so that she could stare out at the sea for a while. She did not know which direction she should go or whether she would be allowed to seek aid should she find a settlement, but knew that either way, she must press on. Rowan sat up, refastened her hair in a bun, as she always did before approaching a day's work or, perhaps, like a knight might adjust his armour before continuing his quest.

'Rowan,' said a voice on the wind.

She started and shuffled back from the cliff edge, alarmed at how she had jumped so close to the edge, fearful of falling. She turned to see who had spoken. Who could know her in this place, so far from home?

'Rowan.' The strange voice was coming from beyond the treeline.

'Who's there?' she called back, shrill and trembling as she stood up.

'Rowan.'

She took a step closer, turning her ear towards the sound. It was a man's voice, low and rumbling. Her skin turned to gooseflesh and something in her stirred. The voice was familiar and yet she could not say why.

'Who's there?' she called again, and this time the tremor was gone, her voice assertive. She steeled herself and drew her new knife then stalked towards the trees.

'Show yourself, if you are a friend,' she called as she strode forward.

Hanging fronds and twigs stroked her hair as she ducked under the low branches of the trees, flicking strands loose from the bun. She scanned all around and turned on the spot with the knife held out, but she could see and hear nothing.

'Show yourself,' said Rowan.

A loud laugh sounded from back the way she came. It echoed all around her then faded until it became indistinguishable from the creaking trees, swaying branches and rustling leaves.

Rowan shivered and shifted her grip on the knife as she stood ready to meet whoever or whatever it was that knew and mocked her. An unpleasant creeping sensation ran down her spine, setting her a-shivering. Her skin turned to goose flesh as she stood alone in the woods, watched by some unknown tormentor.

Nothing happened.

After a time standing ready to pounce, she could no longer stand the tension and decided she must move on, disembodied voices be damned. She pondered which way to go, but there were no ready answers. She did not know Butterfly Isle, did not know the location of its ports and towns. Skirting the coast had seemed to make sense, but for now, Rowan decided she wanted to get out of sight. She abandoned her route along the cliff-tops and set off into the forest.

Dark Oak, King of the Dryads, once Morrick of the Hinterland, watched his wife as she disappeared among the trees.

As soon as Rowan was out of sight, Dark Oak stepped out from a birch tree at the edge of the clearing and took avatar in approximation of his old human form. He shed his skin of bark and the polished wood beneath took shape. Unlike Riark before him, Dark Oak's eyes and facial features were sculpted to near perfection, as though they were a study in fine carving. His body took on the shape of Morrick's old clothing and a wooden hand-axe hung at his belt.

Dark Oak began to walk after Rowan, and, as he did so, he held out his right hand, fingers splayed. The surface of his palm swelled outwards so that it looked as though he held a square block of wood in his hand. That block began to elongate into a length of wood, and Dark Oak gripped it with his fingers, though it was still part of his hand. The wooden handle reached the desired length, and the head of an axe grew and shaped itself from one end until Dark Oak carried a wooden imitation of the old long-axe he had once carried into battle.

Dark Oak brushed the palm of his other hand against the trunk of each tree as he passed by, and in so doing he saw all that the Dryads could see and knew all that they knew, all of those who dwelt within the trees. As for those who were disconnected from the forest, keeping watch over humanity, they were isolated from his perception, and it caused paranoia to grow in him, like a jealous lover speculating on the activities of his heart's affection. He paused with his hand upon a fir tree and closed his eyes, making clear his will to all who felt his presence throughout the world. He opened his eyes and moved onward through the forest, heedless of the pine needles and spindly branches that raked across his wooden eyes now that he no longer had an instinct to blink.

Dark Oak marched through his realm, ever-watchful for Rowan as he advanced. He stopped occasionally to listen for the sound of her feet snapping twigs then followed her when he had best guessed her path.

Dark Oak could have stepped into a tree and appeared ahead of Rowan, but he enjoyed the sensation of hunting her, feeling grim glee in knowing she flew from him, the woman he had fought so hard to get home to, only to find she had betrayed him with Captain Jacob Lynch. He imagined that this was how an eagle might feel, soaring above an open mountainside as a hare attempted to evade it with nowhere to hide.

As he stalked after Rowan, Dark Oak lowered his brow and a grin spread across his face, cracking the perfect surface of the grain. He had felt powerful since his rebirth as a Dryad, and it spilled out of him, showing on his face.

He leant against yet another fir tree and perceived that his people had received his message and were gathering. He gave new instructions with a thought, and before stepping into the trunk and disappearing, he called out her name once more.

'Rowan.'

Dark Oak laughed as he stepped into the tree, and yet somewhere in the back of his mind, he knew that his malevolence towards her was misplaced. His victory felt hollow.

Rowan heard Dark Oak call her name and quickened her pace, her eyes darting about to pick out places for her feet, stepping delicately between roots as she ran. The precision of her fast movements took their toll, and she was very soon out of breath. Rowan forced herself to continue and veered away to the right, attempting to throw off anyone or anything that might be following.

What were these creatures that tormented her, that knew her name and kept her safe, yet would not allow her to find any solace in her grief?

Though she had dreamed of The Isles all her life, there had been no maps of them in the Hinterland. The Isles were settled by those who had fled the Old Continent a thousand years ago, after her people's ancestors had betrayed the rest of humanity and allowed the Dark Lord, Awgren, to march his troops through the Hinterland unopposed, allowing his Creatures of the Devising to strike where the defenders were weakest.

To her knowledge, Rowan was the first from the Hinterland ever to set foot upon any of the islands. It was something she had hoped for all her days, and now that her wish had come true, she hoped in earnest to escape them.

While she and Captain Jacob Lynch fled from the Hinterland after Awgren's defeat, he had told her many tales of The Isles, Stragglers' Drift and of The Folly, but if he had mentioned their precise geography, it had washed over her, absorbed as she was with imagining pretty cottages and free lands where she could start a new life with her boys, Callum and Declan.

Pretty cottages such as the one I have recently picked clean, Rowan thought. Once more the word 'scavenger' ran through her mind.

She walked on throughout the day, lost in the woods, her senses heightened, frightened that at any time a Dryad could appear before her. It was a relief when her feet found a well-worn path cutting through the forest. Rowan looked all the way to the right and all the way to the left along the road, but it curved in both directions so that the view was restricted.

Which way to go?

Rowan thought veering right would take her back towards the coast, but Rowan did not much rate her own reckoning. The path to the left appeared to widen and her heart leapt at the prospect of it becoming a road which might lead to a settlement.

Rowan sat down beside the path cross-legged and rested a while. She sighed, releasing the tension in her shoulders. Her dehydrated lips shrank back to reveal her teeth. It had been several hours since she had last found a stream. Rowan delved in her pack and withdrew a waterskin she had salvaged from the ship that had borne her to The Isles from the Old Continent, now floating abandoned in the inner sea to the south of the Butterfly Isle, the crew presumably killed by the same Naiads who had taken her son. The same sort of creatures who had plucked baby Bracken's lifeless body from her arms as she struggled to stay afloat in the Whiteflow, back in the Hinterland. She still did not understand why she had been allowed to survive, or why Declan had been taken in such a peculiar manner, but dwelling too long on Declan's demise so filled her with grief that she pushed the thoughts aside, forming walls in her mind, partitioning herself off from all that was bad, as she had done before.

Rowan poured water into her mouth, cold against her teeth, and swilled it around her mouth before swallowing. There was no taste like water when you had been deprived of it for longer than usual, she thought, better than wine.

Rowan ate a little salted meat and, though she knew that night was coming and that she should move on, she lay back on the path and closed her eyes for a moment.

Just a brief rest, she told herself.

The screech of an owl shocked Rowan awake, and she shrieked. All was dark about her. She lay upon the path breathing hard, with her heart thrumming like a twanged bow string. Rowan sat up and looked about in a panic, but the dense canopy prevented whatever light the moon and stars provided from reaching her. She was encased within a leafy catacomb and some animal instinct awoke in her, demanding that she escape. She felt around her for the path and, reasonably sure of the direction, she began to walk with hands outstretched.

It did her no good. She tripped on a divot and yipped like a whipped pup. It was, she thought, her night for crying out. She cursed aloud and moved on slower.

'Rowan,' said the disembodied voice in the darkness.

If Dark Oak had expected her to quail and quake at the sound, perhaps curling up into a ball like a hedgehog under a pile of leaves, it was his turn to be out in his reckoning.

'All right, that's enough!' Rowan roared. She drew her knife and widened her stance.

'What kind of coward lurks in the dark taunting a woman alone?' she said. No reply.

'Who are you? What do you want from me? What have I done to offend you so?'

No reply.

'Fine.' Rowan laughed, 'Lurk on! You're naught but an idiot boy peeping on the womenfolk washing at the river, a leper watching a feast from afar. Curse you and yours!'

'Ours,' said the voice, and it chilled her bones.

'What?' she demanded through bared teeth, eyes wide, but seeing nothing. 'What did you say, the Forest damn you!'

A creaking laugh rose up from behind her, and the trees took up the call until the sound was deafening. She felt she could scarcely stand it.

'Laugh then,' she whispered, not caring if the owner of the voice heard, 'but remember what they say about a woman scorned.'

The laughter died abruptly. She heard a twig snap behind her, and she turned on her heels. Strong hands grasped her upper arms, and she could make out the outline of a man. She struggled, but the grip was that of a tree clinging to a hillside.

'Don't,' she said. Nothing happened. Dark Oak held her in his grip and though she could not see his eyes in the darkness, she felt them upon her, that whoever it was both regarded and considered her. A tingling feeling swept up from the nape of her neck, something akin to pleasure.

Rowan gritted her teeth and rammed upwards with her knee, hoping to hit the man in the groin. Instead it connected with solid wood, and she gasped in pain.

Dark Oak inclined his head and continued to stare at her then he leant slowly forward, and she felt smooth wood brush her cheek as he kissed her. Rowan forgot the pain in her knee as she realised the man had no breath. She tried to speak, but was overcome with the sudden fear that she would be raped.

She froze.

And then the strange sterile kisses began to trace her jaw and down her neck.

Rowan knew him then.

'Morrick?' she whispered, comprehending but not believing.

Immediately Dark Oak dropped her and drew back, but without hesitation she advanced upon him.

'Is it you?' she asked, and heard herself snapping impatiently.

It must be him, she thought in one ridiculous moment, *because I sound like his wife.*

Dark Oak took another step back and his avatar almost disappeared from view in the gloom.

'Morrick?' she asked, insistent then.

The owl screeched again, and Rowan felt as though she were trapped in a dream, not knowing what to make of this thing before her that she felt, no . . . that she knew . . . was her husband. They had parted in anger, and yet now that their children were gone, that Lynch was gone . . .

But apologies had always been loath to leave Rowan's lips.

'Fine.' She turned and stormed to the left, hoping her feet would find the path.

'Rowan,' said Dark Oak and this time the word was soft, almost pleading, rather than a taunt. But the walls were building in her mind and heart once more. She folded her arms across her chest and, heedless of the risk of walking headlong into a branch, she lowered her brow, striding onward.

Dark Oak watched her go, and as roots grew from his feet, delving into the soil, he could feel her every footfall through the grass. His first unaccountable instinct was to follow, but, less inclined to act on the memory of habitual impulse now that his brain was gone, he decided not to do so. There was no sense in it. He began to regret ever coming to see her, now that tormenting her had turned to wanting her, and so, stepping back into the woods, Dark Oak returned to more pressing matters, leaving his people to watch over the mother of his children.

The Folly

Far away in the south and east, the Maw Keep looked out over the ruins of The Folly to the south and across burgeoning new forests to the north-east in the previously barren lands. Dark Oak wound his way up the vines that climbed the high towers, and emerged as flowing sap to form a puddle upon the flagstones of the wide gallery of the throne room where Queen Cathryn and Lord Lachlan had once sat.

Dark Oak's human avatar rose from the sap, initially as new green flesh, then taking its accustomed appearance as clothes formed from the new wood which darkened and smoothed. Black ivy hung from his head, and the imitation of the 'T' for traitor which had once been branded across Morrick's face appeared on Dark Oak's cheek.

Rank upon rank of Dryads turned towards him, some of the humans who had died since Dark Oak had turned against humanity, now reborn to the forest. He bowed his head in silence as he climbed the steps to the dais and sat down upon Queen Cathryn's throne.

Whiteflow, formerly Morrick's baby daughter, Bracken, and his son, Seaborn, who had been Declan before he was dragged beneath the sea by his sister, coursed around the dais like a shallow moat, their heads occasionally rising above the surface. His son, Callum, now the Dryad, Red Maple, stood behind the throne.

'Father,' said Red Maple, bowing his head to Dark Oak.

A young Dryad, newly dead as a human, his spirit reborn within his Mother Tree, stepped out from the ranks, and Dark Oak watched as it moved to stand before Lachlan's empty throne. It reached down and caressed the now ragged velvet cushion as though it stirred a memory.

Dark Oak stood and laid a hand upon the Dryad's shoulder and the grains of the two beings flowed into one another. They shared a moment and the Dryad, broad in stature, his face shrouded by a mossy beard, drew back with bowed head. Yet he never took his eyes from Lachlan's empty throne.

Dark Oak returned to his seat and regarded the Dryads before him.

His cheeks jerked and in so doing, his lips split apart, though there was no mouth behind. Roots sprung out from his fingertips and spread across the throne room, finding and merging with the roots of all the Dryads there present.

Soundlessly, though he moved his lips as if speaking, Dark Oak conveyed his instructions, and the Dryads knew his mind. Their roots formed a carpet across the throne room gallery, sharing understanding and yet, vitally, they kept up the pretence of humanity, so recently lost. He had denied them their place in the forest, forced them to take avatar so that the calming influence of the older Dryads would not hold sway. They retained much of their humanity but none of the weaknesses, thanks to their new-found forms.

'We are the firstborn after revolution,' they came to understand through his manipulation. 'We remember many instincts and impulses. We have misdirected prejudices and lingering affections. Humans we were, but now we are Dryad, and our king will guide us into our new lives. He will teach us of our duty to the forest.'

Dark Oak saw both the faces of their loved ones and those who had maligned them. He knew of their suffering and understood their passions. He knew all that they knew. He took all of their memories and desires, along with the associated emotions and bound them anew with his own needs and imperatives, mingling them with grain, root, leaf and bark. He bade them examine their former humanity with the objectivity that their new natures afforded them. He gave orders, and they considered his commands.

There would be balance in the world, at last. No more domination, not by humans nor the likes of the creatures of Awgren's Devising. The forests, the rivers, the skies and the earth would stand watch and maintain the peace.

The young, bearded Dryad stepped out once more, his brow furrowed as he looked at Cathryn's throne. A ripple ran through his solid torso. A mouth formed on his face, and he spoke aloud.

'I remember a slender figure clad in white sitting upon the throne, regal and beautiful,' he said.

Dark Oak turned his attention to the young Dryad, and invaded his mind, changing the image of Cathryn into that of a Dryad, feminine and full of grace, growing from her womanly form into a sapling tree. The bearded

Dryad looked on it with admiration, but still he frowned.

Dark Oak continued to toy with the newborn Dryads and, cut off from the forests as they were, he found he could indeed harness their memories and emotions so that he could convince them as he conveyed the new order of things.

When the council drew to a close and Dark Oak released them, the Dryads filed out of the throne room, thudding down the stone stairs and towards the young forests of Tayne.

Far to the north in Stragglers' Drift, Queen Cathryn lay sleeping on the forest floor, wrapped in a cloak. Dreams troubled her, and she turned on to her side, talking in her sleep. The low sound was enough to wake Aldwyn from his slumber.

He whispered to her, telling her she was safe and not to worry, and the queen settled once more without waking.

Chapter Two

Stragglers' Drift

The forest was like none Aldwyn had ever encountered. Sometimes, as he and Cathryn walked between the trunks, he felt that the trees were approximating a city, not in the fashion of The Folly, but vaguely reminiscent of an architectural design. Archways and corridors lined with pillars formed cathedrals, but of living trees that watched and listened. And, Aldwyn could have sworn, that whispered to one another.

Cathryn walked ahead of him, but she showed scant regard for the marvel. Her eyes were fixed ahead of her, and she strode forward in the direction of one of the wisps of smoke they had seen from the shore.

'Cathryn,' Aldwyn called.

She stopped walking and turned to face him, eyebrows raised in a question.

'We should stop here for the night.'

The queen shook her head.

'No – there's still light left in the day.' She turned back and began to walk.

'Cathryn.'

She sighed. 'I can keep going for a while yet.'

'But I cannot,' Aldwyn said in earnest.

Once more she stopped and turned to look at him. For a moment she appeared annoyed and then, seeing his tired, open face, she softened and nodded.

'Very well. I suppose I am a little tired.' She gave him a weak smile.

Aldwyn dropped his pack and set about gathering fallen branches and dry scrub to get a fire going, while Cathryn considered their rations.

It did not take long to get a small fire going with the aid of Aldwyn's tinderbox. The queen and the duke sat on opposite sides of the fire, but a light breeze blew smoke in Cathryn's direction. It stung her eyes, and she scrunched them closed, rubbing them with her fingertips. Aldwyn watched for a second then shifted over and patted the ground beside him.

Cathryn scrabbled round to sit beside him. They sat in silence, staring into the flames while they ate. She tucked her knees up to her chest and wrapped her arms around them. Aldwyn caught Cathryn shivering out of the corner of his eye, despite her cloak. He unbuckled his own and stood to wrap it around her shoulders.

She looked up at him and smiled. Aldwyn sat beside her once more, just a little closer. The flames roared away from them, enraged by the breeze. Now it was Aldwyn's turn to shiver. Cathryn cast him a glance and laughed. She looked around her, as though someone might see, then shifted towards him and slung half of the cloak around him.

They huddled together in the dark, shoulder to shoulder and yet with a tension in their bodies, unwilling to relax into one another.

Darkness enveloped them so that they became like moths settled by a single candle within a windowless hall. The crackling of the damp wood punctuated the steady rustling of the leaves above and around them.

Aldwyn started to speak, but then shifted where he sat and said nothing.

'Aldwyn?' asked Cathryn.

'It's nothing,' he said.

She did not reply, but she hunkered down and rested her head against his shoulder. He held his breath for a moment then slowly lowered his cheek against her sweet-smelling, raven-dark hair. They both closed their eyes.

In the morning they awoke with stiff necks, and when they continued their march, it was at a slower pace, walking side by side.

'What do you think has happened here?' she asked, then added, 'I have a dread feeling in my heart.'

Aldwyn sighed. Cathryn's fleet had come north to deal with Lord Linwood only to find his land, Stragglers' Drift, covered with new forest. There had been no sign of the populace yet, save for plumes of smoke within the trees, which the queen had insisted they investigate.

'It seems things have gone awry for Lord Linwood. I can only assume that King Riark and his Dryads have acted in our absence,' said Aldwyn.

'What do you think we will find as we venture inland?' asked Cathryn.

'I cannot say. You alone have spoken with Riark. What are your thoughts?' he replied.

'If Riark can be taken at his word, he is not concerned with vengeance. I cannot account for this spreading of the forest,' she said, looking all about her. 'Linwood must have crossed a line if Riark has carried out his promise to keep him in check. But as to the cities and the folk of the Drift, I cannot guess their fates.' She stood, stretching to crack her back and exercise her neck.

'I cannot understand why Riark does not answer my summons,' she said.

Droplets of rain spattered them as they journeyed, beating a steady rhythm on the leaves above them. Both Cathryn and Aldwyn walked with furrowed brows as they turned the events over in their mind.

Later that day, Cathryn and Aldwyn caught sight of movement in the trees ahead of them and before they could react, a shout went up. A company of Linwood's soldiers ran towards them, weapons drawn. The queen and her duke unsheathed their own.

A tall, broad man clad in mail and wielding a longsword, a shield slung across his back, led the soldiers through the trees. He held up his fist upon seeing them and called out to his company.

'Hold!' He stood before them, a little way off, his black hair shaved at the sides, but longer on top; an imposing figure, powerfully built and ready to act.

'Identify yourself,' the man demanded, but there was no anger in his voice. Other soldiers, clad in the mail of the rank and file came up behind them, but he bade them halt.

'Peace,' said Cathryn, and she sheathed her sword, motioning for Aldwyn to put up his blade.

'Your names,' said the soldier.

'I am Cathryn, and this is Aldwyn. Good morrow to you.'

The man in armour sheathed his own sword, much to Aldwyn's relief.

'Cathryn and Aldwyn?' the soldier laughed. 'And I'm Awgren! Tolucan is my name. Pardon our reaction, but there has been much mischief in this part of the world of late.'

It occurred to Aldwyn that their station and power meant very little outside their usual domain. He suddenly felt exposed and foolish for undertaking this journey alone. After all, what were these men to think of them? Anyone could claim to be a queen or a duke. In the soldier's place, would he believe such a chance encounter could occur?

Probably not, he thought.

'Tell me, to whom do you owe your allegiance?' Aldwyn asked.

Tolucan looked both Cathryn and Aldwyn up and down, taking in their fine garb and the quality of their equipment, notably his gaze lingering on their steel blades.

'My allegiance?' he asked, standing with arms folded across his broad chest.

'Aye. Whom do you serve?' asked Aldwyn, standing straight and sheathing his sword. He clasped his hands behind his back and looked down the length of his nose at Tolucan.

The soldier appeared puzzled.

'I serve in the ninth regiment, commanded by Lord Brandreth,' said Tolucan.

'But where do your loyalties lie?' asked Aldwyn, scrutinising the soldier's tanned, scarred face. His nose had been broken more than once, giving the impression of a brawler, but Aldwyn saw intelligence and a thoughtful nature in the man's chestnut-coloured eyes.

Tolucan hesitated and when he spoke, it was clear he was choosing his words carefully.

'I see that the two of you are high-born and perhaps qualified to speak of such things. Allegiances and loyalties are a little above my concerns. I am a soldier, and I serve in Lord Linwood's army. That's all I know. I go where I'm sent, and I do as I'm told.'

Aldwyn smiled, feeling somewhat the fool.

'And if you were to make a guess, to whom would you say Lord Linwood's allegiance lies?' he asked.

'I wouldn't wish to speak for the duke, sir, especially not to strangers. The two of you are plainly not from the Drift. You still have not told me your true names,' said Tolucan, and Aldwyn thought the soldier was remembering his duty.

Aldwyn exchanged a glance with Cathryn. She nodded, and Aldwyn turned back at Tolucan.

'I am Lord Aldwyn, and the lady before you is Queen Cathryn,' he said.

Tolucan's mouth dropped a little open, and the crowd of soldiers began to murmur.

'It is true,' said Cathryn, her voice loud and commanding as she stepped towards the company, 'but being professional soldiers with quick wits, I am sure your instincts tell you to challenge the duke's assertion.'

She brought out her seal and presented it to the soldier. She asked Aldwyn to do the same.

'These are all that we have by way of proof for now, but were you to come with us back to the coast, you would see the Royal Fleet there assembled and awaiting our return.'

Tolucan bowed his head slightly, and Aldwyn noticed his cheeks redden. The man raised his eyes to meet Cathryn's.

'I hope you will forgive my hesitance,' he said finally. 'I have a duty to be watchful and, though I do not call either of you a liar, I must verify you are who you say you are.'

'I would expect nothing less of one of Lord Brandreth's captains, Tolucan,' replied Cathryn. 'He is a canny commander, and the Ninth Regiment did me great service upon the Field of the Scarlet Grass.' She clasped her hands before her. 'What will satisfy you?'

Tolucan thought for a time, and Aldwyn eyed the rest of the soldiers, many of whom still held their weapons ready.

'I think perhaps we should do as you suggested,' said Tolucan. 'I will be satisfied at the sight of the fleet and your folks' response to you and your station, lady. These matters aside, something is amiss in the Drift, as these here trees attest, and it would not be wise to continue without making full use of all your strength of arms – our enemies are perilous.'

'Enemies? We have only lately arrived in the Drift and found things changed upon our arrival. What has happened here?' said Aldwyn.

Tolucan stood to attention as he made his report, and Aldwyn noticed a dirk hanging from the soldier's belt for the first time.

'We were posted with the shore defences, Your Grace. One night the ground beneath my tent erupted even as I sat at my desk. Young saplings grew up faster than I could move. My chair overturned and I was thrown to the ground. I remember scrabbling out just as living trees ripped my tent up, hauling up the stakes as they grew. The same was happening all around. A new forest was shooting up about us, its spreading branches heedless of the destruction they caused. I saw many men carried up high along with the remains of tents. Fearing what would come, I set about mustering my folk,' said Tolucan. He paused, and Aldwyn saw him lick his lips before he continued.

'That's when they came – the men from the trees. They were swift and deadly to any who took up arms against them. We lost many in that assault, though it lasted but a short time. They killed all who opposed them, and they tore down the palisade. I called the retreat and gathered all I could. I thought it best to make my way to Stragglers' End for orders. We've met and joined with others who were heading from there to the shore. The word is that all settlements have been cast down by the men from the trees and that Lord Linwood's army is defeated. In truth, we knew not what to do for the best, but making inland was all I could think to do.'

Aldwyn nodded, but Cathryn spoke first,

'You've done well. You have my thanks and praise for saving so many.'

Tolucan bowed his head in acknowledgement.

'I fear strength of arms will do no good if all you say is true,' said Aldwyn. 'It would be wise to return to the shore. I am loath to continue without speaking more with Riark,' said Cathryn. She turned back to Tolucan.

'March with us and soon you will be satisfied.' She smiled, and Aldwyn noted her features softened, yet when she went on there was an unmistakable gravity to her words.

'And perhaps there will be reward for a man of good faith who took his queen at her word.'

With that she turned her back on Tolucan's company and started walking back towards the shore. Aldwyn nodded to Tolucan, who returned the gesture, then the duke followed after his queen.

'Your Majesty. Your Grace,' called Tolucan as he set out after them, bidding his company do the same. He walked up close to Aldwyn and spoke in a low tone so that Cathryn had also to draw in close. Aldwyn thought the man looked nervous.

'I did not speak of it before as it seemed to me naught but a rumour, but if indeed such folks as yourselves are in the Drift, perhaps there is more to it.'

They waited for him to continue.

'Some of these folk came from the battle where Lord Linwood's army was defeated. They brought with them a rumour that Lord Lachlan had been with the force there. I have heard no more than that.'

Silence.

Aldwyn thanked Tolucan, who bowed his head and fell back to walk with his company. Cathryn said nothing, and Aldwyn walked beside her as she once more set off towards Strewn Men Bay.

'If Lord Lachlan is in the Drift . . . ' said Aldwyn after a few minutes.

'I would not speak of it yet,' said Cathryn, cutting him off. 'I must consider the tidings carefully.'

With the eyes of her people on her back, Cathryn kept up a furious pace during the march back to the shore. Aldwyn was sure that she would maintain it until somebody bigger and stronger of limb collapsed. Sure enough, a little after dusk, Tolucan ran to catch up and suggested they make camp for the night.

Three days later Aldwyn caught the scent of salt in the air and his heart stirred when he heard the calling of seabirds wheeling above them.

He was relieved to see that little had changed on the beaches. Cathryn greeted the guards she had posted, who had established a small camp on the sand itself, just beyond the reach of the waves at high tide. The fleet filled the bay.

Cathryn turned to Tolucan, who clasped his fist to his heart and dropped to one knee, bowing his head.

'Your Majesty,' he said.

Cathryn advanced upon him and drew her sword.

'I promised a loyal captain just reward, did I not?' she asked nobody in particular. Tolucan did not raise his eyes to meet hers.

'You did, Your Majesty,' he said.

She rested the flat of the blade upon his left and then his right shoulder.

'I name you Sir Tolucan. Lowborn you may be, but perhaps now you will find allegiances and loyalties begin to weigh a little heavier upon you.'

'Your Majesty,' stuttered Tolucan, and Aldwyn smiled at how the newly-knighted man trembled.

The queen left him kneeling in the sand and turned to Aldwyn.

'There is much to set in order. Summon the admirals, the chieftains, the lords and the generals to meet me aboard the flagship.'

Cathryn turned her back on him and took her seat in one of the boats.

Tolucan got to his feet and came to stand by Lord Aldwyn, who turned and smiled a grim smile at the man.

'Congratulations, Sir Tolucan.'

'I . . . I'm all at sea,' he said. 'I did nothing to deserve that, Your Grace.' He laughed. 'In truth, I don't even know what it means to be knighted, aside from the "sir".'

'Land and title. The command of men. And headaches,' replied Aldwyn. 'Attend the council and learn a little more. Besides, you are the only one in the fleet with any knowledge of what has happened here.'

Cathryn seated herself at the far end of the table in the great cabin of her flagship, and Aldwyn stood just behind her chair, leaning upon it.

She explained to the assembled council all that she had observed in the forest and called upon Tolucan to recount his tale, as well as all that he knew of Lord Lachlan and Lord Linwood. Though his hands were shaking, Tolucan relaxed as he spoke until he looked as though he were briefing his men instead of the most powerful people in the world. When he was done, there was silence, and Cathryn was the first to fill the void with some housekeeping.

'I want word from The Folly and Halflight Hold on the Long Isle. Three ships to each.'

She drummed the surface of the table with her fingers.

'And now we come to the most pressing matter. I must know what has happened here between Linwood and Riark. I *must* know who here is still loyal to the crown of the Combined People and who would vie for it. I would hear news of Lord Lachlan,' said Cathryn.

'Sir Tolucan's plan to make for Stragglers' End seems wise to me, though it will be an arduous journey through the forest for a large force,' said Aldwyn. 'And yet one will be necessary. Who knows how the survivors will react to us, and if Riark's Dryads attack, we must be able to fight.'

'Little good will fighting do,' said Tolucan, and his cheeks reddened, realising he had spoken out of turn. 'If the queen approves, I am content to lead an expedition into the Drift to seek the information she desires.'

Queen Cathryn nodded.

'I would appreciate that, but you will not be the only party. One will be sent to Stragglers' End, another to the north and west of the Drift and another eastward towards the battle by the forest. Our task will be to gather survivors and news, then to establish encampments near where the largest settlements stood to which my people can rally.'

She sat back in her chair, clasping both of its arms as though she were on her throne in the Maw Keep.

'I must speak with Riark, and he must make an account of himself, but I am unwilling to make any assault upon these trees now that the power of the Dryads has been revealed. I lament the losses of Linwood's people, but there is little that can be done for now. In time they will rebuild.'

There was a murmur of agreement, and Aldwyn spoke up,

'Such is the price that the Combined People must pay for the disloyalty of House Linwood,' he said.

Tolucan shifted in his chair, and Aldwyn held up his hand.

'I refer, of course, only to those who have directly conspired against the queen. My apologies,' said the duke.

Tolucan nodded.

'Very well,' said Queen Cathryn, rising to her feet. 'I want the ships dispatched immediately to The Folly and Isles. We will muster upon the shore and set out at sunrise. Aldwyn will make for Stragglers' End, I will lead a force to the site of the battle and Lord Magregar,' she nodded to her cousin at the end of the table, 'will lead the north-west force. See that it is done.'

Over the coming hours, three ships set sail for The Isles and another three to The Folly. Before they were out of sight, boats began ferrying folk from the fleet to the beaches, and once the larger part of the force was ashore, Cathryn, Aldwyn, Tolucan and Magregar joined the soldiers upon the sand. No sooner were the last of them out of the boat than a cry went up, indistinguishable at first then echoed clearly all around.

'Dryads,' murmured Aldwyn, when first he realised what the troops were shouting.

'Dryads,' he said a little louder to Cathryn, then bellowed for the army to form ranks facing the forest, from which emerged a line of Dryads. They stood just clear of the treeline, silent and still.

A lone Dryad stalked out of the trees. Queen Cathryn did not recognise it, but nevertheless she left her guard behind her and set off to meet the newcomer, feeling as though her heart would escape up her throat and out through her mouth.

'Hold the line,' called Aldwyn to the men, and Cathryn heard him hurry to catch up with her. Behind them, the arrayed soldiers came to order and watched as their queen advanced upon the lone Dryad.

It stopped just beyond the treeline on the narrow strip of grassland before the beach began.

As Cathryn drew near she could see that the figure was cloaked in brown leaves and its face was in shadow.

'King Riark?' she asked, coming to a halt upon the sand.

'Riark is no more,' said the figure. 'I am Dark Oak. Disband.'

Cathryn stood tall and proud, drawing her sword.

'I am Queen Cathryn, and these are my lands. I do not heed commands,' she said, steel running through her words, 'but I will treat with you, as I once did with Riark, if you speak for the Forest.'

'You've not heard me,' replied Dark Oak, sounding, Cathryn thought, almost bored.

The Dryad stood alone before Queen Cathryn's army.

He took a step towards her, but she held her ground despite her desire to step back. This creature had an air of malevolence about him.

'It is said that you alone could defeat Awgren in combat,' said Dark Oak.

'I was not alone,' said Cathryn.

'With your husband then,' said Dark Oak, 'but it was you who struck the final blow.'

'It was,' she replied.

'You must be the greatest warrior in your realm,' said Dark Oak.

One moment he was standing still before her, and the next he had thrust out his hand as though to grab her. His thumb and fingers lashed out towards her like whips, growing faster than the eye could see. Dark Oak's roots seized Cathryn by the ankles, the wrists and the neck. She choked as the tendril constricted around her throat.

She heard Lord Aldwyn cry out and the padding of feet across the sand.

Dark Oak raised his arm and lifted Cathryn into the air.

'Do you see?' he called to the queen's army. 'Do you see that I could tear the best of you limb from limb with scarcely any effort at all?'

Aldwyn drew his sword as he ran to save his queen. Dark Oak did not even turn his head to look at him.

Aldwyn roared and raised his sword to strike, but even as his sword came down, Dark Oak's raised left arm grew into a tall tower shield. The Dryad deflected the blow and smiled at the duke.

'Do you see?' he called to the army. 'How this man's loyalty puts you all in danger? The human heart is a dangerous thing.'

Cathryn, struggling to breathe, could hear Aldwyn panting and saw him raise his sword once more.

'Release her,' Aldwyn demanded.

'I will release her,' said Dark Oak, 'when I decide to release her, and not before.'

He raised Cathryn aloft for all to see.

'Mayri,' called Dark Oak into the sky.

The wind picked up, and a swirl of mist began to coalesce into a vaguely human shape, floating in the air.

'If *this* is not enough to persuade you of the folly in resisting our will . . .' said Dark Oak, gesturing towards Cathryn. He looked up at the swirling ghost of mist and nodded once.

Mayri waved her hand, and the wind dropped.

Cathryn could draw no air into her lungs. She writhed while Dark Oak held her aloft, watching helplessly as Aldwyn and her army fell to their knees, grasping at their throats.

All along the shore, the men and women of Cathryn's army dropped their weapons and descended into disarray as they fought to breathe.

Dark Oak's hood fell back, and the blackened wood of his face cracked and merged once more, his white eyes twinkled at Cathryn, the branded mark of Awgren marring his cheek.

'We are the makers of the very air you breathe, Queen,' he said, as Mayri, Queen of the Sylphs, denied the humans their oxygen.

Cathryn opened and closed her mouth, never breaking eye contact with her attacker.

Dark Oak nodded once more to Mayri, and, with a wave of her hand, the air flowed free once more. The Queen of the Sylphs disappeared with the sea breeze.

Dark Oak lowered Cathryn to her feet and released his grasp, his roots drawing back into his fingers as the humans clambered to their feet.

She turned back towards her army, fearing that they would charge at Dark Oak and his Dryads in anger, but all she could see were frightened faces, cowering behind their shields. Even Aldwyn looked ready to flee as he composed himself.

'Steady,' Aldwyn called to the soldiers. 'Order in the ranks.'

'Listen well, Queen,' creaked Dark Oak, dropping one hand to the head of his axe. As he began to announce his demands, his voice rose in volume so that all there could hear him, and his body began to grow until he towered over Cathryn and Aldwyn as they stood before him. Plates of wooden armour emerged from his body, and the spines of a thorny crown burst from his head.

'The realm of the Combined People is no more. Your army will disband. The world has suffered long enough at the hands of those who seek domination. First came humanity and then Awgren with his many Devised. You have done well in throwing him down, but no sooner had his blood soaked into the soil, than your kind began to turn on one another. And before long, the forest burned. No more of this. No more vying for power, no more loyalties and betrayals, no more heartache and pain, servitude and duty. No more countries. Those times are done,' Dark Oak intoned, a wry smile creeping across his face. Cathryn shivered.

Dark Oak continued.

'We have torn down your hiding place at The Folly. Your cities and strong places are no more. The forest now grows across all of those lands which were never yours and yet to which you laid claim. Humanity has over-reached, and I will redress the imbalance.'

Dark Oak pointed at Queen Cathryn.

'Your kind will be as all other animals. You will join the wolf, the beaver and the mouse, and you will learn your true place in this world of ours.'

Cathryn started to speak, but Dark Oak held up his hand.

'There is new law so heed me well. Your kind will not build great castles and citadels. You will not mine or hew down trees lest it be to survive. You will not gather in great numbers or assemble armies. Humanity will live in harmony with the world, as it did when the days were young.'

Dark Oak strode forward, and as he did so, his form began to diminish once more until he was of a height with her. He reached out and laid a gentle hand on her shoulder then spoke quietly so that only she and Aldwyn could hear his words.

'There need not be enmity between our kinds if you obey me. I was one of your own not so very long ago, after all,' he said, turning to Aldwyn. The duke looked into the eyes of the Dryad, and Cathryn thought she saw recognition in his face. The duke's gaze fell upon the brand on Dark Oak's cheek, and he cursed aloud.

Cathryn frowned at him, and Dark Oak laughed.

'She does not understand,' said the Dryad.

'Are you?' Aldwyn mumbled, and knew the answer before he heard it.

'The woodcutter,' said Dark Oak.

'Morrick,' said Aldwyn.

'You led the men of the Hinterland?' asked Cathryn as she recognised the name.

Dark Oak made no reply to her question.

'Every man for himself now. Every woman too. You may sail where you will, but when you set down, your people *will* disband. If I see or hear any indication that humanity is trying to rise above its station, I will act swiftly and without mercy. The lesson will be learnt either way.'

Then, almost as an afterthought, he said,

'Do not doubt my resolve or our ability to withstand you. Lord Linwood was foolish enough to do so, and Riark executed him in sight of his followers. And yet even Riark could not withstand me. And when your husband drew near to the forest . . . '

Dark Oak turned back towards the trees and gave a wave of his hand.

A lone Dryad formed from the ash tree directly behind him. It was shod in bark, but as it took long strides towards Dark Oak, this fell away and features formed on its face and a full beard sprouted along its jaw. Cathryn's eyes widened as she recognised this living carving of the man with whom she had once shared a bed, the father of her heirs. The Dryad who had once been

Lachlan stopped at Dark Oak's side and looked at Cathryn, his eyes naught but empty polished sockets. He frowned, as though he was struggling with some troubling thought.

'Lachlan,' Cathryn whispered.

'He does not know that name any longer,' said Dark Oak.

Was that an instruction or information, Cathryn wondered. She felt faint suddenly, but shook her head and stood strong.

Dark Oak turned his back on them and walked slowly back towards the forest. The Dryad that was once Lachlan paused for a moment, and Cathryn took a step towards him, but he drew back at a word from Dark Oak. Cathryn reached out to him, but the Dryad stepped into the ash tree, his body merging with its trunk and was gone.

Dark Oak trudged back towards the cover of the trees, but before he disappeared he turned and said, 'Now, children, back to your little boats.'

And with that he disappeared from view.

The line of Dryads began to march slowly forward towards Cathryn's army.

'Do not fight them!' roared Tolucan, forcing his way through the shield wall to address the army.

'Your Majesty, we must leave the Drift. I would take this creature at its word,' said Aldwyn, his words tumbling out as the danger grew nearer.

Cathryn backed away from the advancing Dryads, Aldwyn at her side with his sword still in hand.

She took but a moment to decide.

'Fall back to the boats,' she shouted, and her people heeded her command.

The Dryads upped their pace, and the ranks of humans turned and fled back down the beach as a great uproar of voices and shouts began.

Cathryn backed away, sword still in hand, and Aldwyn moved between the Dryads and his queen.

'Retreat!' he hollered. 'To the boats!'

The once mighty Combined People turned tail and ran.

Chapter Three

Strewn Men Bay, Stragglers' Drift

Cathryn, Aldwyn and the queen's army clambered aboard their ships, and word began to spread of Dark Oak's proclamation amongst those who had not come ashore. Aldwyn noticed morale begin to sink, and the mood aboard the ships soured, many a soul fearing for their home and family in The Isles or at The Folly. Cathryn gave orders that the fleet would remain at anchor and locked herself away aboard the flagship, but before an hour had passed, a mutiny broke out upon the Magpie, commanded by Lord Colwyn. Cathryn was forced to order a boarding action to put down the rebellion as the vessel prepared to put to sea with no order given, ignoring all signals from the flagship. Lord Aldwyn and Captain Jacob Lynch were amongst those who cleared the Magpie's deck and though they were successful in subduing the crew, they found Lord Colwyn slumped over his desk with wounds in his back and neck.

When Lynch reported aboard Aldwyn's ship, the Nightingale, he passed on rumour of secret talk below decks whenever officers were out of earshot.

'Nobody knows what the queen means to do next, but many have their own ideas, and that's dangerous, contrary to discipline aboard ship.'

'And you?' asked Aldwyn, but Lynch just smiled and saluted.

Could the men be blamed for wanting to return home? Aldwyn thought not, yet it was their duty to wait for orders.

He became uneasy that he heard nothing from the queen, who had sequestered herself in her cabin aboard the flagship. She sent no response to his messages and would not receive him when he had his men row him across to her vessel.

Over the coming days while the fleet remained in Strewn Men Bay, Aldwyn began to suspect that Cathryn was delaying the moment when a decision would have to be made.

He received reports from around the fleet and visited other lords and captains, all the time wondering whether Dark Oak had spoken the truth, whether Cathryn's realm had indeed been broken. Did the forests cover the world and, if so, was it also true of his home far away in New Brodack on the South Continent? How could the mighty Folly have fallen? Had Dark Oak truly been Morrick, the man of the Hinterland? He had detected no malice in the man in all of their dealings, and so Aldwyn could not comprehend such a transformation, quite apart from Morrick becoming a Dryad. The last time the duke had seen the man of the Hinterland, Morrick lay injured after Captain Lynch stabbed him during an altercation with the woodcutter's wife; not the happy reunion for which he knew the captain of the Hinterland had longed.

Finally, on the third day, Aldwyn received a summons to go before the queen. He took Captain Lynch with him on the short journey by boat.

He found her sitting by the window of the great cabin, her puffy eyes transfixed by the motion of the waves. She clasped a wine bottle in her hands, and it crossed Aldwyn's mind that she had better eke out her supply because there was no telling when it would be replenished. It was easy to stand in the great cabin with its fine adornments and forget that society as they knew it was at an end, if Dark Oak's words were true.

Aldwyn stood silently, awaiting acknowledgement.

'You must be tired,' she said eventually, looking away from the window. She offered Aldwyn the bottle, but he declined.

'If I never sit in a boat again . . . ' he sighed, and she nodded, smiling weakly.

'I have seen you scurrying about on occasion. How did you fare?' she asked, sipping from the bottle.

Aldwyn cleared his throat and leant across the table, his fingers interlocked before him.

'The people fear for their homes and families. They are anxious to be

AGE OF THE DRYAD

underway. The mutiny on the Magpie was led by a weak-willed captain, urged on by his crew to defy the late Lord Colwyn's orders, he who sought to carry out your command.'

Cathryn nodded.

'Your report said as much, Wyn,' she said. 'Sit.'

He did so, grunting when he heard her use her pet name for him.

'I hanged the captain from his own yardarm,' said Aldwyn. 'Order is restored.'

Aldwyn saw Cathryn's lip tremble, and she looked away. He stood and moved to her side, and, her composure crumbling, Cathryn covered her face with her hands, her shoulders lurching up and down as she sobbed. Heedless of the risk of rejection, he threw his arms about her. She collapsed into him, and he laid comforting kisses upon her hair.

He held her close until the tears were done, and she pushed him away with a light touch and a cowed smile.

'For whom do you weep, lady?' asked Aldwyn. 'I do not think you mourn the captain nor Lord Colwyn.' He paused, then ventured, 'Lachlan?'

She looked up to meet his gaze.

'I do not know what to do,' she confessed. 'And yes, I mourn for Lachlan, of course.'

Aldwyn said nothing for a time. He moved back to his seat at the table.

'In being uncertain you are not alone, Cathryn, but at the very least, there are some small decisions to be made without delay. The consequences of those decisions may well render answers to the bigger questions. We cannot remain at sea indefinitely. Our supplies will not last. So where then do we go? Do we venture ashore? Shall we sail for The Folly or The Isles?'

'What is your recommendation?' she asked.

'That those who have family in The Isles sail for them, and the same for those who have family at The Folly,' he said. 'Redistribute your people throughout the fleet.'

Cathryn raised her head, and he saw she was frowning.

'Is that not overly generous? Will I be manipulated by the will of the people? Dictated to by those who should serve without question?' she asked.

Aldwyn did not reply.

'Cathryn, what will you do if all is as Dark Oak says and our cities are thrown down? If we cannot gather together nor rebuild?' he asked.

Cathryn looked back out to sea, and her chest heaved. Aldwyn steadied himself against the pitch and roll of the ship, bracing himself against a bulkhead.

'I know not. A thousand years the Combined People were unified, rebuilding to overthrow Awgren and reclaim our ancestral homes and to what effect? Linwood has cast it all away. Are we to have nothing?' she said. 'Do I preside over the last days of our realm?'

Aldwyn returned to sit beside her and wrapped an arm around her shoulders.

'We should plan for the worst, though I fear you are not ready to hear what that may mean,' he cautioned her.

She rested her cheek against his shoulder, making no reply. Aldwyn ventured on.

'The mutiny against Colwyn is but the first. The men will look to their own wants and needs, knowing that you will be powerless to subdue them without a force behind you. Some may go off on their own and others may strike at you, believing that they can take power for themselves. If the towns are gone and with them our means of supply, we will be reduced to hunter gatherers, fighting over food, arms and shelter. Our numbers will dwindle as the years go on,' he said.

He squeezed her tight as her breathing slowed, and he felt her shoulders relax, perhaps in resignation.

'You have spent your whole life choosing what is right for your people,' said Aldwyn, 'but it may be that the time has come when they must choose for themselves. The time may have come when you must choose what is right for you as well, if your castles, palaces and armies are gone . . . '

Aldwyn released her and leant round to meet her gaze.

' . . . if your lord husband is gone.'

Anger flashed in Cathryn's eyes, and she looked back out to sea. Aldwyn wondered if he had spoken too fervently.

He pried the bottle from her hands and took a long draught. His thoughts wandered to his home away in the colonies, and he considered how his folk fared there, but now was not a time for indulging in daydreams.

'Do you wish to hear my thoughts?' he asked, his voice quiet and gentle. Cathryn nodded and turned to him as he dropped to his knees before her.

'Listen to your heart, Cathryn. You have spent your whole life putting your duty before yourself. We have come up against an enemy that we cannot defeat with strength of arms. This will not be like before, when we could sail away and, after a brief struggle, build a comfortable new life before sweeping back to destroy our foes. You are of a noble lineage and yet, what does that mean without the trappings to convey such power? What use is that power if you have no people to command? What matters to *you*, Cathryn?'

The queen replied without hesitation.

'My realm.'

'And if you cannot sit upon a high seat to govern your people? If Dark Oak will not permit it,' pressed Aldwyn.

Cathryn shook her head, but he grasped her chin and turned her head back so she was forced to look at him.

'What matters to Cathryn? Not the queen, but Cathryn.'

'They are one and the same,' she replied.

'No, they're not. If you were out there with the men, who would you be worrying about, and what would your hopes be for the future?'

She looked out to the sea.

'If I had no duty to the Crown?' She paused before answering, 'I would wish to see my sons and daughters again. I never had the chance to be a mother to them, and I would relish the opportunity to make amends. I can barely remember their faces, they were so young when we sent them to The Isles to dwell in the halls of Lachlan's fathers.'

'Then we go to The Isles, Cathryn!' Aldwyn enthused. 'Return to your children and keep them safe. And once that is done, would you truly be parted from them again? From your heirs?' he added, mindful that the queen would not be able to shake all thoughts of a continuing royal line.

She shook her head. Aldwyn clasped both of Cathryn's hands in his.

'Then gather them in close,' he continued. 'Watch over them, Cathryn. And allow me to watch over you all.' He heard the tremor in his voice, and after a second he saw her realise his meaning.

'Aldwyn . . . ' she whispered. He heard a warning behind the word, but he had waited long enough, suffered enough.

'I love you, Cathryn, and I know full well you love me. The gods know you have told me often enough when you are in your cups. The queen could not be with Lord Aldwyn, not with a realm to rule and heirs to propagate, heirs I could not sire. Lachlan has given you children, but did you ever love him?' he asked, his pitch rising as he spoke.

'After a fashion,' she whispered, sounding more a maiden than the queen.

'After a fashion,' he repeated. 'Lachlan was a good man, a pragmatic man. He would see the wisdom in my suggestion. Did he not wish to leave behind the throne and return to a simple life together? You dismissed it as irresponsibility and a complicated man's whim. Maybe you were right, but now the world has moved on, and Lachlan's dream could be our reality. Be with me, Cathryn. We will gather our family and look to one another for strength, not to walls, armies and titles.'

She looked into the deep brown of his eyes, and Aldwyn knew she saw his vulnerability. Knew the risk he had taken in making his appeal. His hands enclosed hers, damp from a nervous sweat, yet she made no attempt to pull away.

He knew that he was asking her to change her entire understanding of the world and her role in it. To his eyes, Cathryn looked as though she was standing on the brink of a ravine, waiting for the impetus of his words to carry her over.

'I cannot abandon my charge entirely,' she drew back her hands. Aldwyn realised he had been holding his breath. Her tone and her words surely betrayed a coming concession?

Cathryn stood and began to pace the room. Aldwyn watched in suspense as she walked the length of the table, wondering whether she would accept his proposal. Perhaps he had been too bold?

'We cannot openly stand against the Dryads,' she mused, 'and yet this

Dark Oak said Riark is no more. That suggests Dryads can be destroyed. How else did Dark Oak take power?'

'I know not,' said Aldwyn. He did not like the turn this conversation was taking.

He recounted all he knew of Morrick, Rowan and Captain Lynch, but try as they might, neither he or Cathryn could discern the meaning of the woodcutter's new incarnation as a Dryad.

'It is clear that humans can become Dryads; we have seen as much twice already,' said Aldwyn, not mentioning Lachlan by name.

'Riark once spoke to me of his past life as a man,' mused Cathryn, 'but I can only guess how reincarnation is achieved and at the motives behind it.'

Reminded, she spread out a map across the table, and Aldwyn could see her eyes flitting over it.

'When I spoke with Riark by the orchard within The Folly, he seemed to have no interest in conquest and domination. He made it clear that they are human foibles, not shared by Dryads. And yet if the Dryads have seized power as men are inclined to do, perhaps I should learn from the way of the Dryads. Patience. Growth. Inevitability,' she said with haste then rounded to face Aldwyn, grinning.

'I will bide my time. Appear to be acquiescing to Dark Oak's demands, and yet *we*,' she poked Aldwyn in the centre of his chest, '*We* will know the truth of it!' She spoke fast, and he could hear the excitement in her voice. It wearied him.

Can she not let go?

'Cathryn . . . ' he said, massaging his forehead and scrunching his eyes closed. 'Cathryn, it's over.'

She turned on him, and there was a savage light shining in her eyes.

'Do you still honour me as queen or am I nothing but the object of your impotent affection?' she snapped.

Aldwyn's shoulders slumped as the words caught him unawares, and yet his hurt did not sway her.

'Get to your feet,' she demanded.

He did as she commanded.

'*There* is power,' she hissed. '*There*. I need no armies to command. To rule.'

She moved close to him until her breasts pressed against his chest. His breaths came quick and shallow.

'I have a duty,' she said, her eyes boring into his, and he maintained his eye contact though he felt he might visibly quail at any time.

'I know,' he whispered, 'As do I.'

Her features softened, and she reached up, her hand curling round and caressing the nape of his neck. He closed his eyes. He felt pressure on the back of his neck, and he leant forward. Her lips planted a kiss upon his lips. He savoured the taste of her and returned it, taking her in his arms.

She drew back and put her lips to his ear.

'I love you,' she whispered, and her breath was warm against his flesh. He shivered. 'But do not think that I can sit idle. The day *will* come.'

Caring little for her words now that the moment had finally come when he could hold her without fear of recrimination, Aldwyn poured his heart into their kisses. Soon all conversation ceased, and they became lost in one another for a time.

There came an urgent knock at the door.

'Your Majesty. Your Grace,' said a voice.

'Enter,' called Cathryn, moving to sit beside the window while Aldwyn stood braced against the table.

The first lieutenant opened the door and ducked inside the cabin.

'The captain's compliments, Your Majesty. You are needed urgently on deck,' said the man.

'Thank you, Lieutenant. We'll be up directly,' said Aldwyn, and the officer bowed before he left them.

Aldwyn caught Cathryn ensuring that her garb was in order before she headed on deck. The crew were leaning over the rail, staring down at the water, and the captain only nodded over the side when she caught his eye.

Aldwyn walked beside Cathryn to the rail, the sailors parted, and he looked down into the water.

As though standing on some hidden platform just below the surface, a shimmering woman composed of salt water, with white foam for hair, was visible above the water. Aldwyn felt an impulse to look away, as the creature mimicked the form of an unclothed female right down to the top of her hips. The Naiad appeared untroubled by the thrashing waves around her.

She waved and then, stretching her lithe arms up, she dove forward. It appeared quite unnatural; where one would expect the hips and buttocks to break the surface followed by the arcing legs, there was nothing but still air as though the woman had evaporated mid-dive.

Cathryn turned her back on the sea and leant back against the rail. Aldwyn knew that the queen was conscious that, as always, all eyes were upon her.

'Signal the fleet to hold position and await instructions,' she said to the captain, utterly composed.

Cathryn turned to Lord Aldwyn.

'The muster lists?' she asked.

'Will be sent to your cabin, Your Majesty,' he said.

'Very well, but then see that I am not disturbed,' she said with a nod.

'Send up the signals,' said Aldwyn to the captain, once Cathryn had gone below. He retreated to the taffrail and looked up through the rigging as the signals were hoisted.

'Bloody shambles,' said Captain Jacob Lynch as he approached. Aldwyn straightened up as the man approached, but Lynch moved to his side and leant on the rail. He breathed deeply of the sea air.

Aldwyn almost rebuked the common-born captain, but instead he turned to join him.

'Shambles?' he asked quietly.

'Aye, sure enough,' replied Lynch. 'Like as not we're all that's left of the Combined People, and look at us, floating about like wide-eyed frogs on logs. Fools we look and no mistake.'

'And no doubt you'd set things right if you had the command?' Aldwyn said.

He felt no anger at the captain's presumption, just amusement. Lynch turned to look out to sea.

'Beg pardon, Your Grace,' he said quietly. 'I spoke freely without leave.'

'Speak your mind, Captain,' Aldwyn replied.

Lynch paused and turned to address him, almost confidentially, as though they were conspiring in a tavern.

'Well, what happens now? It's been three days, and I've heard nothing,' said Lynch.

'That will be for the queen to decide,' said Aldwyn.

'Aye, but what options does she have? If the strongholds are gone and her people are to disband, is she . . . '

'Is she what?'

'Beg pardon, no. I have need of my neck without a noose around it,' muttered Lynch, perhaps remembering the captain of the Magpie, thought Aldwyn.

'Speak freely. I would know your mind, Captain,' Aldwyn insisted.

'I'm no traitor,' said Lynch.

'I did not think that you were,' Aldwyn replied.

'But you might,' said Lynch, looking down at his feet.

Aldwyn shook his head.

'Nay, go on and speak free, but low,' he looked about him to ensure there were none nearby to overhear.

'Is she still queen?' said Lynch, and after a moment, he looked up at Aldwyn. The duke saw nothing but genuine concern and doubt in the captain's one good eye, the other scarred and hidden under a makeshift patch.

'Of course,' he said quietly. 'Nothing has changed.'

'All has changed, Your Grace,' said Lynch.

'She is still the rightful ruler and wears the crown, uncontested,' insisted Aldwyn.

'Any fool can put on a tiara and demand to be called king. Nobody knows that better than a captain of men. What stops those under your command from doing as they will? What makes them heed your words?'

Aldwyn faltered. He had no reply.

'A queen needs a nation, castles and an army, does she not? As far as my simple mind can tell, she has none of those if that tree fellow had the right of it. We've had one mutiny already, and did I not hear of minor disturbances aboard several ships only today? This is but the beginning, and among the folk most likely to be loyal to the queen, military folk and such! It takes a lot for a crew to mutiny, seeing how sailors hold their captain's word as the word of a god, but as soon as a crew proper takes against their lawful commander or sees that their rule is failing . . . '

Lynch had no need to finish the sentence for Aldwyn's benefit, and he knew it, it seemed.

The captain drew his knife and pressed the tip against Aldwyn's side. The light pressure drew the duke's attention, and he gripped Lynch's wrist.

'What's this?' Aldwyn hissed, looking about him. He made no further move against the captain, still trusting him despite the alarming move.

'Do you see how close the high ones are from being the dead ones? Do you think I would have had the stones to even feign an attack upon you even a few days ago?' Lynch drew back his hand and sheathed his knife.

'You are no less a man, but far less a lord than you were in light of the Dryads' move against us. Perhaps your blue blood runs truer than mine, but all that empowers you is failing before the eyes of your people. They already whisper below decks, wondering how they might get away and find their families. Sailors and soldiers alike wonder how they will keep their families alive if the shelters and the farms are gone, if they no longer have employment and the means to feed themselves.'

Lynch crossed his arms and leant on the rail, looking out at the fleet, and Aldwyn regarded him with wonder. Were all low-born sea captains this insightful?

'I am not the only man at risk, Captain,' said Aldwyn. 'Have you heard that Dark Oak appears to have once been Morrick?'

The captain frowned, and Aldwyn realised the name was familiar, but Lynch could not place it.

'The captain from the Hinterland. Rowan's husband,' said the duke, and Lynch's one remaining eye widened. 'I would keep a weather eye, if I were you.'

'Interesting times . . . ' said Lynch.

They stood in silence as one by one the ships of the fleet answered the signals from the flagship, all save for the Magpie, as she was manned only by a skeleton crew, her own locked away in brigs of various ships. The sight moved Aldwyn, and he turned to Lynch.

'Would you accept command of the Magpie, Captain Lynch?' said Aldwyn, standing tall, his words formal and direct.

Lynch, still leaning on the rail, bit his lower lip and weighed up the offer, bobbing his head from left to right as he did so. Finally, he too straightened up and faced the duke.

'I'd gladly accept the command, Your Grace,' he said, 'uncertain though times may be.'

Aldwyn stayed aboard the flagship and, later that day, he was asleep in a hammock when the first lieutenant attended him and issued a summons to the great cabin. As much as he loved Cathryn, his heart sank at the words, and he wondered how much talk and hard-headed obstinacy would greet him. How much wine would be left aboard after she had worked so hard alone for so long?

He found Cathryn behind her desk writing upon a piece of parchment. She looked up when he entered, bidding him fetch a drink and find a seat.

When Aldwyn was settled with a glass of brandy, she dropped her quill into an inkpot and sat back in her chair. She stifled a yawn, covering her mouth with the back of her hand and let her hair fall back, her eyes closed.

'Quite the afternoon, Your Majesty,' said Aldwyn. 'You should eat.'

'Soon enough,' she said. 'I need your opinion first.'

'Dare I give it?' he teased, though he meant it and the words came out a little harder than he had intended.

Cathryn raised an eyebrow, and one side of her mouth hitched up in a knowing smile. In return, he raised both of his hands to signal that he gave up, and she pushed two sheets of parchment across the desk.

'Read.'

Aldwyn reached for them and did as she commanded, his brow furrowing as his eyes took in the meaning of the documents, following the delicate lines of her script. She had not heeded him, it seemed.

Cathryn had closed her eyes, and Aldwyn took a moment to look at her. She had aged in the last few weeks, but in that moment, he could forget it. He imagined that she was relaxing as she listened to the creaking of the ship's timbers, pretending that all was as it had been and that a warm bed greeted her back in The Folly. He could not conceive of any devastation being laid upon a place so strong that even Awgren had not managed to damage it in his many centuries of siege, and he doubted Cathryn could either.

Aldwyn read the documents through twice.

'These are your wishes?' he said once he was done, his voice flat and shaking slightly.

'Your thoughts?' she asked.

Lord Aldwyn sighed.

'You do your lineage credit, Queen Cathryn.'

She waited for him to continue, but he simply blew lightly across the ink before rolling up the parchment into two scrolls.

'But?' she said when it was clear he would not speak again.

'You do your lineage credit, but you do *us* a disservice. Twice since Awgren fell, you have asked me what I wanted for myself, and twice you have denied me my desire so that I can serve your purposes. I will not forget it.' The words were sorrowful, not threatening and yet he saw her eyes leap into flame. He looked down at the table before continuing.

'I will see that every available man sets about copying the document until we run short of ink and parchment, Your Majesty. I think it best to address the lords and captains personally before I distribute the decree. And as for the knights – with such a burden laid upon them, I . . . '

'That is for the best,' she conceded, and he saw her struggling with, but finally mastering, her temper.

Aldwyn stood and gave a half bow.

'By your leave, Your Majesty, I will set about the task.'

Without waiting for her to acknowledge him, Lord Aldwyn returned on deck to seek Jacob Lynch. He found the captain still looking out from the quarter-deck.

'I have your answers,' he said and handed Lynch one of the scrolls. The other he kept secure in a tight fist, as though fearful it may be snatched from his grasp. The captain handed the scroll back without a look.

'I am not a lettered man, Your Grace.'

Aldwyn's cheeks flushed, but he carried on undaunted.

'The queen has been through the muster list and is re-ordering the fleet. Anyone who wishes to remain in the Drift will be set down here. Half of the fleet will sail for The Folly. The other half will sail for The Isles. Once there, if all that Dark Oak told us is true, we will disband and go our separate ways.'

Lynch's eye widened.

'She's freeing her people?' asked the captain.

Aldwyn frowned. *He* had never considered them enslaved.

He shook his head.

'She will not relinquish the crown nor turn her back on the Combined People. She has ordered . . . measures . . . to maintain her realm though her people are sundered. New laws. The word must be read and understood by all here then these scrolls burned before ever we go ashore, for the Dryads must not hear of the queen's plans. We have many messages to carry, Captain. The people have new obligations, and there are many systems to be put in place so that we do not lose touch with one another.'

Lynch rubbed his one good eye.

'Never simple,' he sighed.

'Mind your tone, Captain,' said the duke. 'Remember your duty.'

Lynch straightened up reluctantly, but Aldwyn saw the same weariness in his eyes.

'Permission to speak, Your Grace?' asked Lynch.

'If you speak no dissent.'

'Where will you go? And the queen? If I might ask.'

Aldwyn folded his arms across his chest and staggered slightly as the ship lurched.

'The queen sails for her seat at The Folly,' he said.

'If The Folly still stands,' Lynch muttered. 'And yourself, Your Grace?'

Aldwyn turned his back on Lynch and looked out at the setting sun.

'I will sail for The Isles and make my home there to speak in her name and safeguard her children. I will prepare Crown Prince Annan for when he comes of age, and until then I will maintain Cathryn's hold on the islands,' he said, referring to her by name without thinking. If Lynch noticed the gaffe, he said nothing of it.

The captain wrung his leather baldric in both hands and drew tiny patterns on the deck with the toe of his right boot.

'And do I have orders?' he said eventually.

'You are to sail to the west coast of The Impassable Forest and find anchorage. There will be knights put ashore. They will seek you out when the time comes. I would have you bring me news of any word they bring you in the coming days and convey them on, if they ask it of you.'

'With all due respect then, Your Grace, I'll set my men to readying a boat to take us over to the Magpie. Best get an idea of how we fare, provisions and the like.' Lynch tipped his hat to the duke and took his leave.

Aldwyn looked down into the waves and thought, just for a moment, how much simpler things would be if he donned his plate armour and leaped over the side.

Sir Tolucan climbed up the side of the flagship from a small boat and stood by the rail, as out of the way as could be managed, feeling awkward and uncomfortable. He had been aboard ship before, sure enough, but as one of many, never summoned alone to speak with the queen.

Should there be someone to greet him? Should he make his own way to the great cabin?

Tolucan folded and unfolded his arms, clasped his hands behind his back and looked about for someone who might have some answers.

'You look lost.' Tolucan spun round and bowed his head when he saw

Lord Aldwyn approach. He felt his cheeks flush.

Aldwyn studied the knight for a moment before seeming to realise why the man was aboard.

'The queen summoned you,' he said, and Tolucan decided the levity of the duke's tone and his weak smile was an attempt to hide something. Was he to be punished for being one of Linwood's men after all?

'Aye, Your Grace,' Tolucan managed to say, but knew not what else would be appropriate when speaking to one whose station was so far above his own.

The two men stood silently for a moment then Aldwyn nodded his head, resigned, and spoke up.

'I will show you the way,' he said, and led Tolucan to the great cabin.

The knight followed, gripping the hilt of his sword to prevent the weapon bashing against people or bulkheads as he traversed the busy deck.

Aldwyn led him to the door of Cathryn's cabin, but there he paused, and Tolucan could hear a man's raised voice, railing and ranting, only to be shouted down by the queen.

Aldwyn knocked on the door when the noise died down.

'Enter,' said Queen Cathryn through the wood.

Aldwyn pushed the door open, stepped inside, and Tolucan saw the duke bow his head.

'Sir Tolucan of Stragglers' Drift, Your Majesty,' said Aldwyn.

'Send him in,' said Cathryn and with that, Aldwyn ushered Tolucan into the room.

Before Tolucan could step inside, a man clad in finery, but no armour, bearded, red-faced and wearing a furious expression, stormed out of the cabin, his long ruddy hair billowing behind him.

Tolucan found himself standing before the queen as she sat at her desk. Beside her stood Ailsa, her aide, long chestnut hair in a ponytail hanging down over boiled leather armour that utterly hid her form. She steadied herself with a hand on the back of Cathryn's chair.

The queen looked up at him and smiled, but he saw her cheeks were red as well. Tolucan bowed low.

'Please excuse Sir Feran,' said Cathryn. 'He has quite forgotten his manners and had to be reminded of his loyalties.'

'Your Majesty,' Tolucan said, his throat tight.

'You are well?' asked the queen.

'I am, Your Majesty,' Tolucan replied. 'And you?'

He immediately felt his cheeks flush again, heat spreading across them. *You don't go asking the queen if she's well, like she's a mate in a tavern, fool,* he scolded himself. He was just about to apologise when Cathryn gave a little laugh then answered him.

'I am well enough of body, Sir Tolucan, but I think it is plain for all to see that my realm is facing . . . a new challenge,' she said.

'Your Majesty,' Tolucan nodded, his cheeks still hot. He caught Ailsa hiding a smile. She caught him in the catching and suddenly found the map spread across Cathryn's desk too fascinating to look up from.

He scowled momentarily, but then straightened up and paid full attention to the queen.

'Do you have a family, Sir Tolucan?' she asked him.

'I do, Your Majesty. Two boys. Twelve and ten,' he said.

'And they are with your wife? Where do they dwell?' she asked, picking up an inkwell and holding it up to the light, swirling the dark blue liquid inside.

'No, Your Majesty. My sister, Ada, has them. My wife passed last year,' he said.

'I am sorry to hear it, sir,' said Cathryn, but her words seemed cold to Tolucan. The queen was sounding him out, he knew, and he had to stop himself frowning at this line of questioning.

'Now that you are one of my knights, they will be somewhat elevated in station,' she said. 'You will be granted land in the Drift, if you wish it, or elsewhere.'

'You are kind, Your Majesty,' said Tolucan, unable to process the prospect of such a change in fortune and still too wary of where this was leading to be happy or even at his ease.

'Not at all,' she said. 'There may be rewards for good service and loyalty, but the title comes with duties. Sacred duties,' said Cathryn.

'Aye, Your Majesty,' said Tolucan.

'I have a task for you,' she said. 'A task of great import not only to me, but to all of the Combined People, your children and your sister included.'

'I am yours to command, Your Majesty,' said Tolucan, straightening up like a soldier on the parade ground, looking above the queen's head, his hands clasped behind his back.

'I am investing you, Sir Tolucan, this day, into a new order of knights. You will be few, yet your brethren and your sistren will carry all of my hopes,' said Cathryn, pushing back her chair and moving round the table to stand before him.

Tolucan dropped to one knee and bowed his head.

'I have drawn up a list of such men and women who I believe value honour, loyalty and duty above privilege, wealth and renown. I have summoned and laid a charge upon each of them. You are the last,' said Cathryn.

Tolucan's heart smashed at his rib cage, his breathing sped up, but he dared look no higher than the queen's boots.

'I task you with a difficult quest. You will seek the tree to which Dark Oak is bound, his Mother Tree, and you will seek for the means to destroy it.'

Tolucan looked up, wondering at the queen's command.

'To what purpose, Your Majesty?'

'Dryads are invulnerable to attack when they take avatar. Only the swift death of their Mother Trees, into which their human souls were reborn, can kill them. So I have been told by the king, Riark, who led the Dryads before Dark Oak.'

'And how will I know his tree when I find it?' said Tolucan, aware he was accepting this task before he had even given it a thought.

'I do not know. Stand,' she commanded.

She stepped in close to him and took his hand in hers, speaking confidentially to him.

'You will not thank me for knighting you, sir, for this is a nigh on impossible task. I cannot hope to field an army against the Dryads and win, you know this to be true, I deem,' she said, and he nodded.

'And yet they cannot go unopposed. So we must move secretly, by stealth,' she said, her voice low. 'You must not speak of this quest to anyone, not even those in whom you place your trust. You will not know who else has been chosen, lest you are captured and tortured until your tongue spills my secrets. The Order of the Silent Knights will garner no renown unless their task is achieved, for none will know of their labours, though they be long and lonely, for you must needs give up your existing bonds to follow your road.'

Tolucan drew back his hand without thinking, and he saw the queen frown.

'Will you do this, sir knight?' she asked, her eyes imploring. 'For your queen and your people?'

'I will, Your Majesty,' said Sir Tolucan, regretting doing so the moment the words had left her lips. What of his boys?

She nodded and moved back to sit at her desk, breaking his reverie.

'Just so,' she said. 'You will speak of this to no one. Pack your things and have Aldwyn equip you as you see fit. You will be put down on the coast at a time of my choosing, and under cover of darkness. I will assign you a squire to bring me word of your success or your death, whichever comes the sooner.'

She looked up a final time.

'You have my thanks, Sir Tolucan, but time is short, and I have other business. Good luck,' said Cathryn and her eyes dropped to the map once more.

Tolucan stood, uncertain what to do until Ailsa coughed.

'You are dismissed, sir,' she said, barely hiding her amusement.

'Ma'am,' he replied to Ailsa, and offering a final 'Your Majesty' to Cathryn, Tolucan escaped the queen's cabin, making his way on deck under the open skies. Clouds gathered overhead.

There he met Aldwyn once more.

'You are berthed aboard the Seacrest, I believe?' said Aldwyn.

Tolucan nodded silently. A man scurried by, catching his attention. He turned his back to the sea and watched the crew go about their work for a moment, wondering how long it would be before he found himself in company once again.

'We'll discuss what you will need ashore before you return to gather your things.'

Tolucan nodded absent-mindedly, and Aldwyn gave him a gentle slap on the shoulder blade.

'You have my sympathy, sir,' Aldwyn said quietly. 'You are not the first to give up your own desires to go forth at the whim of the queen, believe me.'

When Tolucan looked into the duke's eyes, he saw the truth of it. And pity.

Tolucan was put ashore with his squire, an eager young woman called Cwenhild, on the empty beach at Strewn Men Bay.

He watched as the boat which had carried them pulled for the Seacrest, which was readying to depart along with the rest of the fleet.

Clad in mail and a leather jerkin, a cloak draped over his shoulders, Tolucan wore a longsword on his hip and carried a tower shield. Cwenhild, a girl of no more than eighteen, carried a pack and a longbow in addition to her own spear.

Tolucan took one last look at the sea and turned his back on it. He stood and regarded the endless forest in silence, considering whether he should abandon his quest and set out in search of his sons, Sener and Derian. He thought back on the last time he had seen them, of taking them in his arms before he was redeployed to the beach defences. Could he leave them in the care of his sister? Would they think he had abandoned them?

It mattered not, he decided. He was a queen's man, and charged with a sacred quest, carrying the hopes of all humanity with him. A knight was more than just a soldier, he knew from the tales of his youth; they stood for something greater, never turned from the path. Yes, he had no formal schooling in their way, but his queen had seen fit to reward him, and he would make sure she never regretted her decision. He, Tolucan, born a peasant, would be the one to destroy Dark Oak.

'Right,' he said to Cwenhild, walking towards the cover of the trees, 'Let's begin.'

As Tolucan and Cwenhild entered the forest, another boat pulled for the beach. Men jumped out and hauled it up on the sand before two figures disembarked. Sir Feran, a brown beard covering his face, high on his cheeks and longer at the chin, and his red hair tied into a long plait which hung down his back, was clad in mail, over which he wore a calf-length dyed green leather coat. He carried a longsword. His elderly squire, Dun, a wiry man who wore simple leathers and walked with a stoop, turned to him.

'To it then,' he said.

'If we must,' said Sir Feran, sighing.

The two men made their way off the sand and disappeared into the forest.

Chapter Four

The Butterfly Isle

There was little else for Rowan to do but walk, listening for streams and foraging for food while she travelled. Many of the plants were foreign to her, and she dared not consume them, but she managed to find enough to sustain her most of the time. When her luck failed, she would find parcels of berries laid on leaves beside her when she awoke in the morning - just enough to keep her alive. Her stomach growled constantly, and she lamented every occasion in her life when she had turned down a second helping or regarded her reflection with a critical eye, considering herself grown portly.

Rowan followed the path through the woods of the Butterfly Isle, hoping to stumble upon a settlement yet not knowing what to do for the best if she did so. Could she approach in search of aid and subject another innocent to the old woman's fate, another death on her conscience?

She was alone with her memories, troubled and comforted by the faces of her children, now all lost to her, dead or on the Old Continent. She bitterly regretted her parting with Callum, and it was her determination to reach him and make amends that drove her on.

Her Dryad watchers seemed to have drawn off into the trees, but she knew that they were not gone. She could feel the eyes of the trees upon her.

In time the path widened into a road, and on the morning of the fifth day Rowan spied gates barring her way. She stopped in the middle of the path, planting her hands on her hips and blew a wisp of hair from her eyes. She gathered her breath and looked back the way she had come, as though expecting the Dryads to be coming up behind her.

Was there a town behind those gates? A fortress?

Rowan dared not venture forward to discover the truth of it for fear that her unseen companions would wreak death upon any who dwelt there.

She stepped aside from the path and into the shadows of the forest. Thus hidden she whispered,

'Morrick?'

There was no reply. Rowan laid both hands upon the trunk of the tree and closed her eyes. She imagined that her mind was reaching into the wood and that her essence flowed through it.

'Morrick?'

Nothing. Rowan drew back and gave the tree a petulant little kick. It numbed her toe, and she cursed.

'Damn you.'

She crept close to the edge of the road and stared hard at the gate, scanning for any signs of life and yearning to run towards it. Despair took hold of her, and suddenly Rowan felt tired to the bone. She sagged back against the tree and dropped to her haunches.

'Shades of the Forest preserve us,' she said eventually and pushed herself back up to her feet before returning to the path. She strode on towards the gates, prepared to face whatever consequences she was bringing down on herself or others.

What choice do I have?

She drew near to the gates and still there was no indication of life from behind them or atop the wall into which they were set. Rowan took a deep breath and banged upon the wood with her fist. The wood was thick, and the sound of her thumping did not carry far.

She called out to draw attention, but still she received no reply. Rowan threw her shoulder against the gate and stumbled as, quite unexpectedly, it opened inwards by an inch.

Rowan pressed against the gate with both hands and peered through the widening crack. She could see that the compound which had looked so secure from her side of the gate was open on the far side. The palisade had been torn down there, and the dwellings within had been reduced to naught bigger than matchsticks.

Rowan shouldered the gate once more and succeeded in widening the opening. She slid through and set about searching for anything that might bolster her supplies.

She stooped to pick up a small cast-iron pan, turned it over in her hands, decided it was too heavy to carry and set it down gently, the right side up, on the soil.

Midway through her search, Rowan leant against a post, close to weeping in desperation. She struggled to get herself together, but it all became too much, and she sank to her knees, cupping her face in her hands, as tears rolled down her cheeks. What had happened here? What had happened to the world?

In time her tear ducts dried up, and she exhausted her sadness. An empty vessel, she got to her feet and once more trawled the wreckage for usable goods. Replenished by some meagre finds, Rowan set about preparing a meal in the remains of the house with the most intact roof, its thatching only partially collapsed.

Evening drew in, and Rowan threw shards of timber upon her small fire to stave off the cold. She nestled in a corner and listened to the howl of a wolf, miles distant. The sound provoked no fear in her. If anything, it made her feel at home, reminding her of the Hinterland, and she wondered how the packs, whose territory covered the forest north of her homestead on the Old Continent, now fared.

That wasn't quite right though, she realised, given that her homestead had likely been razed by the Devised.

As she stared into the flames, Rowan became so immersed in her thoughts that she appeared to be in a trance.

What had happened to Morrick? Was he punishing her? Was he making her pay for turning her back on him? Was he right to do so?

Ultimately, Rowan decided, it did not matter. All that concerned her was getting back to the Old Continent and finding Callum. The fighting men of the Hinterland had been bound for Stragglers' Drift with the queen, and Callum should have gone with Morrick if this was the case. And yet Morrick was here, somehow, or at least something that looked like Morrick was lurking in the woods. So where was Callum now? Was he safe? Perhaps he was alone.

She shivered at the thought, despite the warmth of her little fire.

The wolf's howl was taken up by another then another. Rowan closed her eyes and leant her head against the wall of the house.

She had no concept of how long she could survive without the aid of others or how she would cross the wide sea between The Isles and the Old Continent, but she pushed her concerns to the back of her mind, for she knew worrying in a bind was as much use as breathing underwater. She let sleep take her when it came.

Chapter Five

The Folly, Tayne

Weeks passed as Cathryn's fleet sailed south, setting down the Silent Knights along the coast and parting with Aldwyn's ships, bound for The Isles, when the time came to strike away westward.

When first The Folly came into view, and despite the protestations of the captain of the flagship and the first lieutenant, Queen Cathryn carried a telescope aloft. She perched at the masthead and scanned the former bastion of her realm with a sinking heart. The devastation of The Folly was apparent from miles away.

Where once the high stone walls had stood, enclosing the Arduan Peninsula, there was now naught but air, their foundations a row of broken teeth, still formidable in height in comparison with the walls of lesser fortresses, but indicative of utter ruin in the context of the supposed impenetrability of The Folly.

The fleet made swift progress, and soon the devastation could be seen by all who trod the upper decks. A clamour arose amongst the crew, and officers were forced to suppress their own fears in order to keep the men in check, ordering all idlers below deck.

The Folly Harbour had sat inside the walls, accessed by the Sea Canal. The Sea Gate and its towers were all now gone, and the way to the harbour was blocked by fallen debris. Cathryn could see the rocks in the canal quite clearly through her telescope. She spent many an hour atop the mast and studied the wreckage to learn all she could.

The walls and larger buildings had all been thrown down, but it appeared that far to the north atop the slopes, in the gap between the mountains, the Maw Keep was largely intact or, at least, was still standing. She could not see any detail from so far away. The Arduan Peninsula spanned many miles between its northern entrance, the Maw Gate, below the Maw Keep, and its southernmost point at the harbour wall.

Cathryn pondered what to do when the fleet arrived. It seemed that Dark Oak had spoken the truth after all, and that being so, she had instructions to disband her people once they were ashore.

The fleet was forced to heave to at some distance from the coast, and small boats were sent out to establish the best sites to put down troops. Queen Cathryn gave orders that only the steadiest men be set about this task for fear that lesser souls might desert and go in search of their families before permitted to do so.

Once she had received word of the best landing spots, Cathryn determined to lead a party ashore herself. Mindful of the restrictions put upon her by Dark Oak, and unwilling to risk further conflict, she chose her companions carefully.

And so Queen Cathryn left the sea for the last time in her life. She took with her Ailsa, her aide, Lord Magregar and a company of her strongest warriors.

The boats set the companies down with as much dignity as possible on a broken stretch of wall perhaps half a mile from the quayside, where sloping rubble offered somewhere to pull up a boat. With great labour, the soldiers hauled each craft ashore and set them down on the other side, in the waters of the harbour. Once this had been achieved, everyone climbed in once more and the boats made slow progress towards the quayside, manoeuvring carefully because the once well-charted waters were now strewn with hazards. Hidden stone scraped the keels of the boats, and at other times rock spires barred their way. Cathryn could only look about with a grim expression on her face, absorbing the ruination of the strongest place in all the known world, the seat of her family's power, that even the Dark Lord, Awgren, had not managed to destroy.

Before the morning had passed entirely, they reached the quayside with the loss of only one boat, its occupants now distributed amongst the other craft. As they drew near to a set of stairs set into the quay, to Cathryn's relief, she could see a small group of humans assembling and arraying themselves to watch her approach. She looked up at her standard as it danced with the wind and felt some comfort in the people's recognition.

The soldiers went ashore first and cleared a path, followed by Lord Magregar and, lastly, Cathryn with Ailsa at her side.

Cathryn stood silently at the top of the steps until the assembled folk of The Folly were quiet and then she addressed them, thanking them for their welcome and asking them to tell her all that had befallen them. She listened to each speaker in turn and offered such comfort as she could.

'Where are these creatures now?' asked Ailsa of a woman who reported that she had lost her husband, but whose farm had been left largely intact. The woman shook her head.

'There has been no sight of the stone giants since the morning of the attack. They toppled the walls and threw down most of the buildings,' she said before another man interjected,

'And the roads.'

'The roads?' asked Magregar.

'Aye, milord. Great cracks opened up in some of them, and it seemed to me that some buildings were struck down just to block the lanes and highways. Some of us tried to clear the rubble away, but then the tree men came up and offered violence if we continued.'

Upon hearing this, Cathryn felt heat in her cheeks and her chest tightened.

'Are the Dryads still in the vicinity?' she asked the crowd, but got no immediate answer until she fixed her gaze on the man who had spoken about the roads. Her expectant expression caused him to bow his head and stutter before he had fully formed his answer.

'None here have ventured too far afield, Your Majesty. There have been bad goings-on in the last weeks. Raids on farms and groups of men coming by to take what's not theirs to take. Those who have come by who didn't try to rob us knew no more of the tree men than did we. The Dryads, if you please. They seem to appear only when they find cause to, Your Majesty.'

'They have struck hard and retreated, it seems,' mused Lord Magregar.

'Perhaps.' Cathryn took Magregar aside. 'I will be going on to the Maw Keep. Stay here and establish yourself as you see fit. Send word to the fleet that I require the army to be set down here. I want our forces distributed throughout the peninsula in small camps commanded by such captains as can be relied upon to keep fealty.'

'How many men per company?' asked Magregar, but Cathryn placed a hand on his shoulder.

'I have few answers, Magregar. As many as you dare or as many as the Dryads permit before intervening. Make up maps. Name the camps. Give orders for regular reporting of news. We must allocate runners. We must take a census and make an account of our stores. Send out scavengers to gather supplies from amongst the wreckage. Post guards to defend farms and small-holdings. We will see how things fare across the peninsula and at the Maw Keep, then I will return and we will see what can be done to set things in order.'

Magregar bowed low.

'Your Majesty.'

Cathryn and Ailsa took with them half of the company and began the journey across the peninsula. The going was slow and the route so strewn with debris that there was no opportunity to march in an ordered fashion. Instead they picked their way through fallen buildings and tried to keep sight of one another as they moved. Everywhere trees had sprouted up, in the midst of courtyards but also bursting up through the centre of spiral staircases or in the middle of what had been highways or buildings. It seemed that the forest would reclaim the Arduan Peninsula for its own.

Ailsa stayed beside the queen as they walked. The reek of death was ever-present, and there were so many limbs protruding from fallen walls and cadavers mauled by stray dogs, that the queen's company made no attempt to give any of them a proper burial.

Where they found survivors Cathryn listened to their troubles and then imparted what advice she could for protecting their homes if they were intact or invited them to join the company if they were lost amongst the rubble with nowhere to go.

On many occasions they spied people moving ahead of them, armed with bows and wearing mismatched armour. Ailsa would play the herald and call out to them, warning of the queen's arrival, but most of such folk dashed away and hid.

'Bandits,' suggested Ailsa, 'making the most of the disorder.'

Cathryn said nothing, troubled by the thought of such behaviour in the heart of her realm.

They walked on, and when night fell, they made no fires and set a watch. As they lay side by side, Ailsa turned towards her and whispered.

'You seem troubled, Cathryn, and more so since we saw the bandits run from us.'

Cathryn said nothing at first.

'It galls me to hide my own colours upon my own soil, while my company lurk in the dark. Perhaps I should order fires to be lit and announce my presence. It's bad enough that I'm cowed by Dark Oak,' said the queen.

Ailsa shook her head, but there was little light, and Cathryn could not see her.

'Nay, Cathryn. Your lands are like a beach struck by a tidal wave. The waters have hit and swept much away. To be sure, they are receding, but still much is pulled towards the sea. Let the sand settle and see how the shape of the coast has changed before we redraw the maps.'

Cathryn said nothing, so Ailsa continued.

'This is no mere intrigue to overcome. No squabbling baron to put down. We must redraw the maps. Wastelost,' she cursed. 'We must find new parchment and different types of ink! Stalking into the unknown with scant protection against unknown foes, shouting your greatness from the rooftops might be your right, but as we are now, we know not how we would fare against marauding villains and irate Dryads.'

Cathryn said nothing. Ailsa reached out, found the nape of the queen's neck and gently caressed the sensitive skin. She felt the queen relax slightly and continued her work until she was sure her mistress had fallen asleep.

Days went on in this fashion with much labour of walking and clambering, finding survivors and learning a little of the details of how The Folly was brought down. It grew ever more apparent that there was no sign of the armed contingent left when the fleet departed. The Maw Keep, ahead of them on the slopes towards the mountains, loomed ever higher both in reality and dread anticipation.

One morning, Cathryn woke early and began readying her possessions for the day before many of her people. She was stretching and speculating on how far they had yet to travel when a flurry of arrows whizzed through the air and fell amongst her company. They buried themselves in the ground and glanced off mail, but an unfortunate man was struck in the neck and fell, blood spluttering from his mouth.

'Shields!' roared Ailsa and reached for Cathryn, hoping to pin her to the ground and use her own body to protect her, but to no avail. Cathryn drew her sword and, snatching up her shield, she loosed a fearsome roar as she ran at their assailants.

'Preserve us,' muttered Ailsa, then she too gave a rallying shout and hurtled after the queen. Her head down and her legs pounding, she made up the distance, but veered to the right so as not to present a tempting target by staying too close to Cathryn. Another volley fell, but with Cathryn's company so spread out, it did no damage. These were not men experienced in war, Ailsa deemed, and perhaps the queen's assault would take them aback.

Ailsa staggered back, the breath knocked out of her as an arrow struck her chest. Her heel caught on a stone, and she dropped her sword as she fell back. She crashed down on rubble and felt the rush of the soldiers charging by her. She took a second to stare up at the clouds as she managed a breath, looked down and saw an arrow embedded in the leather which covered her breast. She hauled it free and was alarmed to see a hole in the armour, but no blood coursed from the wound, and she realised she was not yet seriously injured. Adrenaline drove Ailsa straight back on her feet, and she set off once more, casting the arrow aside. Before her she saw Cathryn silently dispatch a bedraggled man clad in a mail shirt. The bow had barely dropped from his hand before Cathryn cut down a second man with her blade. Those remaining turned and ran, disappearing between the ruined buildings. Shouts and screams filled the air as Cathryn's troops gave chase, hunting down the attackers.

Ailsa checked her pace, breathing hard as she reached Cathryn. The queen's eyes were wild and her face spattered with blood.

'Come on,' Cathryn growled and set off after her men.

Minutes later they met the soldiers returning.

'We killed all we caught, Majesty,' said Maughan, their captain. 'Most fled.'

Cathryn sheathed her bloody sword.

'To the Maw Keep,' she commanded, and she set off at the head of the group. 'We do not rest until we reach the gates.'

The farther up the slopes Cathryn led the company, the harder the way became, for thereabouts had stood the majority of great stone buildings; gatehouses, temples, libraries and smaller keeps. All of these were crushed to nothing, but to their surprise, the curtain wall of the Maw Keep was intact, and, it seemed, so was the keep itself. The gates through which Lachlan had escaped all those months ago still hung on their hinges and stood open.

Ailsa drew her sword and the company did likewise, but Cathryn snatched up her standard from the bearer and strode proudly through the gate, prepared to die rather than return home humbled. The lane between the outer and inner walls was empty and offset so it could not be seen from outside, the inner gate also stood open, its portcullis raised.

Cathryn strained to hear any movement which might signal an imminent attack, but she heard nothing, and there was nobody to be seen. She marched on into what had been the great stone courtyard and found herself in a lush garden with new trees sprung up all about, young and yet standing tall with outstretched limbs. On the opposite side of the courtyard, the door to the Maw Keep was splintered and had clearly been assailed, but it too stood open. Cathryn paused momentarily to take in the changes then steeled herself and walked towards the entrance to her ancestral seat. Creepers hid the stone face of the fortress, climbing high out of sight. As Cathryn entered into the darkness of the castle's interior, passing under ivy and vine that had grown up since she had departed, she felt a tension in the air and, if pressed, would have sworn she heard them whisper.

The queen stalked inside the Maw Keep and found carnage.

The corridors were strewn with the decomposing bodies of both The Folly troops and those left behind by Lord Linwood. There was scant light to see by, and the allegiances of the fallen remained a mystery to the queen's company as they walked cautiously through the corridors.

She navigated by memory, reaching out with her left hand to guide herself as she moved through the keep, and up the stone stairs. She did not get far before the stench of death made her gag and cough. She paused and hardened her will before continuing. Cathryn was heartened to hear even the burliest of men behind her struggling to keep down their breakfasts. At least she was not alone in that.

Her boots crunched on bones, and on occasion she would cry out as her boots slid in someone's liquefied remains.

Slowly, the queen's company wound their way through the seemingly deserted keep, accompanied only by their echoing footsteps and the stench of death. The hairs on Cathryn's skin stood on end and her nerves grew taut so that she flinched at the slightest movement or noise, barely able to see in the gloom.

Wherever the queen walked, vines traced across the floors and hung from the ceilings, the wet odour of plant life mixing with that of human decay.

From the foot of the final staircase, Cathryn spied a faint glow above. She paused while the company caught their breath and steeled themselves to face whatever was up there. She prepared for what could well be her final moments. Cathryn held her standard high as she stalked on up the stairs towards the glow.

'With me,' she whispered. Ailsa, sword drawn, led the rest of the company behind the queen towards the throne room.

Onward Cathryn strode, head held high while she struggled to master her fears, inwardly commanding her hands to stop shaking. A long corridor lined with her forefathers' tapestries stretched out before her, lit by fires in intricate sconces of silver. There were no corpses although the flagstones were stained with blood. Vines hung from the ceilings, and ivy covered the stonework under the gently billowing tapestries. Cathryn walked forward, straight down the centre of the passageway, making for the great oak doors ahead of her, beyond which lay the throne room.

The Queen of the Combined People stopped short, and two of her soldiers ran forward. They seized the doors and with a single nod from the queen, they hauled them open and drew back.

The morning light flooded into the corridor and shamed the sconces with its power and beauty. Cathryn squinted, and she shaded her eyes with her free hand as she walked forward into the throne room, ivy under foot and vines hanging from the high ceiling. All the world could be seen through the great open wall to the north and though she had intended only a glance, Cathryn was transfixed by its beauty. Where once the barren lands of the Maw had stretched out to meet scorched plains, now a luxuriant green ocean of growth and life could be seen all the way to the horizon.

'Greetings,' said a familiar voice.

Cathryn tore her eyes away from the view and looked in the direction of the voice, down the long room towards the thrones. So many vines hung before her that she could not see the dais or the speaker.

The ivy-strewn flagstones gave way to a thick layer of wet mulch, and Ailsa grasped Cathryn's elbow to steady her as she walked. The mulch gave way to a carpet of springy green moss, and the support was no longer needed. Cathryn swept vines aside with her left hand as she walked.

'Who offers me greeting and sits upon my throne in my own home?' she asked, her view still occluded.

'Nobody sits upon your throne, Queen,' rasped the familiar voice, 'for what good is there in usurping an ornate chair in a forsaken fortress which shelters nobody and protects nothing? This place conveys nothing now. It does not project strength or provide adequate defence. Your throne is but a chair,' it said as Cathryn emerged from the hanging plants and stood before the dais. 'Yet *your* chair it remains, lady. Sit by me, if you will,' said the voice.

'You speak discourteously to a queen in her own hall, Dark Oak,' said Cathryn.

She reached forward and, with the back of her hand, swept a final curtain of vines aside. She caught a brief view of Dark Oak standing behind her throne and another Dryad sitting in Lachlan's, but she was distracted by a sudden pain in the back of her hand, as though she had been pinched, like her skin had been wrung like a wet cloth by miniscule hands. Cathryn flinched and shook her hand, but the vine remained attached. She curled her fingers around the vine and hauled with all her might, but to no effect. She saw Ailsa raise her sword, but another vine reached out and grasped her aide around the wrist. The rest of the soldiers remained behind her, unmoving. She was glad of it, but also concerned. An assault would be ill-advised, but had their courage failed?

The vine drew itself up as though it were a hanging snake with its teeth embedded in its prey and looped itself over the queen's hand, across her palm, and as it did so, the pain lessened. The vine held her hand in a firm grip.

Dark Oak looked up at the ceiling, closed his eyes and in an instant his body shrank down into the mess of vines, ivy and moss that covered the dais, disappearing from view.

The vine holding Cathryn began to swell and took the form of a fleshy green hand which first developed a wrist, then an arm and then Dark Oak's entire body was taking shape before her. Dark Oak bowed his head and gently kissed the back of Cathryn's hand an instant after his lips had formed.

His face and beard snapped into focus, but Cathryn's eyes lingered on the dais where still a figure could just be seen.

'Not Dark Oak, as you can see,' said the figure in its familiar voice, the one who had spoken all along.

Cathryn felt the pressure on her hand release, and she flung Dark Oak's hand away. She strode forward through the vines and up the steps to stand before the thrones.

Her throne was indeed as she had left it, but upon Lachlan's sat a Dryad. It was tall and broad, with a full beard of black ivy and a strong brow. Cathryn drew in a breath and her head began to swim.

Cathryn sank to her knees. The Dryad sitting upon her husband's throne was wearing Lachlan's leather armour over a mail shirt. Atop the Dryad's mossy hair sat a wooden imitation of her husband's circlet, set with an oval stone of jet.

The queen forced herself to stand and look into the face of the Dryad that had once been her husband.

Dark Oak approached her from behind, and Ailsa gasped as she saw Lachlan for the first time.

'Do sit, if you so wish,' creaked Dark Oak, 'and do not let our presence dissuade you in once more making this your home. I have established quarters with the keep, but I am often abroad.'

When Cathryn turned to look at Dark Oak, there were tears in her eyes.

'You see, it is time you understood,' said Dark Oak. 'Understood that *that,*' he pointed at her throne, 'is just a chair. That you and your kind are no better than animals. That this place is nothing more than an elaborate, hollowed-out burrow in which you dwell.' Dark Oak stepped down from the dais. 'I'll leave you to settle in, but remember, your kind are to scatter once ashore. My servant will know if you don't. He will represent the forest here.'

The Dryad that had been Lachlan stood in an awkward motion that reminded Cathryn of sticks being bundled together. He bowed his head and, with a wave of his hand, he ushered Cathryn to sit upon the throne.

Cathryn turned to Dark Oak, moving to stand before him so she could whisper to the Dryad. Only Ailsa could hear her words.

'You were once a man. Once Morrick of the Hinterland. You have been maligned, by Awgren and by Lord Linwood, who has paid for his crimes. You still bear Linwood's brand. I know these things, Dark Oak, but I do not understand why you punish me, why you punish my people. I never sought to harm you or yours, but to overthrow the Dark Lord that oppressed all of us, including the folk of the Hinterland. I sailed north to bring Linwood to justice. Can we not come to some accord?'

Dark Oak stared at her, unmoving, and Cathryn had a strong sense that he was considering her offer, wrestling with it. He looked as though he would speak, his lips parting, but he said nothing for a few more moments.

'I will bring harmony,' said the Dryad, and she heard just a glimmer of uncertainty in his words. 'The world deserves respite from queens and lords. I will see it done.'

FIVE YEARS LATER

Chapter Six

The Impassable Forest, South-East of Stragglers' Drift

The bandits found Tolucan on a river bank in the shade of a weeping willow. His knees were in the mud and his head bowed, his sweat-drenched hair hung lank over his face. He supported his weight on his notched sword, its point thrust into the bank and slowly sinking. The knight's chest heaved with the effort it took him to breathe.

He heard the bandits' feet moving through the undergrowth.

Tolucan's blood-stained jerkin had been slashed to pieces over the years. His shield, rent from the edge right to the tarnished metal boss at its centre, lay face-down on the grass.

The bandits made no attempt to conceal their approach, perhaps emboldened by his weakened state. His body shook as he readied himself, demanding obedience from his bruised body as he attempted to stand.

'Yield,' said a woman, passing her mace from hand to hand. Her husband stood alongside her, crude iron sword already drawn. Both of them were dirty, their clothes torn and bloodied. And they were thin, but thin was too generous. Emaciated.

The husband hollered back towards the forest, 'By the river!'

'Drop the sword,' said the woman. She appeared cautious to Tolucan.

And well she might be, he thought. *She has seen me kill.*

The bandits edged nearer to the knight, the tree to his right and the river behind him.

Tolucan found his feet. He reached down ever so slowly and took hold of his shield. He straightened, withdrew his sword from the ground and, weary, he faced them.

'Yield,' roared the husband, but there was panic in his voice.

Tolucan said nothing, simply glared at the man then the woman from behind a curtain of wet hair. He stooped, but he was powerful, and his determination showed in his stance and his wolf-like, hungry eyes.

The woman called back over her shoulder.

'Get over here!'

The husband stepped forward, raising his sword. Tolucan let the rim of his shield and the tip of his weapon touch the grass, as though his armaments were too heavy to bear.

He said nothing.

'Kill him,' hissed the woman, and she ran forward. The husband saw his wife charge and did the same. He reached Tolucan first, but as he brought down his sword, Tolucan rammed him with his shield, checking his advance and sending him reeling, winded. Tolucan swung the shield aside and slashed with his sword, cutting open the husband's throat before hacking left and parrying the woman's mace. He brought his shield back round with his left arm and rammed its edge into the bridge of her nose. She cried out and fell back a step then arched forward as he buried his sword deep in her guts.

She moaned and cried out as he withdrew the blade. She fell on to her back then curled into a writhing ball. He moved to stand over the woman and then drove the point of his sword through her temple.

The couple, at last, fell silent.

Tolucan fell to his knees once more as he struggled to breathe, forcing his eyes to open after every blink, fighting to remain conscious. He drove both his shield and sword into the mud, and he hung between them, his knees just making contact with the ground.

He groaned, an ugly guttural noise in contrast with the rush over the river and the breeze rustling the willows.

Get up, he told himself, *there are more of them.*

'Get up,' he growled.

He tried to stand, but he fainted, letting go of his sword and shield. Tolucan fell forward atop the body of the fallen woman and lost consciousness.

Tolucan awoke to find Feran's face looming over him.

'You still with me, brother?' he asked, in his amiable, rasping voice.

Feran's long hair flowed over his shoulders as he crouched, balanced on his haunches.

Tolucan closed his eyes and scrunched them tight for a second before opening them wide. He took a deep breath which turned into a yawn then pushed up on to his elbows.

Pain radiated from a wound in his side, and he groaned.

'Cracked ribs and a nasty cut. You'll live,' said Feran, giving Tolucan three quick, but gentle slaps to the cheek. He stood to his full height, and the length of his green coat dropped so that the hem caressed the grass. He carried a staff equal to his considerable height. Between symbols and plant cuttings, secured with twine, small pouches were tied along its shaft. Feran set the staff down and fumbled with one of the pouches. He dipped his finger inside to gather a small amount of the white paste contained within. He crouched once more and applied the paste to a cut on Tolucan's forehead.

Satisfied that he had done all he could, Feran stood once more and tied back his hair so that it hung down to the small of his back. He drew back his coat and Tolucan caught a glimpse of his empty scabbard. Tolucan nodded towards it.

'Perhaps you would consider wearing your sword once more? Perhaps before I end up in this condition once again?' groaned Tolucan as he sat up. He looked around and saw his armour and weapons leaning up against the trunk of the willow.

Feran raised an eyebrow and shot Tolucan a knowing look, but said nothing more of his refusal to fight.

'You killed the others, you know,' said Feran.

Tolucan just nodded at the information. So the other couple were dead then, killed in the frenzy of his initial defence. All four of the robbers had died by his own hand.

He examined the wound in his side. Through a gash in his shirt, he could see it had been stitched and was coated in a green paste.

'Are you healing or seasoning me?' he asked.

Feran grinned.

'Can you walk yet?'

'I'll manage. Damned if I'm staying here,' said Tolucan.

Feran balled his hands on his hips and looked around. They were on a promontory of the river bank, occupied by the lone willow. On the other side of the water, sand martins peered from their burrows. The sky was clear and the air warm.

Tolucan watched as Feran closed his eyes and drew the forest scents in through his nose. A smile crept across his face even when Tolucan continued muttering about moving on. Knowing Feran was ignoring him, Tolucan slowly collected his possessions, one hand clutching his side. His whole body felt bruised, but this was not unusual. His quest had taken him through Stragglers' Drift, where only small cottages and homesteads had been left intact by the Dryads. The towns were gone, and those whose homes had survived often found themselves targets, victims of displaced people turned raiders. He had travelled on into the Impassable Forest, and yet still he found both bandits and folk who had made their homes there and were defensive of what they had. His squire, Cwenhild, had not lasted six months. The forest was a dangerous place. Tolucan had just not expected to be fighting his own people.

He found his pack secreted behind his shield. Tolucan untied the bindings which held his travelling cloak atop it. He readied himself and, subconsciously, gave a particular whistle. He saw Feran smile when he heard the sound, which had become the topic of jest, a sign that the knight wanted to be off. It was the sort of nuance a married couple might notice after long years together.

Comparing Feran to a wife? Tolucan grinned. *Well, it had been a while.*

'Alright, let's move on,' said Feran.

Together the two of them set off along the bank, heading downstream. Neither of them spoke for a while, but then Tolucan heard a cough a short distance behind them.

Tolucan stopped short, but Feran traipsed on, leaning on his staff.

'It's Dun; I'd recognise his spluttering anywhere,' said Feran. 'I've heard it often enough.'

'Relentless,' Tolucan shook his head. 'How does he carry on at his age? And why? I'd have abandoned you years ago.'

Tolucan received no response, and he realised that Feran was not about to criticise the man who followed them. His friend walked on and did not slow for Tolucan to catch up the paces he had lost.

'Hold up there,' Tolucan said, and Feran waited for him. They moved on together.

'The bodies. Did you check them?' said Tolucan when the thought occurred to him.

'I did,' said Feran.

'And?' asked Tolucan.

'Some scraps of food. Assortment of detritus. Little of use,' said Feran.

Tolucan grunted.

'Very well,' he said.

They trudged on throughout the rest of the day, always following the course of the river. Near dusk, Tolucan's wounds were troubling him, and he began to make noises about finding somewhere to camp.

'Just a little farther,' said Feran. 'I don't like the ground here.'

Tolucan took him at his word and walked on, enjoying the proximity of the water and looking all about him from tree to tree, as he had every day on the journey which was now entering its sixth year, though he had lost count of the days. Long he had wandered in the forest which now covered the Drift, over many hundreds of miles, and yet he had achieved nothing. He was no closer to his goal than on the day he started.

How do I recognise a Mother Tree, a single tree in a forest which covers the whole continent? The question plagued him every day.

They found a clearing, and Feran busied himself collecting fallen branches to build a fire, while Tolucan slowly and painfully removed his armour until, finally, he lay back and sprawled on the grass. He panted from the effort, and sweat rolled down his forehead and stung his eyes.

'You took your time,' said Feran, but Tolucan recognised the mocking tone to his voice and did not move. He frowned at the disrespectful words, but their target had long endured such a tone, and Tolucan knew there was little he could do to curb Feran's tongue.

'I too was waylaid by bandits,' said Dun, 'and I am perhaps less able to deal with such matters than you . . . youths.'

Tolucan opened his eyes and attempted to roll on to his side, but it aggravated his wound, and he fell back, only able to turn his head towards the newcomer.

Dun was in his mid-fifties with greasy grey hair hanging down to his shoulders where it had escaped its fastenings. A grey beard covered his face. He hunched as he staggered into the clearing, weighed down under Feran's shirt of mail. He wore an axe at his belt and, disguised by wrappings, a longsword was slung across his back. Tolucan had seen it removed from its shroud night after night so that Dun could sharpen it as he sat by their campfire. Strapped atop the longsword were several packs. Dun stood breathing hard at the edge of the camp as he did every night, stooping to brace his hands on his knees.

Tolucan cast his eyes towards Feran and saw he was busying himself about the fire, paying the old man no heed. Tolucan sighed, defied the pain in his side and forced himself up on his elbows.

'Come and sit with us, man,' he said.

'Thank you, sir,' Dun coughed as he tried to master his breath.

Feran did not look up as Dun sat beside him by the fire, but handed him one of three pewter cups.

'Nettle tea,' he pronounced, then called back the same words over his shoulder to Tolucan as a question.

'If you'll bring me it. I'm down for the night, it seems,' said Tolucan. Feran muttered and groaned as he got to his feet, his knees clicking, but took

Tolucan the cup along with a hunk of black bread he'd filched from a bandit's supply.

'It's hot,' he warned then returned to Dun's side, assisting the older man in removing his various packs, but carefully avoiding touching the longsword.

Tolucan watched his companions as they sipped their tea by the fire as the night drew on and when his own was cool enough, he drank it down in two swallows. Tolucan lay back and looked up at the stars for a while until his eyelids grew heavy. He closed them and listened to the campfire crackle and the busy chirping of crickets.

In truth, the wound was not so painful that he could not have joined the others by the campfire, but Tolucan desired solitude for the moment as he pondered the road ahead, unable to discuss his quest with even a fellow knight such as Feran, let alone Dun, Feran's squire. The queen's quest required he be ever mindful of watchers in the trees. Paranoia? Maybe, and yet Tolucan often felt eyes upon him as he walked the pathless woods. They saw Dryads from time to time, moving through the trees, but they left one another well alone.

Tolucan had decided he was on a fool's errand long ago, but he had accepted the quest, so what choice had he? Honour demanded that he stay true to his word and follow his queen's command. He was a knight, and a knight must keep his word, wasn't that true? He thought so, based on what little knowledge he had of them before he was knighted, though it came largely from stories his parents had told him as a child.

It was why Feran bothered him so much, a knight who refused to bear arms, determined never to do so again, for gods knew what reason, followed by a squire who doggedly refused to neglect his own duty to serve him. He knew little of his companions' past lives, but when they had stumbled into one another on the road two years before, Tolucan had recognised Feran from Cathryn's flagship, and they had formed a company. It was true Feran had given up on the quest, as a knight at least, becoming something of a wild primitive to Tolucan's eyes, meddling in medicines and carrying a staff like some sort of shaman, but he kept Tolucan on his feet so he could continue the quest.

But what use had his determination and vigilance been these years past? He spent each day passing under the boughs of hundreds of trees and yet what move did he make against them? What could Queen Cathryn expect him to do? He had scrutinized every oak, every maple, every ash, every damn tree he passed. He was ever watchful, and yet any hope of completing his task had died before he had been on the road a week.

As Tolucan grew sleepy, he allowed himself to think of Sener and Derian, his young sons.

Not so young any more, he realised. They would be nearing manhood. What kind of men would they become? He had no idea if they were still alive or where they dwelt now, and he worried constantly about their fate. His sister lived in Redbranch, far behind him, and though he was separated from his sons by many miles, they were constant unseen companions, a burden and a joy.

Worse still than the guilt of abandoning them, to pursue his quest, was the fear that they thought he did not care enough for them to return home. It would be better if they believed him dead, he sometimes thought.

Would he be turning away from the righteous path if he made towards Redbranch to find his family? Surely not. There were trees to spy out around Redbranch like everywhere else. Surely he could continue his task and call on his children? No, it made no sense. The trees there had sprung up after Dark Oak came to power. His Mother Tree, Tolucan was sure, would be in the ancient woods, the Impassable Forest.

Tolucan wrapped his cloak tight about him and tried to put the matter out of his mind as he fell into a slumber, only to see his boys' faces once more in his dreams.

Tolucan's snores broke the stillness of the night. Feran chortled, and Dun smiled as he shook his cup at his master. Feran filled it with fresh-brewed tea.

'Quite a day,' mused the knight.

'Aye,' said Dun, and nothing more. He coughed, ragged and painful.

'Lord, don't let your tongue run on so, eh?' said Feran and grinned though the sound of the old man's cough worried him. He decided to brew him a concoction as soon as the necessary plants presented themselves.

Dun shook his head in disapproval at his master's tomfoolery and sipped at the scalding tea. He looked up.

'We should go. The queen did not mean for her knights to travel together. There is too much ground to cover,' said Dun.

Feran sighed.

'Are we to have this conversation again? Be silent, old man,' he growled.

'If you're no longer my master then it's not for you to tell me to speak or be silent.'

'If I'm no longer your master then why do you act the carthorse?' said Feran, pointing at his pile of belongings. His sword was laid atop it, still in its wrappings.

Dun grunted.

'Ah, I see. A true logician,' Feran muttered. 'Good point.'

'Doing my duty I am. One of us should,' said Dun.

Feran's eyes, normally bright and good-humoured, flashed with anger.

'I will not speak of duty with a squire.'

Dun shook his head.

'You're an ungrateful bastard,' he said.

'I should . . . ' said Feran, but Dun cut him off.

'Should what? Cut my head off? How can you, thus unarmed?' Dun laughed, but there was no humour in the sound.

Feran scowled at him.

'Aye. Thought as much,' said Dun. 'Toothless.' He coughed.

'Drink your tea,' said Feran as he sipped his own.

They sat in silence for a while then Feran took the cups to the river and swilled them out. When he returned he lay next to the fire.

'Tolucan needs the company, and what else have we to do?' said Feran. 'He nearly died today.'

'As you wish,' said Dun as he settled down to sleep. 'But if you won't take up arms, we'd be better off finding somewhere safer.'

'And what about him?' said Feran.

'Oh, now loyalty matters? Now you'll speak of it?' Dun grumbled.

'Of course it matters. It does not mean I have to draw blood again. I've had my fill of killing,' said Feran, never taking his eyes from the flames.

Dun rolled over, turning his back to Feran.

'The forbidden conversation,' he murmured.

Feran sighed, feeling the two men would never see eye-to-eye on the issue. How could Dun ever understand the burden of guilt upon him lest he was told the facts? He would not hear them from Feran's lips, he vowed. Never in life. Even though Feran had told his squire the truth of the quest for the Mother Tree, against the queen's orders, he would never trust him with his reasons for setting aside his sword.

When morning came, Tolucan was feverish, and Feran took pains to prevent any infection of his wounds, dabbing at him with salves and making him drink all manner of nasty-tasting liquids from little bottles drawn from who knew where.

'Make yourself useful and scout out the area,' he called to Dun, whose cough was worsening.

When the squire returned with the news that there was no sign of anyone or anything thereabouts, Tolucan reluctantly agreed to make camp until the fever had broken, but only after he made several unsuccessful attempts to stand.

In the end, they spent a full week at the campsite, resting a while even after the fever broke, making the most of the ready water source.

Tolucan soon felt stronger, but it was clear as the days passed that Dun was in greater need of Feran's attention. The old man's cough worsened, wracking his body so badly that Tolucan feared for the squire's ribs. Dun grew lethargic, needing to nap frequently.

'He's getting thinner,' whispered Tolucan across the fire while Dun slept one evening.

Feran sighed, looked back over his shoulder at the old man then nodded slowly.

'He's started to cough up blood as well. My brews are not helping,' Feran conceded.

They said nothing for a time, the fire crackling between them. Tolucan was concerned for the old man, but other concerns were paramount, although he was wary of voicing them.

'I cannot linger here for much longer,' said Tolucan quietly. 'I understand if you want to stay here with him until he is better or . . . '

Feran's eyes flashed, the fire throwing sinister shadows across his face, but he looked back down at the blistering logs and said nothing.

'I have a duty to continue,' said Tolucan.

Feran nodded.

'We will not abandon you,' said Feran. 'Not yet.'

Chapter Seven

Elaris, The Butterfly Isle

'Get on with you,' said the man above the gate. 'Should be ashamed. Dressed all fine when you're nowt but beggars at our gate! If you can't *pay* your way, you can be *on* your way!'

'No disrespect, sir,' said the man's wife, standing beside him above the makeshift gate of Elaris. 'Times are hard for all.'

'And the queen's colours mean nothing to you?' asked Aldwyn, calling up from his horse. A small group of horsemen clad in the colours of the Maconnock clan, natives of the Butterfly Isle, were gathered on the road and awaited his command.

The gates of Elaris were closed to them, and a new palisade had been constructed, a rarity in these times, when Dryads often tore down new works. Mountains rose behind the pine forest-swaddled town.

The man shrugged.

'Don't matter what they mean. Got people here who work for their keep, and we've got nothing to spare just so you can parade around in your finery without lifting a finger. Go on now.'

The bowman standing next to him shifted his weight from foot to foot, and Aldwyn saw him shrugging so that the quiver on his back sat more comfortably.

'Your name?' asked Aldwyn.

'Is my own,' said the man. 'Move on. We're done paying your way, lad.'

He pointed at Aldwyn as he spoke, and the duke struggled to maintain his composure.

'Sir, it is the law that you allow us entry to your lands, and that you pay tithe. If you do not comply, I will return with the sheriffs and force a way through to take what is owed. There will be arrests and consequences for all therein. You defy the queen's own commands.'

The man leant over the wall, and his cheeks flushed as he shouted.

'You bloody well try it, and you'll find what we've got has been hidden or burned rather than give it up to you. Not that I've seen a sheriff in many a month. They've all long seen sense or been shown it at the end of a knife, I'll warrant.'

The bowman grinned, and Aldwyn's heart sank. This was becoming all too familiar a response to his arrival as he made the Tithe Walk throughout The Isles, one of the measures Cathryn had instituted years before to ensure her rule was maintained.

'There are those who farm, those who hunt and those who govern. Those who govern cannot spend their days in the fields. We must spend our days on the road, ensuring that the queen's peace is maintained throughout The Isles,' Aldwyn said, but with little hope.

'The queen's peace? When did you last hear from the queen? You did your best, Your Grace. You are a good man,' said the man in a moment of thoughtless courtesy, 'but we all must look to ourselves now. You've no enemies here, but we're not paying tithe no more.'

'You look well-off enough to me,' said the bowman. 'Don't need no tithe. Clear out now and let us about our business.'

'Hold off there, John,' said the man's wife, stepping up behind him. 'We're not all out of hospitality yet.' The man began to berate her but she cut him off.

'No. I'm not having that.' She turned back to Aldwyn and called down.

'We won't pay tithe, Lord Aldwyn, but you're welcome as our guests if you'll disarm. A meal we can spare you, and a bed for the night. We're not traitors.'

The man began to grumble again, but with a single look, his wife cut him down to size. He went down from the gate without turning back.

Aldwyn considered his next move. By the letter of the law, he'd be entitled to take what he required as soon as they opened the gate, but how would that further his cause? It might instil fear in any who survived and to those whose ears heard about it, but with no army to back him, what would it achieve? Unity was the goal, not disorder.

They could not know how dirty the ragged clothes were beneath his fine armour. They were not to know how his flesh had been rubbed raw by the weight of burden during years on the road or how hunger plagued his men. In truth, Aldwyn and his company were still a sight to behold. They took great pains to care for their armour, which was of the very best quality. Their clothes were washed whenever they happened upon a stream, but no sooner were they gone from a place of strength, than the company would find a quiet place in the woods to remove their fine metal armour and lay it carefully in the cart. If the man and his wife had seen the company earlier that day, there would have been no colours held aloft or a vision of a lord of old Tayne at the head of a band of mounted Maconnock clansmen. Instead they would have seen a troop of wasted beggars tramping onward, armed but in ill spirits. The splendour was for show and to project a power that more and more of the people were realising had no foundations. Where shining armour and standards were once the signal to pay homage and encourage stalwart hearts to do their duty, they became either signs of opulence in times of hardship or fripperies worn by those who wielded no real influence.

Aldwyn knew that his grasp on the settlements of The Isles had never been weaker. What were the queen's colours if not the emblems of a distant woman whose realm had become nothing but an idea, and an idea that no longer had any bearing on their lives, at that? John's guess had been near the mark. It had been years since any ship had arrived from The Folly. When Aldwyn sent the Nightingale, Captain Silas Unwin returned with the news that the Arduan Peninsula was a lawless place with signs of battle visible from the harbour wall. Lord Magregar's banners flew on the quayside and when the Nightingales had attempted to land to gain news, Magregar's archers had loosed a volley of arrows to turn the boats away.

There were no tidings of the queen, and of her fleet, there was no sign. The ships under Aldwyn's command had scattered over the years, seeking new places to put down their crews, for when the vessels remained together, the Naiads demonstrated their displeasure, tearing holes in the hulls, sinking not a few ships. Only the Nightingale remained under his command. Only Silas Unwin heeded when Aldwyn called. He had no army to call upon, only a gaggle of loyal soldiers at various keeps throughout The Isles, acting as emissaries to the many clans.

A chill wind blew and rain beat down upon him. He sighed and called up to the woman.

'I would gladly accept a meal and a bed, lady, but I am loath to disarm. Do you not trust us?'

'Trust the man who just threatened to have the sheriffs break apart our gates and raid the larder?' She folded her arms and smiled. Aldwyn nodded, resigned.

'Fair enough,' he sighed.

He looked back at his people and saw strained expressions upon their gaunt faces. He returned his attention to the woman above the gate.

'I give you my word, we will not draw blades against any inside,' he tried once more and could see the woman considering her conviction.

'Wait a moment,' she said and disappeared from view.

A moment later, a smaller door within the main gate into the village opened, and the man the woman had called John stepped through.

'How many of you are there?' he asked.

'Myself and twenty-two others. Twenty-six horses and two mules there are also.'

'Not short on meat then.' The man huffed then came out from the shadow of the gate, his arms folded across his chest.

'Five may enter at a time. Five we can manage. The rest may make such a camp as you can outside our walls.'

For a moment it seemed he was done as he began to turn, but then he added,

'We will prepare quarters for you, Your Grace. You may stay the night while the others take their turn. Least we can do for one such as yourself. You and the chieftain there.'

John pointed back towards the clansmen.

It was clear the words pained him, and Aldwyn made no attempt to lord it over him. He quit his horse and took the man's hand in both of his own, grasping firmly.

'You have our thanks. We are cold, hungry and weary. I would speak more with you later, if you are willing.'

The man nodded.

'Aye, if ya must. John Comhann is my name. I've trusted you with it. Don't misuse it,' he said as he walked back to the gate.

Aldwyn led his horse back to the road, and Mungan Maconnock, chieftain of the Maconnock clan, leant down to him, his grey eyes fixed on the duke from above his hooked nose.

'Beggars at the door,' he hissed. 'I had a mind to lift yon fellow's head from his shoulders.'

Maconnock resembled Lachlan, tall and proud atop his horse, broad-shouldered but with shaggy hair hanging to his waist, tied at intervals with copper bands. He wore furs all about him and weapons on every limb.

Aldwyn shook his head.

'We have much cleaving ahead if that is to be our approach. How often is this our reception now? Nay, I must take counsel on this matter and think carefully.'

'That may be, but I've a mind to follow a man who won't stand for such words,' said Mungan, and others murmured assent.

'Does my own company turn on me then?' asked Aldwyn.

Mungan's eyes flashed, but his reply was soft enough for Aldwyn's liking.

'I am but watchful on your behalf, Your Grace,' said the chieftain.

Aldwyn reached up and rubbed the neck of the Maconnock's horse.

'And I am ever grateful. Let us take what we can from this encounter and talk more at our leisure on the morrow,' he said.

Aldwyn and Mungan selected two men and three women from among the Maconnocks to accompany them into the village of Elaris, long famed in The

Isles for its distillery. Though Aldwyn had never been inside the village, he had sampled Elaris Whisky both in his quarters at The Folly and thousands of miles away in the colonies. This whisky was better-travelled than most of his company, he mused as he entered.

The gate was closed and barred behind them. Aldwyn took note of the defences, seeing bowmen on the walls and men just inside the gate, who took the surrendered weapons.

Now that Comhann was on his own territory and had the duke at a disadvantage, he found some magnanimity.

'Welcome to Elaris, Your Grace. You and your people are most welcome here.'

He bowed ever so slightly. Aldwyn acknowledged with a nod of his head then looked around him at the town's buildings, visible between the many trees.

'You have fared very well, Master Comhann, said Aldwyn. 'Many villages were left without a building still standing, let alone its defences intact.'

'We were not unscathed, but perhaps that is a tale for later,' he said, and Aldwyn suspected he would hear of something he did not like.

Aldwyn's people took some time washing, as water was in good supply in Elaris. Aldwyn stripped to the waist in the main yard and dunked his head in the peaty water that flowed along a stone channel from the north palisade. He flung his head back and his wet hair slapped his back. He gasped, spat out water and then leant down again to drink his fill. Sitting on the stone ledge by the channel, he looked out over the palisade and his eyes followed the slopes as they climbed up into the high mountains that rose up in the centre of the Butterfly Isle.

'Up yonder is the tarn,' said Comhann's wife.

Aldwyn turned and bowed his head, scrabbling to pull on his shirt, but she held up a hand.

'I've seen worse, Your Grace.' She nodded up towards the mountains once more.

'Eagle's Tarn. Its streams feed this channel and flow into the distillery. How the world has moved on, eh? I'll wager that the last time you drank from Eagle's Tarn, it'll have been distilled before ever it touched your lips.' She ran her trailing hand across the flowing water.

'We distil only a little now. There's no demand for it,' she said.

'I doubt that very much,' Aldwyn replied, 'Demand for it is one thing and means to pay is another.'

The woman laughed.

'True enough, Your Grace. Either way, our barley is for porridge, gruel and bread now.'

'How fares your crop?' The question was innocent, born of genuine interest, but Comhann's wife eyed him suspiciously. Aldwyn realised what she was thinking and held up his hands in protest.

'I am not trying to deceive you into giving something away,' he said and then, sighing, 'What is your name?'

'Matilda,' she replied. 'I was master distiller here before the forests came. I suppose I still am. The crop is good, Your Grace. Better than ever. We've drawn in what folk we can to tend to our needs and protect our interests, but I'll let John tell you the rest. That's his business. Just you pay heed to neither his mouth nor his temper. He's just scared.'

'Scared of what?' asked Aldwyn.

'Of you. Of telling you no,' Matilda replied.

Aldwyn, feeling like a half-drowned and starved cat, as he stood bare-chested in this woman's yard, did not feel particularly awe-inspiring or intimidating.

In the evening, Aldwyn broke bread with the Comhanns. The heat of their earlier exchange had all but cooled, and Aldwyn learnt much from them now that they were more willing to talk. He heard of how the town's founders had been from the Comhann clan of Long Isle, but that after a feud, they had broken away and rowed across the Sound of Nerith to land upon the northern shore of the Butterfly Isle. They had searched for a place of strength, both well-supplied and with fresh water. It took them a few weeks traversing the mountains before they stumbled upon the high tarn.

'It's said that when the first of the founders crested the hill and reached the water's edge, she looked up and saw two great golden eagles wheeling overhead,' said Matilda.

'Hence the name. Eagle's Tarn.' said John.

'Thank you, my love, I think the duke took my point,' she said softly and rolled her eyes so only Aldwyn could see. He disguised a smile behind his hand.

Never the fool, Aldwyn waited until his hunger was sated before broaching more controversial subjects.

'When we spoke earlier you said that the story of how Elaris got through the last years was a tale for later,' he said, and John looked down at the last morsel of his bread as he nodded his head.

'Aye.'

'I'm not blind, Master Comhann. I see your hesitance. What is there in this that may anger or offend me?' said Aldwyn.

'Well, Your Grace, we suffered the same as everyone else with trees growing up suddenly all through the town and Dryads tearing down the stone walls. At first we thought the Dryads were a new type of Devised, that Awgren had somehow survived. We fought them of course and were swiftly put down.' He reached for a goblet of water as he spoke. 'We lost a good many people, but when the gates were broken and the bulk of our standing militia lay dead, they left us be.'

'Not unusual,' said Aldwyn. 'The Dryads seem to kill only to end resistance, to intimidate or inadvertently as they go about their destruction. Destroying roads, strongholds, mines and defences seemed to be their chief interests. Keeping our society simple.'

'Aye,' said John. 'Well, you know we've got by and paid tithe year on year, but as time's moved on, we've had to fight off those who have less or don't want to work for their bread, preferring to rob it from harder-working souls. Some of the clans even began reaving. Trade has dropped off as other villages started to plunder one another.'

Aldwyn nodded. 'I've heard as much. We do not walk the woods without our wits about us these days. Your reaction to the queen's colours is becoming commonplace.'

'Not cos she isn't our queen though,' Matilda broke in. 'She is and always will be, as will be her children after her, bless their living souls. We're not traitors.'

'And yet now I find the Dryads have allowed you to rebuild, and you will not pay the queen's tithe?' asked Aldwyn, setting down his goblet.

'Well, now we come to it,' said John then nothing more until he had drained his own. When he continued, his tone reminded Aldwyn of an abashed soldier reporting some indiscretion.

'Not long after your company last came to collect tithe, I was out in the fields and a movement caught my eye. Looked like a man, hidden amongst the barley. Thought it a trick of the light at first, but then I realised it was one of them, less like a tree and more like our crop.'

'A Dryad,' said Matilda.

'A Dryad,' said John. 'S'what I was getting at, woman.'

Aldwyn waited patiently.

'Long story short,' said Matilda, 'He came back in and told us what he had seen, fearing some new assault. I went out into the field and spoke to it.'

'Oh?' said Aldwyn, but he was not surprised at Matilda's tenacity.

'Aye, and I told it we were hard-working people who meant no one no harm, and it only went and complimented me on our barley fields. Fair quaking I was, but it turned out I had no cause to worry. I told it of the bandits, and how we did not sleep easy in our beds. Asked it about the gate and the wall. It said such things were not allowed no more and little else. It disappeared amongst the barley and I stood there wondering if I'd gone quite mad, talking to the crop.'

'You're a brave woman, lady,' said Aldwyn.

'A little too brave at times,' said John. 'She makes a fine husband.'

She scolded him and swatted his arm, but John grinned and though her expression was stern, Matilda's smile betrayed her.

'Is that all?' Aldwyn said when it was clear they were quite distracted, lost in one another's mischief.

'No, Your Grace. It came back the next day. Appeared right here in the yard and requested an audience, if you like!' said John.

'The council sat down with it, and it explained the futility of building defences against them. We told it we knew, that'd we'd learnt that lesson when we took up arms against them. It questioned us something rotten about our desires and plans. When it was done, it said if we did not overgrow in size nor take more from the woods or the ground than was just, we could have our gate back up and build a palisade,' said Matilda. 'Just to protect ourselves.'

'That's it,' said John, 'and if that makes us traitors then we're traitors. But I say it true, we're still loyal to the queen. It's just things have changed. Seems that's all folk ever say any more, but it's true. The Crown offers us no protection now, and we must look to our own, watch our walls and build up what store we can to last the winter. And quit paying tithe to those who've not earned it, Your Grace,' Comhann concluded.

'And yet it is the law of the Combined People,' said Aldwyn, his voice grave. 'There are ways to change laws and ignoring them is not one of them.'

At this John frowned and looked as though he might stand, but Matilda bade him sit. He did so, but he pointed once more at Aldwyn.

'If we're going to have that debate again, you can bugger off back outside the gate! We're not daft, we know you've armed men camped at hand, but we outnumber you, and we have our walls. We have a good life here, and we're prepared to defend it. So no threats. Elaris has always been a little different. We never had no thegn or chieftain. The council has always been made up of the regular working folk of Elaris, who know their concerns. You can make us an exception again. We're still Cathryn's people, but we'll not pay for the privilege of respecting her colours. We've fed you, and we'll give you shelter, but we'll not give away our harvest. No.'

Aldwyn's face gave little away, but he looked about him to see if any had overheard the exchange. Many sat nearby and looked away as his gaze fell upon them, even his own people.

'I must take some air,' he said and begged their leave. He went out into the yard and leant against an apple tree that grew there, casting his eyes around Elaris and considering all that had been said, considering his responsibilities. When he was suitably calm and could be sure his words would not inflame the situation, he returned to sit across from John Comhann. He too had calmed, and he begged Aldwyn's pardon.

'I give it,' said Aldwyn. 'You have the mettle to speak your mind, and I applaud such strength.'

The Comhanns were true to their word, and once Aldwyn's people had eaten and rested for a time, they left the village and the next five entered. This went on throughout the rest of the evening until all had been fed. Aldwyn was granted the use of a small bed in the Comhanns' lodge, but he did not sleep, troubled by all that had been said.

The next morning, he thanked them and gave them a small bag of coin.

'For your troubles. It does not pay our way, but it's all I have left,' he said.

'Keep it,' said John Comhann. He reached into the bag and withdrew a single coin. 'I'll have this to honour the sentiment though.'

Aldwyn bowed low and mounted his horse.

'I have cause to return this way in a few days. We will not trouble you for food, but if you can offer us shelter for the night, I would be grateful,' said Aldwyn.

'You and your people are most welcome, Your Grace,' said Matilda and curtsied. The Comhanns watched as Aldwyn drew level with Mungan Maconnock, then the two men led the company, composed mostly of Maconnocks, on to the track that led westward.

Aldwyn's company returned before noon on the third day, once more regaled in their armour and with Cathryn's standard flying. The duke made no attempt to demand tithe and made no show of arrogance. Instead, he dismounted at a distance from the gate and called up to the watchman there before knocking on the door. In a few minutes, Matilda opened it and greeted him with a bow.

'How do you fare, lady?' asked Aldwyn.

'Well, Your Grace. I hope the same can be said of you and your people.'

'We are well enough, lady, and have been hunting. We bring meat for your board if you will have us, a few at a time as before. If the offer of shelter is still good, we will stay the night and trouble you no more. I have a mind to settle on Long Isle at Halflight Hold with the queen's children. The days of the tithe walk are over, I deem,' he said, unsmiling.

'You are welcome, Your Grace.' She closed the door, and the gates creaked open.

Aldwyn, Maconnock and the first five of the company led their horses to the stables, and beds were found for each of them as guests amongst the folk of Elaris while the rest of the clansmen made camp near the gate. Aldwyn once more was granted the use of the bed in the Comhanns' lodge. True to their word, Aldwyn made a gift of a great stag, a boar and a brace of rabbits.

'It's a wonder you go so hungry when you hunt so well,' said John when he saw the meat being carried to the cookfires.

Mungan Maconnock took a sip from the whisky that the council had poured for their guests then said, 'We seldom have time for such a hunt, but Lord Aldwyn and I would not be called beggars at your door again. The accusation rankled.'

Comhann's face flushed, and he stuttered some reply, seemingly cowed by the looming chieftain of the Maconnocks, armoured and cloaked in furs.

They had a merry feast, and Aldwyn's company mingled with the villagers, sharing songs and tales until eyelids began to droop. Aldwyn savoured the last drop of his whisky and begged leave to retire. The company took their cue and did likewise, retreating to bed. It seemed to Aldwyn that the Comhanns breathed a sigh of relief that the engagement was near done, and that when the company departed on the morrow, they could go about their business unmolested. Aldwyn had been just, Matilda told him, in the handling of what they knew was a difficult situation.

Just before dawn, Aldwyn rose from his bed and quietly strapped on his belt and sword. He crept across the lodge to where the Comhanns slept upon a thick pile of furs, not far from the embers of the fire. He held his breath, conscious of the noise, and knelt down beside John.

'Comhann,' Aldwyn whispered, shaking John with his left hand.

Comhann started awake.

'What?' he exclaimed. Matilda stirred, but did not wake.

'The queen's word is law,' said Aldwyn then plunged his knife into Comhann's neck three times. John kicked out, striking Matilda, and she yelped, opening her eyes. Aldwyn threw his weight across her. Still holding the knife, he pushed against the back of her head with both hands. Her face sank into the furs, and she writhed as her husband's blood dripped into her greying hair. Aldwyn kept the pressure on until he was sure she was dead.

He wiped the knife on the furs as he begged the Comhanns' forgiveness in a whisper, before he drew his sword and went out into the night.

He stood in the cool night air, his rapid breathing breaking the silence as he looked up and watched wisps of cloud drift across the moon. Aldwyn set off towards the gate, and as he did so, he heard the first shouts and screams.

A door opened in a lodge to his right, and Mungan Maconnock stepped out, still clutching the severed head of his host by the hair. He stood silent, his head low and his axe held high, his long hair dancing in the chill breeze.

Aldwyn nodded to him and together they made their way to open the gate and let in the rest of their men.

When dawn came, the gates of Elaris stood open, and the heads of the Comhanns and the other members of the Elaris council were arrayed atop it, their dead eyes looking down upon their kinsfolk as they set about gathering the tithe, watched over by Lord Aldwyn.

The queen's banner flapped above the gate.

Chapter Eight

Morrick had been a simple man, descended from pioneers and frontier people. He had built a home for Rowan near the banks of the Whiteflow *before* he proposed, felling the trees with his own hands. An offering. He had whittled and embellished the wood until the logs and beams bore the whispering of his heart. Their home was functional, but ornate in its own simple way, a place for shelter, family, work, rest and love, but it could not compare with even the most rudimentary halls of the Combined People, let alone the keeps and temples of old Tayne, Crinan and Culrain.

Now he was Dark Oak, King of the Dryads, and he held the whole world in his sway. He could dwell wherever he desired and craft great palaces with his powers, and he dwelt high in the Maw Keep while his followers did his bidding, yet his thoughts returned to his former family home time and again as the years passed.

He travelled less himself these days, every journey threatening to divert him from his purpose. The calming influence of the forest snatched at him in the fraction of a second it took for him to step into one tree and out of another, miles distant, like hands reaching to grasp him, pulling him back through a doorway. He did not wish to find peace in the acceptance of simply existing. He had a duty to maintain harmony, he knew. Every time he stepped into its trees, the collective weight of the Dryads dwelling within lessened his rage, quelling his sense of hurt and betrayal. Doubts had begun to plague him, doubts about whether he had been wrong to confront and defeat the humans. He knew that prolonged time with the forest would lessen his imperative, that he would be absorbed within the elder Dryads, and he would leave the humans be, so that all would return to as it had been. *That* he could not risk. To admit he had misplaced his anger and deceived himself about his motives? Impossible. And so Morrick, Dark Oak, remained rage and injustice incarnate, not human, but not like other Dryads. An abomination.

To begin with, he had been able to subdue and overpower the Dryads with the force of his newborn will, but as the years passed, the elder Dryads among them, initially led by Nayr, closest to Riark, had begun to return to the trees without Dark Oak's leave. Those who had more recently died as humans and had reincarnated were easier to control, particularly those who had been killed during the purge of human society. They were reborn with fear, grief, a sense of injustice and, crucially, an awe of him that he used to hold them in his sway. Dark Oak still had them in his grasp, denying them communion with the trees, their thoughts and memories twisted to suit his purpose. They eschewed travel through the trees, remaining in the areas where Dark Oak had sent them, each performing their task based on their own interpretation. He was forced to accept that he could not worry about the details. Humanity must not be allowed to regain dominance. That was the message, and he believed his newborns understood. Lord Hawthorn, as he had taken to calling the Dryad who had been Lachlan, had been reassuring. Dark Oak had placed him on the throne of the Maw Keep not only to cow Queen Cathryn, but to test a new Dryad's loyalty and resolve. All had gone well.

Limiting travel himself meant losing touch with his followers, and being disconnected from the forest most of the time meant he was not appraised of the mood within, denied new knowledge. Whenever he *did* travel, he briefly sensed how many of the Dryads had returned home and how the mood was turning against him, their self-proclaimed king, the usurper. Dark Oak grew paranoid that some element, maybe led by Nayr, would rise up against him, and he began to give thought to how he could protect himself, protect his Mother Tree, the source of his life and his only physical weakness.

He relied on Red Maple to travel for him much of the time, but his son was becoming more like Riark every time he saw him; wiser, calmer and less concerned with the doings of humans. When Dark Oak melded with Red Maple to renew his understanding, he found his son questioned his instructions and doubted their philosophy. Worse, those doubts ebbed back into Dark Oak. Red Maple would have to refrain from travelling before long as well, Dark Oak decided. The King of the Dryads could no longer sequester himself at the Maw Keep; he must return to the place which would act as a constant reminder of human suffering and the danger the race posed to the world. Somewhere he could be near the old forest and the Mother Trees of his people, if not within them.

The Hinterland

Dark Oak emerged from an old chestnut tree just inside what had been the bounds of the Impassable Forest, against which he had reclined while fishing the river Whiteflow as a boy.

Red Maple appeared after him, and a short time later, the heads of his Naiad siblings, Whiteflow and Seaborn, broke the surface of the river. The four of them, father and children, travelled towards their former home, no longer recognising the way since Dark Oak's forest covered what had been grassland.

Dark Oak led them to the remains of the homestead, its dry-stone wall, its corral, its barns, workshops and the lodge now deep within the young forest, abandoned and in need of care.

Dark Oak stood for a time at the broken gate, surveying the buildings and the trees, watching the ghosts of a former life go about their business. He recalled sneaking up behind Rowan as she stood on the porch calling to the boys, remembered slipping his arms around her, making her jump, and soothing her by kissing her neck. He could see Callum and Declan play-fighting with wooden swords in the yard. He remembered Acorna, Rowan's mother, cradling baby Bracken, rocking in the chair on the porch.

Dark Oak moved into the homestead through long grasses and flowers, reaching out to touch a fallen beam from the barn as he passed it by.

'Why do we return here?' said Whiteflow, formerly Bracken, looking back towards the river where Rowan had drowned her as a baby and where she had reincarnated as a Naiad.

Dark Oak gave no answer as he ducked inside the open door to the lodge and took in the broken remains of what had been his home. He felt an inexplicable sense that he was on the verge of tears, impossible, for he had no tear ducts. Just the memory of an emotion he could no longer experience, he told himself, but he slumped against the wall, hanging his head so that the blackened ivy of his hair settled on the damp planks of the floor.

'This place causes you pain,' said Red Maple, and when Dark Oak looked back over his shoulder, he saw his son standing in the doorway.

'I need the pain. The anger,' said Dark Oak.

Red Maple said nothing. Dark Oak knew he understood all too well.

'When I am here, I see your mother all the clearer. I remember the life that was twice denied me, first by Awgren and then by your mother. I remember all the pain and betrayal that humans cause one another, the hurts they inflict on the world. I must hold on to that,' he said.

'Must you?' said Red Maple.

Dark Oak turned to face him, tilting his head. He reached for his son, casting out tendrils that took a delicate grasp of his hand, merging their bodies until their thoughts, perceptions and emotions stood bare before one another. Dark Oak frowned, and a fissure split the surface of his face, steam escaping before the wood healed.

Dark Oak perceived that Red Maple knew it was the memory of his mother that made his father feel as he did. Years had passed since she had rejected Morrick, and yet Dark Oak was unable to push her from his mind. Red Maple wanted him to forgive his mother, and if that was too much, to release her from her suffering and end her torment. She was a mother whose children were all dead, though she knew it not. Was that not punishment enough?

Dark Oak released his grip on Red Maple's hand, flinging it from him in disgust.

'You will not listen, Father?' said Red Maple.

'To such heresy? No,' Dark Oak replied in his rumbling voice. 'That woman betrayed me, denied me and stole my hope.'

'You speak like a spurned lover, not the lord of the world,' said Red Maple. 'You should move beyond this, for our sakes if not for hers.'

'What do you mean?' asked Dark Oak.

'My brother and I, we wish to see her happy again. She was a good mother, and a wife in difficult times. You do not fully understand all that she endured,' said Red Maple.

'It is you who do not understand,' said Dark Oak. 'You are but a child.'

Red Maple crossed the room and took his father by the shoulders, trying to fix him with his gaze, though he had forgotten to form pupils.

'I understand all that you understand. We have both been one with the forest and shared knowledge. You have held on to bitterness and resentment too long. There is peace to be had, for all. Your rule is misguided, Father. You have infused your sapling desire to protect the forest with the hurt of a human husband,' said Red Maple.

Dark Oak said nothing for a time. He rested his palm against a wooden post which supported the roof. He let his consciousness pool in his hand and then pour into the wood. It flowed out into the bones of the lodge and breathed new life into them, curing the rot and repairing the cracks. Dark Oak became one with his family's home.

It must have been apparent his father and king no longer heeded him, for Red Maple backed out through the doorway and stepped down among the grass to join his Naiad brother and sister.

Dark Oak dwelt on Red Maple's words. It was true that when he first stepped down from his Mother Tree he had been brimming with rage at the many injustices he had faced in his previous life; slavery, betrayal and, in the end, denial of even the release of death by Riark's intervention. Had he used Morrick's despair and bitterness to wreak havoc, disguising his vengeance as a quest to bring balance to the world and to protect its forests?

Dark Oak reluctantly admitted that he had begun to recognise Riark's conciliatory, acceptant attitude in himself. More and more often he caught himself thinking, why go to this trouble? Let things be. Let nature take its course. Perhaps also, he eventually admitted, he was beginning, just a little, to feel regret.

Dark Oak longed to slip inside the trunk of his Mother Tree and diffuse within it like tea in water. His pains would ease as do weary limbs in a warm bath. There would be no thought, merely existence, and the tumult of these last years would be over.

But the King of the Dryads fought the impulse to return to his Mother Tree, which grew in the south of the Impassable Forest, not far from Oystercatcher Bay. His consciousness ebbed back to his avatar, and Dark Oak departed the lodge. He stood, hands on wooden hips and took stock of the meadow.

'Here is where I will hold court from now on,' he told his children, 'here where we belong.'

One more journey and then back there. Back home.

The Folly, Tayne

Dark Oak stepped out of the very same apple tree through which he, and Riark before him, had first arrived at The Folly years before. Where once there had been a patch of grass surrounded by a high wall, now the tree stood in a ring of broken stone. Ruination was apparent all around him, buildings long torn down and never repaired, the remains of long-abandoned campsites and the skeletons of the dead.

Dark Oak allowed himself a final tour of the peninsula, spying out the various groups of humans who picked a living there, warring with one another now that the queen's control had waned. He stood at the quayside, now devoid of ships, although the wreckage of some of them still washed against the stones upon which he stood.

Lord Magregar's banner, torn and detached at one corner, flapped above the remains of the harbourmaster's office. Dark Oak wondered if the queen's former lord was still alive or whether those who had remained loyal had finished off the traitor. Dark Oak grinned.

Such a petty game they make of life, he thought.

He made his way through the devastation, people fleeing at the sight of him, until he saw the now-broken gate to the Maw Keep and a company of Cathryn's men standing guard there. They saw him approach and stood to attention as he passed by. He smiled and threw them a mocking salute as he did so.

Dark Oak climbed the steps inside the keep and made his way along the torch-lit corridor to the throne room. He passed through the open doors and amidst the vines which hung all around.

Although years had passed, the Dryad that had been Lachlan, Lord Hawthorn, sat upon his throne, still adorned in the armour and circlet he had worn in his former life.

As he had sat upon the wooden chair, living ever more inwardly, his concentration waned and his body became one with the wood of the throne. It was no longer possible to tell where Lachlan ended and it began. His head was slumped forward and bark covered his face. His beard of black ivy hung like a curtain over his knees. His hands and forearms looked as though they had been whittled from the arms of the throne. Dark Oak did not trouble the former Lord of The Isles in his torment.

Queen Cathryn's throne was unoccupied, but nevertheless, two of her household flanked it and stood to attention as Dark Oak approached. Dark

Oak nodded to them, but they did not respond beyond the initial courtesy. They kept their eyes upon the open doorway, looking for any sign of intruders or attackers.

Dark Oak walked around the dais towards the door which led to the queen's private chambers. He turned the handle, but the door was barred from the inside. Dark Oak shook his head, wondering when the queen's aide would learn the futility of such a gesture. He walked into the surface of the wood and out of the other side, appearing at the end of a long corridor lined with other doors.

'Queen,' he called, but there was no response from any of the rooms.

He approximated a sigh, his lungless chest rising and falling, and began to walk towards the closest door when another opened, and Ailsa stepped into the corridor. The woman wore leather armour and was girt with two short swords. An ugly scar now cut diagonally across her forehead. She was far thinner than when he had first laid eyes on her and her eyes were dark hollows.

'What?' she asked. 'What do you want?'

'The queen,' he said, striding towards her aide.

'She won't see you,' said Ailsa.

Dark Oak brushed her aside with his arm and was pushing open the door when he felt something impale his back between where his shoulder blades would have been if he had any. He paused and turned to look at Ailsa. She shrugged, then, after wiggling it loose, she hauled her knife out from the Dryad's back.

'Wait here,' said Dark Oak and closed Cathryn's door behind him.

The queen's chamber was shrouded in darkness. Wooden shutters covered the tall windows that were strewn with heavy drapes.

It appeared to Dark Oak that the chamber had not changed at all in the years since he had thrown down The Folly walls and occupied the queen's keep. The surfaces were devoid of dust, the floor was neatly swept and yet there was something amiss, though Dark Oak had not the ability to discern it. While Ailsa was all too aware of the heavy scent of alcohol in the air, Dark Oak lacked the olfactory sense.

Dark Oak's wooden feet could not find purchase on the stone floor as he crossed the room to the bed, and they slipped a little as he walked. Queen Cathryn was swaddled in blankets and snoring heavily, a trickle of drool had dried a slug trail from the corner of her mouth to the pillow beneath her.

'Queen,' said Dark Oak. There was no sign of reaction.

He reached out and shook her by the shoulder. She stirred and groaned a little, but did not wake. Dark Oak shook her harder. She lashed out at him in her sleep, drawing her hand back with a yelp when she struck his solid body. Her eyelids fluttered open, but she fell asleep again. Dark Oak tilted his head and watched her. He stayed for a few minutes and made a few more attempts to rouse her, then gave up and returned to the corridor, considering the queen's condition and feeling somewhat responsible. It did not hearten him to see her so diminished, he realised. He found Ailsa waiting outside, her arms folded across her chest.

'You were told,' she said.

Dark Oak ignored her and set off the way he had come.

'How long will this go on?' Ailsa called. 'How long will you torture her?'

Dark Oak turned to face the queen's aide.

'What would you have me do?' he asked.

'Go back to the forests! Let us be!' said Ailsa.

'To swarm across the world, rebuild and make war?' Dark Oak replied with scorn in his voice. 'To cut down the forests and kill my people?'

'To dwell in peace! Make what demands you will, and we will see what we make of them. Dryads and humans left each other alone for thousands of years, did they not? Why are you insistent on laying us low?' she asked.

For a moment, Dark Oak found that the answer evaded him. Once more that familiar vague sense of purpose was upon him, which dictated his actions, while not fully justifying their necessity.

He returned to stand before Ailsa and spoke softly to her.

'Do you think I enjoy being in this form, far away from my home?' he asked her. She leant back against the stone wall, yawning, he perceived, to disguise the shaking of her hands. He smiled.

'Honestly?' Ailsa asked. Dark Oak nodded, green tendrils running between his jaw and neck snapping as he did so, his white eyes twinkling in the black wood of his face.

'Certainly I think you enjoy it. Whatever personal cost it might bring to you, you love all of this, the power, the revenge and the enjoyment you glean from watching those who ruled, now cowering in your shadow,' said Ailsa.

Dark Oak pondered her words in silence, and the human woman kept her eyes fixed on him.

'Perhaps,' he mused, 'there is some truth in what you say.'

Ailsa seemed to be hiding her reaction, but a blink gave her away. Dark Oak held out his hands before him and turned them over. As he did so, the shape of veins rose on the back of his hands, and nails appeared on his fingertips. The more he concentrated, the more perfect a wooden carving of a human hand they became. He rubbed his thumbs and fingers together, but felt no sensation from the movement. He looked up at Ailsa, feeling the urge to unburden himself and truly speak his mind as he could never do with his own kind.

'What are you doing?' she asked, still scowling, but her voice perhaps a little softer.

Dark Oak wanted to tell her. He needed to speak the words to another, to hear them as though voiced by somebody else. Perhaps then he could judge his thoughts objectively.

'It matters not,' he said and looked through the door into the queen's chamber.

'What ails her?' Dark Oak asked, nodding in that direction.

'Ails her? You mean aside from the fall of her realm, the sundering of her people, the loss and torment of her husband and her realisation that she has no place in the world?' Ailsa spoke slowly, the malice in her voice undisguised.

Dark Oak said nothing.

'She drinks,' Ailsa said. 'Heavily. And I don't blame her. What else is there for her to do? We are under siege here, surviving only because we retain control of the Maw Gate and so are free to hunt in the forest to the north.'

Dark Oak had no answer to give. What *would* he have her do? It was true enough that he had brought Lachlan here to pain her, preserved the keep merely to demonstrate her own irrelevance. It had seemed necessary at the time, and, he realised, it was true, he had enjoyed her dismay, *all* of the humans' dismay as he changed the world about them. Yet now when he looked upon Queen Cathryn, he saw a bird fallen from the nest or an injured animal. Yes, he had wished for humanity to be reduced to the level of mere animals once again, rather than gods of the world, but had he truly wished to break their spirit? And what of Cathryn herself? She had never openly moved against the forest and, indeed, had proclaimed the forest under royal protection. Perhaps he had been too harsh. And yet if it were so, had his entire reaction been disproportionate? Maybe so.

Dark Oak folded his arms across his chest as something akin to nausea permeated his entire being, a sickness not of the stomach, but of the soul.

He was no longer aware of Ailsa watching him, failing to notice she had discerned his troubled mind.

He wondered if all of this had been a mistake, born out of his own despair and misery. Had he ended an entire civilisation like an angered husband smashing up a room after a dispute with his wife? Maybe it was so, he decided, and the nausea grew more severe. After all, he knew there were humans both on this continent and across the world who lived in harmony with nature. The Deru Weid, who had once advised the rulers of these lands, centuries ago, for instance. He struggled to justify his actions, to put up barriers in his mind to protect himself and fell back on the old logic. If humanity is capable of such malice and such destruction, such irrational action, then it was now echoed in him and was this not why the Dryads had been convinced to intervene? He was a living demonstration of the human capability for destruction, but with balance in the forefront of his mind. And had not those humans who had tried to live in a different way been all but wiped out? Only a handful of the Deru Weid still survived, dwelling apart from the rest of their kind.

It was so, he told himself, just so, though he did not quite believe it.

'Dark Oak,' said Ailsa, clearly uneasy, as Dark Oak braced his forearm against the stone wall.

He regained his composure and bowed his head to Ailsa.

'I will speak with the queen when she has recovered. At sundown tomorrow, we will hold a council in the throne room, and we will discuss the future.'

With that he turned and left her, departing for his own quarters.

Dark Oak found Red Maple, unbidden, waiting therein, accompanied by a slender Dryad who showed no outward sign of respect or acknowledgement when Dark Oak entered.

'What's this?' asked Dark Oak, stepping into the moonlight cast upon the floor by the open window.

'His Mother Tree is dying,' said Red Maple.

'Why am I pulled away from her when time is short?' asked the stranger Dryad.

Dark Oak nodded and sat back upon a table. It made a cracking sound under his weight, but he ignored it.

'Your time draws to a close,' stated Dark Oak. 'I would honour your passing, but I am not at liberty to travel through the forest at this time. My people have standing orders to find me when one of our kind is about to pass. You have my thanks for attending.'

'I would be with her until she dies. Until I die,' said the Dryad.

'I will not keep you long,' asked Dark Oak. 'Tell me, how does it feel to know that your time in the world may be at an end? Do you fear death?'

The Dryad stood tall and unbowed, treelike in his human form.

'I remember being afraid of death as a human,' it said, 'but it was for nothing in the end. I have had a second life, far longer than the first. I anticipate the cessation of growth, which goes against my nature, and the end of my existence. That is all. Though, I wonder what comes next.'

'May you find rest,' said Dark Oak, bowing his head and placing his hand over where his heart would have been.

For the first time, the Dryad looked almost humbly at his king.

'You hold the mastery of the forests and lead the First Council. Can you not say what is next for me? The humans are born and born again until they are ready to become Dryads, but what happens to us when our Mother Trees die? Some believe that our souls end as well, that the Cycle ends, but how can it be so? What purpose can there be in a cycle or rebirth that ends when our most enlightened time is at an end? Do our souls take on new forms, king?'

Dark Oak, who had not dwelt on such matters, bound by the human desire to stave off death, clasped his hands behind his back and feigned wisdom.

'Who can tell, but we all will find out at our allotted time. Go and be with your Mother. Take with you the knowledge that I watch over the world and, though our people may not hear me directly any longer, I will keep the forest safe. Your final task, then, is to be my envoy. Remind our people to maintain the watch over the world. Farewell,' said Dark Oak.

The Dryad bowed his head, more human affectation beginning to emerge the longer he was in their form, and then he departed, disappearing into the ivy which covered the floors.

'I too have wondered what awaits us after death,' said Red Maple, 'but perhaps we should be more concerned with the Eversleep.'

Dark Oak sighed.

'A myth,' he said, 'An idea. Nothing more.'

'The debate grows heated. I fear the elder Dryads will turn on us,' said Red Maple.

Dark Oak said nothing. Civil war amongst the Dryads? Had he brought human discord to the forest?

'There is still no consensus though, so there may be time yet,' said Red Maple. 'We know that sometimes human mothers birth children with new souls. It is their gift to the world.'

Dark Oak said nothing, but his brow furrowed. Red Maple continued.

'It is also known that humans are born and reborn until, finally, they ascend and awake inside a Mother Tree as one of us.'

'A superior species,' said Dark Oak, but Red Maple did not acknowledge him.

'We know no Dryad has ever lived as anything but a human before,' said Red Maple, 'that Dryads are not reincarnated as Dryads or humans, but the debate rages about what happens to *us* when our Mother Trees die, Father. Some believe that when we die, our spirits linger in new forms, in a part of the Cycle unknown to us. After all, none of us recall where our souls dwelled between human lives. Some believe that souls between human lives travel the world unseen until it is their time to take on new bodies, perhaps appearing as what the humans call ghosts; wandering spirits.'

Dark Oak wondered at this. The largely empty Maw Keep sometimes echoed with footsteps when nobody walked. He heard whispers at times, but could find nobody nearby. He paid closer heed to Red Maple's words when his son continued.

'Nayr's faction believes in something similar, but permanent for Dryads after death. She says that to be reincarnated as a Dryad is the last stage before existing without physical form at all, in the long sleep from which none can wake,' he said.

'The Eversleep,' said Dark Oak, and Red Maple nodded.

'Nayr's followers say that your rule endangers humans and that we risk breaking the Cycle,' he said.

'She ever seeks to sow dissent,' said Dark Oak, pondering how he could best deal with the female Dryad.

Perhaps I should send her to the Eversleep, if it exists, as I did Riark, he thought. Dark Oak smiled.

'Perhaps she is right, Father. If the humans die out, there will be no new souls to join the Cycle. The wandering souls will not be reincarnated, condemned to wandering forever, unable to ascend and become Dryads. If that happens, when all the Mother Trees finally die, succumbing to disease or torn down by storms, with no souls to replenish our numbers, the Dryads too will become extinct. There will be no humans. No Dryads. Only wandering spirits unable to ascend.'

A chill wind blew in through the open window and though the Dryads could not feel the cold, it rustled the leaves of Red Maple's hair.

'No more Dryads,' said Dark Oak.

'No more Dryads,' said Red Maple. 'Many of the elder Dryads accept fate, whatever it may be, but there are others who are not as passive. They rally to

Nayr, and their voices grow louder. I fear the forest may turn against you, Father.'

'You say nothing of the Sylphs, the Oreads and the Naiads. Where do they fit into this Cycle? Your sister and brother were human, were they not?' said Dark Oak. 'Nayr makes assumptions without all of the facts.'

'Whiteflow and Seaborn were not reincarnated as Naiads naturally,' Red Maple reminded him, 'just as we died and were forced into Dryad form.' Dark Oak thought he heard bitterness in Red Maple's voice as he spoke. The image of Callum's death at his own hands appeared to him. He remembered laying his son's broken body within the trunk of a red maple tree, transforming his son so that they could be together.

'Never has there been more strife in the world than now,' said Red Maple, 'and it was caused by one family that was not ready to ascend. Riark and the Naiads that saved Bracken may have made a grave mistake.'

'You question me, son?' asked Dark Oak.

Red Maple said nothing.

'Well, perhaps Whiteflow will have more answers,' said Dark Oak. 'Send for your sister and brother. We will have an audience with the human queen before I leave this place.'

Chapter Nine

The Impassable Forest

The forest becomes more treacherous every day, thought Tolucan, as he lay in the undergrowth watching yet another group of armed men parade by. Confrontation was sometimes unavoidable, and when he was forced to engage his fellow humans, he showed them no mercy, as he could not risk the quest. On that occasion, however, the men passed without incident.

A few hours later, he saw a Dryad moving between the trees. It looked at him, pausing only for a moment before continuing its journey. Tolucan realised he had been holding his breath.

He generally walked alone now that he had returned to full health. Feran, as was his wont, had fallen behind, no doubt entranced by a new flower or foraging for something which *he* considered to have value. It was true enough that the green paste had worked wonders on Tolucan's wound though, so he reminded himself to be courteous even in his thoughts. Knights were, weren't they?

Tolucan looked behind him, and he could see nothing except trees and undergrowth in the dim light, an occasional bird or animal breaking the silence.

The day wore on in an unremarkable fashion, spent as he had hundreds of days, trudging along, accompanied by his conflicting thoughts and ideas for what to do next.

Tolucan happened upon a glade ahead of him and took rest there, seating himself upon the grass. He unstrapped his belt and laid his sword across his folded legs. He looked up through the canopy at the blue sky above. He closed his eyes and thought of his children, wondering how they fared in this new world. He thought of their late mother and of his sister, Ada, wondering if she would ever hear word of the charge the queen had laid upon him. He doubted it. The thoughts caused him pain, and so he put them aside and focused on the sound of his breathing, counting every breath in and out. It helped him remain calm and focused.

Time fell away, and Tolucan turned inward until a noise brought him back to the world without. Heavy footfalls broke twigs in the trees ahead of him.

Tolucan jumped to his feet and fastened his scabbard once more at his side as he edged towards the footsteps.

More twigs breaking, and the sound of singing. A young, high voice, free from caution.

Tolucan took cover behind the trunk, his weapon still sheathed. He was all too aware of the sound of his breath and tried to get it under control lest he give away his own position. He flicked his eyes back to the woods behind him, wondering if Feran and Dun would come blundering along, bickering between themselves. He hoped not.

The singing grew louder as the seconds passed. Tolucan's hands were sweating, so he wiped them against his jerkin.

He waited.

The singing continued. Someone was approaching. Tolucan readied to face whatever emerged into the glade.

A twig snapped behind him. Tolucan jumped and turned, but he could see nothing. Feran perhaps?

He turned his attention back to the glade, and at that moment a young girl stepped into view. She was a little shy of ten, thought Tolucan, if the look of his own boys had been anything to go by. Her hair was fair and hung loose about her shoulders. She wore no shoes upon her feet, and she sang freely as though she knew no danger in the world. She paused when she entered the glade, obviously delighted by the sight of a patch of bluebells growing there. Tolucan had not heeded their presence until this moment, nor would he have known the name for them, a man of Stragglers' Drift as he was, a land where naming plants and animals was the business of folk with too much time to waste. They were flowers. They were blue and they looked like bells. If they had a use, he did not know it, but those who needed them would know. There was a stark order to the way of things in his homeland.

The girl clapped, and her face lit up as she ran across the glade. Tolucan looked on with curiosity. Where had she come from? Was she alone?

No sooner had the questions formed in his mind than an answer was provided.

Two Dryads stalked out of the forest and stood openly at the centre of the glade.

Tolucan stifled a gasp and drew back. His armour scraped against the bark of the tree and terrible moments passed during which he was sure he had been given away.

Terror overtook him, but he remembered the girl and her peril. His heart beating hard and fast, his mouth so dry that his lips shrank back over his teeth, he peered back around the tree.

The Dryads had not moved, the girl was still singing and . . .

Tolucan frowned.

The little girl beckoned to the Dryads.

Tolucan remembered to breathe again as the two creatures moved towards her with the long vines of their hair trailing through the tips of the short grass. They were lithe and lean, with carved musculature and clothing. He noted they were not arrayed for war, but one had the appearance of a craftsman, perhaps a blacksmith, and the other wore a long robe of fleshy green material which grew out of the Dryad's shoulders. Their skin was polished, and the colour of pine. Tolucan marvelled at their beauty.

He almost forgot the danger as one of the Dryads leant down and accepted the little girl's gift of a single flower, taking it between a wooden thumb and forefinger. The Dryad looked at the decapitated flower then shook its head and the girl's smile faded. She took the flower back and laid it among the others.

'Tolucan!'

Feran's shout tore through the pleasant silence in the glade, and the little girl squealed. She got to her feet and dashed behind the Dryads.

'Tolucan!' Feran shouted again.

The Dryads stepped forward, and Tolucan saw the robed Dryad's fingers curl into a fist. The limbs of a longbow sprang out from it, a quiver of wooden arrows emerging from his back. A hammer formed in the hand of the blacksmith Dryad. Tolucan saw before him now the same poised look of the Dryads he had seen at Strewn Men Bay, creatures ready to make war.

Tolucan's instincts told him to take up his sword and make ready, but instead he stepped into the glade with his hands up, a worn man emerging blinking into the light, clad in mail with a cloven shield slung across his back, a sword still in its stained leather scabbard. Long, greasy hair hung about his shoulders and his beard reached his chest.

The girl screamed and clung to the leg of the blacksmith Dryad. Both creatures saw him, and as they turned to face him, their fair countenances changed into wrathful expressions. They lowered their brows and raised their weapons. Their faces cracked and split, hot sap spitting from them like water thrown on hot oil. Tolucan observed that their stances were defensive. He had less than a second to evaluate the Dryads' intentions and predict their reactions.

'Well met,' he said, but his voice caught in his throat. He coughed and tried again with a little more success, still showing them his open, empty palms, smiling as he did so.

'My companion calls for aid,' said Tolucan. 'Will you allow me to render it?'

The Dryads both took a step forward, and Tolucan saw a vine from the blacksmith's head reach to grasp a vine from that of the other's. The two vines merged, and Tolucan could see subtle shifts in the Dryads' expressions. Still connected, they advanced towards him.

'I am Tolucan,' he said and clasped his hands behind his back, standing straight. He could feel his body shaking as he stood proud, raising his chin and resisting the urge to step backwards.

So ends my quest, he thought, *and my dead squire is unable to bear the news to the queen and my family.*

'Tolucan, damn you!' shouted Feran, a little closer. 'Where are you?' A desperate roar.

That was too much. Tolucan had never heard such panic in Feran's voice. He dropped his left hand to grip his sword pommel and held up the other, as though he could hold the Dryads at bay like a sheriff keeping back a crowd.

'Wait here. Wait,' Tolucan called as he ran for the trees, shouting Feran's name as he did so.

He expected roots to wrap around his ankles and hurl him face-first into the ground. He expected a branch to impale him through the back and burst through his chest in a mess of gore, but neither happened. He did not look back to see why, instead ducking under the boughs of the trees and running towards the sounds of Feran's continuing calls.

Tolucan found them, Dun lying in the undergrowth with Feran kneeling at his side, rummaging through the pouches hanging from his staff.

'*Hold on*,' Feran muttered to his squire. 'Hold on, damn you.'

Tolucan knew Feran as a playful, sometimes mercurial sort, and so the intense concern on his friend's face told him that Dun's condition was serious.

Tolucan came to kneel beside him. Dun's irises had turned a creamy colour. His skin was mottled blue, like a bird's egg, and his face was frozen in a silent scream. He looked as though he had suffered some sort of horrific death, and yet he shook, blood trailing from his mouth. When Tolucan felt for a pulse, his fingers detected a rapid heartbeat.

'What happened?' he asked.

'How should I know?' snapped Feran. 'It's grave, is what it is. Seen the like before?'

Tolucan shook his head, but Feran was not looking.

'Have you seen it before?' he snapped.

'No, but I'm no healer,' Tolucan said quietly, suddenly and naturally yielding dominance to his senior, giving up the ongoing tussle between them. In this moment, Feran was the knight, and Tolucan but an onlooker as Feran tried to save their friend.

'Have *you* heard of this?' Tolucan asked.

Feran looked up, and their eyes met.

'Only after a few drinks by candlelight when folk are inclined to tell stories and scare each other into dashing to the long drop with loose bowels,' he snarled. 'An illness which cannot be cured.'

Tolucan nodded, and an understanding fell in place between them.

'Help me remove his armour,' said Feran. It took much labour and exertion to accomplish the task, but eventually the old man lay naked before them, discoloured like a corpse pulled from a river, yet gasping and gulping like a fish that came with it.

'Can you do anything for him?' asked Tolucan.

Feran looked his squire over and said nothing, but once more began fumbling in pouches.

Tolucan wiped sweat from his brow and stood.

'There was a girl back there in the clearing,' he said.

Feran looked up and met his gaze.

'What?' he snapped. 'A girl?'

Tolucan nodded.

'Aye, a girl. With two Dryads watching over her,' he said.

Feran frowned and peered down into Dun's widening eyes. There was desperation in his own, when Tolucan caught sight of them.

'Surely they wouldn't help us?' asked Feran.

Tolucan shrugged, feeling helpless, but Feran was not looking at him.

'Who knows? But I gave my word I would return.'

He adjusted his belt.

'I'll return with or without aid as soon as I can,' he said and set off back towards the glade.

Tolucan reached the spot where he had last seen the girl and the Dryads, but now there was no one to be seen. He circled the clearing and, having made a guess regarding their direction of travel, he began to search for them, calling out for aid.

Minutes passed as he followed a trail of crushed grass on to what seemed to be a straight path. An eerie quiet fell about him, the normal sounds of the forest fell silent, and he felt as though he had walked into a cathedral.

Although the boughs of the trees arched high over him as he walked, forming a passageway, Tolucan bowed his head, overcome with a powerful feeling that the place demanded reverence, humility and respect.

Tolucan trudged along the path as it curved to the right, bordered by tightly-packed trees, and before long it opened out. He halted to absorb the sight before him.

Pink and red cherry blossom trees lined an avenue of grass that was hard to look upon, so bright was the sunlight that fell upon it. The knight shielded his eyes until they could adjust. Coloured petals streamed across the way as though confetti was being thrown from on high to mark the significance of his approach.

The avenue stretched for a few hundred yards then narrowed, the trees growing ever closer together until only a gap as wide as a cart was left at the far end.

Tolucan looked all about him and set off up the avenue, closing his eyes as he felt the hot sun on his face.

When he opened them again, there was a man standing at the far end. Tolucan froze momentarily, but then trudged on, holding up a hand in what he hoped looked like a gesture of greeting.

'Well met,' he called.

The stranger bowed his head slightly, but continued to wait in the gap where the trees came closest together. Seconds later he was joined by a woman.

'Well met,' Tolucan called again. Her only response was to whisper in the man's ear then disappear.

The knight set off across the grass, all the time keeping his eyes on the man at the far end. He had taken perhaps ten steps before the man walked down to meet him.

'Well met, indeed, sir,' he said, bowing low. 'What brings you to our door?'

Tolucan returned the bow.

'I am Tolucan of Stragglers' Drift. I spied a girl playing in the glade yonder, watched over by Dryads, it seemed to me. My travelling companion has fallen gravely ill, and I seek aid,' he said. 'Can you help us?'

The man frowned.

'What ails him?' he said.

'An illness that is beyond our power to treat,' admitted Tolucan.

The man frowned.

'Wait here, my son, while I gather folk to assist in bearing your friend hither,' said the man before hurrying out of sight.

Tolucan was left standing in the sunlight, blossom falling all around him as his heart rate slowed. After a short time the man returned with two others. Tolucan noted they were not armed and so led them back to the spot where he had left Feran tending Dun.

The squire appeared to be breathing easier, and his eyes had returned to their normal colour. Feran turned when he heard Tolucan and the men approaching, but he did not object when they started to lift the old man.

The five of them bore Dun upon their shoulders back along the path. When they reached the avenue of blossom trees, Tolucan noticed Feran scarcely reacted to the sanctity of the place, so focused was his friend on the old man's plight. They hurried along through the passage in the trees to the hidden area beyond.

The path widened out into what seemed like a great hall with tall tree pillars set all about it. Around the edges, shorter trees grew close together, walling off the tree cathedral from the rest of the forest. Many people were seated there in the dim light, cross-legged upon the grass.

The men bore Dun away to the right, through a small gap in the trees to a small open area surrounded by hedges where the woman Tolucan had seen on his arrival was waiting with cloths, a basket and a bowl of water.

'Set him upon the grass,' she said.

One of the men who had carried the stricken squire began to examine him, and one of the men dipped a cloth in scented water before dabbing Dun's brow. Feran knelt and began untying and emptying pouches from his staff. Within seconds he was engaged in an intense debate with the men regarding how best to treat the symptoms, while Tolucan watched, helpless, but distracted, too, by his surroundings, a place more magnificent than any he had seen before.

A strange, harmonious calm pervaded the cathedral, and Tolucan felt his cares dropping away, as though his body had already realised he could finally take respite from constant toil and vigilance. He was no longer used to seeing humans in such numbers, and was certainly unaccustomed to seeing contented faces, rather than murderous rage or fear in those whom he encountered on the road. He sighed, feeling both relieved and curious.

The man who had first greeted Tolucan caught his eye and bade him follow. He and the woman led the knight to a secluded part of the cathedral, silent but for birdsong.

The man and woman sat upon the grass and indicated Tolucan should do the same.

'He's being tended by the best we have, though I am sad to say they are not physicians,' said the man.

Tolucan nodded.

'We are glad of any aid,' he said. 'Feran knows his business well enough, and it may be that between them, they can nurse our friend back to health.' Tolucan kept his voice low, feeling the peace was not to be disturbed. He looked about him then back to the man and woman.

'What is this place? And forgive me, I have not asked your names?' he said.

'I am Aspirant Patrick,' said the man, 'and this is Aspirant Meghan.'

The woman bowed her head in greeting. They did not answer his other question, but Tolucan offered thanks for their assistance.

'Meghan, as I told Patrick, my name is Tolucan. I served under Lord Brandreth in the Ninth Regiment. My companions and I have been moving through the forest since the Dryads struck. I . . . '

'Hush!' said Patrick. Meghan flinched and looked about her.

'I . . . ' said Tolucan, flinching at the man's harsh tone.

'Say no more,' said Meghan. She got to her feet and when Patrick reached out for her, she took his hand and hauled him up. He groaned, and his knees cracked.

'Wait here, and we'll fetch the Ascended,' said Meghan. 'It's for them to explain.' Patrick and Meghan hurried under the cover of the low trees and disappeared from view. Tolucan was alarmed by their reaction and loosened his sword in its scabbard, drawing it an inch and re-sheathing it. He was about to set off back towards Feran when he once more heard the laugh of a young girl. Tolucan looked back to where Patrick and Meghan had disappeared and saw the girl emerge into the half-light of the green hall.

The two Dryads he had seen before followed on behind her.

As soon as they appeared, those seated about the place bowed low to the floor and grasped at the grass. The Dryads paid them no heed, seeming to do nothing but watch as the girl wandered heedless about the place, stopping here and there to examine something or other. It was only when Patrick reappeared and pointed towards Tolucan that the Dryads nodded.

Tolucan clambered to his feet as they began to stride towards him. His instinct told him to draw his sword, but instead he clasped his hands together behind his back and watched them approach.

'Feran,' he called, but he choked on the word, and Feran did not hear his plea.

Both Dryads came to a halt some yards ahead of him. Tolucan felt his shoulders bowing, and he straightened up.

'Well met,' he said.

The Dryads said nothing, just looked him up and down, scrutinising him, it seemed. He felt as though hands were running all over his body as their blank eyes examined his attire and armaments.

'You are the Ascended?' he asked, mouth dry.

The Dryads thrust out roots towards one another and entwined, never breaking their eye contact with Tolucan.

'I thank you for your hospitality,' Tolucan persisted. 'I feared my companion was near death.'

The blacksmith Dryad stepped forward and reached for Tolucan's sword. Tolucan fell back a step. The Dryad tilted its head and seemed to frown.

'What are you doing?' Tolucan asked.

The Dryad stepped forward again, and Tolucan, reasoning that a stolen sword would be the least of his worries if these creatures harboured ill-will against him, held his ground and made no move to resist.

The blacksmith Dryad grasped the hilt of Tolucan's sword and unsheathed the weapon.

It stepped back and looked down the length of the blade then tested its balance. Tolucan could have sworn that the wood of the Dryad's face had formed a wistful smile.

The Dryad returned the sword to its sheath. Its lips cracked apart, leaving splinters hanging over the newly-forming chasm of a mouth behind the lips, green flesh visible within.

'Your weapons and those of your companions must remain sheathed here,' the Dryad's voice cracked and creaked, a burbling sound of water over pebbles beneath it.

'Of course, if it is your will,' said Tolucan, 'though we mean no harm to anyone here.'

The other Dryad, the one in the robes, spoke then.

'You may remain until the old one is well enough to walk once more,' it said.

'You have my thanks,' said Tolucan, bowing low, 'but tell me, what is this place? I have never seen humans living in a hall with Dryads as their masters.'

The Dryads' entwined roots curled tighter momentarily then shrank back to the creatures, ending their connection. They turned their back on Tolucan and once more attended to the girl who was lying on her front on the ground, watching a caterpillar make its slow progress up a blade of grass.

Patrick stepped forward.

'You'll come to understand or you won't,' he said, 'but we won't be judged by anyone, let alone men clad for war like the barbarians who brought calamity upon all.' Though his words sounded harsh, there was no unkindness in his face. Tolucan thought Patrick serious, but not unkind. Meghan rested a hand upon his shoulder.

'We know not how tenuous is the peace,' she whispered. 'Come and sit with us for a time, then we will see about finding you food and water before sleep takes you.'

'Thank you, Meghan,' said Tolucan, and the woman gave him an awkward smile.

'It is customary to refer to aspirants by their title, sir,' she told him.

'My apologies, Aspirant,' said Tolucan, and Meghan bowed her head to him.

They left the main hall behind them and settled on a patch of grass beside a flower bed, filled with yellow blooms and illuminated as if by design through a gap in the canopy overhead.

'Come,' said Patrick. 'Sit and pray with us that your companion recovers, but that if it is not to be, that he is ready to ascend. Pray his soul is ready.'

Tolucan, not a religious man, born as he had been in a time that had largely forgotten gods, began to understand what was happening in the cathedral. Concern mounting and implications coming to him by the second, he knelt beside the aspirants, closed his eyes and, reluctantly, he prayed.

Chapter Ten

The Butterfly Isle

The Tithe Walk completed on the Butterfly Isle, Lord Aldwyn stood on a rocky beach on the east coast and looked out at his ship, the Nightingale, that rode at anchor some distance offshore. The sky above him was clear, and the sea calm, but glowering clouds lined the horizon.

He remembered another beach he had visited only once during the Tithe Walk, years ago, against the advice of Mungan Maconnock. Aldwyn had dismissed the ghost stories as nonsense and stepped down on to the pebbles alone. He had looked out towards a rocky island where a witch was said to dwell, and, for a moment, it was easy to dismiss the warnings as superstition, but then Aldwyn had heard her song, drifting in with the waves, an omen of death, it was said. He had stood for a minute, defying his baser instincts, before retreating.

Aldwyn heard nothing so disturbing as he gazed at the Nightingale.

'You look relieved, Your Grace,' said Mungan Maconnock. 'Did ye fear she'd not be here when you returned?'

Aldwyn folded his arms across his chest and made no reply. Mungan Maconnock knew as well as he that in these uncertain times, any asset was at risk, especially ships, which could carry men far from the forests, even if they were perpetually followed by shoals of Naiads. He trusted Captain Silas Unwin more than most, but as for the crew? Well, there was little reward for the toil they endured and they had sat for so long at anchor, only going ashore to find fresh water and supplies; the temptation to mutiny or desert must have been strong, Aldwyn had reasoned, but it appeared he was doing his people a disservice. The Nightingale was where it should be.

Aldwyn turned back to Maconnock.

'You have my thanks for the service you've done me whilst I've been on the Butterfly Isle, Mungan,' said Aldwyn. 'You've once again proved yourself the queen's staunchest ally in The Isles.'

Maconnock arched his back until it cracked, yawning deeply.

'Say nothing of it, Your Grace. We did naught more than I would have done alone to ensure loyalty. The folk in Elaris were getting ideas beyond their station,' he replied, as though perceiving Aldwyn's worries.

Aldwyn nodded.

'There can only be one response to treason,' he said. He knew Maconnock well enough not to speak of his doubts or his regrets.

'Will you be away directly?' asked Maconnock, breaking eye contact. The bigger man looked out across the water, and there was something in his look that Aldwyn did not like, though he could not quite tell what.

'Once I have collected the princes and princesses from your halls, I can be away to Long Isle and see them settled in at Halflight Hold, sure enough, but I'm not in undue haste. If you're offering hospitality for the night, I'll certainly come and break bread with you then be away with Cathryn's children in the morning,' said Aldwyn.

Maconnock nodded, still looking out to sea.

'Aye, we can see that your belly is filled before the morning,' he said. 'Will I signal the Nightingale to send a boat to carry a message for ye?'

'I'd be obliged,' said Aldwyn.

Maconnock nodded and called for his men to start a signal fire with fallen branches.

Gull cries harangued the air, but there were few sounds other than the waves breaking upon the shore. Aldwyn looked up and down the deserted beach, pondering his lingering unease.

He watched as a boat was lowered from the Nightingale and started towards the shore. Aldwyn ignored the Maconnock clan as they busied about, laughing and joshing one another. They had toured with him for many long weeks, but he was not overly fond of the clansmen. No matter though, they would be swapped out with the garrison at Narra, who would begin the long Tithe Walk again, this time without Aldwyn. He would return to Lachlan's family home at Halflight Hold and see Crown Prince Annan and his siblings settled before commencing the Tithe Walk on the Long Isle. He anticipated less resistance there, because of the bond between the ruling house and the narrow island.

When the boat drew close enough that Aldwyn could recognise the faces of the men therein, he walked down to meet it. He waded into the surf and hauled the boat towards the beach. Captain Unwin jumped down to assist him, and once the boat was higher up on the shale, the two men grasped hands in greeting.

'I'm glad to see you, Your Grace,' said Unwin.

'Likewise, Captain. How do you fare?' asked Aldwyn.

Stones crunched behind him, and when he looked back over his shoulder, Aldwyn saw that Mungan Maconnock had drawn in close to hear the captain's report.

'All's well, Your Grace. A few coastal craft about, but we've suffered no attacks. The Maconnocks have been good enough to keep us in good supply.'

The captain bowed his head to Mungan, who merely nodded in response.

'Word from Long Isle? Any news from The Folly?' asked Aldwyn, all too conscious of the sound of Mungan breathing behind him.

'Not a word from The Folly, Your Grace. Small doings on Long Isle. No trouble with the Dryads,' finished the captain.

'Understood,' said Aldwyn, nodding. 'I'll be returning with the Maconnocks to Narra tonight. I'll see to the welfare of the royal children and sleep ashore. Please take the Nightingale round the coast and be ready to collect us off a little after dawn, Silas.'

'Your word is my command, Your Grace. If we find the beach deserted, I'll send some of the men up to let the Maconnocks know we're ready for you,' replied the captain.

The shore party returned to the Nightingale, and, satisfied that all was in hand, Aldwyn and Maconnock mounted their horses before setting off up the beach on to the narrow strip of bare land between it and the forest. Their path followed the treeline north, keeping the Sound of Nerith to their right. Aldwyn took comfort in watching the Nightingale making swift progress along the sound, her sails set to make the most of the east wind. She soon pulled ahead of them.

Hours passed. Maconnock led the way around an outcrop of rock, and Aldwyn could see the land slope downwards towards an obvious westward bight in the coast at the point where the Butterfly Isle was at its most narrow. Nestled between rising hills to the south and north, with only the sea to the east, stood Narra, the ancestral home of Maconnocks. Even from so far off, Aldwyn could see the breaches in the once strong walls, piles of tumbledown rocks beneath them. The archway where the gates had stood appeared deceptively unguarded. Aldwyn saw the Nightingale at anchor in the calm waters of the natural harbour.

'Not long till home now, eh?' muttered Maconnock, his eyes fixed on Narra.

'Not long now, boys,' he said again, this time roaring back to his men.

Aldwyn shivered in his saddle. A ferocious man, thought Aldwyn. A man with whom one should not trifle, as the Comhanns and many before them could attest. He had been a staunch ally, and yet Aldwyn had a sense of foreboding. Aldwyn had been concerned about the challenge at Elaris, that gibe about following a man who would not stand for the late John Comhann's words, and now Mungan's mannerisms on the beach troubled him. Something was not right, Aldwyn felt it in his bones, yet what was he to do? He was a guest of the Maconnocks, and his own people were aboard the Nightingale. How could he summon them without alerting Maconnock if things went amiss in Narra? And even if he could, he relied on the Maconnocks to maintain the queen's law on the Butterfly Isle. Even if he fought his way out, he would lose control of the island, and *that* he could not allow.

Aldwyn rode on in disquiet, trying to keep his mind focused on navigating the path ahead. It ran close to the cliff edge now and was treacherous, scattered as it was with loose stone. Dismissing his concerns as a matter for a later hour, he managed to pay full attention to his riding after his horse missed its footing when his mind wandered and he let it wander too close to the edge.

Aldwyn's company met the first of the Maconnock waywatchers a mile out from the gates of Narra. Two men stepped out from the trees by the side of the path and exchanged words with Mungan. They nodded, seemingly satisfied, and stepped back into the woods. Mungan led the company on. They passed more waywatchers half a mile out and, not long after, the cliff path veered inland and joined the main road leading to the capital of the Butterfly Isle.

Despite his worries, Aldwyn was not immune to the beauties of the Butterfly Isle. The sea was a constant companion to his right, the rustling trees to his left, and Narra's walls stood ahead of him. Behind the trees and the town, the mountains loomed high beyond the foothills, dwarfing all else. Aldwyn looked up at them with the awed eyes of a supplicant, as though the mountains were gods to him, and he was humbled before them.

They drew close to Narra, and Aldwyn saw the broken gates lying at the side of the road where the Dryads had discarded them, years before. Two guards stepped out to bar the way through the arch in the wall. Maconnock halted the company and rode forward alone. He clasped each of their hands in greeting and exchanged words with them before passing through.

Aldwyn chewed his lower lip, resting his hands across the horn of his saddle while he waited for Maconnock to return. This he did in but a few moments, his horse trotting up to stand beside Aldwyn's.

'We'll change the guard before we enter. The Dryads might tolerate our swelled numbers, but I'm not inclined to take the risk,' said Maconnock.

Aldwyn said nothing.

Ere long, twenty men trooped out of Narra and set off up the road, to where Aldwyn did not know. Satisfied, Maconnock stood tall in his stirrups and called to his men,

'Forward and home now, boys!'

With that the company passed in.

Narra was largely deserted, the ruins of many homes swept and piled at points inside the gate to form obstacles to whoever or whatever might enter. Aldwyn led his horse between them and towards Maconnock's hall. When they drew close to the centre of the town, Maconnock's men dispersed to take up the watch around the walls or take rest, according to their lot. Aldwyn wondered for a moment if their families were herein, but then thought better of it. Only Maconnock's household and the garrison inhabited Narra in those days. Maconnock had told him of how its folk had made their escape into the hills and mountains when the forest sprung up around Narra's walls and the Dryads smashed the town's defences. Aldwyn had seen the clan's scattered shelters and hamlets all around the area while making the Tithe Walk. Such was the way of things for all in The Isles now, not just for the Maconnocks.

'I'll see to your horse, Your Grace,' said Maconnock as he dismounted. Aldwyn did the same and handed the chieftain the reins.

'My thanks. Then I'll see the children, if I may,' said Aldwyn, still looking about. Within Narra's broken walls, it was easy to believe that all humanity had been struck down, save for a few unfortunates who picked a living from the ribcage of what had once been civilisation.

Mungan said nothing, but led the horses away into a stable where one of his people took over their stewardship.

His face was grave when he returned to Aldwyn.

'Are you hungry?' said Maconnock. It was a foolish question; of course he was hungry. They were *all* constantly hungry. Aldwyn responded politely.

'I could certainly eat, but I'll see the children while food is prepared,' he said.

Mungan folded his arms across his chest and said nothing for a time.

'That'll not be possible, Your Grace,' he said slowly when he finally spoke.

'Not possible?' Aldwyn frowned. 'Why?'

Mungan widened his stance a little, Aldwyn noticed, ever watchful for such signs, as does anyone who has had to be wary for many a long year.

Now we come to it, he thought.

'Maconnock,' Aldwyn intoned, and though he was diminutive in stature, the look on Maconnock's face was uneasy, the muscles around his eyes slackening momentarily.

'The children are not here, Your Grace,' said the chieftain.

'Not here?' asked Aldwyn.

'Aye,' said Maconnock.

'Where are they then?' Aldwyn cast a brief look back over his shoulder and took two casual circling steps around Maconnock, the better to see around him. There were no armed clansmen crowding around him by stealth as he had feared.

'They're safe and well, Your Grace, but you cannot see them,' said Maconnock.

Aldwyn's temper was rising, a preferable choice to giving in to the fear and dismay that was taking root. What had befallen Cathryn's children, to Annan, the Crown Prince, and the other children?

'Maconnock, speak plainly now,' said Aldwyn. 'I left the children in your care only under your assurance they would be safe whilst we made the Tithe Walk. You have known full well since the beach and before, that I meant to see them and take them off to Long Isle upon the morrow. I will not bandy words now. I have held my tongue long enough. You have evaded my prompts and questions long enough. Where are they? What mischief is afoot?'

Maconnock seemed to steel himself and drew up to his full height.

So that's the way of things, thought Aldwyn.

'Oh, I'll speak plain to you, Aldwyn,' said Mungan, lowering his voice, 'Whatever slight you may perceive, I'll pull out your tongue and stick it up your horse's arse if you speak to me so in my own domain. You understand?' He unfolded his arms and held them tensed at his side, hands curled into fists, Aldwyn noted.

The duke took a small step forward, and he began to ready a punch, but thought better of it and mastered his reaction.

The two men stood at a little distance apart, staring at one another. Aldwyn felt sweat on his brow.

'Mungan, the children,' he said, trying to sound calm.

'They were not safe here, so I put them elsewhere,' said Maconnock.

'Fine. I'm much obliged. But where, and why the deceit?' said Aldwyn, not believing the islander.

'Elsewhere,' said Maconnock, not breaking eye contact. Not blinking.

Aldwyn said nothing. He swallowed hard and once more took a look around the yard, buying himself a precious second by looking down at his feet. When he looked up, Maconnock was still staring intently at him, as though he had not moved at all.

'Break bread with me, and I'll tell all,' said Maconnock. He raised his eyebrows, his jaw tense as though expecting a hostile reaction, yet signalling that turning down the invitation would significantly sour the proceedings, Aldwyn decided.

Seeing no alternative, alone as he was, Aldwyn nodded assent.

Mungan returned the gesture.

'There will be two meals tonight. Half the men will eat first, and when they are back at their posts, strength renewed and as vigilant as may be, we'll sit in comfort therein.' He gestured towards the wooden hall that stood behind Aldwyn, a mere barn in comparison to the stone tower of Halflight Hold, let alone the beauty of The Folly.

Aldwyn's tongue felt rough against his dry gums.

'I'll await word then,' he said, before setting off towards the well.

'Aldwyn,' called Maconnock.

The use of his name without a title told Aldwyn more than Maconnock's words ever could. He stopped walking, but did not turn.

'Mungan?'

'Steer clear of the harbour, and make no signal to the Nightingale. These are not your lands, and your people do not have leave to come ashore,' said Maconnock. Aldwyn heard both sadness and determined resignation in the chieftain's voice.

Aldwyn said nothing, but continued walking towards the well, where, out of sight, he drew up water and drank deep, trying to stem a rising panic.

Bread and butter had never tasted so good, washed down as it was by brown ale. Aldwyn sat at the high table in the dim light of the hall and watched the candlelight dance upon the features of the Maconnock clan. He drank deep of the ale, despite never having had a taste for it and savoured every bite of the bread. A great boar roasted on a spit over the fire, and when it was done, Mungan carved the beast with his long serrated knife then served it to Aldwyn on a pewter plate.

Aldwyn nodded thanks and once again set about his food.

Feeling that perhaps the meal might be his last, Aldwyn gladly accepted everything he was offered, and he drank so much of the ale that his head began to feel a little light. No matter though, he thought, it would assist both his courage and deaden his nerves a little to swords being thrust through them. A smile crept upon his lips.

It did not last long. Maconnock placed a bottle of Elaris whisky in front of him.

Aldwyn stared at it then shook his head.

Maconnock uncorked the bottle and poured a little into Aldwyn's tankard, not bothering to tip out the last sips of ale.

'Drink with me,' he said. 'Drink to their memory and our brotherhood.'

Aldwyn sighed and did as he was bade. Maconnock sat close beside him on the bench, and they drank a toast.

'To business then?' said Aldwyn, still eyeing the bottle and remembering the head of Matilda Comhann looking down upon him with dead eyes from its pike, tongue lolling from between blue lips. The choice of beverage was not lost on him.

'Aye, to business,' said Maconnock.

Voices enmeshed in raised talk, laughter and song filled the room, yet Aldwyn was aware that each of the clansmen glanced at him time and again while they feasted.

'Prince Annan, Princess Aoife, Prince Weylin and Princess Muriel,' said Aldwyn. He spoke slowly, enunciating, so that the names hung between the two men for a moment.

Mungan nodded and poured out more whisky.

'Lachlan is dead,' he said. 'By rights, Crown Prince Annan is Lord of The Isles.'

Aldwyn remembered the face of the Dryad that he had met upon the shore of Strewn Men Bay and nodded.

'And we have not heard from the queen in many a month? Ships do not pass between The Folly and The Isles any longer?' said Mungan.

'Many vessels have been lost in the last few years because of mutiny and rebellion. The queen may not be *able* to send word,' Aldwyn replied.

'Aye, it may be so. Or it may be that Magregar's done for her. If so, then the children of Lachlan and Cathryn are the last hope for the royal line, the only royalty with whom we now have any contact for instruction. And yet Crown Prince Annan is not yet of age,' said Mungan. He leant in close before continuing.

'You have toiled alone for many a year now, Your Grace, maintaining Cathryn's hold over The Isles, but it is time to accept that she is dead or, at the least, Prince Annan must rule in her stead until we can prove otherwise.'

This was an unexpected tack, reassuring and alarming all at once. Aldwyn remained on his guard, still believing Maconnock had ill intent.

'That being the case,' Maconnock's voice became louder as he went on, 'I believe it no longer safe or sufficient for the Crown Prince and his kin to travel around at your heels like a pack of whelps. If an attack upon them was successful, we would lose the entire royal line in a single strike!' He slammed his hand on a table.

'There is truth in that, sure enough,' said Aldwyn, 'but our holdfasts are not secure, and I would not trust just *anyone* with their safety. I have always believed that keeping them close was for the best, trusting only my staunchest allies to care for them. Have I made a grave mistake, Mungan, in trusting you? I am troubled by the events of today, and the direction of this conversation. Where are the children?'

'Secure, safe . . . distributed,' Mungan said, frowning. 'And I remind you once again that I will not have doubts cast upon my honour in my own hall, Aldwyn.'

'Really?' asked Aldwyn, and the corners of his mouth hitched up into a smile. Only candles lit Maconnock's face, but Aldwyn was sure it was reddening.

'Let us not dance around the matter, Mungan. Speak your mind. What are your intentions?' said Aldwyn.

'You mock me and expect me to continue? You'll be lucky if I let you walk out of here,' the islander growled.

Aldwyn said nothing, but refilled his own tankard with Elaris whisky and drank, once again savouring the taste. He met Maconnock's gaze.

'Out with it, Maconnock,' said Aldwyn, his voice low.

It took some moments for Maconnock to gather his wits and calm himself, but once he had done so, he spoke again.

'I have secured the royal children in secret locations, known only to a few of my people and even then, none but myself knows where *all* can be found. I have devoted sufficient strength to protect them, I assure you,' said Maconnock.

Aldwyn nodded, but said nothing. Maconnock finally looked away, and Aldwyn felt relief like stepping into a warm bath at the end of a long day walking in the cold.

'King Annan must be protected until he comes of age, and someone must be named Lord Regent of the Combined People to rule until then,' said Maconnock, with a sigh.

'And who should that someone be, Mungan?' whispered Aldwyn, leaning in close as though he was willingly partaking in this new conspiracy, the whisky hitting him. 'Should it be you, Mungan?'

Maconnock drew back, smiling in the most unpleasant manner, made worse by the shadows and leaping of the candle flame.

'What right would the chieftain of the Maconnocks have to take on such a role? Nay, Your Grace, if any must take on this role, it should be you. You perform it now, even if you have not yet taken on the title,' said Maconnock, sitting back in his chair.

Aldwyn scratched his temple, not yet fully understanding.

'And the Maconnocks will be your strongest supporters, Lord Regent. We shall watch over the precious children on your behalf, and I will ever be at your right hand,' said Maconnock.

And behind the throne, thought Aldwyn, *with daggers at the childrens' backs.*

Chapter Eleven

The Folly, Tayne

Moonlight caught in the water of Seaborn's body as he moved through the wrecked streets of The Folly, leaving wet footprints on the warm flagstones, the only sign that he had passed that way. Whiteflow followed on behind, trickling uphill, spilling into holes and gushing along cracks in the slabs, soaking through patches of earth and enveloping small stones that barred her way. Her brother was a little way ahead, but she was aware of his presence even without ears or eyes to sense him. He retained his human form, but not like the others, who appeared in some approximation of how they wished they had become, had they grown older as humans. Seaborn seemed caught forever in the shape and size of his former body when it died, that of a young boy. Whiteflow remembered snatching Declan from below decks on the ship which bore the Hinterland refugees to The Isles. She remembered carrying him overboard and dragging him beneath the waves. She remembered his last gasps and the screams of his mother . . . of their mother, she corrected herself. Whiteflow remembered, but she felt no compassion, only anger towards Rowan for the life she had been denied.

Seaborn padded on with his arms folded across his chest, like a scolded child storming away ineffectually from his parents. She had found him at the old quayside, humans fighting all around him, and a newly arrived vessel afire in the water. Seaborn had been sitting upon the remains of a wooden jetty, staring into the deep water. Whiteflow knew from her own experience of late, that he was yearning to be one with the ocean, but of far more concern, the boy Naiad wished to seek out his mother.

Arrows passed through Whiteflow's body as she walked towards him. She rested a hand upon his shoulder so that the waters of their bodies flowed together. Their minds opened to one another, more so than was possible between Dryads and Naiads, and they understood one another.

Not yet. Not now, Whiteflow thought for both of them, *but soon you can return to the waters. You heard Father. We will right the wrongs of our past lives, keep the humans in check and then we can return to the waters of the world. Forget our mother. She is nothing to you now and were she to look upon you, you would but drive her insane.*

He began to argue. *I miss Mother. Why does Father punish her if she means nothing to us now?*

Whiteflow drew back her body from his and spoke aloud.

'Come, he has summoned us, and we must obey,' she said.

They travelled from The Folly docks, across the lowlands of the Arduan Peninsula and up the slopes, over the broken concentric walls, towards the Maw Keep.

Once they reached the courtyard, Whiteflow adopted her human form and called out to Seaborn in her rippling voice. The blue marbles of her eyes formed amidst the waters of her head, and she saw that her brother was looking at something. Following his gaze, she found Red Maple was waiting as he had promised. He stood upon a stone slab, perhaps hauled out from the walls, yet his toes and heels had grown out into roots which gripped the edges of the block. His body, still slender, had grown up into the night sky and his head hung down, the tails of his vine-hair swaying down almost to the ground. His arms were thrown up like the wings of a great bird of prey about to catch its meal. From his limbs, narrow branches had sprung, spindly and grasping, thin as bony fingers. Thicker branches still had erupted from his back and were reaching up behind him, curving up and out. Red leaves grew all about his branches.

A cough and the clang of iron on stone interrupted Whiteflow's reveries. She turned and saw Queen Cathryn's guards had backed up against the wall beside the gaping doorway into the keep. They were stationed to defend against raiders coming up the slopes from deeper within The Folly and, in particular, Lord Magregar's traitors. She nodded acknowledgement, and the gesture was reciprocated by the soldiers. Whiteflow turned away from them.

'Wake him,' she said. Seaborn's body dropped suddenly into a puddle where his feet had been. He flowed across the flagstones and up the rock, across the underside of the stone platform until he found the tips of Red Maple's roots. Seaborn flowed into them and was taken up inside the wood.

Red Maple's head jerked, and his blank eyes opened. He lowered his great limbs and the leaves rustled into a crunch as they were compressed against his torso. He shuddered as he attempted to walk, but his legs had melded together and his torso had widened. He closed his eyes and shrank back once more to the size of the man that Callum would never grow to be.

Whiteflow took him in an embrace and closed her eyes as her body passed through the surface of the wood. Inside Red Maple, the spirits of all three siblings nestled together like fox cubs sleeping in their den. The Dryad arched his back and stretched, shedding bark and then passed between the queen's guards as he entered the keep.

Hanging vines obscured Red Maple's view as he made his way through the Maw Keep, but he paid them no heed and made no attempt to brush them away. They slapped against his face, an irrelevance that caused no discomfort even to his unblinking eyes. He climbed to the throne room. More of Cathryn's guards were posted either side of the doorway, but they made no move against him.

Dark Oak stood beside a marble pillar at the northern edge of the room, the long drop to the Maw Gate beneath him, looking out over the trees far below. The ivy of his hair whipped in the wind. He did not acknowledge either Red Maple or Seaborn and Whiteflow when they seeped out from their brother's feet and adopted their human avatars. Lord Hawthorn, at one with the throne, still stared, his eyes downcast and his mossy hair and beard grown down to the floor, limbs indistinguishable from the arms of the chair.

A bolt snapped, and the door to the royal quarters creaked open. Queen Cathryn, pale and sallow-skinned, emerged into the throne room, followed by Ailsa. There were great dark circles beneath the queen's eyes, but she wore her leather armour, her crown and carried her spear with obvious pride. Her dark hair, now streaked with grey and white, was intricately plaited and hung behind her.

The queen said nothing as she circled the dais, but nodded to her guards on either side of the raised platform when they snapped to attention, and she sat on her throne, carefully avoiding looking at Lachlan.

'Council is called,' she said with a power that her frame belied, and only then did Dark Oak pay heed to the room. She watched him turn away from the view of the sun setting over the Maw and move towards the dais. His children came to stand beside him and, as one, they bowed to the queen. The Dryads and Naiads had long since ceased to alarm her, and she nodded acknowledgement.

'Good evening,' said Dark Oak.

'To all,' Cathryn replied. She looked at each of them in turn, except Lord Hawthorn.

'Queen,' said Dark Oak. 'We have been strange bedfellows for a time now, but that is coming to an end. I am returning to the forest, though we will maintain the watch over humanity. I think, and I hope, it will not be necessary for us to meet again. That the lesson has been learnt. '

Cathryn's face remained inscrutable, and she paused before replying.

'I wish to build a new civilisation,' she said, sounding calm at first, but her voice grew louder as she went from stating her desires to making an impassioned plea. 'Can you not see that you have condemned us to a life of violence? For centuries, humanity united to destroy Awgren and take back our homelands. We troubled you little, save to build shelters and ships to rid the world of evil. An undeniable evil, was it not? Did Awgren not lay waste to many a wood south of the Hinterland? Look how we live now, with raiders at our door, harassing my people so that they may not grow their crops or ply their trades. Those without weapons are dead or living in fear, scattered in small settlements all over the continent, and I am unable to go out and protect them. Will you not let me build a strong place? Provide for the weak? Can we not, finally, put our names to a treaty so that we may co-exist?'

Dark Oak smiled.

'We *do* co-exist. We all co-exist. I have no treaty with the field mice or the badgers. It is not necessary. You think in the old ways, Queen. And you ask me to make a decision that you have only recently made yourself? Did you negotiate with the captured Creatures of the Devising that were imprisoned and defenceless whilst at your mercy? They were living creatures that had harmed your people, but begged for clemency. You wince!' he pointed a crooked finger at Cathryn, and she composed herself. 'Did you forget that before my death I too was imprisoned by the soldiers of Cathryn the Merciful? Did I not smell their flesh as the Devised burned? Did I not smell my own flesh as it was seared from my face by one of your high lords?' Dark Oak's face cracked, splintered and steamed as he raged. His white eyes sparkled bright, and it seemed that all other lights in the room had been put out.

Cathryn made no answer at first, bowing her head and rubbing her temples.

'My kind did not harm yours knowingly,' she said after a time.

'The lord in the north did not set a great fire amongst the trees then?' Dark Oak snapped.

'Are the rest of us to be held responsible for the actions of one man and those who followed him?' Cathryn asked.

'Held responsible? If it were so, your kind would be extinct already. The human population is simply being managed, so it does not get out of control, just as the islanders manage the red deer on their estates. Farmers take similar measures against animals which threaten their crops. If you are left to your own devices, your kind will group together and compete. Competition is natural, and I take no issue with it, and yet you are unique amongst the world's creatures in that you have the intelligence to use resources as no animal has ever done before. And there will never be enough. Humans will never hold anything natural in as high regard as they do themselves. Therein lies the danger. Therein lies the threat. Am I not an example myself?' he said.

'You?' asked Cathryn.

'The Dryads have not moved against another people since the time of the First Cleansing, and while Riark did give battle, he would have retreated to the forest. It was only when I was forced into this form before my time, my human instincts preserved, that we have stood up to and forced humanity into submission. If you take issue with my actions, you do so with those of your own race,' said Dark Oak. 'Your defeat was born of human nature, not Dryad.'

Cathryn stood and advanced towards Dark Oak.

'You are not wrong in what you say, but can't you see what you are doing to us now? Yes, we build and craft. Yes, we take more from the world than perhaps any other creature. I concede your point entirely. But as a race we do not wantonly torture weaker creatures, not as a whole, at least. Those who do are reviled amongst my kind. And yet you torture us and condemn us to this life of starvation and violence,' she said quietly, but there was force behind her words. 'You use the powers of the Dryads to act on base human instincts, yet have forgotten any compassion you once had! Your reasoning is flawed,' Cathryn concluded.

Dark Oak shook his head, as though despairing, snapping green tendrils that connected his neck to his shoulders. He raised an arm to indicate the view of the forest far below them, blanketing all of Tayne.

'This is a new world, and humanity must find its place within it or become extinct in the attempt,' said the King of the Dryads. He shrugged and turned back to her.

'Conversation with you is pointless,' he concluded. 'I can assure you that even now, your small folk are out there making do. Surviving. There are warring groups with one another, but many species roam in packs, challenging one another. Before I changed the world, the strong would conquer the weak and those who survived would rally to their banner or form alliances to fight until the strongest became lords, kings and queens. Not so any longer. The strong may conquer the weak and gather strength.' Dark Oak stepped towards her, a hideous expression on his face as he leant in so that his nose was mere inches away from hers. A frond of wet, black vine slapped against Cathryn's forearm, and she shuddered. 'But if they get ideas above their station, I will crush them.'

'Will you not have mercy?' Cathryn said, and it crossed her mind that she should drop to her knees before him, but she ignored the thought and pressed on.

'I wish nothing more than to bring my people together to live in peace. I give you my word that I will guide humanity into this new age in peace. You have nothing to lose, Dark Oak. If I am not true to my word, and I tried to rise against you, you know full well that you could put us down again with little effort.'

But Dark Oak would not hear it.

'If you earn a place in my world, if you can *adapt*, so be it, but I will not change my terms. My people will keep yours in check, but I will no longer waste my years treading your halls, watching you like a schoolmaster supervising a heady, unruly pupil, temporarily at study,' said Dark Oak. He stepped back beside his children.

'Farewell, Queen. I hope we will not meet again.' Dark Oak bowed his head to her then addressed Lachlan by his mockery of a Dryad name which riled Cathryn so. She bit her lip.

'Never abandon your post, Lord Hawthorn. Keep watch for me here,' said Dark Oak.

With that, Dark Oak reached out and took hold of one of the hanging vines, and his spirit issued into it, drawing up the wood of his body as though it were water sucked into a sponge until he had disappeared entirely. His spirit moved along the vines through the barbican of the Maw Keep and down to the undergrowth at the Maw Gate, then on and out into the forest, faster than light travels from the sun to the world.

Dark Oak braced himself to stave off the will of the forest, the calm and the acceptance, the desire to slumber in quiet growth, and though he did feel its pull, his attention was drawn to a sudden silence, such as that which falls on a room when the subject of gossip steps in. The whispers of the forest fell silent, but they could not deny him their knowledge, inexpert as they were at deception. Strife, as Red Maple had warned, raging debate and calls to action.

He stepped out into the meadow of his homestead in the Hinterland and affected a deep sigh. He was back amongst the trees. It was better, yet not enough. He longed to be not just *near* the forest, but to *be* the forest. He would suppress the enemies within, but now was not the time. He began to scheme.

The throne room of The Folly fell silent. Queen Cathryn sat in despair and contemplation as Seaborn, duty done, sloshed down into a puddle and flowed out of the main door. Whiteflow bowed her head to Red Maple, then followed after Seaborn in her human form.

Cathryn felt eyes upon her and looked up to see Red Maple, his head tilted, watching her. Sighing, the queen stood and nodded her head to him, intending to retreat to her quarters where she could weep unseen. Ailsa stepped up beside her.

'Queen,' said Red Maple, his voice lighter than that of his father.

Cathryn turned to face him, clasping her hands together before her and straightening her back. She raised her eyebrows in expectation, looking haughty and proud once more.

Red Maple stood silently for a moment then drew in close, slowly ascending the shallow steps of the dais until he stood between Lord Hawthorn and the queen. Red Maple looked long into Cathryn's eyes, and she searched his face, trying to determine if he had an expression at all, if he was trying to convey something. When dealing with Dryads, who chose what to wear for the world to see, Cathryn had decided to remain cautious in her judgements.

'Red Maple?' she asked when impatience had got the better of her.

'A moment,' he replied. He bowed his head slightly, and the features of his face smoothed until it was but a blank surface, perhaps as his thoughts turned inwards. Ailsa folded her arms in such a way that she could drop her right hand to her sword in an instant.

Little good it will do, thought Cathryn, but Ailsa's desire to protect moved her. She reached out and caressed the younger woman's hand.

Red Maple's fingers began to grow until ten snaking roots slunk across the flagstones of the throne room, moving backward and away from him towards Lachlan's throne. Lord Hawthorn did not move or acknowledge the roots in any way, staring at the floor as he had done for so many years, lost in his own contemplation and bound by the duty forced upon him.

The roots stopped moving mere millimetres from the long black ivy of Lord Hawthorn's beard, its ends piling at his feet. Red Maple's torso heaved suddenly, and Cathryn jumped back a step. Ailsa's hand dropped to her sword. Red Maple's chest seemed to swell and then deflate, as though he had taken a mighty sigh. Cathryn regained her composure, but Ailsa drew her weapon.

'Not yet,' said Red Maple and he withdrew his roots away from Lord Hawthorn as he spoke. 'Follow me, please.'

He led Cathryn and Ailsa to an antechamber and spoke in a hushed voice.

'I will aid you,' said Red Maple.

'Aid us?' said Cathryn. The words came out choked and barely audible, as she attempted to hold back tears. 'Aid us how?'

'Dark Oak does not speak for all of us,' said Red Maple. 'Not any longer. The Dryad nation has grown and overshadowed humanity, it is true, but it is not in our nature to seek out smaller, weaker trees to purposefully overshadow them for fear they will grow stronger. My father has suffered at the hands of many, and I have suffered by his hand.' Red Maple raked his fingers across his chest, and Cathryn saw the shapes of wooden ribs burst out then merge back into his body. She shivered.

Red Maple continued. 'But I do not carry the malice that drives him. I will aid you until his rage cools, as I know it does, slowly. On the condition that you must do as I ask.'

'What would you ask of the queen?' said Ailsa, stepping forward.

Red Maple ignored her and continued staring at Cathryn.

'Leave this place - this graveyard. Gather those who can be trusted and depart. Let go of your old realm, find a new home and show Dark Oak that you have relinquished your hope of rebuilding what was before,' said Red Maple.

'I have not abandoned hope,' said Cathryn.

'And rightly so, but you must appear to do so. There can be a new age where our peoples live in harmony. I have come to know the forest as I travelled as an envoy for my father, and it desires peace. There are many who would rebel against Dark Oak, if he could be outmatched. I see the day when it will happen. He acted in haste all those years ago, driven by animal instincts that are fading day by day. He wishes to return to the forest, but he is in denial; denial that he made a mistake. Come away from here. Let the bandits have this tomb, and start a simpler life elsewhere. We can work together to build a new society. I will whisper to my father, and in time he will relent,' said Red Maple.

Cathryn hesitated and moved to the window, looking down at the Maw Gate and out across the forest, now bathed in moonlight.

'Where would we go?' she asked quietly.

'There is a place where humans understand us better than the rest of your kind. A holy place, but one that could be defended,' said Red Maple. 'It would be a long march.'

'Where?' said Ailsa, moving to Cathryn's side.

'The Isle of Anbidian,' said Red Maple.

'Anbidian,' Cathryn repeated, and she seated herself in a chair by the empty fireplace.

She knew of it. The island lay in the centre of the Firth of Marsh, the great sea bay formed at the mouth of the River Marsh, a place known as the Isle of the Deru Weid, named for its tiny resident population of soothsayers, priests and rangers that dwelled in the groves and hill caves. Anbidian had once been central to the offensive plans of the Combined People, being an island with a small natural harbour where troops could be put down, and amid the Firth of Marsh. The river was sufficiently wide that Awgren's troops would not cross, as the Dark Lord, for reasons unknown, had never equipped the Creatures of the Devising with boats or ships. The Isle of Anbidian had once been covered with sparse forests, with bare hills in the centre, and as was the custom of the Combined People, a palisade had been constructed all around the coast to defend the beaches, should Awgren decide to make an assault.

Once ashore, the troops were in a haven whence they could raid both Culrain and Tayne.

'It is far away,' said Ailsa, and Cathryn heard doubt in her voice.

'I will lead you, Queen. Scout out the way. I cannot travel through the trees without the forest knowing my plans, and I know there are some within who would inform my father, even if most of his followers do not dwell within the forest. We can make this journey together,' said Red Maple.

He looked down at his right hand then offered it to Cathryn.

'Let this be the beginning of peace between humanity and the world,' said the Dryad, 'in some small way, at least.'

The queen reached out and took the Dryad's hand.

'I will do as you ask,' she said solemnly, awash with relief, hope, reluctance and regret all at once. She would abandon the seat of her family's power and seek the Isle of Anbidian, home of the Deru Weid.

Cathryn gave the order for The Folly to be abandoned, and preparations were made for a march. She sent word to her remaining loyal captains, leading their small companies in the surrounding forests, amidst the ruins of The Folly and manning lookouts in the broken mountain fortresses. All must depart and march, in secret, for Anbidian, with the queen and her household guard abandoning the Maw Keep last of all. She would gather any of her people whom she encountered on the way.

On the day of departure, Ailsa mustered the queen's guard in the yard behind the Maw Gate while Cathryn, clad in leather armour and carrying the spear that killed Awgren, went to the throne room alone. Once out of sight of her people, she took a swig of wine to still her shaking hands.

Her footsteps echoed through the halls until she came to stand before the dais, vines hanging all around her.

Lord Hawthorn's eyes bored into the stone at her feet, his body indistinguishable from the throne he hated so, the vines of his mane and the ivy of his beard hanging low. A high wind whipped around her as she stood and looked upon her forsaken husband.

Cathryn knelt before his throne.

'Lachlan,' she whispered, looking up at him. He did not flinch, and his eyes did not move to fix on her.

'My lover, my husband, father of my children, my strong right arm,' she whispered, and tears took her by surprise.

This is no farewell till next I see him, she realised. *This is a final goodbye.*

The queen got to her feet and stroked the back of his wooden hand with her fingertips.

'I won't forget you, my love,' she said. She leant in and planted a kiss upon his unyielding cheek.

Unable to stay in his presence any longer as her emotions rose like a high tide, Cathryn stepped behind her own throne and toppled it forward so that it crashed down the steps to the floor before her husband. Without a look back at him, she strode from the room, mere seconds ahead of her grief.

As she reached the door, Lord Hawthorn's eyes flicked up and watched her retreating. His wooden brow furrowed, showering fragments of bark upon his lap. He raised his head and opened his mouth, splitting his lips, but he made no sound.

Cathryn's echoing footsteps faded, and Lachlan, Lord Hawthorn, was left to govern the empty Maw Keep alone.

The queen mounted her horse and spurred the animal on under the arch of the Maw Gate. Her people trooped out after her, and with Ailsa ever at her side, Queen Cathryn rode on, leaving The Folly to the traitorous Lord Magregar.

Red Maple stood before them on the path, and Cathryn saw his head was tilted far back, so he could look up to the heights of the Maw Keep.

Cathryn dared not look back lest she capitulate to the voices in her mind, the voices of her father and mother, her sires of old who had held this place for time out of mind.

The Maw Keep loomed behind her, a dark tower in the gap between the mountains, with only an undying lord to watch over its empty halls.

Cathryn rode on and tried to forget.

Chapter Twelve

The Impassable Forest

The First Tree called, but Dark Oak, wandering the forest, could not hear. He was not to know the Council had been called, and so the summons went unanswered at first. The First Tree called again, and the King of the Dryads remained unaware.

But Nayr heard. Nayr knew. Nayr who had known Riark longest, and revered him, even if she did not agree with all of his ways. Nayr, birch in the Middle Speech, just as Riark was elm in that same tongue, now long forgotten, just like the humans who had spoken it.

She was still within her Mother Tree when she heard the call, flowing slowly up and down its slender form, gathering in the roots and travelling up to the tips of her spindly branches. She revelled in the warmth and power that dwelled in the leaves. She took comfort and was at ease, despite the cares of the world and brewing angst within the forest, until she heard the First Tree's summons as an impulse in the wood itself.

Come, it ordered, and Nayr paid heed. Dark Oak was summoned, but she did not feel his presence in the forest and knew that he was choosing to be apart. The summons could not go unanswered. Nayr saw her opportunity. She drained out of her roots and, many leagues away, she entered into those of the First Tree. Nayr pushed her way out of its trunk and took avatar upon the shore of the First Island.

She was the last to arrive. Wern, King of the Oreads, Mayri, Queen of the Sylphs and Samura, Queen of the Naiads, were waiting.

She bowed to them and the Council began.

Where is Dark Oak? They wanted to know.

They did not speak, but attuned to one another. The stone of Wern's massive body grew into the likeness of a great grey oak, a living fossil.

Where is Dark Oak? He no longer heeds our call.

He did not hear the summons, Nayr told them. *He no longer communes with the forest.*

Who are you?

They did not know her, beyond seeing her at Riark's side. Nayr broke with tradition, and a mouth formed upon her face.

'Who am I?' she asked. 'I am of the forest as was. I was loyal to Riark, who has been overshadowed by one who should never have been allowed to take his place. Why did you listen to Dark Oak? Could you not see his passion was that of a sapling?'

A pause.

'It is for that reason that the Council has been called,' said Mayri. 'Dark Oak has gone too far. He claimed to seek balance, and yet all is out of kilter.'

'We saw the merit in preventing humanity from becoming too powerful, aiding in the defeat of the road-builder,' said Samura, and Wern finished her thought, 'and in throwing down the walls of The Folly.'

'But we could not have foreseen the consequences of his reaction,' said Mayri.

Nayr slipped inside the First Tree and she drew strength from it as she emerged upon a low branch, mimicking the form of a small bird, shaped like a robin but without the flourishes of colour.

'Dark Oak has inflicted the very damage he sought to avoid. There are too many trees now. The scale has tipped in your favour,' said Mayri.

Nayr dissolved into the branch of the tree and sprang forth from the trunk, pacing forward in an instant.

'Dark Oak never sought to avoid damage!' she said. 'He was newborn to the forest and driven by rage. He sought nothing but revenge and to vent his hate. He was the worst traits of humanity in an unstoppable form and his malice was too strong for us to contend in that moment. He destroyed the true King of the Dryads and subverted all that you are supposed to stand for,' she concluded.

There was silence between them for a moment.

'There are too many trees,' said Mayri again, 'They are changing the nature of the air. The temperature rises. It takes all of my people's power to prevent great fires from burning your realm to ash.'

'All the lands are covered,' said Samura. 'The roots draw up all the water. There is drought. Streams and rivers dry up.'

'The Dryads have become more of a threat to the world than the humans ever were,' said Wern, fixing Nayr with a relentless gaze. 'Balance must be restored.'

'Are you suggesting destroying all that has now grown?' asked Nayr.

'All that was forced to grow,' said Wern. 'Dryads were once content to let trees do their own work, spreading as far as their abilities allowed, yet Dark Oak has used his impetus and mastery to dominate the world beyond what is natural. Do the Oreads throw up mountains at a whim? Do the Naiads raise the oceans to cover the land? Do the Sylphs uproot the forests with constant hurricanes? Did Dark Oak not preach against dominion?'

'What would you have us do?' asked Nayr. 'Dark Oak is no longer one with the forest. He learns nothing of our ways and cannot benefit from being one with the trees. He oversees from afar and will not be swayed by the forest's influence or the natural way of things.'

'Perhaps he must be overshadowed, just as he overshadowed Riark,' said Mayri.

'Killed,' said Wern.

Nayr said nothing for a time, pondering the others' words.

'He can only be killed by destroying his Mother Tree, and he will defend it. Now that I bear the knowledge of this conversation, as soon as I re-enter the trees, all other Dryads therein will know of my intention. Even if the notion is widely accepted, it will only take one Dryad to take the news to Dark Oak.'

'He cannot withstand us,' said Wern, then added, '*if* we move against him.'

'And yet we would rather not do so,' said Mayri. 'We do not wish to wage war, but to restore balance. It would be best if Dark Oak came to realise his folly, just as we have our own. It would be for the best if he listened to the forest, which has long understood that sometimes the loss of trees is inevitable and that what will be, will be.'

'And the humans?' asked Nayr.

'Should be left to their own devices,' said Mayri.

'That is not a message that Dark Oak will eagerly hear,' said Nayr.

'He will hear it, or we will intervene. Do not forget that the Dryads are perhaps the weakest among us, Nayr. He cannot defeat us, we who do not live and so cannot die,' said Wern.

'We have a fondness for the Dryads. Perhaps we have indulged you for too long, like a parent doting upon a child. I remember my time as a Dryad with great affection,' said Mayri. 'Yet though I thought I knew much when I was with the forest, I have learnt much more since.'

'You were a Dryad?' said Nayr.

Mayri, Samura and Wern were silent for a moment, attuning to one another, secretly.

'They need to know,' said Mayri.

Silence again. Samura slipped into the pool, her shimmering form absorbed within then reforming after a few seconds, the blue marbles of her eyes fixed on Nayr. She stepped up onto the First Island.

'Your people know humans create souls which are reincarnated until they are ready to be born Dryads,' she said.

'But that is not the end of the Cycle,' said Mayri. 'Dryads may be higher beings, blessed with grace, patience and acceptance, unfettered by the same fears, weaknesses and imperfections, blessed with as many years as their Mother Tree survives, but they too are mortal. Life as a Dryad is the penultimate form.'

Nayr tilted her head and met Mayri's gaze, realisation beginning to dawn.

'Did Riark know of this? Does Dark Oak?' she asked, feeling both betrayed and curious how they could have concealed this knowledge.

'No Dryad has ever known until now. We conceal the knowledge when we interact with your kind,' said Wern. 'The Council do not wish to condescend to your people. You have a rightful place on the Council, as those who represent the sentience of the living world. But your lives tied to the forest are but preparation for rebirth as a true immortal. The lessons are learnt better for not knowing you will be born again.'

'As one of us,' said Samura. 'Oread, Sylph or Naiad.'

'Riark . . . ' his name slipped out before Nayr could recall her thought.

'He is new to the form, and as it is with your kind, it is best he remains with the waters for a while longer. There is much he can teach us about the tasks ahead,' said Samura.

Nayr, incapable of shock, nodded slowly, but then a new thought came upon her, and she looked up.

'I was wrong. There is no Eversleep,' said Nayr. 'Unless . . . are Dryads all reincarnated?'

'They are,' said Wern. 'The spirits of the earth, the water and the air are many, beyond your reckoning.'

'Even young Dryads, whose Mother Trees are killed prematurely?' asked Nayr. 'They are often rash and retain many human characteristics.'

'All,' said Wern, and Mayri swept around her in a cloud then hovered before her.

'They are sometimes not the best of us,' said Samura, 'but my kind have always claimed those who died at sea and in the waters of the world. Like the woodcutter's daughter, killed as a baby and denied rebirth as a Dryad. Alas, she is a new soul and died so young in her first life; she does not comprehend what has happened to her and what led to her death as well as we might in her place. She will never know peace, I fear.'

'Whiteflow,' said Nayr. 'What of Seaborn?'

'He has spent mere moments with the waters, but he is an older soul. We will see,' admitted Samura.

'Red Maple does not harbour bitterness, except against his father for killing him. He is gradually learning our ways. There may be hope for the Naiad boy,' mused Nayr.

'We will see,' said Samura. 'Your kind have twice made Dryads of humans before they were ready in order to further your goals. Riark had to overthrow the one who made the first when he was newborn to the forest, and yet he made the mistake of creating Dark Oak. Ignoring the Cycle killed him in the end.'

'We do not speak of the first occasion,' said Nayr. 'It is forbidden.'

'And yet Riark did not learn from the mistake, it seems,' said Wern.

'Why do you call it a mistake when the Dryads do as you do? You say the Naiads turn those who die at sea?' asked Nayr.

'The Naiads are different. We are better able to drown out the angst of the newborn among us. They cannot sway us so easily. The forest is so passive. The seas will outlast all else,' said Samura.

'And yet you let Dark Oak sway you?' asked Nayr. 'Let him fool you?'

The Council fell silent as Nayr paced back and forth.

'There may be no Eversleep,' she muttered, then spoke up as she addressed the Council, 'but my concerns are valid. If Dark Oak allows humanity to become extinct, there will be no more human mothers to create new souls or to allow rebirth. Souls not ready to ascend will be trapped in the world as spirits. There will be no new Dryads and, in time, no new Naiads, Sylphs or Oreads at all.'

'It is of no consequence,' said Wern, almost sounding bored.

'Truly?' said Mayri. She travelled as a wisp of cloud, coiling around him. 'You remember your days as a human, I am sure.'

'I do,' said Wern in his deep, rumbling voice.

'And if your friends and family are still caught in the Cycle, living now as humans? When they die, would you have them cast aside as ghosts, the lost and wandering dead, never able to ascend, never able to be one with the world? Never to be seen by their loved ones again?' said Mayri.

The great Wern fell silent.

'Just so,' said Samura.

The four representatives stood in silence for many days, pondering the situation. When finally conversation started up again, it went on for many more until, gradually, the kings and queens of the world came to an agreement.

'The Dryads will no longer force trees to grow. We will not ask you to kill those you have created. Living with the forest and its effect will be our penance and just consequence for our rash action, though our labours will be great,' said Mayri.

Samura slipped into the First Waters and descended until only her head was visible.

'Humanity must be allowed to flourish and a representative must be chosen to sit on the Council with us here present. They too must have a voice, and no longer be the unheeded children of the world,' said Samura. 'That is how we will achieve balance.'

Wern took Nayr by the shoulders.

'You are Queen of the Dryads now. Your duty is clear. Stop Dark Oak and all he commands from inflicting any greater damage on the world. We leave it up to you how you go about this task,' he said, 'and will render aid if we can. If you cannot bring him under your control, we will kill him. He will ascend as one of our people, and we will deal with him ourselves, for he will not overpower us. Stop Dark Oak, and bring a human to represent them.'

'I have someone in mind,' Nayr replied, bowing to the kings and queens of the world.

Nayr returned to her Mother Tree and, therein, she merged with the communal soul of the trees and allowed it to know her mind. Dryads throughout the forest heard her thoughts, gained her knowledge and came to know their appointed queen. Nayr sensed those within who still agreed with Dark Oak, but they were in the minority, and so when she commanded her people to restrain the dissenters, they did so with ease. They were a problem for another day, and Nayr had someone in mind to deal with them.

Days passed while the elder Dryads communed, debating how best to deal with Dark Oak and his followers, as well as how to choose a human to sit on the Council. Surely it should be the human queen, the Dryads argued, but Nayr had another idea.

The woodcutter's wife. She is Dark Oak's weakness. Who better?

Before a week had passed, Nayr had her mandate and something close to consensus. She rallied her people and, together, they travelled to confront Dark Oak.

The Hinterland

'You would deny me my will?' said Dark Oak, standing on the porch to his homestead with steam issuing from the various cracks in his face and body, Whiteflow at his side, her arm draped around Seaborn's shoulders. Green sap dribbled out of the fissures. His face darkened as he lowered his brow. The vines of his mane whipped like angry snakes held by their tails. His wood axe formed in his hand. Like the sergeant Morrick had been, Dark Oak left the Naiads on the porch and stalked along the line of Dryads that had emerged from the trees surrounding his home, looking at each of them in turn. But these were not humans, and they were not daunted by him. They did not know fear in that way any longer, and they knew he was no longer any threat to them. His power had waned.

Nayr stood forward.

'Put away your axe,' she said to him, but he would not listen.

'Are you afraid?' he asked.

Nayr smiled and quicker than could be perceived, her left forearm became a great shield while a long blade formed in her right hand. Her body shifted and layered into bands of armour. A helm formed over her head so her face was no longer visible. In the next moment, she reverted back to her plain, human form, that of a lithe female, like an unfinished carving from a sculptor's workshop, enchanted into life.

'I cannot be intimidated by such trappings, but your desire to hold a weapon says more to me than your incessant speech in the human tongue could ever convey. Put down your weapon. Put aside your hatred and listen to those who have been as you are now for many lives of men, Dark Oak. You cannot triumph here,' said Nayr.

Dark Oak kept his axe in hand but lowered it so its head touched the ground.

'I have the mastery,' he insisted.

Nayr stepped forward.

'You had the mastery, but we have had time to weigh up your actions and our choices. There have been consequences to your efforts to do good. Join with me, unless you are afraid?'

Dark Oak smiled, but did not move. Nayr took this as consent. She knelt, thrust her fingers into the earth and roots grew from them, seeking Dark Oak's own. After a moment's hesitation, he did the same and their roots entwined. Their minds were laid bare, and yet not entirely, for Dark Oak's ability to conceal and dissemble were not fully understood by the elder Dryad, who had lost the need for deception in her long years with the forest, beginning in a time long forgotten by humanity. He could not mask his thoughts for long, but he put up his walls and resisted her with all his might.

Dark Oak learnt all that had been explained at the Council and of the direct threat made against him. Though he retained his anger at the injustices served to him, he began to understand that a world dominated by forest might have seemed idyllic, but it had led to imbalance.

And what of it? Dark Oak thought, and Nayr listened. *Let the Sylphs fall idle. Let the air grow hot and wildfires break out, let them redress the balance, if that is what they wish, but do not let humanity regain their former status as masters of the world, caring only for themselves, exploiting and causing suffering wherever they dwell.*

But he started to recognise his own hypocrisy, and he was about to embark on a new line of reasoning when he heard Nayr's choice of human to sit on the Council.

Rowan.

He thrust Nayr's roots away, withdrawing his own. He advanced upon her even as she knelt upon the grass, furious and growing taller, looming over the queen, but she did not react.

'I will kill her,' said Dark Oak.

'You won't,' said Nayr, 'and even if you were to take back control of the forest, you would not sit on the First Council with her, and that is why she is the ideal choice.'

Steam poured from fissures in Dark Oak's wooden body. His blackened flesh began to smoke and crackle like a log catching fire, but Nayr did not seem perturbed.

'I have my people to guard her. Your followers will withdraw or their Mother Trees will be destroyed. Your wife *will* sit on the First Council, woodcutter, and they will not allow her to be harmed.'

'You mock me by acknowledging the humans! By giving Rowan a seat on the Council! All misery comes from them. All pain. All suffering. All loss. All torment,' said Dark Oak, even as the truth began to slip by his defences.

'The only suffering I endure was perpetrated by you,' said Nayr. 'You killed Riark. I may not grieve as you do, new as you are to this life, but I feel his absence, I feel the shift in the forest that you can never perceive until you have dwelt with us for many long years more. All humans suffer now, and if you continue to persecute them, if they die out, the world will suffer for it.'

He heard a hissing, steaming noise and the slap of water hitting the steps down to the grass. Whiteflow stepped up beside him.

'Let them try to destroy your Mother Trees!' said Whiteflow. 'Your followers can attack hers! You may yet retain control and, if we fail, you will be reincarnated as a Naiad, an Oread or a Sylph, unkillable and immortal!'

'Is this true?' asked Dark Oak.

Whiteflow nodded.

'It is,' said Nayr. 'And the rulers of those people would welcome you, but be under no illusion, they assure me they would take you in hand. You would not dominate their domains as you have mine.'

Dark Oak looked at Whiteflow.

'It is true,' she admitted. 'I am tolerated, but not heeded amongst my people.'

Silence fell as Dark Oak pondered her words. Sacrifice his Mother Tree and become invincible, but lose all influence? No. He was of the forest. It was his domain. Even if he could not dwell within, he would fight to maintain his hold so that he could protect it.

Nayr straightened her back, growing as she did so.

'Your reign is over, Dark Oak,' she said. 'I am the Queen of the Dryads now. If you will return to the forest with us, you have my word that the pain will diminish. Human life is full of misery and suffering, as well as many strange joys, yet it is but a proving ground for greater things. Riark afforded you a great honour in selecting you to be one of us, even if it was also a great mistake. You were not ready to become a Dryad. I know not where your soul would have gone had my king left you hanging by your neck, but I do not think you would have joined us. Not for a life or many lives of men.'

She placed her hands on his shoulders and looked deep into the white stars of his eyes.

'What do you truly want, Dark Oak? To protect the world or just revenge?'

Dark Oak did not reply or make any move against the older Dryad.

'Dark Oak?' said Nayr.

He knew there was no point in speaking with her. She had fallen into her old ways. All of them had. And soon things would be as they had been before. But what could he do about it? Her body would take no injury, and her Mother Tree? He could perhaps mount an assault upon it, and yet did not every one of them know the location of his? He was as vulnerable as her in that regard.

He decided he had three choices, he could fall in line and join the forest, allowing himself to forget the injustice as he became like them, he could attack and risk the Dryads destroying one another or . . .

'I will cede to your will,' he said, 'but I will not return to the forest. My place is here.'

'Father!' objected Whiteflow.

'So be it,' said Nayr. 'but the forest will welcome you when you are ready. Take comfort, Dark Oak. The Dryads will endure, and things will not be quite as they were before. The humans know our power now and will not forget it. We will hear their voices on the Council and move forward in peace.'

'Until they find a way to exploit their new position and take what power they can,' laughed Dark Oak. 'Hard as it may be to conceive, they will find a way!'

'Oh, it is not hard to conceive of such a thing, Dark Oak. Not hard at all when one such as you stands before me. You are but a human with the gifts of a Dryad, some that you misuse and others that you deny yourself, despite the good they would do you,' said Nayr. 'I hope in time you will return to us and come to understand what it truly means to be one with the forest.'

Dark Oak sighed, looked up at the sky for a moment and then met Nayr's gaze.

'Perhaps, in time, once I can leave my old life behind,' he conceded. He bowed his head to the Queen of the Dryads.

'You would throw it all away, Father? Allow Mother her freedom?' said Whiteflow.

'It is the will of the Council, Whiteflow,' said Nayr. 'The Queen of the Naiads has given me her blessing in this matter. Samura is concerned about you and your brother as well. I have no doubt you will be summoned before long.'

'Can I see Mother now?' said a child's voice, high and babbling like a stream.

Dark Oak watched as Nayr turned and attended to Seaborn for the first time. The Dryad's body shrank in stature to match the boy Naiad.

'I think she would like that,' said Nayr and then, louder, to Dark Oak.

'She has been alone for many years, suffering. It may ease her transition if she knows her children live.'

'No!'

Dark Oak watched as Whiteflow held up a watery fist and then swung it a horizontal arc out from her body. The water of her arm flowed out like a wave and washed Nayr away from Seaborn, who disappeared in his sister's embrace.

The Dryads stepped forward, but Dark Oak called out.

'Whiteflow, stop. Heed me,' he said. Nayr regained her footing, water dripping from her body into the grass, and his Naiad children reformed as one conjoined body from the puddles around the Queen of the Dryads.

'We cannot dispute the will of the Council,' said Dark Oak. He strode forward and whispered to his daughter.

'Go to your mother, help bring her before the Council,' he said.

'That woman deserves to suffer,' Whiteflow whispered back. 'Do not betray me, Father. I warn you.'

Dark Oak smiled kindly at her.

'I would never betray you. Your mother has suffered and will again, such is the nature of human life,' he said. 'There is no need for threats. We understand one another. We alone understand what is important. Trust me as I have trusted you, Daughter. Go to your mother. Take Seaborn. But do *not*,' he said, emphasising the word, 'forget your father.'

She stood back, saying nothing, but nodded slowly.

Dark Oak crouched and Seaborn, still appearing as the boy Declan had been, separated from his sister. The Dryad stretched out his arms and the young Naiad collapsed into his embrace.

'Be good for your sister,' said Dark Oak. 'Your father loved you more than anything, you know.' He held Seaborn close, his son dampening his wooden form where their bodies met. Finally, they broke apart and Dark Oak stepped back, bidding his children farewell.

'Whiteflow, Seaborn, I will meet you on the south beach of the Butterfly Isle,' said Nayr. Whiteflow nodded and, taking her brother's hand, they disappeared among the trees in the direction of the river Whiteflow.

'Farewell, Dark Oak,' said Nayr, the vines of her hair swaying as she moved towards the tree through which she had travelled. 'I wish you peace.'

'One favour,' said Dark Oak, and the Queen of the Dryads looked back over her shoulder.

'Send Red Maple to me so I can bid him farewell?' he asked.

'It will not be possible. All of your followers will be found and recalled to the forest. I will not allow you to twist his mind any more than you have,' said the queen.

Nayr left him then. She stepped into the tree and her people followed, leaving Dark Oak standing in the broken remains of his homestead amongst the flowers and grasses, leaves rustling and a raptor calling overhead.

Knowledge of Nayr's encounter with Dark Oak spread amongst her people as soon as she became one with the forest. She felt the tension begin to dissipate, as though taut muscles were relaxing, and the Dryads could breathe easily once more. There was much to do though, Nayr knew, they could not be as passive as they were when Riark ruled. She must bring home to the forest any newborns Dark Oak may have left behind, removing all the watchers of humanity. She must bring Rowan before the First Council and then, Nayr, Queen of the Dryads, hoped, a new epoch would begin, one in which humans and Dryads lived together in peace.

The Hinterland

A badger ran over Dark Oak's feet, but he paid it no heed. The animal circled round him, grunting, before trundling on through the dark forest. An owl screeched in the distance and deer grazed on the grasses around him. The Dryad, alone, and no longer in command of vast forces, reflected on all that had happened. Not constrained by the frailties of a human brain's inadequate retrieval systems, he reviewed every second of his life, starting with the first moments of sentience in his mother's womb, recalling every sensation and instinct before language gave voice to his thoughts and desires. He remembered every face, every word spoken and heard, every laugh, all his joyous moments and traumatic encounters alike. He relived his life as a husband, then a father, before reaching the day when the Creatures of the Devising had conscripted him into the army of the Dark Lord, Awgren.

He evaluated not only his memories, but the collective knowledge of the Dryads, gleant from his brief time with the forest.

There was a place where Dryads could not reach him, a place humans feared, and the wellspring of a forbidden power.

Dark Oak's feet had taken root when he came back to his senses, and his legs had merged together. He had grown in the days since his conversation with Nayr and branches sprouted from his body, acorns hanging here and there. He centred his thought and his body transformed once more into that of a wooden imitation of Morrick, wearing a cloak of moss and carrying his wood axe.

The former King of the Dryads looked around the homestead, said a final goodbye to his life there and set off east towards the Whiteflow. Beyond the river were hills that grew into tall mountains over which, 1000 years ago, the Creatures of the Devising had poured to occupy the Hinterland before going on to crush humanity, suppressing them for a millennium.

Nobody had travelled into The Wastes since the armies of Culrain were lost there when first the Dark Lord rose, and no human who reached Halwende, the Dark Lord's lair amid the desolate wastelands, lived to tell the tale.

But some had reincarnated as Dryads.

Dark Oak began his long journey east.

Chapter Thirteen

The Impassable Forest

Dun was not back to full strength before Tolucan was hungry to move on. The knight told Feran he would need to be leaving soon and with some grumbling and comments about Tolucan's uncaring nature, his friend begrudgingly agreed that if Tolucan kept a slower pace, they could perhaps be off again.

'Perhaps he would be happier if we left him here? The aspirants are kind people,' said Tolucan, but both Feran and Dun scowled at him, so Tolucan instead suggested that perhaps they might barter for one of the horses that grazed around the cathedral.

'The squire shall ride while the knights walk,' Feran said, assembling a poultice for the older man.

'You're a knight again, are you?' said Dun, his skin grey and lips a little blue, as he propped himself up on his elbows.

Feran scowled at him and dropped the poultice on Dun's chest.

'You can finish that, as punishment for your insolence,' he said, and patted his squire three times hard on the head. Dun muttered something and sat up to complete the work.

Feran took Tolucan by the arm and led him away.

'I will not leave him, but perhaps we should all consider staying here,' said Feran.

Tolucan said nothing.

They walked on short grass in a corridor of silver birch trees, which led from the great hall farther into the woods. Tolucan had at first doubted, but now believed that the cathedral had expanded every day, with new rooms appearing from recently emerging hallways. He had seen the Dryads, the Ascended, many times in the first few days, but they had been conspicuously absent for the remainder of the week.

'What do you think?' said Feran when Tolucan did not answer.

'You know what I think. This place is protected by the Dryads, it's enchanting, and both the aspirants and their congregation of enlightened are kind, giving people, but . . . '

He stopped walking and looked Feran in the eye.

'We have other business,' said Tolucan.

'Ah, the other business, yes,' said Feran. 'The futile, hopeless business that keeps us from making lives for ourselves. Tasked by a mercurial qu . . . '

'Quiet,' said Tolucan. 'In this place of all places? Are you a fool?'

Feran winked, and Tolucan began walking again, speaking low.

'You have given up your sword, you are under no obligation to come with me. If you wish to stay here with Dun, I will go on alone,' he said.

'I may have abandoned the . . . ' started Feran, but Tolucan dug an elbow into the man's ribs, and he yelped, rubbing his side.

'I may no longer be as I was,' Feran corrected his wording, 'but I will travel with you while I can.'

'Why?' said Tolucan. 'Why do you haunt me if you do not believe in what I am doing?'

'It is a good question,' said Feran. 'Perhaps I see in you what all knights should be. What I should have been. I may have put aside my obligations, but perhaps I can help you keep yours.'

'Quiet!' Tolucan hissed, but Feran dismissed his concerns with a wave of his hand.

'I would not be at all surprised if you are the only one still honouring your word, you know. We are not so different from anyone else. The world is not as it is in the storybooks, my friend,' said Feran.

They are all I had to go by, thought Tolucan.

Later on in the day, Tolucan left Feran squabbling with Dun and walked towards the great hall of the cathedral, pink blossom drifting down around him and green twilight showing him the way. The enlightened, as they preferred to be called, were seated in rows upon the grass, facing south, while Aspirant Meghan delivered a sermon. There was no sign of the Dryads.

Tolucan paced back and forth, but one of the enlightened turned and glared at him. He realised the clanking of his mail and weapons was disturbing the service, so he sat at the end of the last row, crossing his legs in imitation of those around him. He tried to be as still and silent as the others, but his body ached. When he shifted position, more enlightened would turn and hush him.

A hand grasped his shoulder. Tolucan jumped and drew his knife, but saw Patrick standing over him, one eyebrow raised. The aspirant spoke calmly and politely, but was clearly annoyed.

'Meghan will speak for a while longer. If you are waiting for us, then either go away and we will find you, or take off your armour elsewhere then come back and join us. You might learn something of yourself,' Patrick whispered.

Tolucan felt his cheeks grow warm, and he got to his feet.

'My apologies, Aspirant,' he said.

Patrick nodded.

'If you wish to learn, I'll await you and offer instruction,' he said.

Tolucan nodded and disappeared amongst the trees to remove his armour and his sword, though the latter he would not surrender. He returned in breeches and a torn, blood-stained shirt, but carried his sword in its sheath.

Patrick beckoned for him to follow, and Tolucan followed the aspirant between the trees away from the rest of the enlightened. They stopped in a small glade, and Patrick sat cross-legged upon the short grass between the fragile flowers. Tolucan took up a similar position and laid his sword beside him.

'Do you know why we aspire to become like the Ascended, the gods of the forest?' asked Patrick. The quiet words in the eerie glade sent a shiver up Tolucan's spine, giving rise to a pleasurable sensation near the neck. He shook his head ever so slightly and the sensation flared out and up across his skull ever so briefly.

'The Ascended,' Patrick continued, 'are the dead reborn to the trees. Ascending is an honour afforded only to those who have achieved supreme Enlightenment,' he said, 'those who have turned to the life of the spirit and have made great personal progress over many lifetimes.'

'You speak as though these were hard facts, Patrick,' said Tolucan, 'yet in all my life I have never even heard of your gods until the day the forests came and Dark Oak took power.'

'We have learnt much from the Ascended,' said Patrick and raised a finger to his lips before continuing.

'To become one of the Ascended is a great privilege, for they experience the Duality, the coexistence of sentience and simple existence. While a human might think and know, yet struggle to simply be, a tree may simply be and yet not know it. The gods of the forest may simply exist and yet are aware. They no longer suffer as do we.'

'I do not follow,' said Tolucan.

'It is not an easy concept to grasp. It takes time, but meditation will help,' Patrick replied.

'Why would you wish to spend your days sitting in silent contemplation when there is life to be lived?' asked Tolucan, frowning.

'Says the man who spends his days wandering the forests aimlessly, bruised and without comforts?' Patrick smiled. 'Lord Dark Oak knew that to be human is to suffer. It is his knowledge of our suffering that has led him to make all the world a forest, to foster peace and enlightenment.'

Privately, Tolucan thought that Patrick sounded like many a zealot and priest of the old religions, even if the choice of gods differed, but he did not voice his opinion, instead appearing grave and nodding attentively. The aspirant had been taught by Dryads, and there was a chance he might know something of use.

'Lord Dark Oak wanted to end suffering but decimated humanity? Tore down our homes?' asked Tolucan.

'Very few humans were killed as far as I am aware. We are scattered, yes. Our cities and castles are gone, yes, but humanity persists, and we here have heeded the lesson. We need no more than the forest can provide, as our animal friends know well, or would if their minds were fit to know anything,' said Patrick.

Tolucan opened his mouth to reply, but found a ready answer did not issue forth as expected. He thought for a moment, realising that Patrick spoke the truth. The aspirant smiled, victorious, and carried on preaching.

'Good, you have questions, but do not always have an answer. It means you are more self-aware than I hoped. Human life is but the first step of the Journey, Tolucan, the proving ground and the classroom. We are born and born again until we learn all we can before we reawaken to find ourselves Ascended. We will know the Duality.'

'Surely a tree simply exists better than a Dryad,' said Tolucan, thinking aloud.

Patrick nodded and a smile lit up his face.

'Of course, and yet they are not aware of their Enlightenment. That is the beauty of the Duality. Enlightenment that can be appreciated. No pain, no hunger, no unsated lust, no fear, no ageing, but contentment, growth, learning and existence.' Patrick reached out and rested his hand on Tolucan's shoulder.

'That is why we seek the wisdom of the Ascended. That is to what we aspire,' said Patrick, his eyebrows raised in hopeful expectation.

'I see,' said Tolucan. 'You want to become gods.'

Patrick's face dropped, and Tolucan wondered if he had misspoken.

The aspirant renewed his cross-legged posture, straightening his back and clasping his hands in his lap.

'Adopt this position,' said Patrick, and Tolucan made his best effort, hoping to develop rapport with the aspirant. Patrick set about correcting him, moving a hand here and adjusting the angle of the jaw there. Once he was satisfied, he returned to sitting beside the knight.

'When we meditate, we face in the direction of the Sacred Black Oak, Dark Oak's Mother Tree, in order to focus our spirits on the plan he has for us,' said Patrick.

Now Tolucan *did* attend.

'How can you know where his Mother Tree lies?' asked Tolucan, trying to conceal his excitement.

'It grows not far from where Mount Greenwood once stood, away in the far south,' said Patrick. 'The Ascended have promised to take us on a pilgrimage one day. I hope my old bones can make the journey.'

'That is far, far from here,' said Tolucan, still musing on this new, vital information, as the blood whooshed in his ears. On this unassuming morning, he may have stumbled across the resolution of his quest. Perhaps an end was in sight.

And yet he composed himself and continued to attend to Patrick as the aspirant explained how to moderate his breaths, to clear his mind of all thought, acknowledging and dismissing any images or words that came to him.

And then it was time to meditate.

'Begin,' said Patrick before he lapsed into silence.

Tolucan sat in silence, his thoughts shouting to be heard. He must tell Feran. They must depart as soon as possible! But he knew he must sit for some time if he was not to worry the aspirant and so he did as Patrick instructed.

Tolucan counted his breaths up to ten and back down to nothing. He concentrated on that breathing, to the exclusion of all else and when thoughts intruded, he tried to steel himself against it. At first, he imagined barriers with thoughts crowding behind them, but then the barriers became an idea, not visualised, before becoming an impulse, a transparent medium. Remaining thoughtless became possible for ever-lengthening moments amid the chaos of his mind.

His back began to ache, and he cursed his lack of discipline, fearing he would sag under the pain, displeasing his new mentor. And yet he managed to hold his pose, just, until Patrick spoke.

'Let us end now,' he said.

Tolucan let out a long sigh and arched his back until something clicked.

'Pathetic,' he said, and Patrick looked at him with a puzzled expression.

'How so?' said Patrick.

'To be able to sit for so short a time without my body objecting,' said Tolucan, lying back in the grass.

'I would guess we sat for perhaps half an hour,' he said, 'though it is hard to tell beneath the canopy.'

'It could not have been more than a few minutes!' said Tolucan, propping himself up on his elbows.

'Ah, I've surprised myself many a time at how long I have sat in meditation. When one disengages the mind, one loses the perception of time to a degree,' said Patrick.

He got to his feet and offered Tolucan a hand up. The knight accepted and groaned as he stood.

'Well?' said Patrick.

'Intriguing,' said Tolucan. 'It's always interesting to explore other ways of viewing the world.'

'Our is not just *another* way,' said Patrick, his smile fading, 'it is the *only* way that acknowledges the true order of things, even if you choose not to walk it. If you neglect your spiritual life in favour of the life of sensation and worldly needs, your soul may wander the world until it reincarnates.'

Tolucan said nothing, but turned Patrick's words over in his mind. He did not know it yet, but they would return to him and even trouble him for many days to come.

'Much to take in, in one sitting, at least,' said Patrick, smiling once more. 'Come, let us find your friends and mine. We will take supper together and perhaps you might join us later for our sitting this evening. I hope the Ascended will return soon. They have been gone longer than usual.'

Tolucan thanked Patrick and once they had reached familiar paths, the two men parted.

I'm going to destroy your god, Tolucan thought as the aspirant walked away.

Tolucan returned to the sleeping quarters to find nobody there. Dun's bed was empty for the first time and of Feran, there was no sign.

Has the old man died? he thought as he began to panic.

He looked around for any indication of where they might have gone, and intercepted one of the enlightened, who told him his friends had gone down to the stream, which heartened him - Dun was up and about.

Low branches meant Tolucan was forced to stoop as he made his way along the narrow, moss-carpeted paths towards the stream. The light faded as the trees became thicker on either side of him, but with every step the sound of trickling water grew louder and soon he heard voices up ahead.

Feran and Dun were both bathing in the shallow waters, the former knight fretting and watchful in case his old squire should lose his footing. As Tolucan stepped into view, Dun looked up and slipped as he did so, his right foot flying up out of the water, but quick as a darting fish, Feran caught him under the arms.

'All well?' Feran asked.

'Aye, all well, sir,' said Dun. 'Thought I was getting a more thorough wash than I expected for a moment.'

'Clumsy old fool,' said Feran, but he held the old man's arm for a while longer until he was certain Dun had regained his balance.

'What a sight you two make. A couple of old women slipping about in a bathhouse,' said Tolucan, but he had never been good at delivering banter, and the words fell flat. Feran smiled up at him.

'You could do with a bath yourself, master Tolucan,' said Feran, 'or are you too high and mighty to come down and join us doddering old biddies in the tub?' He grinned.

Tolucan looked left then right, as though prying eyes might be watching from the bank, then stripped down and joined the other two men in the water. He found a cleft in the bank in which the water pooled deeper, and he was just about able to float on his back, fully stretched out. The shock of the cold wore off quickly and his breathing slowed. Tolucan bobbed in the water and looked up at the swaying branches above them.

Feran and Dun carried on their ablutions, not troubling him for a while. He closed his eyes and listened to the water, enjoying the sensation of the current against his skin. Then suddenly he spoke.

'Our business,' he said, keeping his eyes closed and still floating on the stream, the soles of his feet bracing against a rock.

'What of it?' said Feran as he wrung out his long red hair.

Tolucan laughed.

'What is it?' said Feran.

'Oh, nothing really. I just know where to go,' said Tolucan, unable to keep the smile from his lips.

'Truly?' said Feran, sounding perhaps more fierce than he intended. When Tolucan looked up to meet his gaze, he saw that his friend was frowning.

Feran ducked his head forward then snapped it back sharply so that his wet hair slapped against his bare back. He began to tie it back while Dun sat down on a rock midstream and watched Tolucan float.

'If Patrick's word is good, then yes, truly. He mentioned it in passing as though he were referring to a change in the weather,' Tolucan laughed.

Feran and Dun turned to one another, then, offering his squire a supporting hand, Feran led the way closer to Tolucan. The squire paused until a coughing fit had passed. Tolucan noticed a drop of blood hit the water before it was carried away.

'Where is it?' whispered Feran. Dun leant in close.

'He dwells within a black oak at the foot of Mount Greenwood away in the south of the forest,' whispered Tolucan, so quietly that the others had to strain to hear him above the merest burble of the stream, their eyes wide.

'A long way,' said Feran quietly, looking at Dun.

'I doubt I will see the day,' Dun thought aloud, his voice weary.

'None of that, old man,' said Feran cheerfully, as he wrapped an arm around his squire's shoulders, but Tolucan could tell his companion was putting on a good face. He dropped his feet to the streambed and waded out and up the bank, still thinking as he began to dress.

'Come on,' he said to the others, and they followed suit.

Tolucan drew in close to them and whispered,

'Gather your things. We must be away as soon as possible.'

Dun nodded, but Feran paused before answering,

'Which way?' asked Feran.

'How do you mean? The Magpie was given orders to take us off when we returned. The journey south through the forest would take months, if not years,' said Tolucan.

'You really think they will have waited this long? What if she has sailed away or been destroyed?' asked Feran.

Tolucan had not considered that possibility, and it troubled him.

'I see little choice. We head west to the coast and then we will see,' said Tolucan eventually. 'Just think, it could be mere weeks, maybe months, before all of this,' he looked up at the trees, 'is over and life can go back to what it was. I can find my lads.'

'Do you really believe that?' asked Dun, wheezing heavily as he dressed.

'There are hard days ahead, brother,' said Feran. 'I would not trust to hope.' His friend's face looked strained.

'I *will* do this,' said Tolucan, so fiercely that Feran held up his hands in surrender.

'I will prove my worth to the queen,' he continued, 'and then she will allow me to return home.'

The knight set off back towards the sleeping quarters, not seeing Feran and Dun exchange a look.

'He does not understand,' whispered Dun, and Feran shook his head.

The three men accepted the invitation to sup with the aspirants. They were led away from the cathedral to a collection of simple huts, where a central clearing was filled with families, seated on the grass or tending cooking pots. The knights and squire ate with the welcoming community and, keen not to arouse suspicion, Tolucan accompanied Patrick to attend the evening sitting when the meal concluded, leaving Dun to rest and Feran to pack.

He found it easier to concentrate on the meditation, and he felt calm and content when the aspirants broke his trance. He thanked Patrick for teaching him, but told him he must be away in the morning, as his companions were as ready to travel as they ever would be. Tolucan had been concerned the aspirants and enlightened would rise up to stop them going, but there was no need, and he would later feel foolish for thinking ill of their pious hosts. Patrick and Meghan expressed regret that the three companions must go, wished them a safe journey and offered gifts to aid them on their way, food and small items, gratefully received.

The next morning, Tolucan donned his mail and had just hung his sword from his belt when he saw Feran dash to wrestle the mail shirt from Dun's grasp.

'You're not right yet,' he said. 'You'll not wear this again until you are back to full health. Or that!' he added as the old man reached for his sword, still wrapped in cloth.

'You could wear them,' said Dun. 'This is as much your quest as his. You have a duty, Feran.'

Feran said nothing, but after a few moments he donned the mail and snatched up the swaddled sword.

'Carrying it is not using it,' he said, when he saw Dun take a deep breath and smile.

'No, indeed, sir,' said Dun.

Satisfied that all was prepared, Tolucan led them westward from the cathedral towards the coast.

They no longer walked far apart, the knights staying on either side of the squire, supporting him as he required, wiping the blood from his lips when he began to cough.

They whiled away the morning talking and laughing, but all the while Tolucan made plans and fantasised, imagining both Dark Oak's Mother Tree aflame and his triumphant return to the Drift, where he would find his sister and his sons. Where would his new lands be? He would build a keep of his own, Tolucan decided, and keep his family safe until the end of his days. Surely the queen would allow him that?

Chapter Fourteen

The Butterfly Isle

But will the woodcutter's wife be willing?

The thought occurred to Nayr as she flowed up through a pine tree and fell as one of its uppermost needles. She assumed her full form before she hit the ground, landing heavily at the foot of the tree. The long vines of her hair twisted and plaited themselves as she walked, boots and a dress in the style of the Hinterland shaping themselves from her body. She moved swiftly southward until she breached the treeline and saw Whiteflow and Seaborn huddled close together on a rocky promontory, surrounded on three sides by the rough waters she knew they must long for, but with which they had so far been denied communion.

Nayr heard a keening, wailing song on the air. A woman's voice carried on the wind from the direction of a rocky island little more than half a mile out to sea, its cliffs stained with the guano of the many gannets that circled it and dived, wheeling, into the surrounding waters. A sea arch protruded from the west side of the tiny island, and Nayr could see no trees.

The Queen of the Dryads tried to pick out the words of the song as she crossed the stony beach, tiny roots sprouting from the soles of her feet to steady her, but the wind carried the voice away. She climbed up on to the rocks and approached the two Naiads, who were staring out across the water to the island.

'Mother is sad,' said Seaborn. 'My sister will not let me go to her.'

Nayr sat upon the rock and folded her hands in her lap. She could see the rocky island through the Naiads' bodies, the water swirling with sand, shell fragments and seaweed picked up from the rocks. Spray filled the air all around as the waves hit the promontory.

'Your sister was right to wait, little one,' said Nayr. 'We do not wish to frighten your mother. You are very different from the last time she saw you, are you not?'

The little Naiad nodded.

'I suppose,' he said, and his sister ruffled his water hair, like running a hand across the surface of a pond. Whiteflow stood, leaving Seaborn staring at a starfish in a rockpool.

'We will await your summons,' said Whiteflow, the words stark. Her body steamed ever so slightly. Nayr nodded, but she did not trust the Naiad. Not at all.

The Dryad stood upon the edge of the promontory for a moment and then dived into the waves. Her weight took her under, but she bobbed to the surface and began to swim.

The Dryad made slow progress towards the island, the cliffs looming over her as she drew nearer, the wailing song filling the air. She began to circle round and saw a Dryad standing on a ledge just above the water. It raised a hand in greeting, and Nayr swam towards it, finding she could clamber up the rocks to stand before it. The Dryad bowed its head, one of those she had sent to relieve the newborns who had been watching over Rowan for the past five years. Nayr reached out and took the Dryad's hands as they communicated.

Be watchful, it cautioned her. *She has been known to attempt to harm herself in the past. She pays little heed to us, Queen. Her song is unceasing.*

Nayr traversed the ledge, her feet slipping on the wet rock, and she rounded an outcrop to see that the ledge banked inland, following a cleft in the rock island, not visible from the beach. The path led to a sea cave, wide enough for a boat at the base, narrowing to a point at the top.

The Dryad took her time on the path and ducked into the dim light of the cave. A mirror of dark water stretched out in front of her, jagged rocks pointing down from the ceiling above it. The waves crashed, but Nayr could still hear the song above it. The ledge continued around the sea pool, and Nayr spied the broken remains of a little jetty in the water, beneath rough-hewn stones which led up to her level. A tunnel led from the ledge, sloping upwards in places then changing to shallow steps, crudely carved from the rock, filled with the echoing of the waves and the dropping of water on rock. Nayr found smaller caves to either side of it as she followed the sound of the singing. Blankets were neatly folded in one. Shells and some sort of artwork was daubed on the walls in another. She saw two barrels in a third, along with a collection of bird bones, arranged into a pattern on the floor. Finally, Nayr found her way up on to the summit of the rock, where a plateau barred the view of the Butterfly Isle to the north. In a nook of the rock, Nayr saw Rowan wrapped in blankets, sitting with her arms wrapped around her knees, which were drawn up to her chest, long wet hair draped all over her skeletal body like a cloak. She stared out to sea, dull-eyed, and sang a mournful song, not of the sea, but of a loss in the forest. Nayr listened for a while, familiar with the song of the Hinterland.

A Dryad stood a little way off, watching her, but, Nayr noticed, careful not to block the human woman's view of the sea. The two Dryads walked to meet one another, and Nayr bade the other wait below before slowly crossing to stand beside Rowan.

'I have come a long way to see you,' said Nayr.

No reaction. Rowan continued singing, her eyes fixed on the Inner Sea.

'I am Nayr, and you would call me Queen of the Dryads in your tongue.'

No change.

'Your husband, the woodcutter. Dark Oak. He is the one who had our people torment you these years past, Rowan, not I. I have overthrown him. You need not fear him any longer.'

Rowan began to sing louder.

What is wrong with this one? Is this madness?

The queen persisted.

'I have much to tell you. We have chosen you to speak for your people. You will be cared for and will have a home once more - you will live in comfort again.'

173

Rowan paused, and for a moment, Nayr thought she would speak, but the human closed her eyes for a few seconds, cleared her ragged throat and started a new song, one she did not recognise, about a child carried beneath the waves.

Perhaps it was time, Nayr wondered.

'Your children are not dead, Rowan,' said Nayr. 'I have brought them to you.'

The singing stopped. Rowan turned her head slowly, staring out from behind a curtain of greasy hair.

'Do you mock me, wood woman?' said Rowan, her voice rising to a scream. 'Am I not tormented enough?'

Dryads did not flinch, and Nayr appeared unmoved, but doubt filled her even though she had expected something like this. She pushed ahead, slowly.

'Your eldest . . . ' The queen could not recall his name for a moment. 'He is not here, but he too can be summoned.'

Rowan lifted both hands to scrape the hair from her face. Her whole body trembled, Nayr noticed. Perhaps the woman was cold.

'Declan is here?'

'This may not be easy for you to understand,' said Nayr.

'Is he like Morrick?' asked Rowan. 'Like you?'

'Dryad? No . . . ' Nayr considered telling the human about Red Maple, but thought better of it.

'They are of the waters,' admitted the queen. 'Naiads, as I know you have seen before.'

Rowan's trembling developed into shaking.

'They?' she stuttered, and Nayr nodded.

'Your youngest son and your daughter. They are not like you, but they are . . . '

Nayr's sentence trailed off as Rowan hid her face in her hands as she began to sob.

'It isn't true,' the human's words were muffled. 'It isn't true. It isn't true.'

Nayr stood and turned her back, looking out to sea.

What had Dark Oak done to this woman? Nayr did not feel sympathy as humans do, but she could see the human was broken and that one of her kind was responsible. There was only so much time, though, Nayr decided.

'It is true,' the queen said. 'You must accept it and come to understand. You must come to trust me, difficult though it may be. I am not Dark Oak. Not Morrick.'

Rowan looked up and wiped her nose with the back of her hand, her eyes brimming.

'Come away from this wretched place and be with your family,' said Nayr. 'Heal. You are more important than you know.'

The Dryad led Rowan down into the tunnel where together they gathered together some oddments, food and Rowan's waterskin, wrapping them in her blankets. Once her meagre possessions had been gathered, the women, Dryad and human, made their way out of the cave and found a place where Rowan could climb down to the water. Nayr could hear the human singing quietly to herself.

Nayr sat at the water's edge then slipped in so it came up to her waist. Her lower half drew back into her torso as it began to change shape, her head and arms disappearing into it as Nayr's body elongated into a small flat-bottomed boat, all traces of her human avatar gone.

Rowan watched the transformation, wide-eyed, then clambered into the boat and seated herself in the stern sheets. Oars formed from the hull and, unmanned, began to row the small craft towards the beach.

'Over Whiteflow, broad and deep, beyond the mountains, tall and steep,' sang Rowan under her breath as Nayr steered towards the beach under the gloomy skies. She clutched the gunwales, bracing against the boat's motion, her stomach churning, not just because of the sea.

Beyond the pebbles on a thin stretch of sand, Rowan could make out two figures, an adult and a child sitting in the sand. Her heart all but stopped beating as she realised that these were her children. It wasn't possible, surely? She must have finally gone mad, Rowan decided, but then if it were so, at least she would see her children.

But were they? Could she trust this wooden woman after years of torment by her kind?

The boat ground against the stones and, unsteady on her feet, Rowan jumped down into the surf, her blanket bundle across her shoulders. Nayr took avatar once more beside her.

'Your children, Rowan, as I promised,' said the Queen of the Dryads, pointing at the two figures. Rowan could see them clearly now, water in human shape, white foam where there should be hair, their eyes blue marbles suspended in ebbing faces, beach detritus flowing through them. Rowan took one step forward and the stones shifted beneath her feet, scraping.

The Naiads looked towards her and got to their feet. Rowan shrank back, but Nayr wrapped a wooden arm around her shoulders, which startled her.

'Get off me,' she snapped, stepping forward once more.

The Naiads walked off the sand, their feet splashing into the pebbles, the drops flowing towards them and into their feet. Rowan's heart beat fast and she could hear herself breathing, as she blinked, unsure whether to run to them or away up the beach.

The boy Naiad laughed and ran forward. On instinct, Rowan dropped to one knee and took him in an embrace as she began to weep. There was a vague resemblance to her youngest son, but she knew him, she *felt* him. Tears rolled down her cheeks, but her sobs turned to laughter as the Naiad and human cuddled so close that Rowan's limbs were fully submerged in him. They remained that way for some time, finally drawing back, Rowan smiling and glee conveyed by the lilting burble of the Naiad boy's laugh.

'At last you will not have to bathe,' she told him, amazed to hear herself laughing.

'But I want one now!' protested Seaborn, 'but Whiteflow will not let me! You will though?'

Rowan looked up and saw Whiteflow, watery hands flowing into watery hips standing over her, staring at her with eyes a deep, dark shade of blue. The foam of her hair raged like waves against a rock and her body was as a stormy sea.

'Your sister knows best, I'm sure,' said Rowan quietly, as she locked eyes with her daughter and sensed the malice towards her. 'Go and play a while, Declan. We won't be long.'

'It's Seaborn!' he trilled and ran up the beach.

Nayr made no sign of moving, not understanding the need for privacy, she whose every thought was heard by all of her people.

'Please watch him,' said Rowan, and Nayr bowed her head, following the little Naiad along the shoreline.

The human and Naiad women stared at one another. Rowan clasped the necklace she had taken to remember the old woman and lowered her eyes.

'Can't you look at me, Mother?' said Whiteflow.

Rowan raised her head to meet her daughter's gaze. She tried to speak, but couldn't, remembering how she had held her baby beneath the river as Callum and Declan fought to stay afloat beside her. She had . . . it was . . .

Rowan turned away and dropped to her knees, her hands and forearms smashing against the stones. She felt nauseous, and retched painfully, but nothing came up. Recriminations battered her as old barriers came down, no longer able to blame Morrick for the baby's death now that her daughter, all-knowing, stood before her. She wept for a while, but then told herself, *enough.*

You did what you had to do. You must face her. She is your daughter.

Coughing and palming away her tears, Rowan stood. She sniffed, wiped her face with her hands and turned.

The Naiad had not moved in the slightest, and that frightened Rowan unexpectedly. Her daughter had stood silently, observing her with cool detachment, or so it seemed to Rowan.

'Bracken,' she forced herself to say the name.

The Naiad tilted her head and said,

'Whiteflow now.'

Rowan took a deep breath and tucked her long wet hair behind her ears, trying to regain her composure. As with Seaborn, she felt that she was with her daughter, but Bracken had been a baby when she died. She hardly knew her at all and now Whiteflow stood before her, a woman, a creature possessed of knowledge, language and a strange, supernatural beauty all too reminiscent of the Naiads that had taken the baby's body back in the river. Similar, too, to the kelpie Rowan had seen in the Whiteflow when she was a child and that had carried her family to safety as they fled the Devised.

'I love you,' she said in a whisper, and the words sounded awkward to her. Whiteflow nodded.

'I'm sure. I was too young to love you, I think. I know of love, but I am not sure what it feels like. I needed you though. I relied on you for my survival,' said the Naiad, and every word breached Rowan like a stabbing knife, 'but no matter. You are to represent your kind now that Father has been deposed. We will see you home, Mother.'

Rowan was about to ask about Morrick, but the Naiad turned and walked away. Rowan almost followed, but it had taken all her strength to get through that short exchange. She looked for Seaborn and Nayr then smiled when she caught the Queen of the Dryads scolding the little Naiad for skimming stones on the waters that made him.

Nayr gathered driftwood while Rowan sat and talked with Seaborn, who repeatedly soaked her ragged clothing by getting too close, though she did not mind. She managed to start a fire high on the beach and when Rowan lay upon a dry blanket beside it, with another atop her, Nayr sent Seaborn to find Whiteflow. When he objected to leaving his mother, Nayr held up her hand.

'You will have all the time you need, but for now, I must speak with her. Find your sister,' said the queen, before turning to Rowan, whose eyelids felt heavy, lying by the fire.

'Now I will tell you all that has happened in the world, and of the part you must play,' said Nayr. 'For you will . . . '

Rowan began to snore quietly.

Nayr threw another piece of driftwood on the fire.

Chapter Fifteen

The Forests of Tayne

Cathryn had abandoned The Folly, but it seemed that was not enough for Lord Magregar, whom the queen had believed would take up her seat at the Maw Keep.

The queen's company had travelled without incident for many days, joined by many of those they encountered on the road; soldiers, children and many more, and so when the attack came, it was unexpected, so far from the contested lands of the Arduan Peninsula.

Red Maple walked far ahead of the humans, scouting for dangers on the road to Anbidian, which, he assured her, when he returned from time to time, was only a few days away.

A warning cry came from a scout in the trees to the right of Cathryn's party, but it was cut off and became a gurgle before Cathryn could make any sense of his words.

'Protect the queen!' shouted Ailsa, and the soldiers responded without hesitation, forming up around Cathryn's horse. They waited, but not for long.

The onslaught came swiftly. These were no bandits or an unorganised troop, realised Cathryn, despite her foggy head; her wineskin nearly emptied. She could see armoured men charging towards her through the forest in hot pursuit of her scouts. Cathryn nearly cried out, but held back, as the soldiers cut down her people even as they ran, their backs turned. The queen caught a glimpse of Lord Magregar's livery, and the depth of Magregar's betrayal was revealed.

He means to see me dead, thought Cathryn. *He wants my crown, not just my home.*

She wheeled her horse, her spear in her right hand and her shield slung over her back. This was no time to hide behind her people. Cathryn had always believed that a commander could not lead from the rear. This would be no glancing stroke, but a solid blow that needed to be withstood or turned aside. She would lead the way. She would take her people to victory.

'Shield wall!' called Queen Cathryn. 'Skirmishers, tuck in behind and watch the flanks. Be ready to take advantage when they close.'

Her horse reared, and she held her spear aloft, crying her orders above the shouts of both sides. A line of her guard formed between Cathryn and the attackers. The queen moved to the flank and joined the end of the line as the families ran behind her fighters.

The attackers ran on, and Cathryn spied Lord Magregar himself emerging from the trees.

There would be no assault from the rear, not with Magregar in command, Cathryn knew; she had ridden to battle with her cousin at her side many times.

His troops roared, running at a full charge with little caution. There were but seconds before the two sides would smash together. The thunk of shields being raised and locked together in an overlapping, immovable wall came to an end as her troops stood ready. Blades bristled above them and great axes and halberds higher still. The skirmishers gathered at the left and right of the line, ready to defend the flanks should any attempt to charge round.

'Hold your ground!' Cathryn roared. 'Death to the false lord, Magregar! Death to all traitors!' The roar turned into a scream.

And then Magregar's soldiers were upon them.

The bulk of the attackers smashed against the shields and the killing began.

'Skirmishers in!' shouted Cathryn and her lightly armoured soldiers roared as one as they ran from behind the cover of the shield wall to hit Magregar's men in the flank.

From her high position she could see Magregar a short distance away, only stragglers between them.

Queen Cathryn spurred on her horse, urging it into a gallop as she rode out from cover, emboldened by the wine. Weapons hacked and slashed at the horse's flanks, and the beast cried out in a mad fury, but charged on regardless. She fixed her eyes on Magregar and set her mount at a gallop.

'Traitors! Die at the hands of your queen!' she roared.

'Step it forward,' roared Ailsa, ignoring Cathryn's instructions for the ground to be held.

Wastelost, she's not doing this alone, thought Ailsa as she ran a man through and kicked a woman's legs from under her. The woman crashed down on her back, but Ailsa charged forward, leaving her for someone else.

A great call went up and every one of those loyal to Cathryn raised their weapons high and burst forward, any hesitation now at an end. The time for trepidation and fear was behind them. Fate snagged each and every man and woman in that moment. Adrenaline urged them on, driven mad with the impulse to fight, to survive and to defend their queen.

Cathryn rode her foes down if they stood before her. She drove the point of her spear into the throat of one man, skewering him. Seconds passed slowly as the melee fell into disarray. She could see blurs of movement at her flanks, hear weapons clashing and the screams, which sent the birds flying from the branches all around. Sweat ran down Cathryn's forehead and stung her eyes. She blinked, her vision blurring ,and as she did so she felt her horse falter beneath her. She took a sharp intake of breath as the animal stumbled, but it regained its footing. Cathryn saw Magregar preparing to dodge aside, and she raised her spear, preparing her legendary throw.

A thud in her left shoulder threw Cathryn from her horse. She landed on her back and the wind went out of her as the back of her head struck the ground.

She knew no more.

Ailsa had broken through Magregar's men, and she saw Cathryn, her queen and her sometime lover, fall. She had hit a full sprint, screaming for aid, before

Cathryn hit the ground with a thud and a sickening crack. Some of Magregar's people ran towards the fallen queen, but Ailsa managed to reach her at the same time as the nearest of Magregar's soldiers. He started backing away when he saw Ailsa charging towards him, but not before slicing at Cathryn's legs. Ailsa deprived him of one of his own and stabbed him in the side. She stood over Cathryn, fending off any who approached even as the man died in the dirt. Cathryn's guard gathered around her, facing outwards. She looked up to see Magregar retreating towards the trees, knowing he had lost the engagement, no doubt.

Red Maple burst from the trees and lumbered forward as he roared, 'Enough!'

Ahead of her, beyond the backs of her men, she saw Red Maple the Dryad sweeping his limbs in great arcs, bringing them down with terrible force. New roots sprung out, grasping this way and that, flinging Magregar's soldiers high into the air.

'Desist,' intoned Red Maple, and the earth trembled under Ailsa.

'Desist and retreat,' he said, quieter this time, 'or you will all be destroyed.'

It appeared Magregar's men did not need telling twice.

When Ailsa looked back at Cathryn, her eyelids were flickering as one of the men assessed her wounds. The queen's aide saw Cathryn attempt to move her left arm, but with little success.

'Finish them off,' said Cathryn, choking on her words. 'Let none escape.'

'Rest, Cathryn,' said Ailsa. 'They are beaten, and Red Maple has returned.'

'Treason,' said Cathryn, struggling to sit up, her armour slick with blood. She laid back once more. 'Kill Magregar.'

Ailsa took stock of their strength, sighed and cried out,

'Hunt them down! Death to the traitor!

She began to run.

'Your Majesty.'

Cathryn stirred, her head pounding, and immediately winced at the ache in her shoulder.

'Your Majesty,' said Ailsa again.

What had happened? Cathryn couldn't focus. She searched her memory. Then she remembered feeling the arrow as it struck home and tumbling backwards from her horse. Cathryn opened her eyes, but could see little in the meagre light.

'How many made it?' she said.

'Don't try to move. And forget that for now, Cathryn. You're home,' said Ailsa, stroking her hair.

This brought Cathryn back to her senses in an instant.

'Back at the Maw Keep?' she snapped, ready to rage at whoever was responsible for the abandonment of their journey.

'No, no, no,' said Ailsa, smiling, just perceptible in the candlelight.

'Anbidian?' asked Cathryn, scarcely believing, as she propped herself up on her elbows as best she could. She looked around for a wineskin.

Ailsa took the queen's hand.

'For some weeks now. We bore you hence while you were fevered. You have lain asleep, yet healing,' said Ailsa. 'Red Maple says Anbidian means patient in the Middle Speech. Perhaps there is a lesson there, Cathryn. You must rest awhile still, Your Majesty.'

Cathryn may have been healing, but she had little strength and was not able to take to her feet for some days after waking, despite her repeated attempts. Ailsa came and went as her duties permitted elsewhere, for she had taken a far greater role on herself than aide to the queen, it seemed. Cathryn did not begrudge her it, not when the younger woman had saved her life, led her people to a place of safety and had overseen so much in her absence.

One morning, the queen was sitting on the edge of her cot, pulling on her boots when Ailsa arrived. Cathryn saw that her lover's immediate instinct was to scold, but she relented, perhaps deciding that the queen could not be confined to her sickbed forever.

'I would fetch you a walking stick, but I know you would not use it. But perhaps . . . ' said Ailsa. She retrieved Cathryn's spear from where it was propped in the corner of the room and handed it to the queen.

Cathryn paused to catch her breath after her minor exertion, then, putting all of her weight on to her spear and with Ailsa taking hold of her with one arm around the waist for support, she rose. Her aide handed her a wineskin, and Cathryn drank deep.

Together they ventured out into their new home, every step an achievement for Cathryn. The wounds in her legs had become infected and then healed, but muscles sliced and bruised were not as they should be. She had wasted somewhat during her convalescence and her clothes hung from her like sagging sails from a yard on a windless sea.

The queen squinted as she stepped out on to the sunlit, dew-coated grass and looked about her to see the fabled isle where she hoped her people could rebuild.

Cathryn confirmed Anbidian's location without needing to be told. She was surrounded by woodland, but she could see the peaks of mountains rising high in the distance to the north-east. Judging by the gull cries and salt in the air, she was near the sea. Everything looked correct for this to be the island amid the waters of the Firth of Marsh.

She would not see the whole island on that short walk, nor on the many walks on many days that were to follow, getting a little farther with Ailsa supporting her on each occasion.

She had, of course, pored over maps of the island during the war, considered its supply and its garrison, but she had no feel for the place, nor had she imagined its beauty.

'It's been so many years since I've been here,' said Ailsa one morning as she looked around with a smile on her face.

'I have never been,' Cathryn replied.

'Even with its strategic importance during the war?' asked Ailsa.

'There were many such places around the coast and much else to occupy my time,' Cathryn chided.

The two women walked arm-in-arm along a path flanked by olive trees, Ailsa regaling Cathryn with her time on the island before they had ever met, when she had served with the infantry making sorties to the shores of Culrain to the north of the Marsh and to Tayne in the south.

'Where is Red Maple?' asked Cathryn.

'I have seen very little of him since our arrival. He walked with us to the centre of the island, where we make our home, and he has taken root there, yet I sense that he is watchful.'

'Watchful for what, I wonder,' said Cathryn. 'Have there been any further attacks?'

'Not since we drove off Magregar's people, weeks ago,' said Ailsa, 'but the lord survived and may well strike again, if he realises we are here. Yet I think it unlikely. I am confident we were not followed, and he would think us unable to cross the water.'

'How did we?' said Cathryn, standing still as she realised there would have been no boats left on the mainland beaches.

'It had to be seen to be believed, Cathryn. Red Maple can take on many forms, and he ferried our people across the river to the island.'

Cathryn stopped, stooping as she drew a ragged breath.

'I must take a moment,' she said, clinging to Ailsa so that her aide took much of her weight.

'Why not sit awhile?' said Ailsa, then looked surprised when, without a word, Cathryn dropped down upon the grass and lay on her back, closing her eyes.

'Your Majesty?' said Ailsa, and Cathryn heard concern in her voice. The girl was, after all, unused to her showing any sign of weakness.

'It's nothing,' said Cathryn, hoping her churning stomach would settle, perhaps just nausea brought on when she thought of the nasty wound in her shoulder. Her head swam, and she could feel cold sweat on her forehead.

Cathryn folded her arm over her eyes, hoping to take up some of the moisture before Ailsa noticed.

Ailsa crouched down beside her, steadying herself with a hand in the grass.

'We do not have much farther to go. Can you make it, or shall I fetch help?' she said.

'I just need a moment,' said Cathryn.

Ailsa sat beside her in silence, and the two women rested for a time.

'What of the Deru Weid?' asked Cathryn, almost sleepily.

'They are few, but have welcomed us. They revere Red Maple, leaving him offerings, but they tend to keep to their own dwellings in the hills,' said Ailsa. 'A few more minutes upon the path, and we'll reach your new seat so you can see for yourself.'

The remaining walk took considerably more than a few minutes as Cathryn required ever more support as they moved. Finally, after negotiating a slope and cresting the ridge, Cathryn laid eyes upon their destination.

'Welcome to Hengefast, Cathryn,' said Ailsa.

Cathryn had seen the settlement on maps many times, and she was surprised to see that the forest had not erupted through it like The Folly, perhaps because the place had been all but abandoned when the troops joined the invasion of the mainland. But the Deru Weid had remained, she reminded herself, so perhaps that was not it?

Hengefast stood on the banks of a stream which ran south-west down from the hills to the bay on the seaward side of the island. Surrounded by yew trees, the main encampment was composed of circular ranks of dugout pit houses that had once served as barracks and storehouses. Stone longhouses stood between the pit houses and the gradual slopes leading up into the hills, paths winding towards the caves, mines and watchtowers. A circle of great standing stones, protected by earthworks and a ditch, stood at the centre of the concentric rings of pit houses. It clearly pre-dated the rest of the settlement by years untold.

Cathryn could see Red Maple waiting at the centre of the henge. He stood on a great, round, stone table so that his roots did not touch the ground, instead curling rounds its edges and hanging like vines from a cliff edge. His arms were upthrust to the sky, his head drooped as though he was asleep, and his mane of red leaves billowed in the breeze.

Cathryn noticed that her people had taken up residence in the pit houses. They were going about their business, devoid of armour and trappings of war. She spied children playing near their homes, and the sight summoned an image of Annan playing with his nurse on one of the few occasions Cathryn had visited him.

The queen turned to Ailsa as they drew closer to the houses.

'Have we no defences?' she asked, and held up her free hand in apology upon seeing Ailsa's frown.

'The Deru Weid know this island better than any of us, Your Majesty. Their rangers keep a watch on the beaches,' said Ailsa, 'but we are not unwary. I've had our soldiers drilling the villagers.'

Villagers, thought Cathryn as she allowed Ailsa to lead her to the longhouse that had been prepared for her. *All that remain to me.*

They ducked through the low door and stepped down into the dimly lit interior. Partitions blocked the view to the left and right, but Cathryn was too exhausted to look around her new home.

'Is there a bed?' she asked, and allowed herself to be led away to the far end of the longhouse, where Ailsa assisted in removing her boots and getting her under a pile of furs, on Cathryn's insistence, despite her aide's protestations that it was a warm day. By the time Ailsa had fetched her an earthenware jug, filled with cool spring water, Cathryn's eyes were closed, and she had begun to snore.

She did not notice Ailsa reach down and touch her forehead, damp and clammy. She did not see Ailsa frown before heading back out into Hengefast to let her mistress rest.

There was work to be done, people to order, and a new life to build.

Chapter Sixteen

The Wastes

The part of Dark Oak that was still Morrick cried out all the louder as he walked eastwards across the last marches of the Hinterland. The forest became less dense, and the ground sloped gradually upwards into the mountains that barred the way into The Wastes.

It was not until he was over the foothills and had made significant progress into the mountains that Dark Oak paused. The Dryads had no lungs to gasp for breath or muscles to cry out in protestation at overuse, he could march forever if he willed it, and so it was not weariness that made Dark Oak halt.

He had been walking a path looking out across the sheer drop of a crevasse when the memory of standing atop The Folly walls with Lord Aldwyn came to him. Dark Oak remembered being seized by terror, practically unable to move as he clung to the rail and looked down across the Arduan Peninsula, towards the glinting southern seas, as Lord Linwood's ships sailed west. It had been the first time Morrick had been at height, and he had been quite unprepared to be afraid; so afraid that he had begun to sweat, and he had thought he might pass out. Now, standing tall at the very edge of the crevasse, buffeted by wind, Dark Oak felt nothing. He looked down, down into the crevasse until its sides came together in a single black line. The ground did not rush up to meet him as it had when he peered over The Folly walls. He was not dizzy, and he felt no instinct to grab hold of something as the wind pushed at him, teasing that it would push him into the abyss.

After a time Dark Oak resumed his march, and the Dryad did not pause again. Rain soaked into his wooden flesh, and the skies darkened. Still he marched on.

Night fell and yet he found his way along treacherous mountain paths, the darkness scarcely an obstacle to one who perceives without eyes, his wooden feet hammering the ground and drumming birds from their places of rest.

Days passed during which he had only his thoughts for company. Dark Oak lived Morrick's life over in its entirety many times as he journeyed, his mind no longer constrained by the limitations of the human brain, no longer a slave to the all-encompassing library manned by an all too fallible librarian, who without revisiting a route to a certain book, would forget the way in time. It was all here before him now. Dark Oak not only knew the location of every memory but could also review them at leisure, perfect in their clarity of sensation and emotion. He remembered being born. He remembered regarding the face of his father even as he screamed, not thinking but simply feeling that he must eat, he remembered his first tottered steps, he remembered it all as if it were happening in the present. Every piece of information he had ever heard and forgotten was there for his review and his use, but not only that, every piece of information and every memory that every Dryad that had ever been born to the forest had ever known and ever experienced. It was this knowledge that drove his footsteps as he descended the mountains and confirmed that, despite his best efforts to extend the forest across the world, he had failed. The Wastes were as bleak and as barren as they had ever been, stretching out flat to the horizon. And yet Dark Oak knew that out there, many days march ahead of him across the treeless plains, was Halwende, where Awgren had risen. He had the memories of those soldiers of Culrain who had first marched against him and died at his gates, spared the horrors within and fortunate enough to be reincarnated as Dryads.

He remembered Morrick's experience of war beside the Creatures of the Devising; recalled his fear of the snarling beasts - amalgamations of humans, animals and the Dark Lord's sinister imagination. He thought of how Awgren's foul creatures had subjugated the Hinterland through force and terror since before he had been born, of his childhood throughout which loss and atrocity were normal, and of the long forced march to battle across barren lands with abominations as his companions, ripped from the wife who would abandon and betray him.

And now I seek Awgren's home. The part of him that was still Morrick balked at the notion of seeking the Dark Lord's secrets, but he pushed the doubts aside.

Dark Oak knew the way, if not what he would find inside the former home of the Dark Lord who had enslaved him. There were theories of course, put forward not only by the Dryads themselves, but also by the humans, who had passed down tales of the days before The Wastes and of the lost kingdom of Griminish where now the land was dead. Tales of sorcery and the magic that led to the time of the Devising.

Perhaps he would find new methods to protect himself and to take back the forest? But that could wait. For now, Dark Oak reminisced and spent his time looking through Morrick's eyes.

He watched as he met Rowan for the first time as a child, watched her grow into the beauty Dark Oak realised he still considered her to be, caught in an odd echo of an old desire though he occupied a body that did not feel such things. Hatred mingled with affection when her image came to mind, and he knew that she was his weakness and his inspiration. Dark Oak, deluded in his near-omnipotence, mistook perception for insight, and considered that uniquely human propensity for betrayal as the most compelling reason to take the steps he had. Had he not always striven to do the right thing, be a good father and a good husband, a good citizen? He had fought and been injured, he had looked after those under his command. He had been branded for being forced to fight against his will. He had fought to get home to his family, and what reward did he find? His wife turned against him, and in the arms of another man. Lynch. Captain Jacob Lynch.

His time will come, thought Dark Oak, *soon enough.*

It was not just revenge he desired, though, Dark Oak told himself, but the restoration of balance. Awgren's empire or Cathryn's realm, it made no difference, no species should be allowed to over-reach and exert domination. As much as he longed to be at one with the forest, Dark Oak felt not only contempt for humanity, but the human desire to fight and defend his new form and the forest. The Dryads were devoid of humanity's follies and even if they were not canny enough to see it, even they needed to be defended. He,

Dark Oak, would make the sacrifices as Morrick once had. He would defend the world against the human infestation, and in the process, perhaps he would save other true men from suffering as he had done.

Dark Oak marched on across a sun-scorched mudflat.

Days passed. Nights passed.

Still he marched on, across distances that none but the most well-supplied humans could travel before dropping dead of thirst, for there were no rivers or pools, no streams or lakes. The Wastes, this region was named, and rightly so. Dark Oak clambered down into deep canyons and up sheer rock faces, across salt pans and bare rock faces. Nothing grew. There was no sense to the place, no continuity. It was a place of aborted beginnings and misremembered geology, where all was warped and ill at ease, even in its own company.

He arrived without warning or ceremony. The mudflat gave way and sloped down, forming a short road to the mouth of a tunnel leading far, far underground. There, at the gates of Halwende, Dark Oak's memories failed him. Many had died on the approach to the Dark Lord's gates, but no human had survived to breach them. He halted the column and looked down the bare road to the hungry darkness below him.

Were there still Creatures of the Devising lurking below? Probably, but what did it matter, he . . .

His thoughts were cut off by the sound of echoing footsteps.

A figure emerged from the darkness, clothed in a leather jerkin and high boots, as were the warrior cults in the days of the Middle Speech, before even Culrain had risen. He carried a cane, intricately carved with the head of a wolfhound, but his gait was confident and unfaltering. He seemed to pay no heed to the Dryad at his gate. Dark Oak saw that the figure looked human, but his skin was cracked and grey, reminding Dark Oak of volcanic ash, long settled, or perhaps the tough hide of a prehistoric beast, coated in dry mud.

Dark Oak waited. After all, he was a visitor, and it was only polite.

The figure looked up at him and continued walking.

'How things come around time and again,' he said. 'Welcome to Halwende.'

He raised his eyebrows expectantly and, without waiting for a reply, he turned back towards the tunnel.

'Come this way, if tree-folk are not afraid to leave the light,' said the figure, and he was swallowed by the tunnel-mouth as it descended into the blackness. Dark Oak followed, wondering what Morrick would have made of being here, of all places.

It was the first time he had known true darkness as a Dryad, devoid of sun, moon and star, yet there was no apprehension, fear or claustrophobia as Dark Oak strode ever deeper along the widening tunnel, navigating by blindsight. He heard chains clanking, as well as snarling and breathing coming from passages, which led off from the tunnel, accompanied by the ever-present echo of a running underground stream somewhere in the distance.

'Where are you leading me?' asked Dark Oak.

'To what you seek. Where else would I be leading you?' replied his guide.

'You lead me into your halls of your own volition, not knowing who I am or why I have come?' asked Dark Oak, genuinely perplexed. The forest was aware of most things, but this was outside the realm of its experience.

'Such things are cyclical,' said the figure. 'You are not the first of your kind to come here, and thus I know we cannot withstand you, whatever your intentions. Come below. Meet the rest of us, and we will know your mind, lord, though it matters little. All will change.'

'Who came before?' asked Dark Oak, but the figure did not answer. The footsteps recommenced.

Dark Oak followed on.

Who had come before? Not Riark? Not any who had subsequently returned to the forest even for a time, unless they could withhold themselves as Dark Oak could, at least for the time being.

Much time passed, though walking in darkness did not prolong the sensation for Dark Oak as it might have for Morrick. He had no brain to perceive time and was unaffected by such external influences.

The tunnel levelled out, and Dark Oak saw a junction with firelight flickering in both directions, casting a long shadow back from the ashen-faced figure as he walked.

He waited for Dark Oak to draw near then turned left at the junction and led the Dryad through a series of passages, empty caverns and locked doors until finally they emerged into a cavern where many lanterns hung from chains, suspended from the high ceiling. A long stone table sat atop a dais behind which were seven chairs, the centre one more ornate. A throne. It was unoccupied, as was the chair to the right of it. Five more creatures like the ashen-faced figure occupied the remaining chairs, each with a cane, topped with a carved animal head; an otter, an eagle, a fish, a badger and a horse. Their faces, too, were of the same ashen texture, like dry mud on an elephant's skin. All of them were plainly dressed, each wearing a leather jerkin, reminiscent of the Middle Years.

The figure that had led Dark Oak down the tunnel now took up his place behind the stone table, sitting in the chair to the right of the empty throne, still grasping his cane by the wolfhound's head so that a long silver nail came down between its eyes.

Dark Oak moved slowly to the centre of the room and stood before them, still and silent, waiting for them to speak.

He waited while they watched him, strange smiles on some of their faces, grim expressions on others. After a time, the creature with the eagle cane turned to his guide,

'We continue then?' he said.

'That remains to be seen, but he has come,' Dark Oak's guide replied.

'Do you have a name, tree lord?' asked the figure with the otter cane, leaning forward and pointing towards the Dryad.

'I am Dark Oak, King of the Dryads,' he replied, though he knew it to be a lie of sorts.

'It *is* as suspected,' said the creature with the otter cane.

'The work continues,' said the creature wielding the fish-head cane. 'It will always continue.'

'I don't understand,' said Dark Oak.

'You wouldn't, lord,' said the figure with the horse cane.

Now the figure who had led him through the tunnel stood once more.

'We have been waiting for either annihilation by the humans or the arrival of one such as yourself,' it said. 'I am Egil.'

Egil pointed out each of its compatriots in turn. Eluf carried the horse cane, Fiske the fish, Fritjof the eagle, Ovi the otter and Vali the badger.

'Greetings,' said Dark Oak. He looked around the room, casting his eyes over the bare walls and earthen floor.

'Not what you expected?' asked Ovi.

'No, I confess,' said Dark Oak. 'I had pictured tall, black towers and foreboding dungeons, rotting flesh and great works of evil apparent at every turn. This is bare compared with even modest human dwellings,' he concluded.

'In the absence of facts, supposition fills the void,' said Egil. 'Tell us why you have come.'

'What are the six of you?' said Dark Oak, as yet unwilling to speak his mind.

'Will identifying us set your mind at ease?' said Egil.

'I am not ill at ease. I seek information,' said Dark Oak.

Egil laughed.

'How like him. We are the Weavers, and our place was beside Lord Awgren. We are both advisers and instruments of the Devising. Now tell us, Dark Oak, why do you come to Halwende?' he said.

A conflict rose up in Dark Oak, torn between avenging himself against those who had once enslaved him and exploiting any knowledge they might have.

'Are you aware of what has befallen the world? Of how I have expanded my realm?' he asked, the surface of his wooden face splintering like cheap veneer, sap hissing in the cracks and steam beginning to rise.

'Halwende is not yet empty, Lord Dark Oak, and we still have some few scouts abroad. We know of your accomplishments, surpassing perhaps even Lord Awgren's,' said Egil.

'Awgren knew nothing but destruction and domination,' Dark Oak snapped. 'What I have done is for the good of the world. I have undone his destruction and brought forth the forests from the ash to which they burned centuries ago. I would save the world, not destroy it.'

'Indeed. And yet you still have not answered us. What brings you to Halwende?' asked Fritjof.

Dark Oak knew he had no other options. He could not return to Morrick's life, he could not return to the forest, and so he made his choice.

'I have been forbidden from maintaining the equilibrium. I no longer speak for the forests, and the First Council would instate another in my place. Yet I would not so easily surrender my cause. If they have their way, humanity will be allowed to recover their numbers and their dominance. The forests will again be cut back until there are only copses and woodland left. The Dryad nation will falter if we do not fight back - keep them in check. They have grown too intelligent and too dextrous for mammals.'

'I see,' said Egil, exchanging looks with his compatriots at the table.

'I cannot stand against them, for they know the location of my Mother Tree and will destroy me if I do not comply with their wishes. I have come to Halwende seeking methods to withstand their onslaught, in the dungeons and libraries of the Dark Lord who ruled this continent for so many centuries. That is why I have come, Weavers.'

Egil sat back in his chair.

'Dark Lord, you call him? You have much to learn. If you will assure us of our safety, we will assist you, my lord, and the Weavers can continue their work. We carry the knowledge that maintained Awgren's reign for so long. Ovi will show you.'

The Weaver with the otter-head cane led Dark Oak behind the throne and through a small door that led out to the top of a stair. Dark Oak looked out across a cavern so vast that he could not see the far side, though it was well lit by many hanging lanterns. Craters pockmarked the floor and intricate pathways wove between enormous enclosures and cages, nestled up against lean-to shelters that he presumed were for the keepers of whatever lived within. A strange iridescent river ran through the centre of the cavern, branching around an island some distance away. Dark Oak could see a great stone oak tree in the centre of that island, far greater than his own and yet, without need for touch of it, Dark Oak knew that this was no statue, but had once been a living part of the forest. Was it petrified, ossified, fossilised or something else. *Something*. Here stood a part of the living forest in hiatus, preserved in time, hung here and there with talismans and lanterns. And as soon as Dark Oak laid eyes upon the tree, the truth knelled loud in his mind.

Here, he realised, was Awgren's Mother Tree.

Awgren had once been a Dryad.

Dark Oak remembered the oak tree from inherited memory, many years cold, remembered it from when it had grown many miles from here, magnificent and uncontested in beauty. He had the memories of the Dryad that had been born to it, though they stopped at the point when . . .

Dark Oak stared at the tree, ignoring the snarls and growls, the wailing words and the sobs that echoed around the cavern, transfixed by the Mother Tree itself.

Ovi set off down the stairs, his cane tapping on the stone with every step, marking time as the Weaver moved.

'Halwende is the bosom of life itself, wherein intelligence meets creation. The foundation of the Devising,' he said. 'A womb wrought of thought and intent, far superior to those bred through the memory of living flesh.'

Dark Oak made no reply to the rhetoric, aware of something tugging at his mind, an instinct with which he had once been well familiar and now barely troubled him; foreboding. Finally his reverie eased and, fascinated though he was by the tree, he followed on after Ovi the Weaver.

Soon he was walking the corridors of Awgren's menagerie, between barred cages and pits, high walls and barred gates, buffeted from within by something terrible without a name. Dark Oak frowned as he walked, remembering his time serving in an army beside such beasts, Creatures of the Devising he had hoped had met their end in its entirety upon the Field of Scarlet Grass.

Ovi led Dark Oak along paths that wound ever nearer to Awgren's tree, and he did not pause again until they had reached a stone bridge over that iridescent river. When Dark Oak looked down into it, he could see silent, moaning faces and hands reaching up towards him.

'The River of Souls,' said Ovi, urging Dark Oak on. The Dryad stood beneath the Mother Tree's heavy grey boughs, many supported by standing stones in a great circle. Dark Oak walked forward, and as he reached out to lay his hand upon the stone bark, it was like pushing through a thick membrane, crackling with electricity. He drew back his hand and turned it over. A single wisp of smoke rose from the blackened wood and dispersed.

'He was not the first to come to Halwende. He was not the maker of this place,' said Ovi, 'but he was perhaps the most successful in our craft. Certainly the most renowned.'

'Your craft?' asked Dark Oak.

'We are the masters of form and flesh, my lord. We are the Weavers of Souls. We are the Horde Masters,' he coughed. 'Or at least, we have been and will be again. We who are not slaves to the Cycle.'

Dark Oak turned to meet Ovi's gaze, but the Weaver had moved off, circling the base of the tree, ducking beneath the branches. Dark Oak followed and saw the Weaver descend many shallow steps that led to a door beneath the tree, nestled between two arched roots. The Weaver and the Dryad disappeared beneath the Mother Tree, walking a path that spiralled downwards.

'Beneath us are the chambers of the Lord of Halwende, the Dark Lord as you call him, where shades walk the halls,' said Ovi. 'Do not be afraid. They will not harm you.'

The steps opened out into an entrance to a wide hall with pillars in the image of many trees, their branches reaching out to support the roof, through which stone roots dangled.

Dark Oak saw a swirling purple mist filled the hall, and ghostly figures slipped in and out of it, walking between the pillars; men, women and children, dressed in various styles, each looking all around, as if lost and afraid, yet seeming not to see either the Dryad or the Weaver. Some clawed at the walls, their fingertips disappearing into the rock.

Ovi passed between them and led Dark Oak to a small door with no lock. The Weaver pushed it open and revealed a dimly-lit room, small and unassuming, devoid of furniture, but with towers of books stacked against all of the walls but one. A doorway led to yet another room, and Ovi ushered Dark Oak towards it. Dark Oak stooped to pass along a short corridor, and therein he found an armoury of sorts with a forge now standing cold and weapons of many types upon rack after rack.

Two stands were positioned in the far corners of the room. One was empty and the other displayed a huge suit of plate armour, black steel traced with intricate patterns in blood-red filigree. It struck Dark Oak as beautiful, with the designs reminding him of growth, progress and of the forest, though there was little in the colouring to suggest it. He moved closer and noticed that the inner side of the armour was of a thin layer of oak, carved to the shape of the steel.

He turned to Ovi.

'Is the solution to my problem to be found in these chambers?' asked Dark Oak.

'Perhaps, though Awgren himself fell in the fullness of time, did he not?' said the Weaver. 'There are many crafts and there is much lore available in Halwende. Your search will begin here. Awgren knew much that could assist you. Certainly, he knew how to protect his Mother Tree, which stands now above us.'

'That is the only knowledge I seek. I have no love for Awgren or his other methods,' said Dark Oak.

'True enough for now,' said Ovi, 'but tell me, don't your own kind now look at you as an aberration, perpetuating a course of action deemed evil? Sometimes wisdom lies just beyond the tolerable. Even those as wise as the Dryads can be terribly ignorant. They do not know as much of the world as they think. Awgren knew that. Awgren was willing to learn.'

Dark Oak made no reply, looking up at the stone roots. He reached towards them, his fingers growing and stretching until they could almost take hold, but he paused as the tips of his fingers began to blacken and smoke.

'It is no longer connected to the forest?' he asked.

Ovi shook his head.

'Dead?'

'Not as such,' said the Weaver.

Dark Oak grasped the stone root. He relaxed his existence. The will holding his form and the molecules of his fingers teased at those of the tree, working into them. As he did so, the stone root began to relax and understanding began to flow between the Dryad and the Mother Tree.

Dark Oak held back at first then relented as knowledge washed through him, an eon of memories filling him with expertise and experience not shared by any other living being in the world. He tried to protect his essence, his individuality, as he had attempted to do when travelling through the trees, but this was different. The Mother Tree was canny and fully apprised of his ways, expert in concealment and shades of subtlety. Dark Oak conversed with an echo of the dead and strove with the memory of the spirit he found within the stone Mother Tree.

He cried out at the effort. He cried out as a fresh sensation of pain ran through him as though he had nerves to feel it.

Ovi the Weaver watched and smiled.

Chapter Seventeen

The Impassable Forest

Cold winds whistled between the trees and snow fell in the glades, muffling all sound and twinkling in the moonlight. It crunched underfoot as Tolucan paced back and forth, his cloak wrapped tightly around him.

'Will you stop it?' said Feran, 'I'm trying to listen.'

'For what?' Tolucan snapped. 'We've been here for half an hour, and I'm freezing. You expect me to stand and freeze? Let's move on.'

Feran continued to squat down so that the ends of his hair soaked up the snow. He looked across the glade, taking in the paths of the various animal tracks, frowning as he concentrated. He made no reply to his companion, who joined Dun. The old man was leaning against a tree, coughing regularly.

A few minutes passed.

'There. Listen,' hissed Feran.

'What?' said Tolucan.

'Listen!' said Feran, his voice practically a snarl.

So Tolucan sighed and did as instructed, shifting farther away from the shivering, hacking squire.

At first the knight heard nothing, and he was about to rail at Feran when he heard a sound on the wind, a whimpering cry.

'I hear it,' said Tolucan, but Feran hushed him with a motion of his hand. His companion stood and crept through the snow, placing his feet carefully to move as silently as possible. Tolucan followed on behind him, but Dun remained by the tree, sinking down to sit on his heels. The two men separated to circle round as they stalked between the trees, their snow-laden branches listing and swaying under the weight of their burden.

Tolucan heard a whimper to his right. He froze and dropped his hand to the hilt of his sword, but no one rushed him, no animal snarled before pouncing from the undergrowth. He took deep breaths and stalked in the direction of the whimper that had started up again, intermingled with a low whine.

He recognised the sound and relaxed a little, no longer worried by the sound itself. But if a dog was out here, who was to say its master was not? Tolucan crept on, led by the sound of the whining animal.

And then he found it, sitting on its hindquarters by the head of a man who lay face-down on the ground, partially covered by snowfall. Flies buzzed all around, but the dog paid them no heed. It was a huge animal, with snow melting into its shaggy grey fur.

Tolucan knelt and offered the back of his hand for the animal to sniff. It hesitated briefly then reached out with its nose. Satisfied, it seemed, it licked Tolucan's thumb. The knight smiled and scratched behind the dog's ear, still wary and looking all about him.

A few moments later, Feran emerged from the trees to his left.

He looked the dead man over and, leaning on his staff, he stopped to watch Tolucan fussing the dog.

'Have you any of that rabbit left?' asked Tolucan, looking up at Feran like a child asking to stay up just one more hour. Feran relented and passed down a strip of meat. Tolucan fed the animal from his hand.

'You're keeping it, aren't you,' Feran sighed.

Tolucan didn't look up, but unfastened his cloak and wrapped it around the dog.

'I don't know,' he said. 'I hadn't thought about it.'

Feran smiled and picked up the dead man's shield.

'Do you have a name?' Tolucan asked the hound as he looked it over. It was a tall, long-limbed hunting dog with shaggy, dark grey fur and quick, intelligent eyes.

'I suppose you do, but I'll never know it,' said Tolucan. 'Come, let's see what your master had on him and then I'll introduce you to my friends.'

He set about searching the decaying man, who wore no armour and was armed with only a short axe. Tolucan mused on the cause of his death, but there was no sign of any recent wounds.

'I recognise this,' said Feran and when Tolucan looked up, he saw his companion holding up the shield. On it was the faded image of a rampant black wolf with a white snake in its jaws, ivy caught around one of its hind legs.

'This is Sir Maxwell of Main Isle's crest,' said Feran. 'I knew him well. One of us, perhaps. The quest claims another.'

'He isn't clad as a knight, and he only has an axe and a knife that is most likely used for skinning animals,' said Tolucan, puzzled.

'I doubt this is Maxwell,' said Feran, sighing sadly. 'He fell elsewhere, I'd wager.'

Both men stood over the corpse for a moment, paying their respects to both the man before them and Sir Maxwell, whose shield he had acquired by fair means or foul.

'You are keeping his hound so you may as well take his shield,' said Feran, handing it to Tolucan then wandering back the way he had come, calling back over his shoulder. 'Yours has seen better days.'

Tolucan laid his own shield by the dead man, slung the new one behind him and set off after Feran.

'Come on, Randolf. Let's catch him up.'

The big grey hound thought for a moment then padded after its new master.

Later that evening, when the sun had gone down and they had found a relatively sheltered spot, Feran started a fire and the three of them huddled about it, Tolucan fussing Randolf as the hound lay across his feet by the flames. Feran reached for the shield and stared a while at the rampant wolf crest.

'I've never understood why men choose the wolf to be a symbol of terror to emblazon their banners,' said Feran, setting down the shield so he could tend the fire. 'Wolves hunt mere sheep. Tyrants and cowards they are and naught else. A cow defending her calf shows more mettle.'

'The cow will be the sigil of your house then?' asked Dun, trying to disguise a smile.

Feran turned the embers with a stick so that they flared anew.

'Those who need sigils require more fearsome imagery for their purposes. I suspect a wolf, if he became a man, would have need of one.'

Feran yawned, and it caught on around the circle. Tolucan covered his mouth with the back of his hand, and Randolf nudged his leg until the knight began to stroke him again.

Randolf's whining woke Tolucan not long after dawn. He rubbed the sleep from his eyes and rolled on to his front, propping himself up on his elbow to look for the animal.

He saw the dog nosing at Dun's face. The old squire lay still.

No, thought Tolucan. *Gods, no.*

He leapt to his feet and stalked over to Dun's side of the now-cold fire.

'Squire,' he whispered. The old man's face was pallid.

'Dun!' he seized the squire's shoulder and shook him hard.

Dun yelled and struck out with his hand as he woke. Tolucan lurched back to avoid the blow and, his heel bashing against a rock at the edge of the fire, he nearly lost his balance. Randolf barked, and Feran woke, wild-eyed, scrambling to his feet.

'What's happening?' he roared at Tolucan. Randolf snarled and stalked towards Feran.

'Get back, mutt!' Feran shouted and then started as Randolf barked at him. Tolucan laid a hand on the dog's back and knelt down beside him.

'Good boy,' he soothed. Tolucan looked up at Feran.

'I'm sorry, I thought Dun had died in the night,' he said quietly, hoping that the squire would not hear.

'Oh, that's lovely!' Dun exclaimed. 'I'm past my best, I'll not deny, but don't be in a hurry to check on me before you pass water of a morning. I'll outlive the both of you,' he muttered.

Feran stretched out his arms and shifted until his back cracked.

'Never a dull moment,' he yawned, finally smiling. 'Tell me, what have you planned for the day? Have dream fairies brought you new insight and drive, Tolucan?'

Tolucan scratched behind Randolf's ear.

'We head for the coast. It can't be far now,' said Tolucan.

'Ah, good. Another day walking in the same direction,' Feran muttered. 'Joyous.'

The three men and the hound journeyed on at a slower pace for Dun's sake.

One day, Feran stopped walking suddenly and breathed deep.

'What is it?' asked Tolucan.

'The ocean,' said Dun, taking in a lungful of salted air.

'Our journey draws to a close,' said Tolucan.

And sure enough, before the end of the day, the trees came to an end. Tolucan, Feran and Dun emerged on the west coast and looked out over a stormy winter sea.

They all stood, silently, Tolucan, at least, compelled to pay respect to his old, lost life. Randolf gambolled on the pebble peach, snapping at crabs while they stood and looked out over the white peaks of a grey winter sea.

As they walked, the conversation came round to whether or not they would find Captain Lynch and the Magpie, time and again.

'What if we are not the first?' said Feran, airing the thought that had been troubling him for some weeks. It took Tolucan by surprise, the notion that his long toil had perhaps been redundant, another man the first to bring the knowledge to the queen. How could he have been so stupid, he thought. He was carrying another knight's shield, after all.

'There is no use worrying about it,' he replied. 'We press on.'

Feran, Dun and Tolucan, Randolf at his heels, walked the coast until, finally, one day, after the sun had gone down, they climbed a headland and looked out across a bay.

'It's still here,' said Tolucan, who felt he might weep.

Small cottages were scattered along the arc of the shore, some distance apart, their candle lit windows calling their sailor kin home.

And sure enough, Tolucan spied the dark shape of a schooner in the water.

The Magpie rocked in the bay.

Broken Buzzard

The dawn chorus had to be heard to be believed, and given how many birds now populated the coastal forests, it was impossible not to be a believer by the end of your first morning there.

Captain Jacob Lynch, though, had got the better of all those 'bastard' blackbirds, dunnocks, robins, tawny owls and warblers. Over time, his body had adapted to wake shortly before the sun rose each day.

That particular morning was no different, and after waking, Lynch picked his way across the darkened room, remembering the sparse layout of his cottage and avoiding hidden obstacles. He drew back the bolts on the door and stepped out into the salted morning air to be met by the sound of waves lapping the shore and a wren warming up its voice.

'Not today, my wretched friend,' he said to it as he stretched and cracked his back.

Lynch searched in a box just inside the door to his little cottage where he had stowed some dry bark, grass and dead wood, and, yawning, he sat on a stool set before his home and ground a fragment of bark into a fine powder, then piled it onto a larger piece. He used a tinderbox to set the powder smoking before wrapping it in dry grass to encase the heat. Only when the flames took hold did he place the package within a ring of stones upon the ground and begin to work his magic with the broken branches. It did not take him long to get a small fire going.

Lynch returned inside, fetched his pewter mug and drew open a trapdoor in the floor. He descended into the dark of a crude cellar and once more made his way to his destination by memory. His hands touched upon the cold iron rim of a small barrel, and he prised up the lid with the knife he kept stowed in his boot.

Lynch valued the contents of the barrel beyond any other treasures he had accrued in his lifetime. He dipped his mug deep within and then, having secured the lid, he returned to his little fire. It was burning well, but Lynch put on more wood and drew some of the hot coals into a circle at the centre, then, satisfied that the small fire was sufficiently hot, he took a pan across the grass to the stream which ran behind his cottage. He placed the full pan of water upon the coals and waited for the water to boil.

The birdsong rose up with the sun as Lynch sat with his back against a stone wall, his booted legs crossed and a blanket around his shoulders, surveying the world as it came to life all about him. The field before his home sloped downward to the shimmering silver sea, and the beach ran in an arc northwards then out west into a headland. Cottages like his own were scattered along the shoreline as far as he could see. At the midpoint of the bay, a cluster of buildings stood a small distance from the water, into which extended a long jetty from which branched various wharfs. Boats of varying sizes were tied there and small craft were anchored in the bay. The largest of these was Lynch's own vessel, the Magpie, a two-masted topsail schooner, riding low in the water. He watched her for a time then returned to his task, fetching a pestle and mortar to further tend his treasure.

Lynch leant down and lifted the pot of water, just coming to a rolling boil, from the fire. He poured coffee grounds from the mortar into the pan and began to stir.

Captain Jacob Lynch sat back and waited for his coffee to steep, the breeze on his face and the cacophony of the dawn chorus well under way.

He wrapped a piece of cloth around his hands and poured himself a mug of steaming hot coffee. It was smooth yet bitter and although a more careful man could have avoided tipping grits into the mug, Lynch didn't take the trouble. Picking the grounds from his teeth while hot coffee settled in his belly was one of the chief pleasures of his new morning ritual. Coffee tasted of life; harsh, but enjoyable, if you knew how to take it.

Lynch admired the vista, his eye moving from the sea to the trees and finally to the rabbits scampering over the mound of earth in the middle of the field under which they had dug their warren. They belonged here, and Lynch reflected, so did he.

Lynch forgot his cloth when he bent to pick up the pan lid and yelped at the pain in his fingers.

'Idiot,' he said aloud, then, still muttering, covered the coffee to avoid it cooling too fast.

It would be a while before his people came to find him, so he took the opportunity to enjoy his own company, wandering down to the beach, cupping his mug in his hands. The pebbles gave way to packed wet sand nearer the water's edge, lined with discarded seaweed and the coiled sand castings of lugworms, which he went out of his way to step on, remembering the sensation of doing so with bare feet as a child as well as the enjoyment it gave him.

He strolled on the beach for a while, picking through the flotsam and jetsam that still littered the coast even now, the remains of Linwood's fleet and much else besides. He gathered up the planks and anything of use. Planks and logs were a commodity these days; after all, who wanted to risk enraging the Dryads that patrolled the area by chopping down trees?

Lynch took the time to stack everything beyond the high-water mark, pausing every now and then to catch his breath. He headed home to refill his mug, watching his feet as he picked his way across the stones, looking up only as he approached the earthen bank where the field began.

Someone stooped over his little fire, a great shaggy hound at his heels.

That's Larman's dog, though it's grown some, thought Lynch as he stopped short and crouched. If trouble was about to start with the Idlers and Waisters again, Lynch would have his work cut out for him. Those were many of the ships' crews who lacked sufficient seamanship to justify their place aboard the smaller vessels, coasters mostly, that were in more common use these days; landsmen who had carried out much of the unskilled labour back before the Dryads came and the fleet was still up and running. Those folk did not take kindly to being set ashore and left to their own devices. The more resentful among them had formed the core of the Idlers and Waisters, with whom the Magpies and the rest of Broken Buzzard had been skirmishing ever since. He peered through the short grass, wondering whether he'd be visible if whoever it was looked up.

Lynch couldn't make out much detail about the intruder from this distance, but he looked too big to be Larman. When the man turned, he recognised the rampant wolf emblazoned across the shield hung at the intruder's back.

Sir Maxwell, thought Lynch. *What's he doing back and with Larman's pup in tow?*

Lynch dropped to his knees to ensure he was definitely out of sight. He fumbled at a cylindrical pouch and withdrew a small telescope, which he then used to spy on the interloper. His hands were shaking, and he was forced to lean on the bank to steady the glass enough for a decent view.

Still no confirmed identity, but Lynch had a little more to go on. The figure was clad in brown leather over mail with a woollen cloak, fastened with a large buckle at the neck. A longsword hung at his side. The man's greasy black hair hung at his shoulders. A muscular figure and tall. Not Sir Maxwell.

'Well, this could get awkward,' Lynch said to himself under his breath.

But then he saw the man reach for the lid covering his coffee and without thinking, Lynch had scrambled up the bank.

'Morning!' he called in a voice suggesting awareness of an imminent injustice, but civil all the same.

The man by his fire started, and the dog snarled, hackles raised. Lynch raised a hand in greeting, licking his lips as he did so.

Here we go, you idiot, he scolded himself.

He eyed the man's hands, watching for any movement suggesting he was about to go for his sword. Lynch readied himself for a fight.

The man with the shield stood, saw Lynch and returned the wave.

'Good morning,' the man called, and at this, the door to Lynch's cottage swung open.

The captain had not reckoned on this and cursed himself for a fool as another man stepped out, this one with long red hair which was immediately thrown into disarray by the wind.

Lynch stowed his telescope as he made his way across the field, and as he drew closer, it occurred to him that the man with Maxwell's shield had the look of a Straggler. There was trade and some business between Broken Buzzard, Beacon Hall and the Whoreswood, but usually by way of the coast, coasters travelling between the tiny settlements and makeshift ports, of which his own, Broken Buzzard, Lynch believed, was the most successful. It wasn't unusual for small bands of Stragglers to emerge from the forest, but they were rarely armed and armoured as well as this pair. There *had* been Sir Maxwell though. Perhaps these men were of his ilk.

His hands had not quite stopped shaking by the time he reached the newcomers, but Lynch was feeling easier in himself.

'Good morning to you both,' Lynch said. 'Should I be coming at you with my teeth bared and blade swinging, or do you come in peace?' He smiled warmly, wondering how long it would be before some of his own people arrived. Wilson was due up for a talk over breakfast. Somewhat ridiculously, he felt a pang of excitement when he remembered the man was bringing bacon. Where he'd found it was anyone's guess.

I hope it is from a pig, thought Lynch and determined to ask before eating.

'You think a cutlass and teeth would do you much good then?' asked Feran, raising an eyebrow and nodding his head towards Tolucan, who had swept back his cloak and whose hand rested on the pommel of his sword. An imposing figure.

Lynch grinned.

'I can hold my own. I've paid the ladies of the Whoreswood three visits in my miserable life, but I've yet to have my tally etched on any of the girls' tits come contest time, so perhaps a cutlass might serve. As for teeth? None of them complained at having a shoulder gnawed or . . . '

'Jacob Lynch?' asked the man.

'That's me, for my sins,' Lynch replied, offering his hand, knowing he was making himself vulnerable, but hoping, too, that it conveyed confidence.

The man shook his hand. Not an overbearing grip, Lynch decided, just an honest handshake. In short, he thought this fellow felt he had nothing to prove to anyone.

'I am Tolucan of Stragglers' Drift. These are my companions, Feran and, well, those are Dun's legs,' said Tolucan, pointing round the corner of the cottage. Lynch saw boots and realised somebody was sitting back against his cottage. He took a few side steps, mindful not to get too close to the dog, which had settled, remembering his scent. Lynch peered round the corner and saw an older man, grey and thin, his eyes shut and blood spatter down the front of his shirt.

'Is he . . . ?' started Lynch, but Tolucan slowly shook his head.

'I see. Well. Coffee, either of you? Tolucan? Feran?'

'Please,' said Feran. 'And Dun will have one too. He'll be alright in a minute.'

'I've never tried it,' said Tolucan.

Lynch feigned shock then retrieved another mug from the cottage, along with two small bowls. They would have to make do.

'If you ask me, if the only good that came out of Lord Aldwyn discovering the South Continent was him bringing back these magic beans, that still would have been reason enough to make the journey. Course, the likes of me could never afford it before the Dryads came, but coffee isn't worth as much to folk these days. I got mine in trade when a cutter came down from the north. Barrels are stamped with the mark of Stragglers' End.'

'I developed a taste for it at The Folly,' said Feran, accepting a mug from Lynch.

'You have news of the Drift?' asked Tolucan. 'Stragglers' End is still standing?'

Lynch shook his head.

'No, my friend, it's a ruin from what I hear, and it's been looted six ways from Sunday. The contents of Linwood's cellars will have made their way all over the Drift by now.'

'What of Redbranch and the other towns? said Tolucan, eager for news of his family. Clues for when he returned.

'The towns are gone, I'm sorry to say, but the Partisans have a good hold on the area, based out of Beaconhall. Their men have taken to roaming, so sometimes we see them down this way, but not often. Forgive me, but I thought you a Straggler and would know such things.'

Tolucan grunted.

'Shall we?' said the captain, wondering if he had put a foot wrong. He left a steaming mug beside Dun and led Tolucan and Feran a short distance from the house, so as not to disturb the old man, beside whom Randolf stretched out when the knights bade him stay.

'So . . . ' said Lynch, cradling his mug in both hands and looking from one to the other of his guests. He said no more and waited for an explanation.

The morning was advancing and sheets of mist hung over the field as the dew warmed. The trickling water of the stream accompanied the intermittent sound of breaking waves. A mewing call cut through the still atmosphere and all three of them looked up to see three buzzards circling overhead, soaring with their great wings outstretched.

Tolucan smiled, and Lynch queried what had made him do so.

'We've spent many years in the forest. There isn't a lot of open ground, and it's not often we get to see birds doing anything but flitting between branches. Truth be told, it's nice to get a sight of the wide blue sky and the sea.'

'What brings you to Broken Buzzard, gents?' asked Lynch, growing bored with dallying. 'And, if I might come to the point, how came you by Tom Larman's hound and Sir Maxwell's shield?'

Tolucan frowned.

'How do you know of Sir Maxwell? And who is Tom Larman?' said Tolucan, then added, 'the hound is mine now.'

'Sir Maxwell came by here a month or more ago. Travelling the forest, like you, but wouldn't say much about it. He stayed a week or so. Needed the company, I think. As for Tom Larman, he's no friend of mine, not any more, and his dog is your dog as far as I'm concerned, so have no fear on my account,' said Lynch. 'He's one of the Idlers and Waisters. Ragtag lot. Real pain for a few years, but we saw them off. There's a fair few settlements up and down the forest coast, but after the first major fall-outs, we've pretty much set our borders and for the most part, they're respected. We have to keep a weather eye, but we're alright. We have no high walls to keep us safe, but there's swift justice in Broken Buzzard. One of our own gets hurt, we band together to deal out punishment, and that knowledge dissuades most who'd hurt us. We've had it quiet for a while now.'

'Broken Buzzard?' asked Feran.

Lynch pointed at the circling birds overhead.

'Found one of those with a broken wing not far from where my cottage stands now. Decided the bay would suit our purpose and built a home. Good a name as any. Bird died though. Wilson says it's an omen, but who ever asked Wilson anything?' Lynch laughed.

'We found a dead man in the forest. The shield and the dog were with him,' said Tolucan.

'Not Sir Maxwell,' said Feran. 'I knew him.'

Lynch nodded.

'Ah, that's a sad affair. Doesn't bode well for the knight, does it? Maybe Tom Larman's copped it or perhaps someone stole his dog,' he said, 'but what brings you here?'

Tolucan and Feran exchanged a glance.

'We were told that you might give us passage south,' said Tolucan.

'Oh aye?' asked Lynch, suspecting his moment had come. 'Business or pleasure?'

'The queen's business,' said Feran.

Lynch took a swig of his coffee, sighed then looked out across the bay and at each of the cottages in turn before his eye fell on the Magpie.

If this conversation was going the way he suspected, would he really leave home? Broken Buzzard could be overrun by the time he came back. He'd found his place here.

Lynch turned back to Tolucan.

'Tell me more . . . '

Chapter Eighteen

Halflight Hold, The Long Isle

Halflight Hold stood on a clifftop peninsula at the northernmost tip of Long Isle, with nothing but the open ocean visible from half of its windows. Aldwyn, who had occupied chambers that had once belonged to Lord Murdock, Lachlan's father, looked out across the sea towards the Old Continent, searching for a glimpse of the Nightingale. He knew there was no chance of such a sighting, given that, under Mungan Maconnock's direction, Aldwyn had ordered Captain Unwin to sail for Stragglers' Drift bearing the news of King Annan's impending coronation and demands for the tithe to be paid. Still, sometimes the eyes search for what the heart desires, even when it has little chance of success.

A deliberate cough sounded behind him.

Aldwyn ignored it and continued looking out to sea, but the moment's spell had been broken. He sighed, looked down at the rocks below momentarily and then stepped back into the room.

His Maconnock guards stood with their arms folded in the doorway. One faced towards him and the other kept watch over the spiral staircase that came up from below, wary of the Hold's garrison.

Aldwyn almost apologised for the delay on instinct, but defied his better nature and ignored the men, his captors, he reminded himself. He continued packing his possessions into a wooden chest which stood open on the bearskin that covered the floor, offering some protection against the cold stone below.

He paused only once more, while going through a drawer, when his fingers touched upon a broken silver chain of a type no longer crafted in the known world, as labour on fripperies had been labour wasted during Awgren's reign, according to popular belief, wasted when all toil should be directed at preparing for the invasion of the Old Continent and the overthrow of the Dark Lord. This chain, then, was centuries old and had proven to be too fragile for daily wear. Aldwyn dragged it across the drawer with the lightest of fingertip touches and lifted it out. The tarnished silver had snapped midway along the chain, not far from the small pendant, a ruby encased in silver.

Aldwyn let the chain's length pool into his left palm and closed his fingers gently over it, closing his eyes and remembering his first touch of the thing. He remembered Cathryn just after she had given it to him as they stood on the sandy shore just outside The Folly walls, her hands clasped before her, her head bowed with a long plait hanging over her shoulder, he knew *now,* dreading delivering the news of her engagement to Lachlan.

Once more the cough behind him.

Aldwyn whirled round, his face ravaged with anger.

'Do not hurry me,' he barked.

The Maconnock guard showed no reaction at all, save to lean back against the door jamb, massive arms still folded.

Aldwyn closed the shutters to the window and then looked around the room that had been his home for the last few years, bidding it farewell, for he suspected he would not live to see it again. Mungan Maconnock had insisted that Aldwyn relocate to Narra, no doubt because the chieftain knew that the people of Long Isle were close kin of Lachlan's and thus would be likely to rally to Aldwyn's banner should he decide to make a stand. It had crossed Aldwyn's mind, but how could he object without putting Cathryn's children at risk? One false step, and Maconnock could have any one of them killed and seize power using the threat of violence to the survivors to maintain his hold.

Aldwyn closed his chamber door and descended the tower's spiral stair followed closely by the Maconnocks.

'Lord Regent!' said one of Halflight Hold's own soldiers, Lachlan's kinsmen, who remained loyal to Cathryn, when Aldwyn stepped into the great hall.

Aldwyn raised his eyebrows expectantly as he approached the woman.

'I know you mean to be away, Lord Regent, but a woman has come ashore in a boat,' she said, bowing her head as she spoke.

'What of it?' replied Aldwyn.

'It's an open boat, Your Grace, with no sail or provisions,' said the soldier.

'What of it? The Lord Regent is needed in Narra. We sail at once,' interrupted one of the Maconnock guards.

'Quiet,' Aldwyn snapped, then turned back to the soldier and awaited the answer to his escort's question.

'She claims to have come direct from the Butterfly Isle, Your Grace, but can't have rowed all that way,' she said, frowning, Aldwyn realised, because of the tense exchange.

'No, indeed,' he said, forcing levity into his tone and even smiling. 'Thank you. Where is she now?'

'She awaits you on the beach, lord,' said the woman.

'Awaits me personally?' asked Aldwyn, frowning.

'Aye, she says she will speak only to the lord of Halflight Hold, Lord Regent. Will you attend her or shall we send her on her way?'

Aldwyn thought momentarily then nodded.

'I'll see her. Show me the way,' said Aldwyn, and held up a hand when the Maconnocks objected. 'This may concern the Butterfly Isle, and if so, Mungan will wish to hear of it. We are not in such a hurry that we should turn down tidings of import, are we?'

The four of them strode through the hold towards where the main gate had once stood, now propped against the adjacent wall, its hinges bent and broken. The soldier walked ahead of Aldwyn and the Maconnocks behind him. He could feel their eyes upon him, watching his every move.

They passed out under a stone arch and crossed the bridge spanning the deep ditch that divided the slope on the southern approach to Halflight Hold, that was surrounded on all other sides by sheer cliffs and crashing waves. The turbulent waves sent foam high enough to reach the walls. The soldier led them west down the slopes, and long before they reached the beach, Aldwyn saw the woman sitting in a small boat, still far below.

A keening song rose up from the beach, and Aldwyn shivered when he heard it.

The slope eased as they reached sea level and the soldier returned to her post, while the Maconnocks followed the Lord Regent as he approached the stranger who had made such wild claims and whose song echoed off the rocks, seemingly striking fear into all around.

The soldiers on the beach had drawn back a little, and Aldwyn recognised relief on their faces as he approached. *Now this is your concern*, their expressions said.

As soon as his feet were upon the sand, Aldwyn stood and took stock, his thumbs hooked inside his belt, and his cloak whipping back in the wind. Before him, a stretch of white sand sloped down to the water's edge. There, bobbing in the shallows, being drawn out and pushed back in by the tide, was a small rowing boat. Inside sat a lone figure with the longest red hair that Aldwyn had ever seen. It lay, lank and wet, across her back and over her shoulders, hanging over her face so that the woman beneath was barely visible to him, though he caught glimpses of skin through the strands, which dripped salt water on to her knees. She seemed not to care whether the boat was dragged out to sea or whether it was pushed ashore, and she paid no heed to the presence of so many armed soldiers. She simply sat with her head bowed in the boat, leaves in her hair, her shoulders rising and falling with her breaths as she sang.

The woman lifted her head when Aldwyn set off across the sand towards her, his feet sinking and knees buckling as he strove to maintain his stride.

Aldwyn walked into the water and took hold of the prow, pulling the boat towards him. Still the woman did not move. It was only when the soldiers and the Maconnocks rushed to assist him that he looked back at her, their gazes meeting. A tickling, creeping feeling ran up his spine at the sight of those eyes behind bars of sodden hair, staring dolefully back at him.

'Good morrow,' said Aldwyn, his feet back on dry land.

'I know you,' said the woman from under the hair. Aldwyn thought she sounded surprised.

'Forgive me then, for I do not recognise you at present. Perhaps if I could see your face a little better?' he said.

The woman swept aside her hair, but it took a moment to recognise her, for he had only met her once before and briefly. Her name eluded him even when he did.

What is she doing here? What business can she have with me?

'You're the Captain of the Hinterland's wife? The two of you quarrelled at Oystercatcher Bay before I set sail for Stragglers' Drift?' he said.

'Aye. Morrick was his name. Rowan is mine,' she replied.

'I remember now,' said Aldwyn. Dark Oak's wife. Here. This was no small matter, and his concerns for Cathryn's children were momentarily pushed aside. 'Will you come ashore?' He extended his hand to her.

Rowan nodded and stood, her red hair like slick blood pouring from some unseen head wound. She took Aldwyn's hand and stepped onto the beach.

'We're expected elsewhere,' said Malcolm, the bigger of the two Maconnocks.

'They'll wait. In fact, send word of a delay,' said Aldwyn.

The Maconnock man stared back at him, weighing his options, then nodded acknowledgement with the slightest nod of his head.

'I have orders to watch over the Lord Regent. One of the Langilanders must go,' said the Maconnock man, referring to the Hold's guards, all of whom were Long Isle natives. Aldwyn cursed inwardly, but acquiesced. He could ill afford to make a scene.

'Send for a rider,' he said to one of the Halflight guards. 'They must ride to find the Maconnock ship at Traive. Tell them I have been delayed and that they are to wait, then haste you back.'

The man set off up the slope to the Hold.

'Will you come up to the halls? I'll arrange dry clothes and a meal, for you are soaked through and half-starved, I deem,' said Aldwyn to Rowan. Rowan leant into the boat and retrieved a single bundle of clothes and a waterskin before heading off up the slope towards Halflight Hold.

She had gone but a few steps when she turned and spoke, louder than was necessary for anyone nearby to hear her.

'And is my escort welcome also?' she asked, looking straight into Aldwyn's eyes.

'Your escort?' he asked, immediately becoming uncomfortable and suspecting Rowan had gone mad, but then he realised the boat may have come from a ship somewhere out of sight.

Rather than phantoms conjured by her own mind, thought Aldwyn.

'Are they welcome?' asked Rowan.

'All who honour the line of Queen Cathryn are welcome. All who pay homage to King Annan, her son,' said Aldwyn.

'They do not pay homage, for they are of high standing in the world, but they will honour guest law, and they will do none here any harm, lest they give cause for me to fear my life or imprisonment,' said Rowan.

'You are free to come and go as you please, as long as you do not break our laws,' said Aldwyn, perplexed. 'Where must my messengers go to summon your friends?'

'Not far,' said a child's singsong voice, muffled as though speaking through a door. 'Not far.'

Aldwyn started and turned to look at the boat, expecting to find a small boy had stowed away in some hidden, inconceivable compartment in a craft so small. He saw nothing.

When he looked back at Rowan, the sight before him shocked him so that he cried aloud, and he stumbled back and fell on his rump in the sand. His palm scraped across a shell and drew blood. He clutched it to his chest, dripping blood across the leather of his tunic.

The Maconnock guards, Malcolm and Rathe, held up their shields and unslung their axes, but Aldwyn grabbed Malcolm's boot. The Maconnock looked down at him, and Aldwyn shook his head.

The voice had belonged to a small boy indeed, yet no human. Rowan had poured water from her wineskin on to the sand. Whiteflow and Seaborn's bodies rose from the beach as though they had been moulded from wet sand. Once they were at full height, they tensed their arms and all the sand fell away, revealing their true watery forms, their eyes shining the blue of an equatorial sea amongst the grey waters of The Isles. Seaborn ran to take Rowan's hand, but Whiteflow slunk forward, the sway of her hips mesmerising, her brow lowered and a knowing expression upon her face, locks of white foam tumbling over her shoulders.

Aldwyn clambered to his feet, and found himself looking into the Naiad's blue marble eyes, like two gems beneath the curtain of a waterfall.

'Lord Regent?' she laughed a rushing laugh, rapids over sharp stones.

Aldwyn could only nod.

'Has the queen died then in the short time since I last saw her?'

His heart nearly stopped. He tried to speak, but his mouth dried out.

'Humans,' she said and grinned, before walking to the shoreline and wading into the sea.

She took hold of the boat's stern and drove it forward from the waves so that it ploughed into the beach as though hurled by some giant creature. Whiteflow returned to stand beside Rowan, and Aldwyn was about to begin questioning her, but the spectacle was not complete.

The boat began to creak and crack, at first seeming to collapse in on itself, and yet there was no hint of destruction. The planks melded together, sinking down into the bottom of what had been the boat as yet another being took form, rising up from the centre of the dwindling craft until Nayr stood on the beach before him, the green vines of her hair braiding themselves even as they grew, arranged around a shapely crown.

Rathe Maconnock inched forward, his axe held high, but Aldwyn seized the man's upper arm.

'No,' he said, and the Maconnock turned to him with a scowl upon his face.

Nayr bowed to Aldwyn and moved to stand beside Rowan.

'Greetings, Lord Regent,' she said. 'I am Nayr, Queen of the Dryads.'

Aldwyn looked about him, but his people had drawn back in fear. Only the Maconnocks stood beside him.

'You need not be afraid,' said Nayr. 'We are but passing through and seek shelter for our companion, as well as supplies for our forward journey.'

Aldwyn composed himself and tried to think clearly.

'Dark Oak is King of the Dryads, is he not? I would know who you are before taking you into my hall,' he said.

Aldwyn noticed the female Naiad was grinning, somehow, without a mouth, a suggestion of the expression from the current of the waters of her face.

'Dark Oak has been deposed. I was a friend to Riark before he was murdered, and, thus, to your queen,' she said.

'This,' Nayr pointed, 'is Whiteflow, a Naiad of the Hinterland, daughter of Dark Oak and Rowan, who now stands before you.' She saw Aldwyn stir, ready to speak, but she continued, pointing to the boy Naiad, 'And this is Seaborn, their son.'

Aldwyn bowed his head to each of them, but then walked towards Rowan.

'These are the woodcutter's children? How do they take these forms?' he asked. 'How does Morrick? What has befallen your family?'

Rowan looked up at him, her hair hanging down and salt water trickling down her forehead. She turned to Nayr, who nodded and then focused on Aldwyn once again.

'See me warm, dry and fed,' said Rowan, seeming to look through him, 'then we will talk.'

'Very well,' said Aldwyn. 'If we follow yonder cliff path it will lead us to the main gate of the castle. You are all welcome at Halflight Hold.'

Having negotiated the arch of the great gate and pacified the garrison as best he could, Aldwyn led Rowan's company through Halflight Hold to the great hall, once the heart of the castle and now barely used at all, with numerous holes in the thatched roof. Pools of rainwater had formed on the flagstone floor. Some of the windows had been smashed by falling beams and the wind swept around the hall, yet there was nowhere better to receive his guests. The high table set upon a dais at the far end was intact and maintained, yet for all to sit on one side and look out on an unattended feast seemed forlorn and not conducive to conversation, so instead Aldwyn led them to one of the long boards that ran the length of the hall. Having seen the others seated on benches, he sat upon a stool meant for guests of lower standing than his own. He could see the appeal of such a position during a feast, allowing one to remain anonymous and the focus of as little attention as one desired.

Malcolm and Rathe Maconnock did not sit, but stood behind Aldwyn at a little distance, still within earshot. Without having to look, he knew they were standing, arms folded across their chests, watching and listening. Aldwyn felt their eyes upon him at all times.

The Maconnocks presented a problem to him, given that clearly the arrival of such guests heralded movement in the events of the world, movement and events that he did not necessarily want Mungan Maconnock to know. And yet how to deal with the guards? If he excluded them or had them killed, there was every chance that Mungan would believe Aldwyn had reneged on their agreement and would kill Cathryn's children. He saw no way to speak candidly with Rowan and her escort without endangering those whom he was duty-bound to protect, as well as his own standing with the Maconnocks.

One of the garrison brought a plate of meat and bread, and another, a bottle of wine and two goblets. She set one in front of Rowan and one before Aldwyn. He thanked the woman, and she retreated without ever having dared to look at Nayr or the Naiads.

Rowan set about the food, but Aldwyn simply filled the goblets and swilled some wine around his mouth.

'What brings you here, Rowan, and in such company?' he asked.

'I was summoned,' was all she would say, returning immediately to her meal.

Aldwyn watched her for a moment, seeing a half-starved animal gorging itself on a filled bowl newly set before it. He turned to Nayr, looking at her emotionless face, waiting for an answer.

'We will escort her across the sea to the Old Continent, but unless she eats raw fish, we have little for the journey. Can you aid us, Lord Regent?' asked Nayr.

'Lord Regent,' Whiteflow laughed.

'Be quiet,' Nayr commanded.

'Why does my guest laugh at my title?' asked Aldwyn.

'Of what are you Lord Regent?' said Whiteflow.

Aldwyn set down his goblet and leant forward on his elbows.

'Of the Combined People,' said Aldwyn, 'until King Annan comes of age.'

Whiteflow laughed again then asked,

'The son usurps the mother then?' and her voice burbled as she spoke. Aldwyn straightened up.

'Are you saying that Queen Cathryn still lives?' he asked.

Whiteflow said nothing. Aldwyn turned to Rowan, then Nayr, asking the same question. Rowan shrugged, but Nayr nodded.

'Your queen lived when last I communed with the forest. She has dwelled at the Maw Keep, under siege, since she returned there years ago.'

This was news indeed, and Aldwyn gave the Queen of the Dryads his full attention, almost forgetting the Maconnocks.

'And what of Dark Oak? You said he has been deposed?' asked Aldwyn.

'A mistake was made in making the woodcutter one of us. A mistake we seek to remedy. I speak for the forest now, and we will suppress your kind no longer,' said Nayr.

'The restrictions he put upon us? We can rebuild?' asked Aldwyn, waving a hand at the leaking roof and the fallen beams.

'We have appointed Rowan to speak for humanity on the First Council. We will seek her counsel before deciding on how things will unfold,' said Nayr.

'Forgive me. But Rowan?' said Aldwyn.

'You think it should be you,' said Whiteflow, laughing once again.

'If you cannot sit under what is left of my roof without showing discourtesy, you will step outside where your laughter will cause me no offence and dishonour me no longer,' said Aldwyn, getting to his feet. Whiteflow grinned, but said nothing. She stood.

'Ignore her,' said Nayr. 'How should we choose one human to represent your kind? You are all individuals without the ability to share knowledge and experience. One is as good another, but Dark Oak is not destroyed, and Rowan is his one weakness.'

Aldwyn turned to Rowan, who looked back at him through emotionless eyes, shark eyes, and he was not comforted in the least.

'I see,' said Aldwyn. 'And what of those of us who govern at present?'

'No doubt I will have cause to seek your opinions and require education, Your Grace,' said Rowan. 'I have no desire to rule and I know little about the

Combined People, but I am to be a voice for humanity, not an overseer.'

Aldwyn rubbed his eyes with his fingertips, trying to absorb all of the information, wondering how this would play out.

'You don't seem pleased,' said Rowan, raising her goblet to her lips to drink.

Aldwyn made a tiny motion with his head, indicating the Maconnocks.

'We thought the queen dead,' he said. 'I rule the Combined People on King Annan's behalf until he comes of age. The young king is with the Maconnock clan. For safekeeping.'

'None of that concerns us,' said Nayr. 'You are born, you squabble, you live, you die. The individual players mean little in the greater scheme of things. We are here to fetch food for our onward journey, and to inform you of how things will be. Once Rowan is ready, we will depart so that she might take up her seat on the council.'

Aldwyn said nothing, but his cheeks grew red and his shoulders tensed up. He did his best to think clearly, but there was so much to ask and to tell, and he felt the Maconnocks' eyes upon him.

Aldwyn could not think how he could extricate himself from his current predicament, under the heel of Mungan Maconnock, without risking hurt to Cathryn's children.

He desperately wanted to convey a message, but the clansmen's presence confounded him. He decided to take matters in hand.

'Malcolm, with me,' he called. 'Please excuse my absence momentarily, Queen Nayr. Rowan.'

He bowed to them and led Malcolm out of the hall. Once they were out of sight he turned on him, leaning in close.

'They will tell Queen Cathryn that we have declared Annan king, and that I have been acting as Lord Regent. The queen will know I have been told she lives on and name all of us traitors. She will raise a force and retake The Isles, no matter the cost to her kin,' whispered Aldwyn.

'Surely she'll not risk the lives of her children?' said Maconnock.

'Don't underestimate Cathryn's devotion to duty. She will not compromise,' said Aldwyn. He pinched the bridge of his nose, shaking his head. 'I don't know what to do.'

He took Maconnock by the shoulders.

'You're Mungan's man. What would he have me do?'

'I've no idea what he'd say, no idea at all!' said the clansman

'Everything hinges on this moment, Malcolm. Everything. I can't make this decision without a Maconnock's say-so. What would you have me do?'

Malcolm Maconnock, unaccustomed to such responsibility, looked as though he might faint where he stood. Then, gathering himself somewhat, he replied, hope in his eyes.

'I will fetch Rathe,' he said.

'Rathe will know no better than do you!' said Aldwyn, raising his voice.

'I can't give you an answer I don't have!' barked Malcolm.

Aldwyn put on a show of taking time to think.

'Perhaps . . . perhaps we send word to Cathryn that we rejoice at the news of her ongoing reign? There has been no mention of her coming to The Isles, thus far,' said Aldwyn. 'She trusts me and will believe I crowned King Annan only because I believed she was dead. It might buy us some time.'

Maconnock frowned.

'Do you attempt to deceive me?' asked Malcolm.

'Malcolm, if they leave Long Isle knowing what they know, mark my words, Queen Cathryn will sail to retake the isles and Mungan will have your head if we do not at least attempt to dissuade her. You heard them. With Dark Oak deposed she can rebuild her army and her fleet. What choice do we have?' pleaded Aldwyn.

Aldwyn ordered the garrison to gather dried meats and other supplies. He saw to it that Rowan was bathed and dressed in dry clothes, and when all was ready, Nayr informed him that they would be departing, and she would entertain no argument to the contrary.

Just before nightfall, Aldwyn, escorted by the Maconnocks, led Rowan, Nayr and the Naiads down to the beach. On the way they passed a copse, and

Nayr broke away from the party, disappearing inside a fir tree and reappearing a few moments later with two Dryads.

'I will leave you in the care of my people,' she said to Rowan. 'I can ill afford to spend weeks at sea, unable to return to the forest at need. I will go ahead and make preparations for your arrival.'

Rowan nodded and addressed her children.

'Will you travel with me?' she asked, and Seaborn immediately ran to her side, but Rowan held up her hand before he could embrace her.

'I am only just dry, Declan,' she smiled. 'Later.'

Whiteflow stood, the waters of her body churning like stormy seas.

'Bracken?' asked Rowan.

'I am Whiteflow,' said the Naiad. 'Do not forget it. I will escort you.'

She walked down to the ocean and stared into the water. Aldwyn wondered what was running through her mind, she who appeared so disdainful even of her mother, and so full of wrath.

The rest of them followed on after Whiteflow, and once they were on the beach, one of the Dryads strode into the water. Aldwyn watched in amazement as its body grew into that of a great tree, resplendent with strong branches and green leaves, towering above them. The tree crashed into the water, smashing against it and sending up spray. It dipped beneath the water and even as it appeared on the surface once more, Aldwyn saw the branches thickening then merging, the tree shaping itself, morphing and growing until a great galley bobbed just offshore. Its mast was a trunk and a great furled sail of green leaves hung upon a horizontal branch. Vines ran down to the deck like rigging.

The second Dryad transformed into a small boat upon the shoreline, just in the water.

'Thank you for your hospitality, Your Grace,' said Rowan. 'I will send word when I am settled.'

'Please convey my unending loyalty to Cathryn,' Aldwyn looked to Nayr, 'should you or *any* of you be willing to pass the message. I am her loyal servant.'

He wondered if he had just signed his own death warrant, feeling the eyes of the Maconnocks upon him still.

Aldwyn helped Rowan climb into the boat without soaking her fresh clothes and Seaborn climbed in beside her. Whiteflow disappeared into the water and then Aldwyn caught a movement by the galley, and he saw the Naiad climbing up the side of the hull.

Aldwyn and the Maconnocks pushed the boat into the water and then watched in amazement as oars grew from the gunwales. The boat pulled for the galley, then Rowan and Seaborn climbed aboard. The boat, bumping against the galley's hull, absorbed into the ship and disappeared.

Aldwyn watched as the sail of leaves unfurled without any sign of a crew moving on deck. Rowan and Seaborn stood, the little Naiad waving as the sail filled and the galley headed out to sea. A kingfisher flew over Aldwyn's head and perched upon the galley's bow, just visible to Aldwyn. The galley rose and fell on the swell of the choppy waters, but the kingfisher took flight once more and flew ahead of it, and the waters seemed to calm as it passed over. White foam churned at the stern, and Rowan was borne away north before rounding the headland and turning east towards the Old Continent.

Aldwyn stood on the beach, his boots sinking in the wet sand, and watched it go, feeling that were it not for Malcolm and Rathe Maconnocks' eyes upon him, he would weep.

Chapter Nineteen

Anbidian

Sunrise coaxed the Isle of Anbidian into bright colour and sweet scent. A multitude of flowers sprung up amongst the grass and sunlight twinkled on the rushing waters of the stream that ran down from the inland hills. Cathryn awoke to the sound of a buzzard mewing for its mate as it circled high above Hengefast, and she lay for only a short time before seeking the light beyond the gloom of her windowless lodge.

Cathryn shivered in the chill air even with a blanket wrapped around her shoulders. Gone were the days that armoured guards waited either side of her door, and Cathryn walked out under the sun unimpeded. She could not see Ailsa, but her folk were busying themselves around the various pit houses of Hengefast.

Cathryn's head swam, and she leant back against the lodge for a moment, her body trembling, before returning inside to fetch her spear.

It once opened Awgren's throat, but is now reduced to a walking stick, she thought.

Small campfires blazed between the pit houses, and Cathryn nodded to those seated around them, cooking or talking. They found their feet as she passed, bowing their heads to her and not a few offered her sustenance, though she declined. Her appetite had waned since sustaining her injury, and at times she was glad there were no mirrors in which to see how emaciated she knew she had become.

Cathryn walked on alone, following the path beside the stream towards the coast. Clouds blew clear of the sun, and she felt its rays warm her cheeks while she walked. Cathryn closed her eyes and savoured the sensation for a moment, then stumbled a little and leant heavily on her spear as she shuffled on.

'Your Majesty,' said a man sitting upon the rocks by the water, washing out his clothing.

'Good morning,' said Cathryn with a smile, and she passed on down to the sea.

The stream cut through a riven cleft in the hillside so that steep banks formed above it on either side, and it used up much of her energy to reach their summit. Cathryn perched upon the edge of the crag, letting her legs down, and was reminded suddenly of how she had used to do the same in moments of privacy in her throne room, where the drop below was ever so much greater and her seat afforded her a view of the wide expanse of the southern Old Continent, the twin mountain ranges of the Maw stretching away from her, their lonely fortresses hidden in the clouds which shrouded the mountain heights.

She thought of that throne room when last she had seen it, its ceilings writhing with vines, and creepers growing across the flagstone floors. Ivy wrapped around the stone columns that held up the ceiling and gone was the view of wasted rock plains, replaced with the young forest that the Dryads, that Dark Oak, had commanded to spring forth. Cathryn had never denied that the vista was much improved.

Her thoughts turned to Lachlan, a man who had been loath to sit on his throne and yet had now become one with it, the wood of his body indistinguishable from that of the chair. The irony was not lost on Cathryn, and she pitied him, wishing she could offer him some reprieve from his long wait in the Maw Keep. Perhaps the day would come.

'Queen Cathryn?' A voice startled Cathryn, and she blushed, feeling foolish at jumping so visibly. She started to twist so that she could stand, but she no longer had the energy and was forced to content herself with looking up the slope towards the trees from where a man was approaching. Cathryn relaxed upon seeing his attire, recognising him as one of the rangers of the Deru Weid, who for generations uncounted had spent their days protecting the island from invaders. He was clad in grey with leather bracers covering his forearms. He carried a longbow and a quiver of arrows, and a short sword hung at his belt. His beard was long, grey and plaited intricately with small bones tied within. The man's face, ears and neck were smeared with mud so that only his eyes and lips were visible. Leaves and feathers were tied into his hair, and he wore a golden torc around his neck.

Cathryn shielded her eyes from the sun and squinted up at him, smiling.

'How fare you this morning, sir?' she said, but she was weak, and she doubted that her words had carried far enough for the ranger to hear.

When he was a few yards away, he squatted down in the fashion of a much younger man, sitting back on his heels. No nod of deference, but his manner was respectful.

'I am well. It's perhaps the first day of the year that I've been able to walk without a cloak.' He smiled, and she pulled her blanket closer around her.

'You have a hardier constitution than I, sir,' she smiled, and as though to emphasise the point, a shiver ran through her.

The man frowned.

'You shouldn't be wandering out of Hengefast alone, lady,' he said. 'If you were to fall, you'd do yourself a mischief.'

'I know the way well enough,' said Cathryn, and was amused to find herself justifying herself to this wood-wanderer whom she would have once thought of as a mere resource to deploy.

'No doubt, lady, but you're not long off your sickbed, and the terrain is uneven. If you should fall alone . . . ?'

'It is my risk to take, sir,' said Cathryn, straightening up somewhat as she spoke. The ranger held up his hands in defeat.

'On your own head then,' he smiled, eyes twinkling, 'but I'd feel a sight better if you'd let me walk you on to where you're going, or, if you prefer, I can keep out of sight and keep an eye more discreetly?'

'You are good to offer, sir,' said Cathryn. She was about to turn him down, but as she shifted in preparation to stand, she once again found her energy depleted. She laughed to herself and raised an eyebrow as her eyes met his.

'I'd be grateful,' she said, 'but even more so if I might trouble you to help me stand?'

The ranger sprang up and extended both hands. Cathryn took them, feeling the roughness of his skin as she did so.

Once she was up on her feet, the ranger bent down and fetched up Cathryn's spear, and she shifted her weight to it.

'My thanks, sir,' she said.

'My service is a given, my lady. But might I ask something by way of reward?'

'Reward?' she asked.

The ranger grinned.

'Aye, I am no 'sir', my lady, but I do have a name. Magan. Perhaps you would use it,' he said.

Cathryn laughed.

'A suitable reward, I deem! If you can get me down to the sea to bathe and safely home again, Magan, you would be in the queen's favour.'

She witnessed a knowing smile briefly lighten his face, as well as a twitch of the eyebrow, but the ranger fell in beside her, and they continued following the stream down to the sea.

Cathryn was not one for conversation with the lower ranks, but once Magan began talking, he seemed unable to stop. She found the ranger put her at her ease, and, thus disarmed, conversation began to flow easily, even if Cathryn's breathing did not. He told her of his doings of late, and asked after her lodging and general health. She expressed gratitude for the former and to begin with she lied about the latter, but as they walked her face betrayed her pain, and Magan pressed her until finally she was forced to admit that her wounds still troubled her, and she was much diminished physically and in spirit. Magan listened attentively and took her arm in the manner of a lover rather than a servant as she made her confessions. Cathryn made no objections and, in fact, paid little attention to the gesture, for with no eyes upon her in this strange land in which her companion was so at ease, she felt no desire to enforce her role or status upon him. She suspected it meant little to him, as she listened to him go on to speak of the various plants, trees and animals that could be found on Anbidian.

Another hour passed and, with Magan's assistance, Cathryn descended to the beach.

'I will come away now, lady, and await you behind the treeline while I resume my watch,' said Magan.

'I would not object to some company, if I do not keep you from your duties?' said Cathryn.

'What man could resist such an offer?' said Magan, and they settled in the sand just close enough to the waves so that the water lapped Cathryn's toes when she removed her boots.

The queen sighed, uplifted by the beauty of the place, the view of the sea to the south with not a ship upon it.

'Had you seen anything of the Dryads before Red Maple arrived?' she asked, looking out south to where grey seals could be seen in the bay, their long-nosed, dog-like heads just visible as they seemed to bob up and down in the water, mere flyspecks from the beach.

'Not in many an age, though we have long honoured them,' Magan said. 'You took counsel with their king, I hear tell?'

'He came to The Folly once. Riark, not Dark Oak, though I have met him as well.' She massaged her throat where the root had wrapped around it.

'The King of the Dryads of old,' Magan said, shaking his head, but Cathryn detected awe in his voice.

'How do you know of Riark?' she said, giving him her full attention.

Magan smiled and laughed, looking out at the seals.

'I amuse you?' said Cathryn, lying back in the sand.

'Nay, lady,' said Magan, 'but I cannot help but wonder at how much you and yours have forgotten.'

Cathryn closed her eyes and sighed.

'Are you going to tell me, or have you finally grown weary of the sound of your own voice?' she teased, smiling as she did so.

A wave reached a little higher, wetting the hem of her dress, and a curlew cried out as it flew low overhead. The rhythmic sound of the waves made Cathryn sleepy, and when Magan finally spoke after a long pause, it was as though he had broken a spell.

'All of the Deru Weid have heard stories of Riark, and it saddens me, though it is no surprise, that you have not, lady. Your line has long dismissed the lore which the Deru Weid possess. We once advised kings and queens, but your ancestors turned their backs on us, even putting some of us to the sword. Our numbers dwindle. How long before our knowledge is lost?' he said.

'That is not what I was taught,' said Cathryn, frowning and looking at Magan whose eyes were fixed on the sand. 'My father told me the Deru Weid, forgive me, were savage followers of an old religion who sought to subvert those they advised and to prevent the success of the countries that were beginning to form. I recall tales of blood sacrifice and betrayal.'

Magan shook his head, smiling as he traced an image in the sand with his fingertip.

'No wonder you dismiss us as eccentric madmen, even if you saw fit to use our sacred place as a staging point,' he said, making eye contact. Cathryn felt ashamed and closed her eyes again.

One of the seals, similar in shape to the others, but with blue marbles for eyes and no substance but mere water to its form, looked towards the beach. The head disappeared beneath the water as though the seal had dived, and the spirit which had formed it flowed towards the beach.

'Long before Awgren rose to dominance, there were Deru Weid living throughout the lands, honouring the old rites and passing down lore. Your forefathers thought to put an end to our teachings as they fought to consolidate their kingdoms, wresting power from the fief-lords and the Deru Weid priests who advised them. Anbidian is the last known refuge of the Deru Weid,' Magan said, his voice soft as he was caught in the memories of the past.

'I faintly remember reading about it as a child,' murmured Cathryn. She could taste salt on her lips as she spoke.

'Only as a child?' said Magan.

'I was raised to launch an invasion and overthrow a Dark Lord. The Combined People have had little time for study for its own sake,' said Cathryn, hearing the edge to her own voice.

'We have forgotten much, no doubt,' she conceded, thinking of the great architecture of The Folly and the grand rooms, maintained from the age of glory, yet never reproduced or re-created. Her folk were a lesser people, inhabiting the halls of those far more advanced than themselves, concentrated as they were on building enough strength to contest Awgren.

'What do you know of us? And of this place then?' said Magan.

'Truthfully?' asked Cathryn, opening her eyes and turning her head to look at the ranger.

'Aye, always,' he replied, drawing his hair together and tying it with twine as he spoke.

'I knew that Anbidian was a useful refuge and a watchtower upon both shores of the River Marsh. A staging point, just as you said. And of the Deru Weid? That they were a misguided spiritual people, who believed they were bound to Anbidian and that they communed with the spirits of nature. I thought their rangers fearsome in battle and deadly with their longbows. Folk who followed an old way, believing in superstition and magic,' she said.

'And of the superstition and magic?' asked Magan.

'It served no useful purpose in overthrowing Awgren,' said Cathryn.

Magan huffed.

Cathryn forced herself to sit up, her arms shaking at the exertion.

'If it were otherwise then perhaps the Deru Weid should have spoken up?' she snapped.

Magan held up a hand to placate her, but she remained sitting, looking straight at him.

'The Deru Weid gave up counselling queens a long time ago,' said Magan. 'Besides, we could not advise you how to overthrow Awgren, though we have stories of him, and of those who have unmade all your line has built. It was made clear to us by a king long dead, your grandfather, I believe, that our teachings were not welcome in the throne room of The Folly, and so we have served as best we could in our way. We have kept Anbidian safe and done right by those you sent here as a garrison.'

Cathryn laid back on the sand, propping herself up on her elbows.

'You knew of the Dryads all along then? And of Riark?'

Magan nodded.

'Not just the Dryads, the Immortals too; the Oreads, the Sylphs and the Naiads. They are courtiers of greater powers, unnamed and unknown, even to them. We honour Danzi, who we all shall meet one day. And we know of Torla, the Godhunter,' Magan broke off, realising he was wandering far from Cathryn's question.

'Riark became King of the Dryads, we think, not long after Culrain was founded and before The Wastes were barren as they are today. Legend has it that he overthrew his predecessor after something went amiss and the forest that had been there died away. Nothing has grown there since. It is a dead place.'

'Awgren killed it,' said Cathryn.

'Perhaps,' said Magan, 'or maybe he made use of whatever caused it. Who now can tell? But there is a legend.'

'Tell me,' said Cathryn.

The Naiad that had appeared as a seal now rushed up the beach in the foam, swirling around Cathryn's toes then sinking back towards the sea. It listened with interest.

Magan lay on his side by Cathryn, propping up his head with his hand.

'Legend has it that the queen of the lost kingdom of Griminish gave birth to twin sons, one hale and hearty, the other sickly and prone to wailing, unable to keep down his milk. The first, the queen named Arden and the second, weaker child, she named Arawn. The queen was fearful that her younger child might die and so lavished him with attention and, in time, the boy grew stronger, and yet she kept him confined to her library and availed him of the finest schooling Griminish could offer. Arden was left to his own devices and became a great swordsman, archer and hunter. He loved nothing more than to ride in the woods that once covered those lands and to be alone with the spirits of nature. As the years passed, Arawn grew bitter at his well-intentioned incarceration until, one day, he ran from his tutor and sought out his brother, demanding that he teach him how to fight, so that they might be well matched. Arden agreed to teach his brother in secret as long as Arawn continued his studies to please their mother,' said Magan, while Cathryn lay back, enraptured.

'Yet for all the hours of practice,' continued Magan, 'Arawn could never best his brother. He realised that prowess at arms would never be his strength, but his mind was keen, and so he turned to his studies afresh, seeking out new tutors and philosophies, turning, in secret, to sorcery.'

'Sorcery,' said Cathryn, dubious, but Magan ignored her.

'When the twins turned 16, Arden mounted his horse and went hunting in the great woods of Griminish while Arawn met in secret with his tutor, Ovi, a Weaver, whose craft was the summoning and binding of souls. Under Ovi's direction, Arawn began his first ritual of summoning, whereby he wished to draw a lost soul to capture and bind to a body anew. And yet, as the bond was so strong between them, twins with a shared soul, his mind turned ever to Arden as he chanted. As his brother rode through the trees upon the trail of a white hart, he heard the whisper of his brother's voice in the rush of the leaves, and his senses left him for a moment. He fell from his saddle and was killed when his head struck the ground. And yet he was not gone. Perhaps it was just his time or perhaps a consequence of the ritual, but Arden awoke in the Impassable Forest inside the trunk of an elm tree, reincarnated as a Dryad.'

The Naiad soaked into the hem of Cathryn's dress and flowed out again.

Magan took a swig from his waterskin and passed it to Cathryn.

'It took many years to accustom himself to his new form,' said the ranger, 'and he was ever troubled by memories of his past life, and drawn to seek out his twin. Arawn was bereft at the loss of his brother, convinced that he had snatched the very soul from him with his wayward thoughts during the rite, but he took comfort when he walked in the woods of Griminish where his Dryad brother would seek him out and keep watch over him, tormented that he could no longer be with his brother, for it was not the Dryad way to reveal themselves to humans, not since the time of the First Cleansing. Somehow, though, Arawn felt his brother's presence, it is said.'

Magan looked back at Cathryn, who appeared asleep.

'Shall I tell you the rest another time? You are weary, and your dress is getting wet,' he said.

'No, do go on, but perhaps you could help me move a little farther from the water's edge?' she suggested, and Magan helped her to shuffle back before continuing his story.

'In time the Queen of Griminish died, and Arawn came to power, but his reign was marred by rumour of sorcery and sins against nature, as he strove for new methods to seek power other than with weapons upon the battlefield. Arawn set his people to invading the neighbouring country of Culrain, and his doom was wrought, as they were a hardy and numerous people. All of Arawn's sorcery came to nothing and his brother, constrained by the laws of the Dryads, could only watch as his brother was drawn into malice and ill choices. Eventually the armies of Culrain laid siege to Arawn's castle and, despairing, he unleashed his monstrous creations on his attackers. But they were overcome and Arawn was smote by an arrow between the shoulders.

'He crawled from the field and took shelter in the woods, where he lay at the foot of an oak tree and began to weep. His tears soaked into the bark of the tree, and his twin felt his need from afar. Knowing that it was against the Dryad's laws and yet desperate to save his brother, the Dryad opened the great oak, and he laid his dying twin at its heart, sealing him inside.

'There in the darkness, Arawn died, and his soul became one with the tree, and he became a Dryad, calling himself Awgren, which was oak in the tongue of Griminish. And yet not all who die are ready to move to the next incarnation, and Arawn's soul had been corrupted through his work with the Weavers. When he stepped down from his oak, he was filled with wrath against his enemies and yet he was fearful of them, so accustomed to weakness and defeat was he, felled in the shadow of his own keep.

'Shunning the forest, refusing to return to his oak, Awgren watched as Griminish was overthrown by the armies of Culrain, and skulked in secret to seek out Ovi and his other tutors, blessed with a new form and new knowledge to aid his cause. And when his twin returned to find his brother, he could find no sign of him. In despair, the twin returned home and, to our knowledge, never saw his brother again.

'In the years to come, the lands once belonging to Griminish began to die. The soil would yield no crops and nothing that grew could survive. Animals and livestock began to die, and the people of Griminish abandoned their lands, taking their tale with them when they took up new homes in Culrain. Before long, there was nothing left of Griminish but The Wastes we know today. And we know not what happened to Awgren between then and his marching forth many centuries later when he drove humanity from the Old Continent, naming himself lord.'

Cathryn realised she was wide-eyed when she saw Magan smiling at her.

'Of course, this is legend, but there is no doubt some truth to it. Other versions tell of Arden dying in his mother's womb and Arawn searching for a way to resurrect his brother. As I said,' Magan returned to drawing in the sand, breaking eye contact, 'we know something of Awgren and the Dryads in our lore.'

Cathryn felt vaguely familiar with the story, as though she had been told it in childhood by a nursemaid.

The Naiad drew away upon an errand, for it knew that there was one who would be interested in hearing this conversation and speaking with the queen.

'Surely these are just ancient myths?' she said, interrupting the ranger, who nodded in response.

'Perhaps, but there is often a truth at the centre of a myth. Who can tell where the truth lies in the story? What's important, though, is the lesson that has been passed down with the story even as it changed over the years. Denying Arawn's soul its natural fate, forcing Dryadhood upon it, was a grave mistake.'

'It was frowned upon?' asked Cathryn.

Magan nodded, burying, uncovering and reburying a pebble in the white sand.

'There is a natural progression for the soul from its first inception, through life and beyond death. If one is removed from the Cycle and dropped elsewhere in it, well, this legend teaches us or at least implies that there will be consequences. It is said that the Dryads, Naiads, Oreads and Sylphs sometimes break the Cycle to suit their own needs, denying a human their death and their natural fate, making them ascend to a higher form before they are ready. The Naiads, in particular, are mercurial by nature, and it is told that they accept those who die at sea as their own, regardless of the consequences. Who knows what mischief those reclaimed souls make upon the waters. It is said that such a transformation led to the First Cleansing long before the events between Arden and Arawn, in which the Oreads were forced to intervene to prevent the Dryads and humans destroying one another. They never seem to learn that lesson.'

'What?' said Cathryn, seeing Magan was grinning.

'You are scowling,' he said. 'Do my words trouble you?'

'Not trouble me so much as make me wonder,' admitted Cathryn.

'Wonder?' said Magan.

'How knowledge of such import can have been dismissed by my forefathers, and, I suppose, it makes one consider the true nature of life and death. A year ago, I'd have told you that there was no place for the soul after death, that all comes to nothing in the end,' said Cathryn.

'That kind of thinking is the product of a desolate, utilitarian age,' scolded Magan. 'Look about you? See the mountain heights and the green of the forest. Listen to the song of the sea and feel the water caressing your skin. Doesn't your heart respond? There's more to life than survival, always seeking to postpone the inevitable end of one's current life, just for the sake of a few years more. Here, of all places, you surely feel that nature has power?' he asked.

Cathryn nodded and gave a short, humourless laugh.

'These years past, it has been impossible to ignore, and we have paid the price,' said Cathryn, thinking of her broken realm and her lost husband. Of Dark Oak mocking her from the dais.

'Perhaps, but I think in time you might come to see things differently. You are alive. Your people are alive. Life here is simple and hard, but nourishes the spirit. Humans don't need empires to be fulfilled, Cathryn. And they don't need a queen . . .'

She sat up at that.

'It's true, lady,' Magan persisted.

'Nonsense,' she said, 'and you speak treason.'

'Lady, of what are you queen? The Combined People? That union no longer exists. The countries do not exist. The world is changed, your people scattered and fending for themselves. Your influence extends no farther than the sound of your voice. No, wait,' he said as she struggled to stand, 'listen to a greyhair, who has no axe to grind with you or yours.' Cathryn found herself settling in the sand once more, though she still scowled.

'Your people have carved out their own lives under the new order,' said Magan, 'and no doubt many of them are content. Perhaps if you can find acceptance of this, your new home and the new way, you too could find contentment? Let the years and the legacy and the entitlement slip from your shoulders like a discarded cloak. You'll be happier for it. And what alternative is there?'

'To fight. To rebuild,' said Cathryn.

'To fight what? The world itself? The woods, the hills, the waters you drink and the air that you breathe? And rebuild what? Great cities and trade, thinking ever of expansion and progress? What more do your folk need than they have here? Peace? They have it. Sustenance? Anbidian provides it. Companionship? We have one another. Lead your people into a new era, Cathryn. Settle,' he concluded. 'Listen to the Deru Weid, as the kings of old once did, before they turned from wisdom,' said Magan.

'You really think that the world Awgren destroyed was so terrible? Tayne, Crinan and Culrain were co-existing peacefully. Our arts, our culture, our science were advancing apace, all to be set back centuries by Awgren.'

'That is how your ancestors tell the tale, sure enough, but the Deru Weid remember it differently. Your people prized wealth and possessions more than living well and respecting the world. They neglected the spiritual life, just as you do. The Deru Weid were put aside and our counsel ignored,' said Magan.

'You are clearly biased,' said Cathryn, feeling attacked. Magan fell silent at the rebuke. He sat up and looked out across the water, but then, seemingly troubled, he turned back to her.

'May I ask you something?'

Cathryn nodded.

'I cannot guarantee I will answer, mind,' she replied.

Magan spun and sat cross-legged before her like a child eager for a story to begin.

'We received word that you personally felled Awgren,' he said.

'That's true. Alongside my husband,' she said quietly, wondering where this line of questioning was heading.

'How did he appear to you? Was he a Dryad? Or a giant man with a snake's body?'

Cathryn blew air from between her pursed lips, her eyebrows raised. Quite a question.

'To me, he appeared to be nothing more than a man,' she confessed.

'Truly?' whispered Magan. 'How can you be sure it was him?'

'It was him,' said Cathryn, but would say no more on it.

'And how did you kill him?' asked Magan.

'By burying my spear in his throat,' she said.

'And he just died?' said the ranger.

'Like any man would. The Creatures of the Devising immediately fell into disarray, as though a spell had broken,' said Cathryn. 'Why do you want to know?'

Magan cleared his throat.

'The legend spoke of Awgren being forced into rebirth as a Dryad before his time, but even *they* live only as long as their Mother Trees. And there was mention of the Weaver and the teachings of soul craft,' said Magan.

'And yet I spoke with Riark? He would have lived almost as long as Awgren if the legend is true?' asked Cathryn.

'As king, he would have been ancient and powerful among them, but perhaps coming to the end of his days,' said Magan. 'Ailsa tells us he was overthrown by another, by this Dark Oak? Perhaps a sign of Riark's power waning.'

Cathryn nodded.

'If it was, I could not tell. But I know little of Dark Oak or how he usurped Riark,' she said, 'other than he was once a man of the Hinterland who served under both Awgren and Lord Aldwyn when war was done.'

'Whoever he is, or was, he has no regard for the natural order of things, as do true Dryads,' said Magan.

'What can you tell me of them?' asked Cathryn.

'Less is known than is believed,' said Magan. 'Our lore tells us that there was once a time when the Deru Weid were in communion with them to a greater degree, though I do not know if it is true. I can only tell you what *we* believe.'

'And what is that?' asked Cathryn.

'The Deru Weid believe that over the course of many lives our souls are nourished and improved. Between lives, our souls are cast free in the world, eventually to be reborn to have another chance to seek enlightenment. Eventually, our souls are ready to be reincarnated as one of the Ascended. We are reborn inside a Mother Tree, or the rock of an Oread, the waters of a Naiad or to the air as a Sylph. The latter three are known to the Deru Weid as the Immortals, for they do not die and their souls cannot be parted from their forms. The Dryads, however, are bound to their . . . '

'Their Mother Trees, I know,' said Cathryn, thinking of the Silent Knights, wondering how many of them were still upon the quest. It had been so long that she could not even remember some of their names. If they had any sense, they had long abandoned the cause and found what peace they could, she thought, and was then surprised by her own attitude. Had she changed so much? The Cathryn of yesteryear would never have thought such a thing.

'Aye, and we do not know what happens when their Mother Trees die. I'm not sure the Dryads know themselves. Perhaps the Weavers knew. They were alleged to have mastered the art of snatching lost souls and bonding them with animals, with the dead and with forms they had created themselves,' said Magan. 'They put souls where no soul should dwell.'

'The Creatures of the Devising,' Cathryn realised. And she had burned them, thinking them no more than monstrous creations and denizens of a Dark Lord, but if this was true, then what? These were the souls of the dead, tormented and trapped in foul forms? Had she released them to rejoin the Cycle or condemned them to some other fate?

'It's possible that Awgren used soul craft in some way to change his own form, then,' Cathryn said eventually.

'It's possible,' said Magan, nodding, 'but so are many things. Our view has become so narrow. There is much, much more to the world than we know.'

Cathryn stifled a yawn. Magan got to his feet and extended a hand.

'You'll have been missed by now, my lady. Ailsa will be concerned, and I had best return to my watch in the woods. Can I assist you back to Hengefast?'

Cathryn sat up and smiled, then shook her head.

'Thank you, Magan, but no. I wish to sit alone for a while to think about all you have said. Return to your watch,' she said.

'I'll leave you, lady, but I'll stay in the woods nearby. Call when you wish to return, and I'll hear, if it pleases you?' said the ranger.

'It does. I have enjoyed our conversation. Perhaps you can teach me more, and I can visit the Deru Weid in their own abode?' said the queen.

'Your wish is my command, lady,' the ranger smiled, and without another word, he trekked back across the beach, hopped up the bank on to the grass and disappeared up the slope into the trees.

Cathryn sat alone in the sand. She closed her eyes and listened to the rumbling waves and the peeping of the wading birds by the shore. Gradually, she drifted off to sleep.

'Queen,' lilted a strange, rolling voice.

Cathryn started awake and looked about her, but could see no one. She realised she must have dreamt the voice.

'Forgive the intrusion,' it said, and this time Cathryn knew that it had come from the sea. She reached out for her spear, fearing what was to come.

Then she cried out in surprise. A dark shape, like the shadow of a shark, was gliding through the water towards her. When it reached the shallows, it began to rise out of the sea, drawing itself up to its full height, a figure in a hood and cloak of slimy wrack, dripping upon the surface of the sea. The waves seemed to draw up inside the cloak, filling the voided body of an insubstantial man. Cathryn took her spear in both hands and drove it into the sand, determined to stand, and yet she fell back when she tried.

'Do not be alarmed, Queen,' said the figure. It reached out two watery arms and threw back the hood to reveal a likeness of a human head sculpted in white foaming water, with two blue eyes swirling and fixing Cathryn with a stare.

Cathryn attempted to look as statesman-like as she could whilst barefoot with her rump in the sand, hanging on to her spear as though she were a small child barely able to reach its mother's hand.

'You know me?' she managed to say.

'We know each other,' said the Naiad.

Cathryn looked closer but it was impossible to distinguish features in the ever flowing, changing face, and yet, there was something in the Naiad's bearing.

'We meet again,' it rumbled, 'but not in an orchard.'

And suddenly Cathryn knew him.

'Riark?' she whispered.

The Naiad bowed low.

'It seems we have much to discuss.'

Chapter Twenty

Halwende, The Wastes

Dark Oak woke feeling as though an insidious poison was being drawn up through his arm, as though his outstretched limb was taking sick from the point where his hand mingled with the root of Awgren's fossilised Mother Tree. With an effort he managed to wrench his hand away and stood cradling his arm, never taking his eyes from the root.

Something brushed across Dark Oak's shoulder blades, the faintest of touches, and if he had still been Morrick, with a man's skin, he would perhaps have shivered and broken out in gooseflesh, startled and left perturbed. Not so Dark Oak, and yet he turned with foreboding.

He saw nothing. Dark Oak stood alone in the dimly lit cavern.

Where was Ovi the Weaver? How long had the Mother Tree held him entranced?

Every instinct told him that there was something amiss here in this chamber, deep within Awgren's stronghold, this anteroom of the Dark Lord.

Dark Oak heard footsteps approaching, and Ovi stepped into the room.

'You are back with me, I see,' Ovi smiled that sunless smile and his face, textured like sun-baked clay, seemed almost to crack anew. 'Have you learnt much?'

Dark Oak moved to stand before him.

'How is it I can see Awgren's mind when I touch his Mother Tree if he is truly vanquished?' asked Dark Oak.

Ovi frowned leaning heavily on his staff.

'It has been many years since I have been confronted with new lore,' said

Ovi. 'I know not. And yet he *is* vanquished, for his soul resides there no longer. Perhaps you perceive the residue of his memory within the tree. Tell me, my lord, what do you remember of Awgren's last days?'

'I remember much. I recall the ceremony during which his Mother Tree was isolated from the forest. I remember feeling his Mother Tree ageing and approaching death many centuries later. I remember his frantic search for a way to prolong her life then the gradual acceptance that he could not, realising that he would cease to exist unless he turned his art upon himself. I remember him selecting from amongst his human prisoners . . . '

Dark Oak broke off suddenly, as though the memory had just come to him.

'There were once humans in Halwende?' he asked.

'There still are,' said Ovi. 'In the farm. Go on, lord . . . '

Dark Oak paused momentarily, but then continued.

'I remember him anticipating the loss of his Dryad form and the fear of rendering himself weak again, yet also his decision to go ahead with the final rite. I remember him guiding the chosen man from his cell to the temple where the rite would be performed, I remember you and the rest of the Weavers beginning the ceremony. Then nothing,' said Dark Oak.

Ovi nodded slowly as he considered Dark Oak's words.

'His Mother Tree appears to remember as much of Awgren's life as it experienced when his soul resided within it,' said the Weaver. 'We severed that link and thereafter, Awgren passed his soul from form to form as necessity or his desire dictated.'

'And it proved his undoing,' said Dark Oak, thinking of Awgren's downfall upon the Field of the Scarlet Grass.

He paced the room, taking in his surroundings.

'I would see more of Halwende,' Dark Oak said quietly, his white eyes twinkling in their dark sockets. Ovi the Weaver bowed low.

They returned through the library up the stairs to the island where Awgren's Mother Tree stood.

Ovi led him around to the far side of the island where another stone bridge led to the other bank. They followed a path across the subterranean cavern and this time, with his back to the tree that had so transfixed him, Dark Oak attended to the enclosures. Inside were packs of dog-like creatures such as those kept with the garrison near Northall before Morrick had been conscripted. In other cages, Dark Oak saw a variety of creatures, some many-limbed, some winged, covered in fur or scales, some shaped like animals, others like men and the rest like nothing else that walked under the sun.

Dark Oak reflected that not so many years hence he had fought as a slave alongside these creations under Awgren, quietly hoping that humanity would prevail, and yet now he walked the halls seeking a way to suppress all humanity. As though Ovi had read his thoughts, the Weaver began to point to each variety of creature in turn, describing the process by which they had been Devised and how that planning had come to bear fruit. Some, Ovi said, were normal animals with souls grafted to them and others were amalgamations of acquired flesh. That was how the Weaver put it, and Dark Oak wondered as to the meaning. Some were creatures of rock or of metal.

They walked on for nearly an hour, and it seemed to Dark Oak that Halwende was far from emptied, each barracks, cage, enclosure teeming with all manner of Devised.

'Why did Awgren not unleash his full fury when the Combined People invaded? Why go off to war, risking his life, and yet not reveal his true might?' asked Dark Oak.

Ovi continued walking, his staff thudding in the dust of the ground before them as he did so.

'Lord Awgren took all that were ready when the moment came. We have been busy in his absence. Of course, there were already those Devised that were not yet full-grown and have now reached maturity, but we have Devised many, many more creations in the intervening years, Lord Dark Oak. We have been readying ourselves for the next to present himself at our gates.'

'You talk in riddles,' said Dark Oak.

'You have questions?' said Ovi.

'Will you assist me or not? Do you have the means by which I can protect myself? My Mother Tree is a weakness that I cannot afford, and though Awgren did not fear the Dryads, it is they who could be my undoing. Every one of those who would stand against me knows where to find my beating heart, and if any one of them should decide to pierce it, I will be undone and my cause will be lost. I do not seek immortality or to extend my allotted span of years, merely to receive assurance that those years will not be cut short by the burning of my Mother. Can it be done?' he asked, seizing Ovi by the shoulder and hauling the Weaver round to face him.

'It can be done, and we can do it,' said Ovi, unperturbed.

'Then show me,' said Dark Oak, and walked on, entering a section of the cavern in which hundreds of animals were kept alive, many Morrick had seen in his lifetime, but others that Dark Oak knew only through the experiences of Dryads in lands as yet unknown to the Combined People. There were elephants, rhinos, lions, gorillas and all manner of creatures in Halwende, locked away from the grass and the light, in a place with no water and no obvious source of food.

So it was that Dark Oak took up residence in Awgren's halls, becoming known as lord in his own right. And while he was no less single-minded in pursuing his cause, he took no pleasure from dwelling in the home of one who had tormented his people in a previous life. Here was a place where no living thing would grow, and Dark Oak felt even more disconnected from the forest and, indeed, the world, than he had high in the Maw Keep, where at least he could look over the trees he had caused to come to life.

Ever Ovi walked beside Dark Oak in those days, and with the Weaver's assistance, he picked from amongst the Devised and set a guard around Halwende made up of those who could think autonomously and whose motives were closest to his own. Once more then, Creatures of the Devised roamed, in part, the Old Continent, let loose by one who in his previous life had hated them beyond reckoning.

Dark Oak withdrew to Awgren's chambers and locked himself away, and with no need of food, drink or sleep, he read on, day into night, week after week, until he had read the entirety of Halwende's library. All that Dark Oak read, he remembered.

On the allotted day, though Dark Oak had lost all sense of the passage of time, Ovi sent word for him, and Dark Oak followed the Weaver towards the cavern wall, into which were carved a tall doorway, stairs and pillars as though it were a building. Ovi led Dark Oak through the doorway, into the temple, up a narrowing stairway and into a tunnel, which sloped downwards.

The passage led to a corridor with doors to either side. The light was dim and water dripped from the ceiling, soaking into Dark Oak's body.

Ovi marched straight on towards the door at the far end of the hall, and Dark Oak followed, but then he heard a distinctly feminine sound through one of the doors.

The farm, he remembered.

Dark Oak turned the iron ring in the door and pushed it open. There was no light inside at all, but it did not hinder his vision. Dark Oak found himself in a room that reminded him of the barn in which he had once kept cattle, with locked stalls either side of the main walkway. The air reeked of urine and faeces. The female's voice had stopped as soon as he pushed open the door.

Dark Oak moved to the bars of the nearest cage and peered through. Huddled in the corner, naked and covered in her own filth, was a human woman. Her long hair masked her face, and she muttered to herself in the dark. The cell was unfurnished, save for a filthy mat of some kind to prevent her skin gaining sores. Dark Oak saw that she was not malnourished despite her filthy appearance. He saw that she was pregnant. How different she looked to Rowan when she carried his sons. What were their names then? Dark Oak could no longer remember. Red Maple and Seaborn.

One by one, he surveyed the cages, finding a woman in similar condition in each. He looked on the women, knowing he should feel pity, but it was just beyond his grasp. This was wrong, but it was as it was. Reality.

Once he had viewed them all, Dark Oak returned to the passage and closed the door behind them.

'You're breeding them,' he said simply.

Ovi nodded.

'Awgren would choose from among the human population of Halwende whenever he needed to rehouse his soul. And we make use of their organs and flesh in the crafting of new, superior creatures,' said Ovi, 'but most importantly, they carry souls with which we can experiment and transplant as need dictates.'

'And there are men here, too, I presume?' said Dark Oak.

'Segregated,' said Ovi, and he opened the door to their destination within this, the Temple of the Weavers.

Dark Oak recognised the room as the very same as that where Awgren's last memory of a ceremony took place. It was circular, with many work benches, glass vials and beds with leather straps. A great altar took up most of the far wall, around which were laid various body parts, skins and pelts. A statue stood atop it, dominating the room, an image of the lesser courtier of the gods, Danzi, the collector of souls. He was carved in basalt, pixie-like, appearing as a young boy of the woods, in a jerkin and ankle-high boots. He had no facial features, and yet his face was sculpted to suggest a smile. One hand extended out and above the head, as though it were awaiting something to drop into it, and the other was held out before him. From that hand dangled an iron lantern and a blue flame therein cast an eerie light around the cavern, sending slender shadows to dance upon the walls. The other Weavers were knelt in prayer before the statue.

Dark Oak could not free himself from the images of the pregnant women, cowering in their cages, awaiting who knew what fate, but he thought also of Rowan and of how her belly had swelled. Something stirred in him, remembering how happy she had been, his pride and love for her. He gasped as the memory of emotion washed over him. A past life, he told himself. Nothing more.

'You have a solution to my problem?' he asked, paying no heed to the Weavers' reverence. One by one, they concluded their prayers and came to stand before him.

'We have many solutions, lord,' said Fritjof.

'We have Devised many new methods to seek out and destroy the humans, this time without limitation. We have merged wolf and man so that he can dwell with the humans, infiltrating their society, only taking on his more powerful form when the moon is full. We have designed great wyrms and flying dragons. There are ways that can hold the Dryads, the Naiads, the Sylphs and the Oreads at bay should they attempt to move against you,' said Egil. 'Awgren would not use them against his own kind.'

'Tell me,' said Dark Oak.

'Our miners delved deep and broke through the world's crust. We found the last of the Immortals; the spirits of fire that dwell there, who seek to consume.'

'I do not seek to burn the forests,' said Dark Oak. 'I wish to command them.'

The Weavers exchanged glances.

'Perhaps the threat of annihilation would serve?' suggested Vali.

'And my Mother Tree?' he said. 'The one task to which you were actually assigned.'

Egil and Ovi exchanged looks.

'There are several choices, lord,' said Egil. 'We can transplant your soul into another body, as we did for Awgren when his Mother Tree came to the end of her days. Thus you would be protected unless your body be assailed.'

'I would no longer be a Dryad?' Dark Oak asked. 'That's no good to me. I will need to be able to stand before them and travel freely without fear of attack.'

'Then,' said Egil, 'perhaps you can make the location of your Mother Tree a strong place that none can enter? A fortress?'

But Dark Oak shook his head.

'There is no fortress that can withstand such an assault as I envisage. The Oreads would rend the ground beneath my Mother Tree, the Naiads poison the waters, the Sylphs stifle the air,' said Dark Oak.

'Just so,' said Ovi. 'It appears that there is no difficulty providing you with solutions, lord, but that you are having difficulty choosing between them. Tell me, what do you truly desire? Halwende is at your disposal. You have the means here to wage war across the lands, and yet you are not content.'

'I do not wish to destroy, simply to place limits,' said Dark Oak.

'And you can only do so by retaining the mastery, lord,' said Egil.

Dark Oak lowered his eyes, deep in thought. He stared down for so long that some of the Weavers moved off and went about their own business at their benches. Finally, his head snapped up like a carving suddenly gifted life.

'Awgren had no quarrel with the Dryads, and their disinterest protected him. I am not afforded that luxury,' said Dark Oak.

'That is true,' said Fritjof, 'yet I surmise that the Dryads and the council will be content if you are not seen to be contesting their will. They will not move against you, and perhaps you can grow your strength in secret.'

'And they will grow complacent and placid once more,' said Dark Oak, 'but when I come forth in strength, they may stir . . . '

'They did nothing when Awgren drove humanity from these lands,' reminded Ovi, 'even when the lesser woods and forests burned.'

'Just so,' said Dark Oak, knowing they feared Awgren. He began to pace back and forth, taking his axe from his belt and turning its haft in his hands.

'And while you bide your time, there is much that can be done to keep humanity in check, but secretly and without any connection to you. We have created many new creatures these past years, and can Devise many more, subtle and effective, unlike those Devised by Awgren, made for butchery and brute power. Abide here with us, Dark Oak, as Lord of Halwende. Together, we will maintain our watch over the world and prepare.'

'I cannot leave my Mother Tree exposed. I believe I know what must be done, though it pains me. We will assemble when I have considered for a little longer,' said Dark Oak and without another word he turned his back on them and walked out of the chamber. They heard cries and sobs and the squeal of contorting iron. Ovi started to go after him, but Egil bade him stay.

After a short time and much commotion, Dark Oak returned, leading a straggling line of naked, stooped, pregnant human women into the light of the room.

'Fritjof, find these ladies accommodation more suitable for guests. No more will they suffer the barbarity of these halls. Clothe them, feed them and allow them to walk in the light of day, under supervision, of course. See to it that all of the humans of Halwende are freed from such dungeons as they may now endure.'

Dark Oak turned to the women, who stood unabashed and seemingly unashamed of their nudity. He spoke to them.

'Fear not. They call me Dark Oak, but my true name is Morrick, and I too was a human. The Dark Lord is dead. I have come to root out the evil from Halwende and set right all ills. I will clear Awgren's dungeons and set all things right. A new era has begun in the world now that Awgren has passed away. Where barren lands of poisoned dirt and ash could be seen to the horizon, I have raised forests. Life returns. I will protect and tend you, then, when the time is right, you will be free to stay or go as is your wont.'

The women stared at him, their wits dulled by their long incarceration. Then a few began to sob and cry, but they did not shed tears of sorrow. It was evident in their faces that they were relieved and overjoyed at this news of the Dark Lord's defeat and their impending freedom.

'Follow Fritjof. He will lead you to a place of comfort, where you can recover. Your true freedom will come in time. I will allow you to rest and recuperate, then visit you when I am able. There is much to occupy my time here, and there are the remaining Devised to re-educate,' said Dark Oak. Some of the women thanked him as they filed past, those who were able to master their emotions enough to speak, and those who were brave enough.

Once they were gone, Dark Oak turned to Fritjof, and it seemed his starry eyes burned even brighter than they had before.

'We must make this a place of strength, but also of refuge for the humans, so that they live with my kind and under our control. We will feed them, clothe them and make this a place of splendour after a fashion, so that they will not wish to leave. They will work and they will build, and Halwende will become strong, peopled by humans, Devised and, in time, Dryads.'

And as he spoke, Dark Oak began to grow in stature, his face growing ever darker, the ivy tendrils of his hair curling and hissing as they grew so long that they brushed the floor.

At the sight of their new lord, the Weavers stepped back and bowed low.

'I have another task for you. Awgren's library contains tomes that suggest combining your rituals with weapon-craft. His first attempts at forging weapons that might bear the magic are in his chambers. I believe he was not far from success. Complete his work,' said Dark Oak.

The humans of Halwende cautiously rejoiced at their new-found circumstances, praising Dark Oak for his benevolence, while he plotted his offensive. The Dryad wandered the menagerie, viewing the Creatures of the Devising and contemplated their uses.

At dawn, Dark Oak would climb out from Halwende, sometimes granting a grateful human his favour, taking them to stand upon the plain and look east to watch the sunrise.

He thought of all the options for protecting himself, the risks and the benefits, the potential personal loss. He wished to remain a Dryad for as long as his Mother Tree lived, but if he stayed as he was, he would forever be at risk. If the First Council decided to kill his Mother Tree, there was nothing he could do from Halwende, and if he returned to the forest, he would be subdued. He did not wish his life as a Dryad to end, to ascend to become like his daughter or the other immortals. There was no guarantee he could exert any control over his new kind, but more importantly, Dark Oak *loved* the forest and wanted to protect it just as much as he wished to suppress humanity. If that meant he denied himself communion, just like Awgren, then so be it. Awgren had been able to disconnect and move his Mother Tree to a nearby place of safety, though, beneath Griminish, dwelling with her until the end of her days, but the Dark Lord had not been at war with his own kind. The Dryads would never allow Dark Oak to do the same.

He thought of his Mother Tree, so far away and vulnerable in the midst of the Impassable Forest. He felt the connection between them, and it pained him, but to travel to her would mean joining with the forest and risking being seized by the Dryads and indoctrinated. And even if he could get to her over land, Nayr's people would prevent him from removing his weakness. The longer Dark Oak thought about his Mother Tree, the greater his desire to be with her became.

But he had to protect the forest. Had to keep humanity under his boot. And what was his personal loss compared to achieving those goals, no matter how unnatural the means?

He looked all around at his treeless land, and he felt not only malice, but a secret glee flooding through him. And power. He had decided.

Chapter Twenty-One

Halflight Hold, The Long Isle

Aldwyn had known since Mungan Maconnock had suggested he become Lord Regent that one day, or more likely, one night, the clan would kill him. It was inevitable, and as such, he had spent his days preparing for death. Every night he had pondered the situation, wondering what he could do for the princes and princesses, acutely aware that if this was the day Mungan Maconnock decided he was secure enough to seize power, it might be his last. Time would run out for him and for Cathryn's children. His final memory might be the view of the moon through his window from his bed as he drifted off to sleep, before some unseen assassin went to work with a knife in the dark or a pillow over his face.

And then what of Annan and the rest of Cathryn's children?

The Maconnocks had wasted no time in spreading the news from isle to isle that the queen was dead, that Annan would soon be crowned, and that Aldwyn ruled as Lord Regent until the boy king came into his majority, but a few years hence.

A knock at his door, gentle at first, then harder. Aldwyn imagined a Maconnock pressing his ear to the wood.

Perhaps he thinks to find me swinging from the rafters . . .

Aldwyn went to the door and opened it a crack.

Malcolm Maconnock stood between the two clan guardsmen, clearly in his cups. He braced himself against the wall.

'Forgive the hour, Lord Regent,' he said and pushed the door open. Aldwyn gave way, allowing the Maconnocks in before bolting the door behind him.

'I wasn't sleeping,' said Aldwyn.

'Something on your mind, Your Grace?' asked Malcolm, taking a swig of his ale.

Aldwyn returned to his window and sat upon the sill, regarding Malcolm for a moment before answering.

'I was pondering how long it would be before you or one of yours puts an end to me while I sleep. Is tonight to be the night?' asked Aldwyn.

'Would you have it so?' asked Malcolm, his face expressionless for a moment before breaking into a smile.

'You think too little of us, Your Grace,' he said.

'Malcolm, I'm not a fool. Mungan will be done with me soon enough, and when you no longer have need of me, well . . . ' said Aldwyn. 'Have you come for a reason?'

Maconnock moved back to the door and drew back the bolts then stood between it and Aldwyn.

'I've come to bring you fair tidings, Lord Regent. King Annan has decided to strengthen the ties between The Isles and the royal line. Mungan has sent word that his daughter, Fiona, is to marry Prince Conrad, and King Annan's coronation will take place tomorrow on Main Isle.'

Aldwyn said nothing, but turned to look out of his window upon the thrashing moonlit sea far below.

'The news does nothing to lift your spirits, I see,' said Malcolm. 'I thought not, but I am instructed to ensure you voice your support for the union. Perhaps a speech to the nearby settlements.'

Aldwyn turned to his captor.

'The Maconnock clan consolidates its hold through marriage then? How long before Annan dies of a sudden fever or in a riding accident, so that his brother might take the throne with your kin at his side, and, perhaps, your kin in her womb?'

Maconnock shook his head.

'Such a suspicious mind, Your Grace,' he said. 'You'll want to prepare a few words before morning. We'll ride out then. Perhaps you'll get a little sleep, Lord Regent, but needs must.'

AGE OF THE DRYAD

And with that Malcolm Maconnock strode out, closing the door behind him. Aldwyn slid the bolts home once more then braced himself against the door, his forehead resting against the wood. He felt powerless to intervene and bereft at his inability to do his duty to Cathryn and her children. There must be something he could do, but not trapped in the tower.

He returned to the window and once more looked down at the sea and the rocks below, wondering if a man would survive such a fall even if he was lucky enough to hit the water.

And then, before he had a chance to think better of it, Aldwyn clambered up onto the sill and, turning to face into the room, he dropped to his knees. He dangled his right foot out over the edge and swung it about until it found purchase. Aldwyn tested his weight against the ivy that grew beneath his window then swung his second foot out. Hands shaking, Aldwyn lowered himself out until one hand was grasping ivy and the other was gripping the window ledge by its fingertips.

A tremor ran through his whole body as he began his descent, his breaths shallow and fast as fear seized him. He knew he must move swiftly and yet be quiet and careful, for he feared both a fall and discovery by the Maconnocks. Either would mean death.

Down and down Aldwyn climbed until finally his feet touched upon the rocks at the base of the castle wall.

Bearing no arms and wearing no armour, he scrambled around the base of the wall, all the time casting glances behind him to check he had not been followed. Halflight Hold loomed above him, and there was nobody in sight. The crashing of waves upon the rocks masked any sounds of his movements as Aldwyn made his escape. Spray soaked him through and he palmed water from his eyes as he moved, considering where to go and what to do. Remaining on the land meant more chance of being seen, but to drop into the water near the rocks would surely be suicide. Aldwyn reached the ditch that ran under the bridge by the Hold's gate, and he crouched in the dark for a while, listening, aware that the Maconnocks would have posted guards on the bridge. To his left, the deep ditch ran across the slope, its steep sides difficult to climb. To his right, the cliff fell away to the beach below. There was no easy way.

Aldwyn once more got on his knees, and backed over the edge of the cliff, his heart in his mouth, his whole body shaking and sweating.

I must survive, thought Aldwyn. *I must get to at least some of the children.*

The descent in the dark seemed to last for hours, but finally, by some miracle, Aldwyn felt his boot touch sand. Unsure if there would be guards on the beach, he wasted no time and with a final look back up at Halflight Hold, the Lord Regent strode out into the sea.

When the water was up to his waist, he ducked under so that only his head was above the surface. The freezing water knocked the breath out of him, but he gradually acclimatised. Aldwyn began to swim with a powerful, controlled breast-stroke to disrupt the water as little as possible. He powered southwards, parallel with the beach, all the time hoping and praying that the moonlight would not betray him.

Eventually, the cold became too much. Aldwyn knew he had to go ashore or his body would give out, and he would sink to join the stones rolling on the ocean floor. He had lost all sense of his position, at times not knowing whether the beach was to the left or right of him. He was all too conscious that arriving at shore in the wrong place might bring him directly to the attention of the Maconnock patrols. Nevertheless, he altered course and swam towards the beach once he'd got his bearings. Dark clouds obscured the moon, and Aldwyn swam blind, able only to make out tall shapes, vague and ominous ahead of him. At one point, he realised at the last second that he was powering straight towards a pinnacle of rock and changed direction with only a couple of feet to spare. As he swam round the shard, thinking it could not be long until he would be able to put his feet down, his kicking legs, trailing deeper in the water now that his energy was nearly gone, scraped against something hidden beneath. A sharp, urgent pain tore along his lower foreleg as it was drawn across a boulder below him. Aldwyn cried out then rolled on to his back and floated for a second, raising his leg from the water. Ripped though it was, whether by rock or barnacle, he could not see the wound in the dark, and he imagined the seawater coursing across it was a tide of blood. Ignoring the throbbing, stinging pain, Aldwyn kicked out like a frog, slowly, to avoid propelling himself headfirst into yet another unseen obstacle.

Aldwyn rolled and began to swim once more. He counted down from thirty and when he reached his chosen number, he stopped and felt beneath him for ground. His boots long discarded, his toes touched upon slimy weed, covering smooth pebbles. Aldwyn swam forward for a few more strokes and then found he was able to put both feet down. He began wading towards the beach, carefully, as he would tread sometimes upon sharp points and sometimes on slippery weed that made him lose balance.

A few minutes passed before Aldwyn found himself free of the ocean's grip. He shivered uncontrollably and wondered if he had made a grave mistake, if he would simply die of cold having made himself nothing but a castaway on the beach of the Long Isle. He longed to venture farther up the beach and drop into the dry sand, perhaps burying himself in it for warmth, and yet he knew that by morning at the latest, he would be pursued.

Leaving the sea behind him, Aldwyn crouched low and ran for the cover of the trees, thinking to make as much progress southward as he could.

The tall dark shapes he had seen from the water proved to be the beginnings of the woodland that Aldwyn knew lay less than a quarter mile south of Halflight Hold. There were hamlets scattered across the Long Isle, as well as isolated crofts and cottages, but although Aldwyn suspected their loyalties lay with Lachlan's children, he could not predict how they would feel about him, a stranger who had ruled in the queen's stead these past years. He was freezing, wet, bootless, unarmed and without food or water. Aldwyn was a learned man, comfortable at sea and considered to be a just leader by most he had commanded, but he was no ranger, and what he had gained in seamanship over the years, he had lost in woodcraft. While Lord Lachlan had felt at ease making his own journey across Stragglers' Drift, viewing it as a return to the wild roaming and freedom of his youth, Aldwyn had been raised within stone walls and under a roof. He stumbled through the woods, cracking fallen sticks beneath him, his feet in constant pain, so bad that he sometimes fell, thinking only of how he could find someone who could feed and clothe him and perhaps set him in the direction of some kind of assistance.

He walked in constant anticipation of hearing the thundering of hooves and the baying of the Maconnocks' hunting packs. They would chase him down and then what, an imprisonment more formal than before, or even death?

Aldwyn trudged on throughout the night, learning to move more quietly as the time wore on, at first taking fright at the hoot of every owl and creaking limb, then growing gradually accustomed to the recurring sounds. He heard no sound of pursuit, but he forced himself to go on despite his weary limbs, his thirst and the desire to lie down and sleep. He feared that if he allowed himself to do so in his current state, then he would die of cold.

Aldwyn's legs began to tremble with every step, and he was forced to brace himself against a tree. He slumped against the trunk, breathing heavily and shivering.

I must keep moving, he thought. *I must.*

But when he tried to do so, his body betrayed him, and he sank down on to the moss-carpet of the woods.

Only now, when he was still, did Aldwyn hear the strain of a fiddle above the night sounds of the forest. His first reaction to the sound of the music was alarm, knowing that there were folk near at hand, and yet would the Maconnocks be making merry whilst set on hunting him? He thought not. And perhaps, just maybe, whoever was playing might help him.

Aldwyn steeled himself to meet his fate, and with an effort he stood then made his way on through the wood, following the eerie sound of the fiddle.

Ere long he could see firelight ahead of him through the trees. The jig seemed to accelerate and become ever more urgent with every step he took. The swipe of the bow matched the beating of his heart.

He had not heard a fiddle played since departing The Folly, and even there it was a rarity to hear such an instrument, remnants as they were of a time long forgotten even before Dark Oak came to power, back when all crafts, arts and trades were more advanced. It occurred to Aldwyn that therein might lie a clue to the nature of the mysterious fiddler, who was surely of high rank if he had obtained such an instrument.

Time would tell. Aldwyn pressed on. His teeth chattered as he walked, drawing closer to trees upon which firelight danced.

By the time he had drawn so near that he could hear the tune clearly, Aldwyn was resigned to whatever might happen to him, unable to think of any course of action other than throwing himself upon the charity of whoever he might find gathered about the fire ahead of him. And yet, concealed by a final tree, Aldwyn paused a while, resting his shoulder against the bark and peering round to see what could be seen.

Aldwyn looked out across a glade lit by a campfire, around which a fiddler danced. A man and woman sat together between him and the flames, tapping their fingers and hands in time with the wail of the fiddle. At first Aldwyn was transported to childhood stories of travellers meeting fairies making merry in the wild woods, but the soldier in him shouldered these aside and saw the scene for what it was. They were all dressed simply in leather armour and armed with crude iron swords and axes. Aldwyn noticed quivers of arrows leaning against a young tree, and bows unstrung in pouches lay on a nearby log.

Aldwyn thought all looked at their ease in this pocket of firelight in the woods, surrounded by the watchful trees, in a land so tenuously governed.

He mustered his courage and stepped out into the light, his hands held out open towards them.

'Well met,' he said, as softly as he could manage and yet still be heard, hoping not to startle them.

Their heads turned almost lazily and the fiddler ceased his circling, but drew out three final notes from his fiddle before lowering it, along with its bow.

'Well met,' Aldwyn said again, his voice shaking. He staggered slightly.

The seated man rose from the ground slowly, yet Aldwyn noted he made no move to draw his sword. He was a hulking man with a shaggy brown beard.

The fiddler eyed Aldwyn warily.

Aldwyn realised what a desperate figure he must have looked, bedraggled and sodden with nothing on his feet and blood staining his ripped breeches.

'I am in need of aid,' he said, stepping closer.

'I know your face,' said the fiddler.

'May I sit by the fire and warm myself a while?' said Aldwyn.

'You alone?' said the bearded man.

Aldwyn nodded.

'And in need of your kindness,' he said.

The fiddler moved to the fire and beckoned Aldwyn to draw near, never taking his eyes from him, scrutinising his face. He reached down to his pack and threw Aldwyn a blanket.

'Hang out your clothes by the fire. Never mind Greta. She's no innocent,' said the fiddler.

Greta scowled at him, but did not deny it.

'I'll avert my eyes,' she said. 'How come you to be so sodden on such a night as this? We've not been troubled by rain.'

'Were you wrecked?' said the bearded man.

'Hush, Tam,' said the fiddler.

'Who're you hushing? Hush yourself. Reasonable question,' said Tam.

Aldwyn pulled off his shirt, and the fiddler set down his instrument so that he might rig a line by the fire between the branches of the surrounding trees. Aldwyn wrapped the blanket around his middle before removing his breeches, conscious of his scar, for none had seen it bar those who treated him on the battlefield, and Cathryn on that one night they had spent together aboard her flagship so many years before. His clothes hanging by the fire, Aldwyn sat with his back against a log, so close to the fire that he felt his face might melt. Greta and Tam sat together, and the fiddler stood on the other side of the fire from Aldwyn with his arms folded across his chest, apparently no longer in the mood to make music.

'So?' said Tam, draping an arm over Greta's shoulder and pausing only long enough to take a swig from a wineskin. 'Wrecked?'

'Tam,' said the fiddler, not taking his eyes off Aldwyn.

'Bloody what?' said Tam. 'What?'

The fiddler leant forward, and flames danced across his furrowed brow.

'What's happened, Your Grace?' he said, and Aldwyn knew his identity was betrayed. He hung his head and let out a long breath.

'Your Grace?' said Greta, asking the question of the fiddler, frowning as she did so.

'Hush,' said the fiddler, giving her a hard stare.

'He's hushing you now!' said Tam. 'Hark at him!'

'Hush!' said Greta and shrugged off his arm.

'Well, I like that,' Tam grumbled then drew down from the wineskin so that his cheeks filled.

Aldwyn took a deep breath and closed his eyes, as yet unable to lift his head and meet the fiddler's stare.

'This is Aldwyn, the Lord Regent,' said the fiddler. 'I've seen you making the Tithe Walk, unless my wits are failing me, haven't I, Your Grace?'

Aldwyn mustered what was left of his will and met the fiddler's gaze.

'Aye, I'm Aldwyn. You have my gratitude for the seat by your fire. You'd have yet more if you have water to quench my thirst and food for my belly, though at present I can offer no payment,' he said, glad to hear his voice sounding a little more like his own and less like the death knell of the sea.

Greta and Tam seemed not to know what to do, looking from one to the other, to the fiddler, to Aldwyn and back again. Tam handed Greta the wineskin, and she raised it to her mouth then thought better of it. Greta circled round the fire and, holding it out at arm's length, she offered the wineskin to Aldwyn as though trying to feed a tame lion for the first time. He took it gladly and drank deep. He started to stand, but the fiddler darted towards him.

'No, Your Grace, stay where you are.' He rummaged in his pack then handed Aldwyn a cloth bundle. Aldwyn unwrapped it as best he could with numb fingers and found strips of a salted meat therein. He nibbled at first, but his constricting stomach urged him on and within seconds he was tearing at the meat like a wild dog. He wolfed down the scant meal and felt all the better for it.

'Thank you,' he said, then as an afterthought he added, 'What's your name?'

'Luthier,' said the fiddler, offering a playful salute. 'Named for my father's trade, but I chose to play fiddles rather than building them. I'm still not sure if Father was proud, embarrassed or both. I had the honour of playing for Lord Lachlan in his youth, up at the Hold, you see.'

'I can see why. My compliments,' said Aldwyn as he held out his hands to the fire. Luthier bowed his head in thanks.

'I must be away again in a short while,' said Aldwyn, and his heart was heavy at the prospect, knowing full well his clothes would still be damp and that he still had little by way of a plan.

'Are you pursued?' asked Luthier as he settled on the log beside him. Tam and Greta watched them both with interest, but said nothing.

'If not, I soon will be,' Aldwyn admitted, seeing no point in subterfuge. If these folk had half a brain between them then the manner of his appearance would be all they would need to determine the truth.

Tam shook his head. Aldwyn saw Greta curl her fingers around his bicep, taking his arm and leaning her head against his shoulder.

'If that's the case, we'll all need to be away and without delay,' said Luthier. 'We've tarried overlong on the Long Isle as it is.'

'You have a way off?' said Aldwyn. 'What do you have to fear from any who might pursue me?'

'Let's not dance around the matter, Your Grace. It'll be the Maconnocks that are after you, sure enough,' said the fiddler as he set about ordering his pack, readying for the off. He stood, slung his pack over his shoulder and met Aldwyn's gaze once more. 'And there is no love lost between them and us, as you can imagine.'

'Why?' said Aldwyn. He stood and, with regret in his heart, he fetched down his clothes from the line. He was starting to dress when Tam laid a hand on his shoulder and passed him some of his own spare clothing.

'I can't do anything for yer feet, m'lord,' said Tam.

'Wrap em round with something, mate?' said Greta. 'Might have something.'

'You all have my thanks,' said Aldwyn, 'but what's this all about?'

'No time for that now,' said Luthier. 'As I said, we've tarried overlong. We head south through the woods and find somewhere to hide out while the pursuit is fresh. We can talk on the move, if you're willing to come with us?'

'Gladly,' said Aldwyn, knowing he had no other choice.

As the night crept on, Luthier the fiddler led Aldwyn into the heart of the wood. The trees became close-packed, and the dark became ever more impenetrable, though the width of the wood itself was not so very great, for, as the name suggested, Long Isle was a lengthy, narrow island save for the mountains at the very centre. Tam and Greta, apparently inseparable, followed on behind them.

After what seemed like hours, Luthier turned westward and headed towards the coast.

'Surely they'll be searching the beaches?' said Aldwyn, breathless as he tried to keep up the relentless pace.

Talk on the move? There was no fear of it for the time being, Aldwyn thought.

'Like as not,' said the fiddler, 'but they do not have so many men that we can't slip by them undetected. We know these woods better than any Maconnocks from the Butterfly Isle.'

Ere long they emerged from the trees, and Aldwyn looked out upon the moonlit waves once more.

'Tam?' asked Luthier as the other man caught them up.

'Lemme get my bearings,' said Tam and he picked his way down across the dunes to the beach then began to look about him.

'He's a Langilander. From here,' Greta explained. 'I'm from the Main Isle, yonder,' she nodded towards the ocean, 'and your man here,' at this she poked Luthier in the chest, 'is naught more than a court dandy.' She grinned, and Aldwyn found that he too was smiling.

'She's not wrong. I can find my way alright, but Tam knows the place better than I, for sure,' said Luthier.

The three of them settled on the sandbank and watched Tam pace the beach for a time before he shouted for their attention and ran back up towards the trees. When Aldwyn arrived he saw Tam darting into the woods and disappear from view. Luthier and Greta jogged after him, and so the Lord Regent followed on like a dutiful dog. He made up the ground between them and found his three companions hauling a small boat towards the shore. Aldwyn seized hold and put his back to it.

They dragged the craft into the shallows and jumped in. Aldwyn joined Greta in the bows whilst Tam and Luthier took up the oars. They hauled, and the boat moved out to sea before turning southwards.

'We'll follow the coast a-ways then rig the sail and head out yonder for Main Isle,' said Greta. She closed her eyes and nestled down in the boat seeking comfort and sleep.

And so Aldwyn left the Long Isle and the Maconnocks behind him, for the time being at least.

Chapter Twenty-Two

Broken Buzzard

The Magpie stood out to sea before dawn on a black, cloud-covered night.

Captain Lynch spared only a short while to look back at the home to which he feared he might never return, whether it be because of his death or the whim of some nobleman keeping him away. His headland and his cottage receded gradually from view, their features blurring into the background of the forest as though the churning wake of the schooner was casting some spell of forgetfulness over the land they were leaving behind.

Yet Captain Lynch was mindful of the many reefs in the bay and so abandoned nostalgia to stand beside the quartermaster, keeping a watchful eye on the trim of the sails and satisfying himself that the Magpie was holding to his chosen course.

When he was content that everything was as he desired, Lynch sought out his passengers. He found Feran below decks, settling Dun into a hammock despite the older man's protestations. He offered the services of the Magpie's surgeon, and Feran thanked him with honest appreciation and a firm handshake, but Lynch noted the weariness in Feran's eyes and the wet pallor of Dun's skin. He feared the hammock and the old man would make a lasting acquaintance, with the former encasing the latter while he sunk to the ocean floor.

Lynch found Tolucan leaning over the rail and looking out to sea, watching the small islets as the Magpie passed them by, his hound, Randolf, lying between his legs. The animal whimpered, but would not be parted from its master. The knight braced himself against the lurch and roll of the schooner, his knuckles white and his arms rigid. He seemed entranced and it was only when Lynch spoke that he blinked and seemed to regain his senses.

'Have you decided?' asked Lynch, rubbing at his blind eye, the scar still itching five years on. 'We'll be clear of the reefs before long and one way or the other, I'll need to give the quartermaster a heading.'

Tolucan sighed and scratched his temples briefly before an unexpected lurch sent him reeling. He grabbed for the rail as though someone had kicked a chair out from under him. Lynch stifled a smile and steadied the man with a hand on the shoulder.

'We'll do as you suggested, Captain. Make for The Isles to report to Lord Aldwyn, if that is what he ordered. We can seek his counsel before we decide to sail for Oystercatcher Bay or The Folly, and you can resupply for the second leg of the journey. It all depends on what we can learn of the queen's fate,' said Tolucan, saying nothing of seeking the means to destroy the Mother Tree.

Lynch nodded. He'd heard no news from The Folly in a long time by that point, and had expressed his doubts as to whether or not the queen would have survived the war there.

'I for one would be glad of a chat with Lord Aldwyn,' said Lynch, 'before I commit to taking you south without understanding what burden you are under and the risk it may pose to the Magpie, though there are not a few risks when visiting The Isles.'

Lynch saw Tolucan frown and turn to look at him, still clinging to the rail with his left hand.

'What sort of risks?' asked the knight.

Lynch raised an eyebrow and blew air between pursed lips.

'None too chivalrous of me, and I'm mightily ashamed to say, now I come to think of it, in the presence of the likes of yourself, a knight and all,' said Lynch, his laughter lines deepening as he spoke.

'I couldn't care less,' said Tolucan. 'What risks?'

'The wife was living on Main Isle when last I saw her, and the mistress made her living on her back in Eastport on Long Isle. The whore will be fine, but I suspect the missus won't give me a warm welcome after such an absence, but I fear Rowan is the one to actively avoid,' Lynch confessed. Seeing Tolucan frown, he went on, 'In the dying days of the war against Awgren, my last command was wrecked on the east coast of the Old Continent. We made our way inland through the forest and wound up falling in with some of the Hinterland folk. I met Rowan there, and we escaped to Oystercatcher Bay together. Our affections grew, as they tend to between a woman and a man, and despite her husband's fate being unknown, me and her fell in together. Husband turned up though and it ended with a scuffle, and him finding my sword point in his shoulder. By then I'd started to see her for what she was and I'll admit I was not sorry to pack her off to the Butterfly Isle along with the other folk from the Hinterland, offering a promise of a reunion before she left.'

'There was no reunion,' said Tolucan. It was not a question, and Lynch supposed the knight felt he had quite taken the measure of the captain.

'Not as such,' said Lynch, drawing himself up to stand straighter, his tone becoming a little defensive, 'You know, what with the end of the world as we knew it n' all?'

Lynch thought it best not to mention that Rowan was the former wife of Dark Oak.

Tolucan said nothing, but nodded slowly, turning to look back out to sea. Neither of them spoke for a moment, and then Tolucan asked,

'You don't think Rowan would be grateful you survived the turmoil and returned to her?'

'There'll be no returning. Well shot of that situation. Complicated,' said Lynch. 'and I'm well rid.'

'You're a true gentleman, Captain,' said Tolucan.

'Aye,' said Lynch, 'and you're so bleeding perfect, aren't you?'

Tolucan made no reply, and Lynch clapped him on the back.

'Thought not. I'll leave you to your business and speak to the helmsman.'

'Quiet,' said Tolucan suddenly.

Midway in turning, Lynch tottered on one foot and, balanced once more, he returned to Tolucan's side. The knight caught his eye and nodded discreetly towards the water.

There were shapes in the foam displaced by the Magpie's bows, the fine curves of womanly forms, white hair coursing down their bodies as they dived then once more broke the surface like a pod of playful dolphins ahead of a ship. Dolphins Lynch had seen many a time, and they had stirred his heart in wonder and brought a smile to his face. This? The sight of Naiads escorting them, silently, ever watchful, bearing them up? The thought sometimes filled him with horror and, sometimes, comfort.

'Our departure does not go unnoticed,' said Tolucan.

'Seems so,' said Lynch. He slipped a coin from his purse and tossed it down to the Naiads. It disappeared in the foam.

'What are you doing?' whispered Tolucan.

'An offering for the sea goddess,' said Lynch, and he tipped his hat to the Naiads. 'May she see us safely to port.'

'Surely you don't believe in a sea goddess?' asked Tolucan with a laugh.

'Seeing is believing, my friend,' said the captain, turning his back to the rail.

'Is this unusual?' asked Tolucan. 'You don't seem surprised to see them.'

'Not unusual, no. My guess is they've always been with us, but they don't hide it no more,' said Lynch.

He'd seen less of them in recent days, though. The Magpie had spent more and more time at anchor as the years went by. Once, Lynch had felt more at home at sea than he did ashore, but that wasn't right entirely, he thought. He doubted any man could feel at home on the ocean, but it'd be true to say he'd adjusted to it. He'd learnt its mercurial ways, and he was as comfortable as one could be, knowing that each day survived was a defiant spit in the eye of the sea's every attempt to drag you under and drown you. He felt no comfort now, none of the joy he used to feel at the beginning of a voyage, with the freedom of leaving obligations behind. He wanted to be back in Broken Buzzard, where he had found peace. His mood darkening, he left Tolucan and retreated to his cabin.

The days passed slowly. Each morning Tolucan would take up the same position at the rail, watching the Naiads. He called out to them and spoke to them in a low whisper, but though he suspected they could hear and were listening, not one of them ever chose to reply. He wondered about their motives, as he stood with the spray wetting his face and clothes, but wondered if the captain wasn't right and that the Naiads were seeing them on their way, for good or ill.

At mealtimes he would take food below for his travelling companions, as Feran only left Dun's side when nature called. The squire had deteriorated at sea, drifting in and out of consciousness, his skin and eyes losing their colour and his bloody coughing worsening. It went unspoken between Tolucan and Feran that Dun's time in the world was drawing to a close. Tolucan knew his friend could not speak of it. Feran would barely eat, spending his time trying to feed the old man, dribbling fresh water on his lips and mopping his brow, telling him stories and speaking of their past together, but only when they were alone, and so Tolucan caught only snippets as he passed by.

Chapter Twenty-Three

The Tinkers' Camp, The Fell Wood, Main Isle

'No,' said Aldwyn.

'Whatya mean no?' asked Tam, shrugging Greta's hand from his arm and standing before the circle of Luthier's band of outlaws.

'If we station archers on both sides of the road, they'll like as not kill each other as often as they do the Maconnocks, that's why,' said Luthier, before Aldwyn had a chance to reply.

'Only if they're a piss-poor shot,' spat Tam, hands on hips. Greta quieted him by slipping her hand in his. Then she had her say.

'We'll position half the archers on either side of the road after the turns. That way we'll be on high ground and shooting down into them. We'll wait till the Maconnocks are in plain sight and let loose a volley that'll take them by surprise. They'll be looking both ways and have to come uphill to get at us. We'll place half of our skirmishers so they burst out behind the Maconnocks and half ahead of them. After the archers have let off two volleys, Phoenix and Luthier can lead the skirmishers in. Attack them on four sides,' concluded Greta, and then kissed Tam on the cheek. He reddened and frowned.

Luthier nodded.

'It's one idea. I'll think on it,' he said, rosining his bow, with his fiddle lying on a log beside him.

'This is all very well,' said Aldwyn, 'but how does it advance my cause? We deplete the Maconnocks' numbers, yes, but it tells us nothing about where they are keeping the princes and princesses,' said Aldwyn.

His time in the highlands of Main Isle had left him looking no different from the commoners. They had fed him, clad him and armed him, but as one of their band, not as a lord. At first it was to his chagrin that he found his authority diminished, that all of them looked instead to Luthier for commands, and yet after a while, he realised it was also a relief. He still had Luthier's ear, and so influence, but some of the burden of responsibility had been lifted from him.

The band of outlaws had originally been made up of those who had been driven from their homes by the Maconnocks as they brought The Isles under their control, rallying smaller clans to their cause. Most had mined or worked tin on some of the smaller islands, which the Maconnocks had invaded and occupied, driving out or enslaving the occupants. The tinkers hiding in the Fell Wood of Main Isle came to be known by the locals as the Tinkers of the Fell Wood, and they would aid them when they could, for they had no love for the barbaric Maconnocks and were sympathetic to the Tinkers' plight. That was true of folk throughout The Isles, which had led to wandering folk such as Tam and Greta joining the band.

The Tinkers had already garnered something of a legendary reputation throughout The Isles when Luthier fell in with the group by chance as he made his way around The Isles, scratching a living as an entertainer. He had quickly risen to prominence, Aldwyn guessed, because of his likeability, his patience and his cool head, but the man was bold, and he knew how to delegate. He also knew tales of the Lords of The Isles and could recount meeting Lachlan and Cathryn themselves in Halflight Hold before the final offensive against Awgren. He could stir hearts and inspire his followers.

They gained new people every day, with loyalists from all over The Isles making the journey to Main Isle when Mungan Maconnock announced that Aldwyn was a traitor and that Mungan himself was now Lord Regent, rightly suspecting a plot.

They had, however, been too few to prevent either the coronation of King Annan or the marriage between Prince Conrad and Fiona Maconnock.

Luthier's band built their strength in secret, moving camp regularly in the highlands of Main Isle and the Fell Wood, which encircled them.

'We'll take prisoners. Prisoners talk or prisoners die,' said Phoenix. He was sitting just outside of the circle with his golden eagle secured between his legs, a hood over its eyes. Another man held the bird's legs together while Phoenix trimmed the excess growth of her beak with a small knife.

Lachlan's brother, Hadwyn, had kept a hunting lodge on the Butterfly Isle, and Phoenix worked there as head falconer before the Maconnocks came to power. His head was shaved, and he stood far taller than any other man in the band. He was all muscle, and Aldwyn thought he was the strongest man that he had ever encountered. His one bare arm bore scars from the wrists up, the other, Aldwyn knew, looked the same underneath the great leather gauntlet he wore when handling his raptors. Phoenix rarely joined in with conversation or merriment, preferring to spend his time either with his birds or alone, and so when he spoke, people listened.

'He's right,' said Luthier, setting down his bow and carefully laying it beside his fiddle, 'but there's no need to make any of these decisions in haste. We have a while before Mungan Maconnock walks the Tithe on Main Isle. We'll be ready. Until then, we prepare, we scout, we make plans to fall back on should we fail. Get about it now, ladies and gentleman,' he concluded, and without another word spoken, the Tinkers drifted off in their own directions leaving just Luthier, Phoenix and Aldwyn still seated in the glade.

Satisfied with his work, Phoenix put away his knife and allowed the eagle to perch once more upon his arm.

'I can't tell you how grateful I am,' said Aldwyn to Luthier, but the fiddler shook his head in response.

'You have nothing to thank me for, Your Grace. I was sworn to service with the Lord of The Isles, and it's my duty to see things set right here.'

'Nevertheless, I will see to it that Queen Cathryn rewards all of you,' said Aldwyn.

'You'll not see her again,' said Phoenix. 'Have you not come to understand yet? The world has changed. It won't change back.'

Over the coming days, Aldwyn and the Tinkers moved farther inland, deeper into the Fell Wood and on up the slopes that led, eventually, into the barren granite mountains that dominated the centre of the Main Isle. A number of the band spent their days fletching arrows until every archer had more arrows than any could hope to use in a long day of battle.

Eventually they made their way beyond the treeline and after a steep ascent, Aldwyn found himself cresting a ridge beyond which lay a freshwater tarn, hidden from the slopes below and circled by steep mountains. Luthier set a watch upon the slope, for it was the only point of approach and that done, the Tinkers made camp by the waters of the tarn. Aldwyn slept under the stars when night fell, and he dreamt of that day when he was young, when Cathryn had given him her necklace.

One day, after the sun had sunk behind the mountains, Aldwyn saw one of the scouts clamber over the ridge and, huffing and blowing, head straight for Luthier. Aldwyn followed.

'The Maconnocks reached Bellanoch this morning,' said the scout, and he set down a pack loaded with mackerel, caught fresh that morning by the folk of the village.

'How many?' said Luthier.

'Was Mungan with them?' asked Aldwyn simultaneously.

'Aye, he was. Around twenty,' said the scout. He knelt in the sand at the side of the tarn and cupped water to his mouth.

'Tomorrow then,' said Aldwyn. 'We'd best get about it.'

'What news?' asked Phoenix, thumping over to them.

'The Tithe Walk has reached Bellanoch,' said Luthier, quietly.

Phoenix nodded.

'Gather round,' he called, and the Tinkers abandoned their business to crowd round.

His heart beating fast, Aldwyn recovered his voice and his standing somewhat. Before Luthier could say a word, Aldwyn was on his feet and addressing the fiddler's folk.

'It has come to it. Tomorrow we ambush the Maconnocks as they travel the road through the woods towards Princefall. Every man and woman here has a score to settle with Mungan and his brethren, but I ask you all to remember this; we are not settling personal vendettas, at least, not as a band. Annan is Lachlan's son, the rightful Lord of The Isles and the heir to the throne. He is being used by Mungan in a scheme to seize power, as are Prince Conrad and his new wife. Cathryn still reigns as queen. The Maconnocks merely seek to take advantage of a momentary weakness, and while the queen is abroad and unable to intervene, you and I are all that can prevent these islands coming under Maconnock rule. We fight for a bloodline that has led our ancestors through centuries of hardship, bringing us at last to victory against the Dark Lord. Clad though we may be in leathers at best, carrying crude weapons and bows, tomorrow each and every one of you fight as warriors of the realm. So fight hard in the name of Queen Cathryn, fight true and together, perhaps, we can wrest back these islands from your oppressors,' he said.

'Hear, hear,' called Phoenix, and the cry was taken up by all assembled. All, Aldwyn noticed, except for two men who stood together with their arms folded across their chests, Randall and Caplin, two of Greta's archers from the Butterfly Isle. Caplin caught Aldwyn's gaze and nodded to him, but before Aldwyn could think more on it, Luthier had begun to speak, sitting in the grass beside his little fire as he began to prepare a mackerel to cook over the small flame.

'Noble sentiments, true enough,' he said quietly, his words barely audible, he was so softly spoken. The Tinkers ceased their talk so they could hear him.

'And while I am here out of duty to Lord Lachlan and his children,' continued Luthier, 'I am not eager to throw your lives away in the name of any cause. We will do what we can tomorrow, but I'd not have any one of you die trying to act the hero. We have done our best to gather what strength in numbers and in arms we can manage. Listen to your captains; to myself, to Tam, to Greta and to Phoenix. We are not the prettiest and not of noble birth like the good lord, Aldwyn, and yet we will see you through if seeing you through is possible. Now get some sleep, all of you. I'll take the first watch. We set off before dawn.'

Aldwyn could not stay asleep for long. He would drift off for minutes at a time, but wake suddenly imagining he had heard something approach. He was both fearful and determined, mulling over the different ways the ambush could play out as he tried to find sleep again, picturing his own part in the action, wondering how he would acquit himself and whether he would gain glory or find shame. Whether he would do right by Cathryn. By the time Luthier came to wake him, he was exhausted but as alert as he was going to be until the fighting started and his body flooded with adrenaline.

'It's time,' said Luthier.

Breakfast was hurried, but every one of them ate their fill, dually conscious that they needed the energy for the fight and also that it could well be their last meal. They drank water from the tarn until they could drink no more and then, once everybody was clad and armed, they gathered by the waterside.

'Tam, Greta, take your archers and scout out the way, but do not string out so far apart that you lose sight of one another. Phoenix, lead the rest of them on behind.'

Luthier stowed his fiddle in a cloth bag, which he threw over his shoulder, and he bound his hair tightly before pulling up his hood, taking up his longbow.

'Are you ready, Your Grace?' he asked Aldwyn.

'Ready as anyone can be,' said Aldwyn. He sheathed his iron sword and took up a short axe to wield with his less dextrous left hand.

The Tinkers made their way down the mountain and into the Fell Wood, moving swiftly through the trees, ever watchful in case the Maconnocks were scouting the area surrounding the road. They met no one as they made their descent.

Before dawn, they reached the turn in the road that Greta had suggested some weeks before.

'Good luck to all,' said Aldwyn before the Tinkers moved off to take up their positions.

'And be careful,' said Luthier, a stern expression on his face. He pointed his finger at the man farthest to the left then swept it across to the right so that it encompassed all of his people. 'Do not sell your lives cheaply.'

Aldwyn lay flat behind a ridge with Luthier and his half of the skirmishers while Tam and Greta ran on to position their archers on the Princefall leg of the road. Phoenix led his skirmishers after them. Aldwyn's mouth had dried out, and he licked his lips as he drew his sword.

And then, lying in the undergrowth, silent and hidden, all he could do was wait.

Aldwyn heard the sound of hooves. He felt Luthier shifting beside him.

'Keep still,' he whispered. 'Our heads stay down until Greta starts the killing.'

Luthier, perhaps feeling his own inexperience in battle for the first time, nodded. Aldwyn closed his eyes and concentrated on listening.

Hooves. Feet tramping. The sound of clanking steel. Carts to carry the Tithe.

The sounds drew closer, and Aldwyn held his breath. They began to fade as the Maconnocks passed around the bend in the road.

Any second now, thought Aldwyn. He wanted to run or to hunker down and wait it out, but he wouldn't. He knew that, a veteran of many campaigns.

Do it for Cathryn, he thought. *Do it for her children.*

A great cry went up, and Aldwyn heard a volley of arrows whizz through the air and screams further broke the still of the Fell Wood.

Luthier shifted onto all fours, still low.

'Wait,' ordered Aldwyn in a hiss, 'Wait for it . . . '

He heard the second volley and, just seconds later, a great roar over the din of the shouting Maconnocks. It could only be Phoenix.

Aldwyn's arms shook as he pushed off against the ground into a run.

'With me!' he roared as he burst from hiding, axe in his left hand and sword in his right. Without checking to see whether anyone had come with him, Aldwyn ran down the slope and around the bend in the road towards the huddle of fur-clad Maconnocks, some dead or dying in the road and those who were standing attacked now on four sides.

Aldwyn saw nothing but what was ahead of him as a red mist came over him.

Here was his chance.

He saw the archers on the bluffs throwing down their bows to draw their melee weapons. A bellow from Phoenix drew his attention as he ran. The Maconnocks were forming a circle, shields and weapons readied even as the sound of ringing metal began.

There were far more than twenty of them.

Aldwyn charged the Maconnocks, putting his head down to close the remaining distance. The man ahead of him raised his shield, but Aldwyn jumped into a kick which sent his enemy flying backwards. Aldwyn landed heavily on his side and swung out right with his sword, hacking into the back of a man's knee. Still lying on his side, he parried a blow with his axe and then scrambled to his feet. All around him, the Tinkers set upon the Maconnocks. All was a blur around him. Aldwyn's sword rose and fell, flicking blood in all directions as he gave battle, his heart beating fast. His limbs began to tire, but he pressed on with the fight, clansmen falling before him, Tinkers dropping by his side. The archers ran into the fray.

Aldwyn caught a glimpse of Greta lying on the floor. She held her sword in both hands, impaling a Maconnock through his chest. Near her, Mungan Maconnock rode amongst the Tinkers, mounted on his black stallion, preternaturally calm as he sliced down with his axe to either side of him, splitting skulls and shattering shoulder blades.

'Greta!' Tam screamed, sprinting towards his lover and felling all in his path.

'Forward!' roared Aldwyn, and he started to cut a path straight for Mungan, calling the chieftain's name over the screams and the clash of weapons.

But it was no use, there were too many Maconnocks barring his way. Aldwyn realised they must have reinforced after the scouts had left Bellanoch to bring news of their numbers. The Tinkers were fighting as well as could be expected for tin-workers and miners, but the Maconnocks were pushing them back. They began to press their advantage.

Luthier stepped to his left, dodging a colossal blow, and half severed a Maconnock's neck with a slice of his sword.

'Fall back!' Luthier shouted, 'Fall back to the trees!'

'No!' shouted Aldwyn, but the Tinkers had already begun to respond to Luthier's command.

Aldwyn knew they were beaten, that they could not carry the day, but also that he could not give up. There was Mungan, right there before him. The consequences for Annan and the other children would be too severe if Aldwyn did not take him down.

Aldwyn grabbed the wrist of his next attacker then swung a kick which lifted the woman's feet from under her. Her head slammed into the ground. Aldwyn looked up, ready to fight on, but the Maconnocks were forming up.

'Aldwyn!'

From Aldwyn's right, Mungan Maconnock rode towards him. Aldwyn began to back away, stumbling over the injured and the dead.

This is it, he thought, *this is the end.*

Phoenix stepped into view. He hefted his great black axe and swung it with a roar. The axe cut into the stallion's side, and the rearing beast sent Mungan flying from the saddle.

'Run!' Phoenix roared and took to his toes up the slope into the trees.

Aldwyn started towards Mungan, who was groaning and struggling to get to his feet, but the Maconnocks were advancing. Two arrows flew from behind Aldwyn, one embedding itself in a shield and another felling one of the clansmen. The Maconnock advance was checked momentarily and, his instincts finally taking over, Aldwyn turned and ran towards the trees.

Ahead of him, farther up the slope, he saw Caplin and Randall nocking arrows, covering the Tinkers' retreat while the rest of the archers disappeared into the woods.

Aldwyn put his head down and drove forward, his tired legs beginning to respond less and less to his efforts. He was slowing by the second.

Up the slope Aldwyn climbed, with shouts and cries following on behind, his feet slipping in the mud, his hands grasping for any root or trunk he could grasp to pull himself higher. He cast a look back over his shoulder and, with relief, he realised the Maconnocks had halted.

Perhaps I can rally the Tinkers and launch a new assault, thought Aldwyn.

He ran between Caplin and Randall, both men standing with arrows ready, taking aim in case their enemies charged again.

He had just stepped past them when Caplin seized his arm.

Aldwyn turned to look at him, pulled off-balance.

'I ever tell you where I'm from?' said Caplin.

Aldwyn heaved himself free from Caplin's grip, but Randall wrapped an arm around his throat from behind, dragging him back as Caplin nocked an arrow. Aldwyn struggled to breathe, dropping his weapons and grasping Randall's arm.

'Ever tasted Elaris Whisky?' Caplin said, his voice low. Aldwyn realised what was happening and was about to drive an elbow into Randall's gut when Caplin loosed an arrow into his thigh. Aldwyn sagged, gurgling as Randall's chokehold intensified.

Caplin looked up the slope and, reassured the Tinkers were out of sight, he turned back to the Maconnocks.

'Take this one as part-payment for the butchery at Elaris!' he shouted.

With that, Aldwyn felt strong hands propelling him forward. Randall hurled him down the slope, and Aldwyn tumbled towards the waiting Maconnocks.

Chapter Twenty-Four

Halflight Hold, The Long Isle

Lynch gave orders for the Magpie to drop anchor a safe distance from the rocky west coast of Long Isle. He and Tolucan took a boat ashore then drew it up on the white sands near to Halflight Hold, crossing the very path Aldwyn had swum many weeks before.

They had made no secret of their approach, and before long a party came down from the Hold to intercept them.

'Evening, lads,' called Lynch, salt water dripping from his fingertips.

'Who goes there?' said the fur-clad leader of the group.

'Captain Jacob Lynch of the Magpie,' said Lynch, tipping the brim of his hat in salute.

'Angus Maconnock,' said the man.

'Maconnocks on Long Isle? Did you drink the Butterfly Isle dry at last?' Lynch smiled, but it was not returned. Lynch reached into the boat and withdrew a sack.

Tolucan tucked his thumbs into his belt as he weighed up the men, deciding in which order he would kill them if it came to it.

'What's your cargo?' asked Angus, but Lynch shook his head.

'No cargo today, sir. I'm here to see Lord Aldwyn. He up there?' Lynch pulled a bottle from the sack and held it out to Angus, who examined it, but could find no clue as to its contents.

'Brandy,' said Lynch. 'Acquired from the cellars at Stragglers' End, courtesy of the ladies of the Whoreswood as was.'

Angus tucked the bottle inside his tunic.

'You have my thanks,' he said, 'but you'll not find Aldwyn here, and truth be told, those who ask after him would do well to be wary these days.'

'How's that?' asked Lynch, frowning. Tolucan untucked his thumbs and draped his left hand over the pommel of his sword.

'Lord Aldwyn has been charged with treason. Word from Main Isle is that he led an attack on the party walking the Tithe. They say he's been gathering rebels to seize the crown from King Annan,' said Angus.

'King Annan?' Tolucan interrupted. 'Queen Cathryn is dead?'

Angus shrugged.

'Dead or as good as. Annan's been crowned in her stead. Aldwyn was acting as Lord Regent, but seems he had ideas above his station,' said the Maconnock.

'Annan's surely not reached his majority?' said Lynch, still frowning. He did not like the turn the conversation was taking and felt a strong desire to be away. Halflight Hold in the hands of the Maconnocks and Lord Aldwyn named a traitor?

'He can't be more than 16,' added Lynch.

'Our chieftain acts as Lord Regent, being Prince Conrad's father-in-law,' said Angus.

'And where might we find the Lord Regent?' said Tolucan.

'Who's asking?' said Angus, turning his full attention to the knight.

'Sir Tolucan of Stragglers' Drift. I was tasked with an errand by the queen and was due to report to Lord Aldwyn,' he said, heedless of the danger that Lynch easily perceived.

'Then your business *is* with Mungan. You will find him at his residence in Princefall with the king,' said Angus.

'Fair enough,' said Lynch, adopting a lighter tone than came naturally. 'I'll pay my respects to the princes and princesses whilst we're here then be off to the Butterfly Isle with anything you wish me to convey.' The captain started up the slope, but two of the Maconnocks barred his path.

'They're not accepting guests, Captain,' Angus warned Lynch. 'These are troubled times. Even Lord Aldwyn could not be trusted.'

'I see,' said Lynch. Tolucan was about to speak, but Lynch seized him by the arm.

'We'll be off then. Would you have me take a message to Princefall?'

'There's no message I'd trust you with, Captain,' said Angus. He turned his back and set off back towards the Hold, leaving his people to see Lynch and Tolucan off the beach.

The two men pushed the boat back into the shallows without a word exchanged between them and, indeed, they remained silent until nigh halfway back to the waiting schooner.

'You think there is something amiss, I take it?' said Tolucan.

'Traitor, my arse,' said Lynch. 'I've known the man for years and never met one so loyal to the Crown. The Maconnocks have taken Halflight Hold. If the children aren't dead and buried, I'll be pleasantly surprised.'

'We must seek Cathryn without delay,' said Tolucan, disturbed both by the captain's grim tone and his own inability to detect deception.

'We can allow for a little delay. She'll want to know what's gone on here, not to mention the fate of her children and Lord Aldwyn. Let's head down to Brookmouth and get the true account from those that know best, those with no skin in the game,' said Lynch.

Then as an afterthought, 'Aldwyn may need our help.'

Princefall, Main Isle

The sun sank low in the west behind the mountains, and two of the Maconnocks took a rough hold of Aldwyn by the arms and then hauled him, gagged and still tied at the hands and feet, to the edge of the wooden stage in the town square, lit by the flaming brands in the hands of the watching clansmen. A crowd had gathered, no, been assembled, and stood murmuring as the Lord Regent was dragged before them.

King Annan, a scared boy, his former guardian trussed up before him, was flanked by Mungan Maconnock. He alighted from his throne to stand upon the simple lower dais, but it was Mungan who read out the king's decree, towering over the boy.

'Let it be known that even the noblest are beholden to the law. In these wild times, we must all remain true to one another. The former Lord Regent, Aldwyn, Duke of Culrain, has murdered my brothers and sisters and attempted to murder me. His regency has been marred by a brutality hitherto unknown to The Isles, not least among his deeds being the sack of Elaris and the murder of that town's folk.'

Aldwyn looked down and saw a great oak barrel full to the brim.

He realised what was coming. Aldwyn tried to step back, but strong hands kept him in place. He began to panic and struggle, becoming light-headed.

'Aldwyn's land and goods are forfeit and will be paid as weregild to the people of Elaris. They will also pay for the method of his execution,' pronounced Maconnock.

And with that, the Maconnocks wrestled Aldwyn forward. He struggled against them, his heart pounding and his eyes wide, frantic in terror.

Cathryn, he thought. *Cathryn.*

'Just as the people of Elaris died by his hand, let him die by the work of the people of Elaris,' said Mungan. The men holding Aldwyn's arms kicked his legs out from under him so that he sunk to his knees.

Tam started forward in the crowd, reaching for the hilt of his sword, but Luthier held him back. High on the battlements, Greta nocked an arrow and looked down into the courtyard, but when she met Luthier's eye, she saw him shake his head. There were too many.

One of the men grabbed Aldwyn by the hair and, aided by his companion, they threw him from the stage, headfirst into a barrel of finest Elaris Whisky.

Aldwyn held his breath, but his head struck wood, and he gasped. His lungs filled with the finest whisky Elaris could produce, burning his nose and throat on the way down, tearing into his eyes.

It took all of Luthier's control not to spring forward, not to unleash the fury of his band upon the gathered Maconnocks. His fingers dug deep into Tam's arms as Aldwyn thrashed, his legs kicking frantically at the air.

He watched King Annan's mouth fall open. The boy trembled as he turned his back on the drowning lord and climbed the steps back to his throne, but Mungan Maconnock moved to the edge of the stage, his arms folded across his chest, and watched Aldwyn drowning below.

He beckoned to one of his clansmen.

Aldwyn willed himself to die, his body riddled with pain, his lungs crying out.

Yet one memory persisted as his consciousness began to fade, of Cathryn huddled up to him by the firelight, the trees of the Drift encircling them and the stars wheeling overhead.

Go there now, he thought, already beginning to fade. *Leave this life and go.*

Luthier saw a clansman holding a burning brand cross the stage to stand at Mungan Maconnock's side.

At the last moment, Luthier realised what was happening and turned away.

Maconnock snatched the brand from his man, and, waving him away, he tossed it into the barrel, leaping backward as he did so.

Cathryn, thought Aldwyn as his world exploded, but then he was no more.

Luthier had seen many executions in his time, but this was the first where the crowd had let out a collective groan instead of a cheer. Many turned away or cried out.

'Bastards,' growled Tam, and Luthier could feel his friend driving forward. Luthier held him back.

'Not now. It's not the time,' he said.

The flames from the barrel licked up at the night sky, the fire hissing and giggling as it burned. Aldwyn's charred legs lay prostrate against the wood of the tun. A strong smell of alcohol and burning flesh filled the air.

Maconnock, who had been forced to jump back when the barrel went up, walked forward again. His grim expression looked demonic in the firelight as he spoke.

'Now go from this place and remember your allegiances. Any from Elaris may return in the morning and take a dram of this noble distillation when it's cooled,' he said, while King Annan looked on, his face pale and mouth hanging open.

Luthier's stomach churned.

'Come away now,' he said to Tam, leading him by the arm. 'We must go.' Tam relented and went with him. Seeing them make for the gate, Greta made her way down the steps from the palisade to join them. Phoenix was waiting just under the cover of the trees.

'Is it done?' he asked.

Luthier ducked under the low branches, and the others fell in behind him.

'Aldwyn may be dead, but this is not the last that Mungan Maconnock will hear of us,' Luthier said as they entered the cover of the trees. 'I'll rid The Isles of that man if it's the last thing I do.'

Brookmouth, The Long Isle

Tolucan called upon Feran when they reached Brookmouth, a small port, largely intact, but found him sleeping, in a hammock beside Dun. Tolucan checked on the old man, whose skin was mottled blue, his irises fading as they had in the forest. His breathing was shallow, and he groaned in his sleep.

He took Randolf with him ashore.

'You want to be off that accursed tub as much as I,' Tolucan told him as he tied a rope around the hound's neck.

Lynch, Tolucan and Randolf took to the smaller of the Magpie's two boats, barely able to hold four men, and Lynch rowed them to the jetty. Folk were already gathering there, excited to see a strange vessel in port.

'Best not mention your true name until we get a sense of how things are in this part of the world,' Lynch advised as they approached a two-storey tavern with The Dripping Bucket painted carefully above the door.

The captain turned back as soon as he had planted his boot upon the first step, and Tolucan had to rear back to avoid crashing into him.

'And if you see any woman bearing down on me with death in her eyes and any manner of weapon in her hand, do me a favour and shout up?' he said, with no hint of humour in his voice.

The two men ventured into The Dripping Bucket's dark bar. Tolucan found they were in a large room, dimly lit by hanging lanterns which illuminated swirling smoke. A fire burned in a circular brick pit in the centre of the room, beneath a hole in the roof. All of the long, crude tables were populated by folk of all sorts who sat on shoddily-built benches. The odd one or two were perched on upturned buckets or stools, wherever they could squeeze in.

Lynch tipped his hat to the left and to the right, then removed it and crossed the room to lean on the bar. Tolucan stood beside him, upright with his arms folded across his chest.

'Any brandy?' asked Lynch when the innkeeper approached.

'If you're not choosy,' said the innkeeper.

'Have you seen my wife?' said Lynch, indicating Tolucan with his thumb. Tolucan sighed and looked up at the ceiling.

'Brandy,' said the innkeeper with a perfunctory smile before turning to find a bottle.

'Would you ease up? You look like a sheriff, nosing out a pickpocket or sensing a brawl brewing,' hissed Lynch to Tolucan.

Tolucan let his arms drop, then, not knowing what to do with his hands, crossed his arms again without thinking. Seeing Lynch raise his eyebrows, Tolucan turned to lean on the bar and reached down to scratch behind

Randolf's ear until the dog settled at his feet.

Once Lynch had a drink in his hand, he scoured the room for familiar faces, and when he had found one he moved off to see what he could find out. Tolucan remained at the bar, sipping his drink under the innkeeper's judgemental eye.

He had yet to drain his glass before Lynch returned.

'Finish up,' said the captain.

'Why?'

'Business elsewhere,' said Lynch, who promptly walked out of the bar without a farewell to any within, all jocularity dissipated. Tolucan abandoned his unfinished brandy and followed. Lynch waited outside in the middle of the street.

'Annan had Aldwyn executed,' he whispered, his face flushed. 'Drowned and burned in a barrel of whisky.'

'I am sorry,' said Tolucan, knowing the duke and the captain had been close, but the words came out without feeling, he was so occupied with considering his quest. 'Perhaps I should report to King Annan and the Lord Regent,' he mused.

'No, you idiot,' snapped Lynch, and Tolucan wondered what he had said that was so foolish as he led Randolf back to the boat.

Once aboard, Lynch took Tolucan to his cabin and sent for Feran. When they were all assembled, he made his feelings clear.

'The word is the queen is likely dead,' said Lynch. 'There has been no word of her for years and ships that approach are seen off. The Folly is at war. If we go there, we'll struggle to land and have to fight our way to the Maw Keep. Only other choice is landing elsewhere and travelling through the forest to approach through the Maw, which will take weeks, if not months.'

'Surely if the queen is dead, I should seek an audience with the Lord Regent,' Tolucan said again.

'And aid Mungan Maconnock? That boy is nothing but a hostage,' said Lynch.

'And in great danger,' concluded Feran. 'Lynch is right.'

'Forgive me,' said Tolucan, genuinely confused, 'then to whom do I owe fealty?'

Feran sat back on Lynch's desk, gripping its edge. He sighed and closed his eyes for a moment.

'We owe fealty to Annan if Cathryn is dead, that much is true,' he said, 'but the Maconnocks were bloodthirsty rebels even before the world changed. Lachlan had to put them down by force before the final offensive against Awgren. The Lord of The Isles took Mungan Maconnock with him on that campaign as a hostage in all but title. For my part, I am loyal to Annan, but we must find out if the queen has fallen before we decide what to do next. I will not turn my back on her.'

Tolucan frowned. There was something about the way Feran was speaking.

'*You* will not turn your back on her? You, the wildman of the woods?' asked Tolucan, raising one eyebrow.

Feran did not smile. He strode out of the room.

'Well done,' said Lynch.

Tolucan rubbed his eyes. Was he to invade The Folly alone?

Feran stepped back into the room, and Tolucan saw his cloth-wrapped sword in his hands. His travelling companion laid it on Lynch's desk and untied the bindings. Feran unfolded the cloth to reveal his sword. Tolucan moved up beside him.

'Feran?'

His companion picked up the weapon, testing its weight in his hand.

'He made me promise,' said Feran, and he slipped the blade into the long empty scabbard which hung from his belt. 'He is not long for this world. I cannot deny the old goat forever.'

Tolucan grasped the knight's shoulder, smiling. Feran met his gaze and gave a sad smile.

'Together then?' said Tolucan.

'For a while, at least,' said Feran. 'Captain, could we have a minute alone?'

Lynch straightened up and headed out.

'Oh by all means, kick me out of my own cabin, noble knights,' he muttered as he closed the door behind him.

Tolucan stumbled as the Magpie rolled. He circled the desk and sat in Lynch's chair.

'I do not know where my duty lies,' he said.

Feran adjusted his belt, and, for the first time, Tolucan saw him as a knight, clad all in mail, his duty at the forefront of his mind.

'No more uncertainty,' said Feran. 'Let us sail for Oystercatcher Bay at the southern boundary of the Impassable Forest. I have seen Mount Greenwood from there in years past. From there we can land safely and test the truth of the aspirant's assertion, see for ourselves if Dark Oak's Mother Tree truly does grow where he believes it does. Perhaps destroy it,' said Feran.

Tolucan considered all Feran had said, and it made sense to him, but for one aspect.

'We have, forgive me brother, both lost our squires on the road. We have nobody to carry the word whether it be to Cathryn or Annan,' he said.

'I believe we should take the captain into our confidence, lest we do not return from the Mother Tree. He must get word to Cathryn if she is alive and to Annan if she is not,' said Feran. 'I am torn, I admit. Should we trust the tidings to someone in The Isles?'

'That is not the way of our Order,' said Tolucan. 'That much I understand. If Dark Oak hears of our attempt, of the queen's orders, who knows what he will do.'

'True, but if we die then the knowledge dies with us,' said Feran.

'A difficult choice,' said Tolucan.

Both men fell silent.

'I am decided,' said Tolucan. 'We will do as you suggest and trust the captain. If we fail, the burden will be his to bear. We will find it and burn it.'

'Agreed,' said Feran. He extended a hand, and Tolucan stood to take it.

'Our path is decided then,' said Tolucan. 'Let's drink to it.'

The Magpie remained at Brookmouth long enough for Lynch to secure fresh water, food, and to his amusement, the copious quantities of oil that the knights had requested.

The captain left Wilson in command of the schooner, and his passengers drinking on deck, while he took the opportunity to go ashore and drink in an actual tavern, the patrons hungry for news. He denied the men shore leave, and they were sore about it, he was certain, but he could not risk tongues wagging overmuch. Was he a hypocrite for heading to a tavern himself?

Most surely and certainly, yes, thought Lynch, but it didn't stop him ordering another brandy.

The next morning, the crew of the Magpie waved farewell to the people of Brookmouth, who had gathered to see them off, and the schooner set off for Oystercatcher Bay.

Chapter Twenty-Five

Anbidian

The Naiad moved through the water as if it caused him no impediment, like a knife slicing up a still pond.

Queen Cathryn, her body flooded with adrenaline, managed to stand fully upright before Riark's insubstantial foot touched dry sand.

He bowed his head to her, and his seaweed beard dripped on her bare feet.

She could think of nothing to say, and for a time they held one another in silent regard even as the queen heard Magan, the Deru Weid ranger, approaching at a run.

He came to a stop beside her, struggling for breath.

'Step back please, Naiadlord,' he said, stern, but with respect. Cathyn noted there was a tremor in his voice.

'If you please, lord, step back,' Magan said again.

Riark did as the ranger bade him.

'Well met, Deru Weid,' said Riark, bowing to Magan. 'Queen,' said Riark. 'I come from the depths of the ocean in a guise that, unless memory fails, should be familiar to you. We were not friends in my former life, and yet we reached accord. I would honour it, if others do not.'

'Surely, you are welcome here, Riark,' said Cathryn. 'I have long thought you dead.'

The Naiad before her smiled.

'I am a long time dead, and yet I endure,' said Riark. 'Born a man, born a woman, born to the forest and, finally, born to the seas.'

Cathryn caught a movement on the periphery of her vision. She turned to see that Magan had dropped to one knee and was looking up at the Naiad with a reverence she had not noted in the ranger's interactions with her. Annoyance flared up, reddening her cheeks and yet, without giving it consideration, she too dropped to one knee before Riark.

'I have drifted shapeless and formless in the deeps and lapped against every shore since my Mother Tree died, learning of the ocean and her mercurial ways, listening to her laugh and rage and play. I felt no need to walk upon the earth and yet tidings have reached me that compel me to act once more, but this time in defence of humanity, for my mistake cost her dearly.'

'Will you come to our halls at Hengefast, lord,' asked Magan. 'Red Maple of the Dryads sleeps there amidst the henge itself.'

Riark nodded to the ranger, but fixed his blue marble eyes on Cathryn.

'There is much to discuss,' said Riark. 'I will meet you at the henge.'

The Naiad's body fell away in a shower of seawater. The ocean caressed Anbidian as though Riark had never been there at all.

Cathryn leant upon Magan all the way back to Hengefast, her feet scuffing the ground, sweat beading on her brow and her wound radiating pain as she walked.

Each obstacle, even the smallest step, required a pause, steadying of the nerve and a concerted effort to traverse.

They drew close to Hengefast, and Cathryn paused to catch her breath once they had crested the final ridge, her hands balled on her hips.

Then she saw she was in trouble.

Brace yourself, thought Cathryn.

Ailsa bore down on her from the centre of the settlement. Cathryn could not help but smile, her heart fluttering as the younger woman approached with her jaw set, teeth clenched and her face fixed in a frown. Flanked by members of Cathryn's guard, Ailsa's booted feet pounded towards the queen.

She is magnificent, thought Cathryn.

'You've been gone hours. I was worried sick. You are in . . . ' started Ailsa in a tone she would never have dared to use in public just a few weeks ago.

Cathryn held up her hand before Ailsa's remonstrations could become a tirade.

'I know. I am sorry to have worried you, but Magan has kept me in one piece,' said Cathryn.

She took Ailsa gently by the shoulders and when the younger woman lowered her head, Cathryn planted a full kiss upon her brow. She savoured the woman's sweet, familiar scent. Cathryn instantly felt she was home whenever and wherever she smelt it.

'I am weary, but there is urgent business,' said Cathryn, looking at the short distance between her and the henge and thinking she could not face another step. She sighed and, with a glance at Magan, understanding passing between them, she eased herself to sit in the grass beside the stream with his assistance.

She looked up at Ailsa.

'Please go to the henge with Magan. He will explain what has happened. Wake Red Maple, and please pass on my apologies to Riark. Tell him I can walk no farther. If they would both meet me here, I would be grateful,' said Cathryn, and saw Ailsa reeling.

'Riark? He's not dead?' said Ailsa, eyes wide.

'No, but . . . well, you will see for yourself,' said Cathryn. 'Please extend him every courtesy. And if you could have some food and water brought to me, I would appreciate it. I am not feeling at all myself.'

Ailsa crouched down beside her.

'Perhaps I should help you back to your lodge?' she said, but Cathryn shook her head.

'I will need to sleep, but I must give Riark an audience before I do. His news may be of the highest importance,' said Cathryn. She lay back on the grass and closed her eyes, heedless of the guards. 'I may just take a moment . . .'

Ailsa stood and sighed, meeting Magan's gaze, who met her concerned expression with sympathy on his face.

'Wait with the queen,' Ailsa said in a hushed tone to the guards.

'A little way off, if you please,' said Cathryn. 'I would not have you hear me snore if I drift off. That is a king's privilege.' She smiled.

Nothing.

Then, awareness of the absence of thought.

Thought.

Red Maple came to his senses upon the stone table, his body resembling that of his Mother Tree, his legs part of the trunk, his toes gone to roots and his arms just two of many branches. Leaves hung all around.

'Dryadlord,' said Magan again, a little louder.

Red Maple concentrated, and with a single shake, he shed his bark and every red leaf fell, floating down to carpet the grass between the standing stones. His body diminished as he reversed the growth until he stood in human avatar, the carved image of the man he had hoped to become had Dark Oak not murdered and changed him, standing in the centre of the stone table. He yawned, a mouth appearing on his face for him to cover with the back of his hand.

'You have been missed,' said a rolling voice; the depths of the sea. 'Your people have been searching.'

Red Maple looked up and saw a Naiad standing before him, flanked by Ailsa and Magan. He recognised Riark immediately, despite his new form. Riark bowed his head, the foam of his hair hanging down before him.

Red Maple tilted his head and stepped from the edge of the stone table, his feet thumping into the ground below. Before him stood the being that had intervened when Morrick attempted suicide before reincarnating him as Dark Oak. Red Maple had watched as his father and sister burned Riark's Mother Tree, but here he stood before him. His soul, it seemed, reincarnated.

Red Maple stood silently, staring at Riark, who regarded the Dryad with a steady gaze. Neither moved.

'Lords,' said Magan, as the people of Hengefast gathered on the outside of the henge.

Red Maple turned his head to look at the Deru Weid.

'Queen Cathryn awaits you on the stream bank, yonder,' said Magan.

Red Maple returned his gaze to the Naiad.

He knew he should feel something towards Riark. He remembered how he *should* feel, but his experience of the emotion was muted. The flattened affect left him conflicted, knowing that in days past, before the forest had begun to calm him, he would have been angry at this creature. Surprised to see him. Not so now. The entire experience seemed somehow academic to him. Riark was a Naiad. All that had happened could not be changed. The moment was the moment.

'You have many questions,' said Riark. 'Rightly so.'

Red Maple began to speak, but the Naiad held up his hand.

'Much has changed since you last saw your father. Dark Oak has been deposed, the forests reclaimed,' said Riark.

Father, thought Red Maple. Dark Oak. Again, not the rush of concern he might have expected, but there was lingering loyalty. What had happened to him?

Red Maple strode from the circle, the people of Hengefast parting to let him through.

'What's he doing?' he heard Ailsa ask.

'I think . . . ' said Magan, but the words trailed off as Red Maple approached a silver birch.

He laid his hand upon the trunk and as his fingers merged with the tree, the Dryad bowed his head, his features smoothing so that his face disappeared. He became one with the forest and absorbed the knowledge of his kind throughout the world. He felt the change immediately; the calm which now permeated their realm. The peace and the acceptance was a sweet relief.

He could sense his father's Mother Tree, but Dark Oak had not been within the forest for a long time. He had last been seen in the Hinterland when Nayr deposed him.

Those of Dark Oak's newborns who had been found and recalled to the forest were content, becoming as they should always have been. Most of them. There were still a few abroad, but Nayr's people were working to bring them home.

Red Maple could feel his own desires and emotions calming as he realised the Queen of the Dryads had ended his mother's torment. Even now, she sailed towards the Old Continent with Whiteflow and Seaborn at her side, travelling to sit on the First Council.

Welcome home.

He heard Nayr's wordless greeting and realised the Queen of the Dryads was right. He was home.

But you cannot stay, she told him, *for you have tasks to complete before you can rest. You must speak to the last dissenters. Your thoughts carry weight.*

Red Maple lifted his head, looked back at Riark and nodded once. He stepped inside the birch tree and disappeared just as Nayr stepped out in human avatar. Her bark fell away and a gown of leaves fell to her ankles as her crown formed upon her brow.

She made for the centre of the circle and her reunion with Riark.

This place, the warm air, the blue seas, the woods and the mountains beyond. I have never seen the like, thought Cathryn, relishing the sun on her skin while she paddled her feet in the stream, watching rabbits chase one another on the other bank. The Isles were beautiful, but cold, rainy and rugged, whereas this felt like . . .

What an afterlife should be, she realised. She sighed a deep, contented sigh and finished the last morsel of food that had been brought down to her. She heard people approaching from Hengefast and looked up the slope to see Ailsa and Magan walking beside a female Dryad. Cathryn thought her beautiful and admired her dress, its leaves of many shapes and colours. When the queen saw Nayr's crown, she pondered the meaning of it and knew she should stand, but could not find the strength.

And why bother? The Dryads and Naiads care nothing of human

ceremony, she decided. She smiled and looked down at her feet, splashing in the stream.

If Lachlan could see me now . . .

At any rate, Ailsa and Magan do not seem troubled, Cathryn realised. She drew from her wineskin while she still had the opportunity.

Cathryn started then laughed as Riark's head appeared from the water. The Naiad drew himself up from the water, and a fish jumped clear of his chest as he sat cross-legged, as one with the current.

'Your Majesty, may I present Nayr, Queen of the Dryads. She brings tidings that Dark Oak has been deposed,' announced Ailsa from a short distance away. Cathryn had barely had a chance to react before Nayr leapt across the stream and took up the same position as Cathryn, mirroring her across the brook.

'Queen Cathryn,' said the Dryad, and she bowed her head.

'I . . . I find myself about to bid you welcome, Queen Nayr, and that surprises me given all that has transpired between our peoples. Perhaps it should give me hope,' said Cathryn.

'Hope indeed,' said Ailsa quietly, as she and Magan came to stand behind her.

'I do not know hope as you do,' said Nayr, 'but there have been many wrongs on both sides, and I seek to right them. Dark Oak should never have been made,' the Dryad's eyes fell on Riark, who did not react, 'should never have been allowed to subjugate your kind as he did. He exploited our passive natures. Overwhelmed us with his grief. He too was wronged, denied his natural progression through the Cycle. He no longer speaks for the forest and though I cannot unmake him, all of the world's peoples must come together to forge a new future.'

Cathryn looked between Nayr and Riark, her smile turning into a little laugh.

'Forgive me, but there could be no gladder tidings,' she said. She felt herself about to cry, she was so overcome with emotion, but swallowed, took a breath and composed herself.

She found herself unable to hate the Dryad who sat before her and unwilling to list the many hurts inflicted upon her people, her personal losses and grievances. The prospect of living free of suppression so heartened her that she was at a loss where to begin; a feeling quite alien to the woman who had ruled the Combined People for so many years, who had thousands upon thousands under command not six years before. Cathryn poked her toe from under the water.

'I don't know where to begin, Nayr,' she said, finally looking up. 'Perhaps you would tell me of how it has come to this?'

Between them, Riark and Nayr told Cathryn of all that had happened since her last meeting with Riark in The Folly years before, when her only concern was taking wayward Lord Linwood in hand. *All of this over one man building a road through the forest,* she thought.

Riark told of his desire for Morrick to act as an advisor when dealing with Linwood and of his decision to save the woodcutter from death when he tried to end his life. He told of how he had created Dark Oak, hoping to benefit from the woodcutter's human insight, then left him to deal with Lord Linwood, who was burning the Impassable Forest. He told her of how he had felt his Mother Tree burn and his first moments as a Naiad, born in the ocean to the east of the Old Continent.

Nayr picked up the tale, explaining how Dark Oak had denied himself communion with the forest, instead taking the heat of his sorrow, jealousy and fury to overpower the Dryads, burning Riark's Mother Tree and manipulating not only her people, but the First Council itself, until the Naiads, Dryads, Oreads and Sylphs decided to follow Dark Oak in his attempt to diminish humanity for the sake of the world.

Cathryn beckoned Magan and Ailsa forward, asking them to sit beside her while they listened.

The Queen of the Dryads told of her own return to her true nature as the years passed, the growing dissent with the forest, Dark Oak's absence and of the First Council's decision to replace Dark Oak as the voice of the forest.

'I stood forward and now speak for not only my people, but the First Council in this matter. Dark Oak has left the forest and his followers are gradually being brought home,' she said.

'So he still lives,' said Cathryn quietly, troubled by memories of his white eyes and his twisting mane of black ivy.

'He does,' said Nayr, 'but even Dark Oak's resolve was gradually weakening. He knows he cannot enter and contest the forest now that the Dryads have come to see him for what he is, one who should not have been among us for many lives. He may not have been a bad person in his last life, but he was not ready to be one of our kind. His anguish was the world's undoing.'

'I made a grave mistake,' said Riark. 'I was naive and had forgotten more of the dangers of human emotions than I realised.'

'Naive still, I fear,' said Cathryn. She sat back, sitting cross-legged on the bank, feeling more like the Cathryn of old. 'You say he has disappeared from the view of the forests, the rivers and the seas. Where then has he gone? What is he doing? You said his resolve was weakening, but did he seem as though he had given up his cause?'

Nayr said nothing.

'Cannot the Oreads or the Sylphs find him? Where was he last seen?' Cathryn demanded.

'He was seen in the Hinterland, crossing the Whiteflow, heading east,' said Riark. 'That was the last my people saw of him.'

'Towards The Wastes,' blurted Ailsa. Cathryn turned to look at her aide, who began to apologise, but Cathryn shook her head, coming to the same conclusion as Ailsa. The thought filled her with dread.

'He has disappeared into the Dark Lord's domain,' she said, barely louder than a whisper.

All sat silent for a moment.

'The Oreads? The Sylphs?' asked Cathryn, remembering her question.

'I had thought Dark Oak defeated,' said Nayr. 'My people watch for him, but I had not asked the others.'

'I can see how the Dryads were so easily overcome by the force of the woodcutter's emotion if you so readily accept what you are told. He is not like you, Nayr, or you, Riark. Have you not learnt? If he has not abandoned his purpose, he will be seeking a way to wrest back his power,' said Cathryn, suddenly remembering her old sense of superiority. These creatures were so wise and powerful, yet she saw clearer than any of them. She had taken precautions years ago.

Riark and Nayr stared at one another in silence, and in that moment, Queen Cathryn remembered those she had dispatched years before and given up on not so long after.

'If only the Silent Knights had found his Mother Tree and had the means to destroy it. I fear our troubles with Dark Oak are only just beginning,' said Cathryn.

'The Silent Knights?' asked Ailsa.

'An order of knights I tasked with finding and destroying Dark Oak's Mother Tree. They were to tell nobody of their quest, lest the forest become aware of it,' said Cathryn, looking at Nayr as she said it.

She lowered her gaze, wondering what had happened to each of the knights, overcome with guilt that she could not remember all of their names, all of their faces, those she had condemned to a hopeless quest. They never had a chance, she knew now, while she had been so certain that decisive action was needed as she schemed in the cabin of her flagship out on the waters of Strewn Men Bay. She had been so determined to hold the Combined People together, she had rejected Aldwyn and wasted her knights' lives. All for nothing. She had failed.

'It is well that they did not succeed,' said Riark, and Nayr looked at him sharply.

'I will not tell all, for it is not my place,' he continued, placating the Dryad, it seemed to Cathryn, 'but suffice to say that if his Mother Tree had died, he would have been reincarnated as one such as I; a Naiad, an Oread or a Sylph. He would have become truly immortal, with no such weakness as a Mother Tree.'

'I did not know he would be reincarnated,' said Cathryn, horrified. 'I could not have foreseen it. I sought only to protect my people.'

'That has long been the world's greatest threat, those who seek only to protect their own kind,' said Nayr, once more looking at Riark.

'Will we never be free of Dark Oak then, if killing him will only make him invincible?' said Cathryn. 'Would he not dominate the Oreads, the Naiads or the Sylphs, turning them against us once more?'

'He might become invincible and immortal, but he would have no influence,' said Riark. 'I knew immediately how different the waters of the world are to the forest. Naiads far outnumber the Dryads, and we are not as passive by nature. Trees will stand for a lifetime, and a Dryad might sleep within, but the Naiads are as mercurial, changeable, ever moving and unforgiving as the seas. We may abandon our unfinished business from our past lives in time, as do Dryads, but we are not as passive or as crushed by the weight of acceptance that one experiences in the forest. Whiteflow is an abomination like him, reincarnated immortal before her time, with the same desire for vengeance, but she has little influence over our kind. One insistent voice can be drowned out by the crashing of the waves, and we do not fear the loss of our realm as do Dryads. Neither do the Oreads with the relentless strength and endurance of the mountains or the Sylphs, so ethereal is their nature. Dark Oak would have been reincarnated with an angry voice in a world full of kin who tolerated and ignored him until he eventually lost all interest as his true nature took hold.'

'Then there is no danger?' asked Nayr, her Dryad nature blinding her to the need for power and influence, her forgetfulness and placidity already putting her at a disadvantage.

'Do not forget what the human queen told us, Nayr,' said Riark. 'If Dark Oak has not given up his cause, even now he may be seeking a way to gain power. He cannot be one with the forest, he knows that, but he can fight on its behalf, sacrificing his own peace to do so. If his Mother Tree is killed, he will live forever, unkillable, without influence among his people, but no less able to seek other ways to gain power.'

'He will not stop at suppressing humanity,' said Cathryn. 'He will need to bring down those who stand in his way.'

'He cannot overwhelm us again,' said Nayr, her wooden face creaking into a frown.

'But he may have travelled to Awgren's lands,' cried Cathryn. 'Who knows what dark magic he might learn there?'

She grasped Magan's shoulder as he sat beside her.

'The Deru Weid tell tales that Awgren was a Dryad who disappeared in the country The Wastes now cover, is it not so?' said the queen.

'It is so,' said Magan. 'Queen Cathryn has the right of it, Naiadlord, Dryadqueen. The threat from Dark Oak is as great as ever. He must be found.'

Once more the summit fell silent, and a bird singing interrupted Cathryn's thoughts, reminding her she was no longer queen of a united people, with armies at her command, seated in a strong, high place.

'I will put it to the First Council,' said Nayr. 'They were right to offer the humans a seat beside them.'

'I will make the case myself, if you wish it,' said Queen Cathryn, but Nayr shook her head.

'I am here because Red Maple told me Riark was here, and I wished to be reacquainted,' said the Queen of the Dryads. 'I have stayed out of courtesy to one who formerly ruled this continent and the islands to the west, but it will not be you who sits on the First Council. I did not intend to mislead you, Queen. I will speak with all who lead in the days, weeks and months to come, but I deem you do not rule beyond Anbidian.'

Cathryn fell silent, her cheeks growing red, embarrassed rather than angry.

'Has nothing I said to you been of value then?' she asked.

'It has been of great importance,' said Riark, and Nayr nodded before speaking,

'And you will be represented, do not doubt it. I have chosen a woman who does not seek power in her own right and has no title from the days of the Combined People. The woodcutter's wife will not only represent you, hearing your opinions and communicating them, but provide insight into Dark Oak's nature as well as acting as a barrier to him returning to the forest, for she is his greatest weakness,' concluded the Naiad.

Cathryn laughed.

'We are to be represented by a woodcutter's wife,' said Cathryn, but nobody else was smiling.

'Very well,' she said. 'I will be content if we can make Anbidian a haven for my people hereabouts; a strong place to withstand Dark Oak, for he will move against us, I do not doubt it.'

'And we will aid you,' said Riark. 'We will all watch over one another from now on.'

'The First Council will help you to rebuild,' said Nayr, 'as long as you do so with respect for our domains.'

Cathryn struggled to get to her feet, succeeding only when Ailsa and Magan lifted her by the arms.

She stepped down into the stream and stood before Nayr.

'Allies?' she said, offering her hand.

'Allies,' said Nayr, and she took it.

Cathryn stepped back up onto the bank, struggling to breathe as she did so.

'I fear our summit must draw to a close, my friends,' she said. 'My health is failing for all to see, so I see no point in either denying or trying to hide it.' She smiled, her eyes bright with a mischievous twinkle.

'I will send word when the woodcutter's wife has reached the Old Continent,' said Nayr.

'Perhaps then we can discuss just how Dark Oak's wife will represent our needs here,' said Cathryn.

'I will dwell for a while in the waters surrounding Anbidian, Queen,' said Riark. 'Call for me when I am needed.'

'Farewell, Riark,' said Cathryn, bowing her head to him. The Naiad, still sitting in the stream, lay back and disappeared into it, flowing down over the stones to the sea.

'Will Red Maple return?' asked Cathryn, as Nayr walked slowly towards a young willow which overhung the stream a little way up the slope.

'If he desires it,' said Nayr, 'and I will send someone else in his stead if he does not. It will not be a hardship, for my people have a great respect for the Deru Weid. Farewell, Queen.'

'Farewell,' said Cathryn.

Nayr pressed her hand to the tree, merging with the wood and then suddenly withdrew it.

'I have been remiss. I have news which concerns you,' she said.

'Concerning what? You have already told me much,' smiled Cathryn.

'I do not think I am the one to deliver it,' said Nayr, 'and it can wait until you have rested. Return to this tree when you are ready, and I will send one who can explain better to wait for you within. He will bring word from The Isles and The Folly.'

Without waiting for an answer, Nayr bowed her head and stepped into the willow, disappearing from Cathryn's view.

Cathryn was grateful that neither Ailsa or Magan attempted conversation while they helped her back home. She worried what she might hear of her heirs and of Aldwyn's rule in The Isles.

Safe within her lodge, she slipped beneath her blankets and fell into a deep sleep that yielded no memory of dreams upon waking.

When she finally did open her eyes, she had no notion of how long she had slept.

For a time she lay on her side, looking at the crack of daylight beneath the door and then, in an instant, she became aware of a presence beside her.

'Ailsa?' asked Cathryn, but her throat was dry and her voice came out as a croak. She licked her lips, swallowed some saliva and tried again.

'Ailsa.' This time the word sounded clear, but there was no response.

Cathryn sighed, flung back her blanket and began the torturous effort of rolling over.

'Be still,' said a man's voice, as though echoing from the past.

Cathryn froze, her waking dullness gone in a second. Her body tensed, expecting to feel the imminent needling of a knifepoint.

Magregar?

But fingers brushed the downy hair on the nape of her neck. A touch and gesture both familiar and yet impossible.

She rolled to face the other occupant of the bed, crying out as she did, pain running throughout her body.

The other side of the bed was empty. Cathryn patted down the furs and stroked up and down as though searching for a hidden body underneath. Then it occurred to her that whoever it was might be beneath the bed. She groped beneath her pillow for her knife and drew it forth, ready to fight and die if need be.

'Who goes there? Show yourself!' she demanded, getting to her knees so that at least she could dive forward to attack or sideways to evade. The effort left her sweating and gasping as she looked frantically from shadow to shadow.

Do the guards not hear?

'Cathryn, be at peace,' said the voice softly, chiding, wryly amused. And she knew him at once. It was a placating tone she had heard many times in the privacy of their night meetings in his candlelit room, where others might not hear him address his queen in such a manner.

'Aldwyn,' she whispered, unconsciously lowering the dagger, and yet not quite fully, for she still could not see him.

She flinched at the softest of unseen touches upon the thumb steadying the knife, felt non-corporeal fingers encase her hand and firmly lower it for her.

Cathryn said nothing, her mind racing, but her body still, waiting.

'Aldwyn,' she said again, not comprehending what this could all mean, but it was as though she had a weight upon her chest, crushing her, for her mind was slower than her heart.

She felt hands cupping her face then caressing the line of her jaw ever fainter until the touch became imperceptible just before the unseen fingertips reached her chin.

A breeze upon her lips, and he was gone. The accustomed absence was restored.

Cathryn breathed fast and heavy, still upon her knees, sitting back on her calves. She dropped the knife on to the bunched furs and began to weep, every sob racking her body with pain, her wounds issuing nascent warnings.

When she called, the guards *did* hear, and she asked them to gather all the folk of Anbidian at the henge.

A while later, Ailsa came to tell the queen that the gathering was awaiting her presence. Cathryn emerged from her lodge, leaning heavily on her spear, with Ailsa at her side; the younger woman close enough to seize her if she should stumble.

They approached the henge itself, where the people of Anbidian were gathered around the altar at the centre. The rangers of the Deru Weid were not in evidence, save for Magan, who stood with the elders of his kind as close to the altar as they could.

All turned to watch the queen approach, and Cathryn steeled herself, forcing her back to straighten, the effort barely perceptible on her face, though she knew if Ailsa had seen it, her aide would have frowned and hastened the gathering to end it all the sooner. But Ailsa, walking beside her, could not see, and Queen Cathryn stopped before the crowd.

'Here on the Isle of Anbidian, we have found a haven,' she began, 'hosted by the gracious Deru Weid, of course.' Cathryn bowed to the elders, who returned the gesture of acknowledgement. Cathryn continued,

'This place is to be the spring from which all future civilisation will flow, and yet humanity is still under threat. I have held counsel today with both the new Queen of the Dryads and the Naiad whom I once knew as the King of the Dryads. I have good tidings,' she said.

She intended to allow a pause for dramatic effect, but a cough ruined it so she continued.

'Dark Oak has been overthrown!' she said as loudly she could manage.

A cheer went up from all assembled, and she allowed them a moment of joy before tainting it.

'Yes, we have much to be grateful for today. A safe home. Generous hosts. And now humanity will work with the Dryads, the Oreads, the Naiads and the Sylphs to walk into the future together. But Dark Oak is not dead,' she said, her tone grave.

Cathryn felt her legs beginning to shake, and she clutched at her spear, knuckles whitening. She felt Ailsa's hand in the small of her back, and instead of stepping away or shrugging her off, Cathryn accepted the support.

'It will not be long before Dark Oak will move against us, for his malice has not diminished. We will prepare to meet his forces, but this time with the support of our new allies,' she said. 'With the blessing of the forests, the rivers and the seas, the winds that blow, the mountains which tower above us and the ground below,' said Cathryn, pausing to survey the faces of the hushed crowd.

She stood as straight as she could manage and addressed them all.

'All here assembled have shown great loyalty and courage, for which I will always be grateful. You have followed me, though so many others have long abandoned any desire to follow a queen or have even turned against me. Indeed, they may have laid me low,' said Cathryn.

She paused for a second then turned to Ailsa, meeting her gaze.

'It has taken many years for me to realise that the old world is gone forever. What is to follow will be unlike anything in the history of the world, with humanity and the older races living in communion. Nations are a thing of the past, perhaps. Maybe very soon, crowns too will be melted down and put to better use.'

She turned back to the crowd.

'I issue no commands, for what am I, but an ageing woman empowered by a collective memory? But I ask you all to consider, shall we stand together and make Anbidian a place of unity and rebirth? Or do we scatter to the four winds? I, for one, will stay,' Cathryn intoned, 'but I am no longer strong enough to lead, nor does my blood count for much. I will stand with you, beside you and learn your names, if you will have me. But others must lead in the days to come. I recommend my aide, Ailsa, to you. She is fierce and loyal, strong and quick-witted. I relied on her long before I needed her help to walk. It is she who led you here, not I. She would lead you well, but ultimately, you must all decide for yourselves. And now I must rest before my body fails.'

Cathryn's shoulders sagged, and she turned back towards the stream.

When Ailsa, still reeling from Cathryn's words, moved to assist, Cathryn told her no and bade her stay.

Cathryn left her people to decide amongst themselves.

Alone, Cathryn shuffled down the path beside the stream to the willow.

She stood panting, leaning on her spear, and rested a hand upon the tree trunk.

'I am here,' she said.

Nothing.

'Nayr? Red Maple?' said Cathryn.

The breeze rustled the willow's leaves.

Struggling to breathe, and unable to stand any longer, Cathryn sat down with her back to the tree and dangled her feet in the cool water of the stream. She laid her head back against the wood and closed her eyes, listening to the gentle movement of the water, the wind in the trees and the birds singing all around. She thought she could make out the crashing of the ocean.

Perhaps she fell asleep, she wasn't sure, but the voice startled her.

'Your Majesty,' he said, and she knew him.

Lord Hawthorn stepped down into the stream before her, and he dropped to one knee, bowing his head as he did so. Tears filled Cathryn's eyes as she looked upon him, tired as she was. The Dryad was the very image of Lachlan, with a carved jerkin over wooden mail, a circlet upon his brow. When last she had seen him, he had been one with his throne at The Folly, his beard touching the floor, but now he looked as he had when he was a man. A full beard, but trimmed. He looked strong again.

'Your Majesty,' he repeated. 'Nayr has granted me leave to see you.'

She wiped her eyes with the back of her hand and grinned at him.

'I have missed you so,' she said, reaching out her hand, and he stood to take it.

'You were ever the queen of my heart in life, but I was not strong enough to withstand Dark Oak, and I sat idly by as our realm crumbled,' he said, his voice as gravelly as it was when he was Lachlan. 'That I can forgive myself, or indeed, that I see no need for forgiveness, tells me that I am dead. No longer the man who was your husband.'

'Not dead,' whispered Cathryn, moving her hand to her heart. She released the Dryad's hand and rested her head back against the tree, closing her eyes, her breath shallow. 'You stand here before me.'

The queen smiled.

'Aye,' said Lord Hawthorn, 'but I cannot stay over-long, for I am but lately returned to the forest, and to it I must return. Nayr met with your lord, who sits at Halflight Hold. I cannot recall his name, but you know him well? A friend since childhood?'

Cathryn did not respond.

'Your Majesty?' said Lord Hawthorn. He stepped closer and placed a hand on her knee.

Cathryn did not react.

The Dryad stepped up onto the bank and caressed the queen's cheek with his smooth fingers.

She stirred no more.

'The queen is dead,' said the Dryad that had been Lachlan in a flat voice. 'Long live the king.'

He stood, bowed his head and disappeared into the trunk of the tree.

Cathryn, just Cathryn, lay in the shade of the willow tree, little fish dancing around her feet amid the cool waters of the stream.

Chapter Twenty-Six

An easterly wind spirited the Magpie quietly away from The Isles, her canvas spread and her crew working steadily. The schooner made fine progress. All aboard were glad to be away from what the crew termed 'that unpleasant piece of business' in The Isles. Tolucan felt it clear that Captain Lynch was attempting to distract himself from the loss of his former commander. He seemed utterly enthralled by the wind and the weather, on directing the crew in maintaining the ship, but the knight suspected that the captain was unable to stop the image of a burning barrel intruding into his waking thoughts and night-time dreams.

Tolucan, on the other hand, only really knew Aldwyn by reputation as an explorer and a general, so the loss was not as personal to him as it was to the Magpie's crew. He avoided their sombre attitude whenever he could. It was sad, yes, but he had to focus on his task.

He could find little to occupy himself at sea, having no interest in learning seamanship or 'skylarking' as Lynch referred to it. He kept himself to himself, either watching the schools of Naiads, or he sat wrapped up out of the way to listen when the crew eventually began to sing and play their instruments once more. At those times, it was difficult not to think of happier times and to yearn to be with his family once more.

One night when all were either sleeping or up on deck, working and skylarking, Tolucan shared a bottle of brandy, which the captain claimed had come from a Folly trader in the early days of Dark Oak's reign. The knight suspected looting or piracy.

Both men well in their cups, Tolucan finished off another glass.

'We should get Feran up here,' said Lynch.

'He won't come, and you know it,' said Tolucan.

'There's quite a bond between those two, sure enough,' said Lynch. 'More like father and son than knight and squire.'

Tolucan stifled a belch and pointed an unsteady finger at the captain.

'You're right on that score. There's more to it, for sure. To begin with I thought the old man ridiculous and that Feran merely tolerated him, but it's more than that,' said Tolucan.

'What's his story? Looks more like a Deru Weid priest from the old tales than a knight. Why was he carrying his sword around in a rag?' asked Lynch.

'I don't know!' said Tolucan, frowning. 'They won't say!'

He stood, unsteady on his feet, and beckoned for the bottle.

'Here, give me that. I'll get it out of him. He needs some clean air,' said Tolucan, and the captain handed over the brandy.

Tolucan found Feran sitting on a stool beside Dun's hammock, visible by the light of a swinging lantern, his hands on his knees and his head bowed.

Voices raised in song floated down from the weather deck, and Tolucan tripped as he made his way to his friend.

Feran looked up at him, and Tolucan offered the bottle. Even in the dim light, he saw the sorrow and anger on his companion's face.

Fearing the worst, Tolucan reached the hammock.

Dun lay within, still and quiet. No rasping breath. No coughing.

Tolucan reached forward to touch his skin, but Feran grabbed his wrist.

'No man touches him,' Feran whispered.

Tolucan drew back, instantly feeling more sober.

'Feran, I . . . ' he started, but Feran stood, staring him down.

'Leave us,' he said, and Tolucan did as he was told.

He drank no more, but stayed on deck, mourning the old man's passing in his own way and worrying for Feran while he stood at the rail and waited for dawn.

When morning came, Tolucan heard Feran calling his name. The knight yawned and, blinking to stay awake, he went below.

'Will you help me take him down?' asked Feran, his eyes red from weeping.

Together and in silence, the knights unslung the hammock and lowered it until Dun lay upon the floor. Tolucan stepped back as Feran knelt beside his fallen squire as if in prayer, and then leant down to kiss the dead man's forehead. Then, ever so carefully, Feran folded the material of the hammock over him. Tolucan helped Feran carry Dun's wrapped body up on deck.

Tolucan watched Feran weigh down the hammock. His friend had insisted on sewing Dun into it, even the traditional last stitch through the nose to ensure the man was dead. Tolucan approached once, thinking of helping to hold the material, but a hard glare sent him turned about. He maintained a safe distance from then on. Feran made no objection, however, when Randolf slunk over, sniffing at the hammock. The hound began to whine and lay down beside Dun's body.

Eventually, when all was ready, the crew prepared for a funeral. The Naiads circled the Magpie like sharks, just visible under the water. Two of the crew placed a wooden board on the deck and Feran allowed Tolucan to help him lay Dun upon it. They carried the board to the ship's side, and as they set it in place, four Naiads' upper bodies rose from the water as they circled, their eyes fixed on the leading edge of the board.

Tolucan stood on one side of Dun, his heart heavy, watching Feran, who seemed utterly emotionless, the skin of his face taut.

'Will you say anything?' asked Captain Lynch.

Feran lowered his head and stepped back.

'Very well then,' said Lynch. 'We give him up to the sea. Send him down.'

The two sailors began to tip up the board, but suddenly Feran darted forward and pushed it down.

Tolucan clasped his hands before him and waited.

'This man died a squire, but he was much more,' said Feran. 'Dun could have been a knight. He *should* have been a knight. We both came from noble families. He schooled me at arms when I was a child, and he a squire. His family had fallen from the king's favour, though, and while he remained a squire, it was I who was anointed. Against my objections, he insisted on becoming *my* squire when his master fell in battle.'

Tolucan heard Randolf beginning to whine. Feran continued.

'I am both proud and ashamed to say that Dun was my squire. He was by my side for many years, riding out on sorties and eventually taking part in the final strike against Awgren. We were there, fighting side by side, upon the Field of Scarlet Grass when the Dark Lord fell. He saved my life many times, and I his.' Tolucan scratched behind Randolf's ear as the dog's whining momentarily turned to a mournful howl. Feran's voice began to break, but he took a breath and continued.

'I turned my back on my sacred duty and tried to dismiss him from my service, but he chose never to abandon me, even as I scolded and berated him. Many years he has trailed after me, wearing my armour and carrying my sword, as I made my own way in the world, fighting a battle of a different kind. Never has anyone had such a belief in duty, both that of a squire and of a knight. No man I have met has been as dedicated to truth, honour and justice. He taught me what it meant to be a knight. And I failed him. I only took up my sword and donned my armour again when he could no longer carry the burden he bore for me, year in and year out. He died on the quest. He died my squire. And he died a better man than any here today, including me. I am a knight once more, but only because of the stubbornness of the old man who lies here before you. If I regain my honour, it will be because I feel his eyes upon me from the next life. Goodbye, Dun, a knight in all but title,' he said, but the last few words were barely audible through his rising sobs.

Feran moved to the head of the board and, seizing it by both corners, he tipped it up and, slowly at first, Dun's body, encased in the hammock, slid down. The old man's body toppled and fell between the waiting Naiads.

They reached for him, grasping the hammock with insubstantial hands then dived, taking Dun below. The sea swallowed him.

Feran cried out in horror and began to clamber over the side, but Lynch and Tolucan ran to haul him back.

'They've taken him down,' said Lynch. 'It's an honour.'

Feran said nothing, grasping the rail and staring down into the water.

'I had no idea that . . . ' said Tolucan, moving to Feran's side, but the other man turned his back and went below decks to find solitude.

Tolucan stared down into the water, waiting for the Naiads to surface.

After a few seconds, Tolucan saw something rising up.

Dun's hammock floated to the surface, its stitches broken.

Tolucan straightened up, frowning.

What did this portend?

He watched the water for some time, but the Naiads did not return until later in the day.

Chapter Twenty-Seven

The Impassable Forest, North of Oystercatcher Bay

How long since we landed and how long have I been walking?

Rowan had lived beside the Impassable Forest her entire life until the Devised drove her away. It had sheltered her family as she fled her home, the home Morrick had built for her with timber felled from the Impassable Forest.

It has taken the husband I rejected for its own and he, Callum, before the forest also turned its back on him, she thought, watching Whiteflow's shimmering form slink ahead of her through the trees.

The forest permeated her life, and yet here, in these unfamiliar tracts, she felt a stranger to it.

And now it is to be our home?

Her party moved in a procession towards the First Tree, the Dryad who led them on had told her, so that she could be presented before the First Council and they would teach her all that she needed to know. Another followed at the rear. Rowan and Seaborn walked together, as it seemed to her that her son would not be parted from her. If anything, Seaborn seemed younger than he had as a human boy. Not Whiteflow. The Naiad had been a sullen companion on the sea voyage, often standing at the prow, watching the crashing waves.

That evening, the Dryads halted beside a river, and there they set about making camp for Rowan. She watched, as fascinated as she was every night, while one Dryad picked up a fallen branch and, merging with it for a few moments, he shaped it into a chair for Rowan to sit upon. He set it down, and Rowan took her seat just as the Dryad placed a rough table before her, three-legged and entirely covered in bark. The other Dryad, a female, Rowan had realised, picked up another piece of wood, and it grew into the shape of a simple bed frame. The bark split in places and long green shoots sprang out, arced up and curled themselves around the other side of the frame until a soft green weave hung between the wood for Rowan to sleep upon. The Dryads went in search of food for their human charge.

Whiteflow stood on the rocks looking into the stream while Seaborn played at her feet, fashioning a puddle with one hand and turning the other into a boat to sail upon it.

'You always stare into water,' said Rowan, calling to Whiteflow, who was facing away from her. The Naiad's face emerged on the back of her head, the marbles of her eyes fixed on Rowan, but she said nothing.

'First the rockpools and the ocean. Now streams,' Rowan persisted, determined to get to know her daughter.

'I am of the water,' said Whiteflow. 'I desire to be within. We both do.'

Rowan looked down at Seaborn. He looked up.

'But I want to be with you too,' he said, and Rowan heard the child's desire to please.

'What stops you?' asked Rowan, and Whiteflow walked to stand on the other side of the table from her.

The Naiad said nothing for a moment, tilting her head.

'Being one with the water makes you forget what was once important,' said Whiteflow. 'Father asked that we remain apart.'

Rowan nodded.

'What will happen to Father?' asked Seaborn, looking up at her.

'Yes,' said Whiteflow. Steam rose from her, and Rowan could have sworn the words hissed, 'What will become of Dark Oak?'

'I don't know,' she said, and she didn't. Nayr had told her so little. Perhaps when the First Council convened she would fully understand.

'If they kill him, he will become like us,' said Whiteflow. 'Naiads, maybe.

Nobody will be able to kill him then.'

Rowan said nothing.

'Perhaps I should drown his Mother Tree?' said Whiteflow. 'Protect him. We should protect our families, shouldn't we? Remain loyal?'

Rowan heard the edge to the words.

'I . . . ' she began. She had been unable to process having drowned Bracken; had blamed Morrick for the baby's death. But here was her baby, reincarnated, and Rowan could no longer lie to herself.

'Oh, don't worry,' said the Naiad. 'The others wouldn't let me.'

'Stop it,' said Seaborn, standing up. 'She has suffered enough.'

Whiteflow laughed.

'Everything that has happened. To me, to you, to Father and to the world. It all comes down to this woman,' said Whiteflow, spitting the words.

Seaborn stepped forward and, faster than Rowan could perceive it, he took an adult form.

She gasped, seeing him as he had once hoped he would become, a living water sculpture of a knight in plate armour.

Whiteflow grinned.

'Enough. Both of you,' said Rowan, standing. She rounded on Whiteflow.

'Do you think I wanted to be parted from my husband? I loved him dearly, but after all that had happened . . . ' she trailed off, but seeing Whiteflow smirking, she continued, shouting.

'You are angry with me! Jealous that I chose the boys over you, but I did what I had to do! The Devised were seconds behind us. Your cries would have brought them to us and then our whole family would have perished. I saved all I could!'

The smirk dropped from Whiteflow's face.

'I should kill you,' she steamed. 'You denied me life. Why should yours continue? You betrayed Father.'

Whiteflow raised both hands, her fingers all fanned out, and as she did so, a rushing tide flowed from them towards Rowan.

Seaborn stepped between them, raising his shield. He swept his water sword down in an arc, and it drew the tide within.

'Enough!' shouted Rowan.

'Is it?' said Whiteflow.

Seaborn raised his shield, and Rowan sensed he was about to attack his sister.

'Don't you dare,' she said in a voice he remembered well from his human life; the voice that all human children take as the word of a goddess - his mother's voice.

Both Naiads lowered their hands and looked at her.

'I killed you. It breaks my heart, but I did it because I had no other choice. I would do it again,' said Rowan, and tears began streaming down her face. 'Whether you can forgive me or not is a decision you must make, but we have an opportunity to know one another that was denied us.'

'That you denied us,' said Whiteflow.

'You are not an innocent, Whiteflow,' said Seaborn. 'You denied me life, and yet I accept it.'

'You were older than she,' said a deeper voice. A voice of the forest. 'She is less able to reason.'

Rowan turned to look at the speaker and clasped her mouth as Red Maple emerged from the dark between the trees.

'Callum?' she asked, immediately recognising his features, aged as they were and carved in wood.

He stepped towards her and opened his arms. Rowan edged around the table and embraced him, but she drew back quickly. There was no warmth to him, no give in his body. She could not pretend they were falling into one another as she could, in a strange way, with Seaborn.

'Mother,' he said. 'I am glad that you can be with us again.'

Rowan looked up at him, her body shaking, and she reached out to hold him by his shoulders. His flesh was polished wood to her fingertips. She shook her head and began sobbing.

Whiteflow laughed.

'She grieved hard for you,' said Red Maple to his sister. 'I remember it well. Do not be cruel, Whiteflow. I know you are loyal to Father, but he too will forget his hurts soon enough. They fade in me.'

Whiteflow said nothing as Rowan returned to her chair.

'We will have to get to know one another all over again,' she said, sniffing as her tears subsided. 'A human, a Dryad and two Naiads.' Rowan shook her head. disbelieving. Her family.

'Perhaps you could have twins with the sea captain then kill them too?' suggested Whiteflow. 'Maybe we could get a little Sylph and a baby Oread to complete the set?'

'Whiteflow,' scolded Red Maple, and Seaborn dived forward, disappearing within Whiteflow's body. There was a brief contest, and she spat him back out in a spray that pooled together once it hit the earth. The Naiad re-formed into his child avatar from the puddle.

'I am far, far stronger than you. Stronger than most Naiads,' said Whiteflow.

'No more fighting,' said Rowan. 'I have apologised, Whiteflow. Your death broke me, and I am only lately recovering now I know you all go on. Did I wrong your father?'

She looked at each of their faces.

'Yes,' she concluded, 'but I had been through more than I could bear. I apologise to you all.'

'All will be well in the end,' said Red Maple. 'We will set things right. And Nayr has tasked me with speaking to Father. We may bring him back to the forest in time. He may yet be saved.'

'No,' said Whiteflow. 'He would not want that.'

'He may not have a choice,' said Red Maple. 'Nayr has spoken with the First Council. They are sending Sylphs and Oreads into The Wastes to seek him out even now. I will go to him when they succeed. Accept it. His revolution is over. We all must fall in line.'

'No,' Whiteflow hissed, her body partly turning to steam.

Whiteflow stepped into the stream, intending to flow away a short distance, but as her body merged with the water, she gained all knowledge that every Naiad had brought to the world's waters since last she was home, when she had stepped down from the Dryadship upon arrival on the Old Continent. She knew all that the oceans knew.

And of all those who had recently been reborn to the ocean.

Those who had died, and been buried at sea.

Dun. The youngest Naiad.

Tolucan and Feran, the names came to her.

They meant to kill her father's Mother Tree. They knew its location.

It did not concern her so very much. Father might end up like her. But the Dryads would not allow it anyway. No matter. It only proved Father's theory. The queen had ordered his destruction while feigning compliance. The humans were not to be trusted.

And then another name appeared in her mind.

Captain Jacob Lynch.

He carried the knights to destroy her father. The very man who had cuckolded the woodcutter and who had led her mother astray.

She knew it all. And she knew where Dun had been made.

She would kill them all.

For Father.

As Whiteflow raced down the stream, on into a river and down to the sea, the Naiads of the world heard her. Dun heard her. Riark heard her.

Samura, Queen of the Naiads, heard one of her people contravening the will of the First Council. She issued the command.

No sooner had Whiteflow's body fallen into the stream, than another Naiad burst up in her place, a crown rippling around her brow.

Rowan jumped, but Red Maple and Seaborn bowed their heads.

'My queen,' said Seaborn, once more assuming his form as a water knight. 'This is my mother, who travels to join you on the council.'

Samura looked Rowan up and down and bowed her head in what appeared to be respectful acknowledgement.

'Rowan, Queen of theHumans,' she said. 'Dark Oak's Bane, I am honoured.'

'Queen?' Rowan laughed. 'I'm a Hinterland girl! No royal blood in me.'

'I have no blood at all,' said Samura. 'None of us do.'

The Queen of the Naiads turned her attention to Red Maple.

'I cannot linger,' she said. 'We have learnt that two humans have discovered the location of Dark Oak's Mother Tree and that they mean to destroy it. Whiteflow is on her way to attack the humans on Dark Oak's behalf. I am sending my people to stop her and will aid them myself. If the humans survive, it may be best if Nayr intercepts them and explains how all has changed.'

'I will tell Nayr at once,' said Red Maple.

'We should meet them at the Mother Tree,' said Rowan. 'They will want to see for themselves.'

'I must away. Dark Oak's daughter is close to the human vessel. I do not know how long I will be gone, for her will is strong,' said Samura, 'but I will see you, Queen Rowan, at council.'

The Naiad's body flowed away with the stream just as Whiteflow's had done.

'Look after Mother,' said Red Maple to Seaborn. 'I will return.'

He dived inside the trunk of an ash and was gone.

Despite it all, Rowan worried for her daughter.

Chapter Twenty-Eight

The Ocean North-West of Oystercatcher Bay

'Land ho!'

A frenetic energy ripped through the crew, and the decks came alive with sailors joshing one another and busying loudly about their work. The one island of calm stood at the bow, leaning against the heel of the bowsprit. Feran's long red hair was tied back into a single plait, bound with cord into intricate stages, each different from the last. It hung down beyond his waist. Tolucan saw him when he emerged from below decks and approached with caution. He held back at some distance, grasping the rail, and watched for a while.

He grew bored as the minutes passed and craned his neck over the side to see what the other man was looking at.

A school of Naiads swam ahead of the Magpie, leaping in dolphin form from the waves.

'I have an ill feeling,' said Feran, turning back to look at Tolucan, who, after a moment's pause, moved unsteadily towards the bow, eventually stopping beside his friend.

'An ill feeling?' Tolucan asked, staring down at the Naiads.

'I just . . . foreboding, I suppose,' Feran replied, but even as he finished, their world was thrown into disarray.

The dolphins had been leaping in a synchronised pattern, some in the air, while others dived under. Now those that dived did not return to the surface.

They disappeared from view.

'Look,' said Tolucan, but suddenly he was sliding backwards as the bow of the Magpie rose up as though it had sailed straight on to a sandbank, her timbers creaking and splitting. The knight grasped for Feran and between the two of them, reaching for rails and ropes, they secured themselves as the deck lurched to larboard, hurling the crew into the air before crashing down once more. Tolucan heard a yelp, but could not see Randolf.

'All hands on deck!' Lynch roared as he ran towards the bow.

The Magpie began to right herself and Wilson, the master, ordered the crew to shorten sail as men went below to check the hull for holes.

Tolucan found his feet and called over to Lynch, but the captain was standing, apparently dumbfounded, staring across the water. Tolucan frowned and turned to look for himself.

There, just fathoms away, the water stirred and thrashed. Tolucan's eyes widened as he saw the Naiad dolphins hurled from the foam skyward before breaking into a million droplets of water that rained down onto the waves.

Tolucan may have been speechless, but Feran found his voice.

'Make sail! Make sail, now!' he roared as he ran down the deck. Tolucan watched him go then set off after him.

'Disregard that,' shouted Wilson, but Feran grabbed him by the shoulders.

'That there, out there,' he pointed towards the thrashing waters in which various forms could be seen locked in combat, 'that there is the end times. We must get away now, or we will not leave at all!'

'He's right,' said Tolucan, then again to Lynch as he advanced on him. 'We must get away now. I must make it ashore. Give the order.'

Lynch, returning aft, hesitated for a second then nodded.

'Make sail!' he shouted, then whispered, 'What's happening?'

Tolucan made no reply, for he had no answer.

'Something is coming for us,' said Feran, his voice a low growl. 'Something we can not outrun with all the world's winds behind us.'

All three men were standing at the rail when Whiteflow finally broke free to attack. The Magpie was back under way and, for the moment, still whole, making good speed on a larboard tack towards the Old Continent, still distant and out of sight except for those atop the mast.

'Randolf!' Tolucan called. 'Randolf!'

'Here he is, sir,' said one of the crew, and the knight saw the big grey hound trotting across the deck towards him, limping ever so slightly. Tolucan crouched and fussed the dog, who allowed him to lift his leg. It seemed whole.

'You'll be alright,' said Tolucan.

'But will we?' asked Feran in all seriousness. 'Tolucan, fetch anything you need while you can.'

The waters grew still, and all became quiet save for the flapping of canvas and the Magpie's customary creaking.

'How long before we reach the coast?' asked Tolucan as the knights made their way across the deck, planning to go below.

'Too long,' said Feran before Lynch could reply.

'Will you keep quiet with your prophecies of ill omen?' Tolucan snapped. 'What do you suggest we do?'

Feran rubbed his eyes then the bridge of his nose between his thumb and forefinger as he replied.

'Ready the boats,' he said, 'and if you have a god, pray. Our quest may be at an end.' Tolucan opened his mouth to rebuke his companion, but stopped short as something caught his eye.

Four great, translucent tentacles burst from the sea on both sides of the Magpie, towering above even the crow's nest. Their probing ends met above the schooner, like fingers coming together in prayer. Tolucan shivered as salt water dropped from them and fell like a hard rain upon his face. He looked about him, desperate to act, but anything he could do would be futile.

The tentacles drew apart and then those on the starboard side began to close in so that they pushed against the hull, and the Magpie rolled to larboard. Lynch took the wheel and clung on while both Tolucan and Feran could find no purchase and slid down the steepening deck beneath their feet. Randolf slid with them, yelping and whining. The crew shouted and screamed, wood splintered and ropes snapped.

The tentacles on the larboard side drew back to a great height and then swung violently across the length of the deck in a sweeping motion, carrying away the rigging and smashing against the masts, showering the crew with seawater.

One of the tentacles drew back then plunged down towards the Magpie once more, pulling down the foresails as it wrapped around the bowsprit. The Magpie began to lift at the bow, and the knights staggered back, grabbing anything they could. The other tentacles curled around the masts. They convulsed and heaved. Tolucan heard the masts begin to crack.

Lynch threw the helm to larboard, but the tentacles held the Magpie in place, and once more Whiteflow attacked. She curled her water-tentacles around the masts even tighter and heaved until they snapped. For a moment, Tolucan thought she would cast them aside, but instead she wielded them as battering-rams and drove them against the hull, puncturing the Magpie beneath the water-line.

'We're done for,' said Feran as he struggled to his feet.

'Abandon ship!' shouted Lynch as he regained his voice. 'All hands, abandon ship!'

Lynch left the wheel to join Feran and the crew in running to ready the boats.

'Useless,' cried Wilson as he reached the first. A spar had punched a hole straight through its hull.

'This one's intact,' shouted Feran as he reached the longboat. Lynch stood off, looking at the boat, his skin pale, as the crew set about launching her as best they could, doing their best to ignore the steady beat of the masts upon the hull. Yet Whiteflow was not blind to their efforts.

She lashed out at them and with the first blow, she caught Wilson in the midriff, hurling him over the side. She struck out again and again as the men worked. Her tentacles curled around the cowering sailors, plucked them from the deck and tossed them far out into the sea. Tolucan, mindful of their importance, grabbed Feran and tried to pull him to cover, but his companion shrugged him off and helped Lynch to release the longboat from the debris that covered it. Tolucan wrapped an arm around Randolf and kept a watch on the tentacles. He would jump overboard if it came to it.

Tolucan retreated to the starboard side and looked east towards the shore. What were his chances in the water?

He spied a movement in the water farther off, way beyond the tentacles. A stirring as though a great creature was approaching at speed. As it drew closer, Tolucan saw a great dorsal fin form from the sea-foam.

He wanted to warn the others, but his voice failed him, and he could only watch as the creature swam straight at them.

And then it dived and the tentacles exploded into a fine mist that dropped all around them. The Magpie rolled back and all was silent for a moment. Tolucan could see no sign of the dorsal fin or the tentacles.

He was heartened for a moment, thinking now they had a chance to sail away, but the splintered stumps of the broken masts reminded him of the true situation. He ran to help them with the longboat, Randolf at his heels.

What remained of the crew managed to get the boat over the side and they began to clamber in.

Tolucan glanced at the men crowding into the boat and frowned at how little space was left.

'Come on, boy,' he said to Randolf, shoving a sailor aside, and jumped in. The dog followed.

Tolucan took up a seat at the stern, calling for Feran to join him. His sword, shield and mail remained below decks, but he wore a dirk on his belt. The other knight, helping the crew climb aboard, was similarly attired and not armed. Tolucan noticed that Lynch's face was ashen-grey while he stood surveying the slope of the deck. The Magpie was sinking.

'Look!' shouted one of the sailors as they continued to fill the boat.

The water thrashed before the Magpie's bow.

The gargantuan head, arms and torso of a giant woman with foaming white hair rose from the sea, fish and sand swirling beneath the surface of her form. Samura, Queen of the Naiads, appeared as the avatar of some forgotten sea goddess, holding Whiteflow's spirit below the water and, forming a great spear in her right hand, she drove it into Whiteflow's being. She pierced the Naiad with her will as it flowed through the weapon, striving to contain her.

Samura fell back as a huge watery forearm drove into the queen's throat. Whiteflow burst out of the water, a water giant, steaming and churning. She grabbed Samura's throat with both hands.

'What the . . . ' hissed Tolucan.

A third and fourth arm formed from Samura's torso, grappling Whiteflow, who was pulled in close so that the Naiad's bodies merged.

'It's helping us get away,' said Feran, climbing into the longboat, squeezing between the men. Tolucan felt his ribs protest as the men either side of him shifted backwards to accommodate yet another of the crew. Randolf growled, curled by Tolucan's leg, and he snapped his teeth at a sailor who had inadvertently crushed him.

The longboat jolted as Lynch helped to lower her, bracing himself with one foot and feeding the rope through his hands, aided by a sailor.

The longboat hit the water and the sailor jumped in, landing atop his crewmates. There was no seat for him, and the boat was perilously low in the water. Lynch looked over the side.

'Come on, man,' shouted Feran, but Tolucan realised why Lynch's expression had been so grave.

'Pull for shore,' shouted the captain.

'What are you doing?' called Feran.

'There's no room in the boat,' said Tolucan. Feran did not hear him and Tolucan roared again, 'Feran, there's no room in the boat!'

Feran turned towards him, clearly about to spit some rebuke, but as the crew jostled to follow the captain's order, he seemed to realise that it was true, that there were too many already and the boat rode very low in the water.

Feran looked at Randolf.

'Come back for me if you can,' called Lynch, 'but go. That's an order.'

By then the crew had pushed off and the longboat was drifting away from the Magpie, and Tolucan could see that the schooner was going down. Lynch stood alone at the larboard rail for a time, silently watching, seemingly oblivious to the great match between the Naiads behind him, Whiteflow growing with every second. Other Naiads, smaller, appeared and seized Dark Oak's thrashing daughter, like the unliving rising up from the river of the dead to pull her under.

Tolucan noticed one of the Naiads had a white beard and unkempt hair, his foaming body reminiscent of armour, and he held a watery sword in his right hand. It looked back towards the boat, nodded and then plunged its weapon into Whiteflow's side.

Surely it couldn't be, thought Tolucan as the old man Naiad disappeared into Whiteflow's body. Scores of Naiads were climbing up her from the ocean and gradually, they pulled Whiteflow slowly under, even as tentacles which had sprouted from her shoulders plucked away some of their number, hurling them into the air. Samura seized both of the tentacles with her fifth and sixth arms. The Naiads roared as they fought.

Tolucan watched as Lynch clung to the rail, shouting something inaudible to them before he clambered out of view.

The Magpie's bowsprit and bow were fully under, her stern out of the water now as she went down.

The crew hauled for shore.

The deck sloped at an unnatural angle while Lynch watched the men in the overcrowded longboat pull at their oars.

'Still too many,' he shouted over the din of the roaring Naiads. It was no good, he realised, they could not hear. He watched the boat pull away, the water nearly up to the gunwales.

Two wrecks in the last seven years, thought Lynch as he clambered away from the rail towards his cabin, now all alone aboard the Magpie. He could not bring himself to watch the Naiads, so great was the fear they roused in him, and as a man about to meet his fate, Lynch did not wish to dwell on such emotions. He managed to haul himself through a hatch near the stern before the angle of the deck became too severe. He clambered on all fours up the deck and into his cabin by lamplight. He could hear the water rising behind him.

Lynch took a moment to compose himself and right his tricorn upon his head, then searched among his possessions, fallen against the most forward bulkhead that was fast becoming horizontal. He found the small cask he was looking for, and, holding it, he peered down through his cabin doorway. He could see only dark water beneath him.

He knelt and pried open the lid of his cask.

Lynch could hear blood rushing in his ears as he cast the lid aside. He dipped his hand inside and withdrew a fistful of coffee beans. The captain dropped the cask through the doorway into the rising ocean.

'A final offering to the sea goddess,' he said and laughed aloud.

Lynch sat back against a bulkhead with his legs dangling through the doorway, his boots just above the rising water.

The sea captain held up his hand and unfurled his fingers then buried his nose in the coffee beans, closing his one good eye and savouring their scent.

Thinking of his cottage in the north, Captain Jacob Lynch felt cold water soak through his boots. Shoulder-first, he rolled through the doorway and into the water. He swam down and breathed deep, the ocean filling his lungs.

Still miles from shore, the Magpie slipped below the surface, and she, along with her captain, went down to the depths as the Naiads' battle raged on.

Tolucan watched the sun cross the sky and eventually dip into the western sea.

The daylight faded away, and the blackening sky was populated with ever more stars, save for a patch of looming cloud coming in with the wind. Tolucan felt his stomach lurch as the boat began to pitch and roll more and more as the waters grew choppy. There were so many men crowded into the boat that he couldn't even see that his feet were completely submerged in the water that continuously slopped over the side. Randolf whined. Tolucan could not see him properly, tucked between men's legs, but he feared the animal was soaked in the cold seawater, which kept sloshing over the side.

It did not take long for the issue to come to a head.

'We're carrying too many,' said one of the Magpies. 'We're not going to make it at this rate.'

'He's right,' said another.

'Wastelost,' said a third.

Tolucan caught Feran's eye and the two of them exchanged a moment of understanding as more of the men chimed in and the shouting began, an acceptance that a situation was about to develop.

'Look here,' said Green, the coxswain, who sat beside Tolucan. 'Facts are these. Boat's too small for those we have. Water's rising. Weather's worsening. Only gonna get worse, lads. That's what we know. This is what we got.'

'What do you propose?' asked Tolucan.

'Do I need to say it? Who doesn't know? Raise yer hand if ya don't,' said Green.

Nobody moved, save those pulling for shore.

'Now,' said Green, 'It comes down to who stays and who goes. By my reckoning, the hound and ten of you are going overboard. Only thing left is deciding who . . . '

To a man, the Magpies began shouting at one another, and the boat tipped as they jostled one another, allowing more water in as the debate became heated.

'Put the knights over!' said one man.

'Aye, they're no use at sea!' said another.

Tolucan knew his options. He could wait to see the Magpies' verdict, he could join in the debate, or he could take the situation in hand. Tolucan drew his dirk and held it low, out of sight. He waited until he was sure everyone around him was engaged in arguing and then he launched into a frenzied attack.

Tolucan plunged the dirk into Green's neck then punctured the eye of the man to his right. He swung his left forearm into the throat of a sailor who lunged at him over the dying coxswain, halting the man and giving himself time to stab him twice in the chest. Dead or dying, they slumped around him. Tolucan twisted, scanning the boat's occupants, and saw that most of the remaining Magpies were still frozen in shock and Feran was staring at him, wide-eyed. His companion clambered over a dead man to sit beside him in the stern sheets.

Randolf growled, snapping at legs so that the sailors cried out and moved forward.

'It seems I will not regain my honour today,' said Feran solemnly. He reached down and, with some manoeuvring, helped the hound up to lay across his lap.

'That's three,' said Tolucan, his eyes savage. 'You pick the rest. Feran and I will make sure things don't get uncivilised. We are on the queen's business and any man who attempts to waylay us is a traitor.'

'What about the dog?' asked one of the sailors.

'Try it,' Tolucan snarled. 'He's worth ten of you.'

'Tolucan . . . ' said Feran, but Tolucan shook his head and shot him such a fearsome look that he fell silent.

Tolucan watched as the sailors hauled their dead comrades overboard and then kept a wary watch upon one another. Would they decide on merit? Would those with greater seamanship or knowledge of the land win out? Would they choose the strong over the weak?

Somewhat inevitably, Tolucan felt, the injured were the next to go over the side. And they did not go quietly. They kicked and punched, wriggled and screamed, but to a man, the three Magpies injured during Whiteflow's attack were unceremoniously flung overboard then fended off as they tried to regain the relative safety of the boat.

Sailors manned the oars and pulled for shore. The rest drew away from Tolucan and the snarling dog, which gave the knight grim satisfaction.

Tolucan never once dropped his guard while they chose, arguing amongst themselves. Feran, Tolucan noted, stayed silent throughout the proceedings, wary and ready to pounce, judging by the look of his posture and the tension in the muscles of his neck, but silent.

A brief respite from the ritual sacrifice of the Magpie's crew came in the form of the suggestion that with six men over the side, they could complete the voyage with no further loss of life. Tolucan, hard-hearted, watched with almost amusement as the sailors engaged in a collective delusion until finally the quartermaster broke the silence by standing and diving overboard, unwilling to partake any longer.

Seven down, thought Tolucan, *three to go.*

It appeared that those who remained felt too strong a bond with one another to advance the issue any further, and more than once he caught Feran shooting him a significant look before nodding in the direction of men whispering amongst themselves.

This was dangerous, Tolucan knew, for they were still greatly outnumbered by the Magpies, and their continuing survival depended on fear alone. To that effect, he waited until there was a lull in conversation then lunged for the nearest man and sliced his throat.

To Tolucan's surprise, some of the remaining sailors not only cried out in protest, but they actually jumped up and tried to get to him, setting the boat rocking perilously. Tolucan crunched his fist into one man's face before finishing him off with his dirk, and he was pleasantly surprised to see Feran jump on another as Randolf pounced on a third. Catching his sailor off balance, Feran wrapped an arm around his throat and, spinning round, walked him straight over the side.

The man clawed at him as he dropped into the water, but Feran shoved down on his shoulders and hastened his departure, with a blank expression on his face. Tolucan's opponent clutched at his broken nose and throat, slumped over the side.

'Get him over,' said Tolucan and waited for the Magpies to comply while Randolf's victim screamed, protecting his genitals with now torn and bleeding hands.

'And him,' said Feran, quietly.

The Magpies complied.

'Any other volunteers?' asked Tolucan, flicking the blood from his blade into the sea.

'You're a monster,' hissed one of the Magpies, tears streaming down his face.

'Hush now,' said Tolucan. 'We're all in the same boat.'

The night passed and morning came, the Magpies occasionally trading places at the oars.

Tolucan settled back in his seat and watched over them, for the first time wondering what would happen when he slept.

As time passed, it became apparent that the boat could cope with those that were left, and so the survivors had but ten lives on their conscience as they drew close to the land, weary from hard effort and lack of sleep. None had dared to drift off with the eyes of their crewmates upon them.

By the evening, the boat had reached a beach on the tree-covered northern headland that extended south across the mouth of Oystercatcher Bay. Tolucan knew they were close to what had been the southern border of the Impassable Forest.

'Mount Greenwood is gone,' he whispered to Feran.

Feran spent a moment considering the distance and nodded to his companion.

Tolucan raised his dirk and pointed it at each of the sailors as he spoke.

'Well gentlemen, I thank you for your labour and your losses. It will offer you no comfort, I am sure, but in transporting us, you have offered great service to the Combined People and your queen. I wish you safe onward travel. But rest assured, if you come after us, I will gut each and every one of you. Go on your way, and may it take you far from mine.'

Both of the knights leapt into the surf. One of the sailors started towards Randolf, but the hound growled menacingly, so he thought better of whatever notion had taken him. When Tolucan called his name, Randolf leapt out of the boat.

Chapter Twenty-Nine

The Old Continent

Two bedraggled, sodden figures and a hound emerged from the ocean and collapsed on the beach in the late evening. Tolucan watched the longboat pulling away south, concerned the crew would come for retribution on land, where their numbers might even the score, but it disappeared from view.

'Come here, boy,' he said to Randolf. The hound shook the water from its fur, showering Tolucan in the process, then came to lie in the sand beside him.

Tolucan's attention was distracted by Feran first retching then vomiting a little way off, before his companion fell to sobbing. Tolucan clambered to his feet and went to his friend, pulling the other man's hair away from the mess on the ground then placing a comforting hand on his shoulder.

He wanted to offer words of solace, but could think of nothing, and so he waited for Feran to compose himself.

Perhaps he will talk, thought Tolucan, *perhaps he won't.*

Eventually Feran mustered and the two men sat shivering together on the beach, listening to the roar of the waves and the sound of seabirds as the day wore itself out, Tolucan taking up handfuls of sand and letting it slip between his fingers so that he could marvel at the many coloured particles of shell and grit of the sand.

'I have lost count,' said Feran, 'of the distasteful tasks I have performed in the name of duty.'

Tolucan made no reply.

'I donned the armour and picked up the sword believing I could do some good in this world, but that was all a fairytale. I've killed innocents, murdered good men, I've burned those who had surrendered, and I've fought, but for what?'

'I think,' Tolucan replied, 'you are forgetting the part where you helped overthrow the Dark Lord. Not to mention all the other good deeds you have performed. Not to mention keeping me on my feet. That was a hard thing in the boat, but what choice did we have?'

Feran looked at Tolucan and saw the smile on his lips.

'Still feel like a knight from the stories you heard at your father's knee?' asked Feran.

Tolucan, sitting shivering in boots, breeches, a shirt and cloak, armed with nothing but a dirk, snorted a grim, quiet laugh.

Feran stood and offered his friend a hand.

'Come, let's gather wood and get a fire going if we can before we all freeze to death.'

They sat by the fire in silence, both men staring into the flames, and Randolf lying across their feet.

'We're very near to the end now, brother,' said Feran, not taking his eyes from the sinking sun. 'Whatever that might be.'

'More days on the road and then the deed,' Tolucan replied.

'Or death in the attempt. Why did that Naiad attack us? And why did the others stop it?' asked Feran.

Tolucan shifted and looked down at a bird bone he had been turning over in his hands.

He considered telling Feran that he believed Dun had been among them.

'Perhaps it would be prudent,' said Feran. 'if we were to part ways now.'

'Part ways?' asked Tolucan, raising an eyebrow. Was his companion planning to abandon him? Anger rose, but reason kept it in check.

That, thought Tolucan, *is not the Feran I know.*

He saw Feran was smiling.

'Dun always maintained that I would need a squire again, that I would once more take up my sword, don the armour, bear the burden,' said Feran. 'I took him for a romantic fool, but he was right all along, even if I only managed to look the part for a few weeks.'

With a groan, he stood and offered his hand to Tolucan.

'Let's get this done,' he said and pulled Tolucan to his feet.

'I thought you wanted to part ways?' Tolucan asked, reaching down to tousle Randolf's furry head.

Feran nodded.

'We must, both for the quest and for my own sake. A hard decision you made in that boat, and I supported you, but I will not regain my honour in your company, I know that now. You are the man to bring our foe down, I am sure of it. You are determined, strong, but utterly ruthless. A fine soldier, it makes you, but not chivalrous. Your hands are stained with innocent blood now, brother, as mine already were. I mean to wash mine clean, but I am not so sure you will,' said Feran, 'or even that you wish to do so.'

Tolucan started to object, but the words hit him, and Feran held up his hand, shaking his head and smiling wistfully.

'You find shelter while I find food,' said Feran. 'Tomorrow morning, you continue your quest alone. I will set off on the long road south and go in search of the queen lest you fail.'

Tolucan thought they would perhaps lie talking by the campfire embers into the small hours, but both men fell asleep long before the flames died down.

They were ill-equipped to hunt and so made what breakfast they could of the crabs they could find in rock pools on the beach, drinking from a stream that ran down to the bay on the lee side of the headland.

They delayed parting as the morning advanced, but before long each man came to realise that it was time to say farewell.

'How far? For me, I mean,' asked Tolucan.

'I could not say,' said Feran. 'Back to the Impassable Forest you go for a time.'

'You have the longer road to The Folly,' said Tolucan, then, after a brief pause, 'are you sure you will not come with me?'

Feran came to stand before him and placed both hands on Tolucan's shoulders.

'Brother, with all my heart I wish we could do this together, but we are pragmatists, not romantics. This needs to happen, and this way. Our fates are sundered. Perhaps we will both fall on the road and fail in our duty, perhaps we will both survive and one will have journeyed in vain due to the success of the other, but we must not fall together, for no good can possibly come of it,' said Feran, smiling.

Tolucan said nothing, but sighed.

'Time then,' said Feran. 'Goodbye, Randolf. Look after this brute.'

He squatted and wrapped his arms around the dog's neck.

Feran stood and after an awkward second, their eyes brimming with tears, the two knights embraced there amongst the trees, offering silent concern and affection for one another.

Seconds passed, and they moved apart again. Feran bowed his head.

'Farewell,' he said. He turned east to seek and follow the coast around the bay.

Tolucan watched him go, holding back tears that would inevitably come. The cloaked figure with the long red hair soon disappeared amongst the trees.

Tolucan knelt down beside Randolf. They were alone.

Tolucan had intended to set off north through the trees immediately, but instead he returned to stand by the sea for nearly half an hour, thinking about his earlier life, and the now-distant memory of his late wife and sons. He sighed as a flock of oystercatchers flew by him and landed in the shallows, peeping, as they do.

Is my family still alive? Will I live to see them again?

He thought of his many battles, the loss of Cwenhild, his squire, and the weary time alone in the northern forest before he had met Feran by chance, back before he had carved his staff or tied pouches upon it. He thought of Feran and Dun bickering around so many campfires. Tolucan grieved for his past and then, unable to delay any longer, he turned north and began to walk, his hound by his side, leaving footprints behind them in the sand.

Days passed. Man and hound trudged onward, Tolucan sometimes talking incessantly to Randolf, but sometimes not uttering a word for hours at a time, his mind entirely occupied either with his memories or by the task ahead.

How would he know the Mother Tree when he saw it?

How would he destroy it before Dark Oak or his guard tore him into a thousand pieces? Not with a dirk, that was certain. He pondered how he might make a fire which burned swift enough for the task, lamenting the oil that no doubt lay with the Magpie on the ocean floor.

Before long, the woods of the headland gave way to the ancient Impassable Forest, which he entered without ceremony. Five years he had walked in this forest, away in the north, and this was nothing but a return home, if through an unused door to a neglected room.

The forest did not welcome him, but he met no immediate opposition. He walked warier than he had ever done before, knowing full well that the attack on the Magpie might signify that his quest was betrayed. He wondered what had become of the Naiads, locked in battle when he had last seen them. What had happened to Dun?

The trees swayed and creaked. Twigs snapped. Animals darted across his path. He tramped on, and Randolf ranged about him, playing, sniffing and occasionally pricking up his ears and staring intently through the dim light afforded by the luxuriant canopy.

He kept his reckoning in the direction of where Mount Greenwood had once emerged from the trees, once visible for miles all around.

Moss was his mattress when it came to sleep, and he would wrap his cloak about him, sleeping close with the hound so that both might benefit from the other's heat.

To begin with, the unseen eyes of the Dryads watched him with fleeting interest – wanderers and humans making subtle homes amongst the trees were not uncommon in these times, yet that interest heightened the closer he drew to Dark Oak's Mother Tree, and the more apparent his course became to them. Very soon the eyes watched him night and day.

Until eventually, one day, just after dusk, when he was considering stopping to sleep, Tolucan heard singing.

Tolucan stopped dead and listened. For a moment he thought he had finally gone mad, but Randolf too had frozen mid-stride, his ears pricked up.

It was a woman's voice, still some distance away, singing in the manner of the cattle-folk's kulning calls. Her voice rose and fell. A shiver ran down Tolucan's spine.

Tolucan walked onwards and realised as he did so that the woman singing was up ahead, in his path. Randolf stood still.

'Heel. Heel, boy,' Tolucan commanded, and the hound ran to his side. 'Easy now. Easy.'

Randolf whimpered in reply, but kept pace with his master.

The forest opened out into a moonlit glade with a single oak tree at its centre, but he paid it little heed, as at its foot lay a woman with hair so long that it lay all across her body like a cloak. And she sang.

Tolucan approached the towering oak tree and found himself reminded of boyhood autumn walks along the dirt path through the graveyard to his father's resting place. The air had that still, solemn quality.

As he drew close, he saw that the tree was grey and dead, with limbs fallen away as though sheared off by lightning. It had the look of black charcoal burned white. Fallen branches lay all about the glade, acorns and dead leaves scattered about them.

The woman turned to look at him, and he raised a hand in greeting, feeling awkward and exposed.

She peered out at him from under her hair, eyes reflecting the moonlight.

'He's here,' said Rowan.

'Is he a knight?' asked little Seaborn, stepping out from behind the tree, pale light refracting in his Naiad body, the mulch of leaves forming boots over his feet.

Tolucan gasped and drew his dirk.

The quest was betrayed, he realised. Randolf snarled, his hackles rising.

'Put it away,' said Nayr as she stepped out of an ash tree behind him. Tolucan spun round, surprised, and Randolf sprang forward, sinking his teeth into the Dryad's leg. Nayr looked down at the hound then back up at Tolucan.

'Such a loyal dog,' she creaked.

'He is,' Tolucan said, his throat suddenly dry.

'The hound too,' said Nayr, and she smiled.

Tolucan frowned, then took her meaning. His cheeks reddened at his slow wits, but he made no retort.

'Your quest is at an end,' said Nayr. 'This,' she motioned back at the oak tree, 'is Dark Oak's Mother Tree.'

Tolucan said nothing. He felt his body shaking as the adrenaline flowed. He felt an unaccountable need to weep, but set his jaw and fought the impulse.

'We were warned by the Naiads that you were coming, but I'm afraid you have journeyed in vain, silent knight,' said the Queen of the Dryads.

'I will fight you if I must,' Tolucan said, pointing his dirk at her.

Nayr smiled, but not unkindly.

'I am not here to stop you,' said Nayr. 'Dark Oak's Mother Tree is already dead.'

Tolucan stepped back and looked up at the gnarled, dead oak, finally registering what he had already seen.

Seaborn had sat beside Rowan, and she stroked the surface water at the nape of his neck, her voice now lowered to a lullaby.

Tolucan shivered again. He did not know what to do or say. How was he to know if the Dryad was telling the truth? What was he to do? He had no way to tell one tree from another. Tolucan began to despair.

'How can I know you speak the truth?' he asked Nayr. 'That you do not seek to deceive me before you kill me on his behalf? Perhaps Dark Oak will not face me? Perhaps he is a coward.'

'Of course he would. He'd obliterate you before you had a chance to think. No, I do not serve Dark Oak, I serve the forest. I am the forest.'

Tolucan said nothing, but his bewilderment was clear.

'Dark Oak is no longer King of the Dryads, and I wish you no harm, silent knight,' said Nayr.

'Perhaps if you stop talking in riddles, he will understand,' sighed Rowan, fiddling with her necklace. She stood and looked up at the tree.

Nayr took pity on him then and explained all that the forest knew, of Riark and of Dark Oak's awakening and his eventual exile and of how he had last been seen heading into The Wastes. She told him of how the Naiads claimed Dun as their own and that it was in that way that their quest was betrayed. He learnt of Whiteflow and her mission to waylay her father's enemies and to gain vengeance on Captain Lynch. Tolucan learnt of Anbidian and of the queen's death. His heart went out to Feran then, knowing that his friend journeyed to The Folly, which was now abandoned.

'And now it is feared,' she concluded, 'that the woodcutter seeks to take up Awgren's mantle as the Dark Lord of Halwende in order to retake the forest and move against humanity. Queen Cathryn suspected that as long as he lives, your kind is at risk of extinction. Were that to happen, silent knight, there would be no more new souls and no more vessels into which old souls can be reincarnated. There would be no more new Dryads and when the existing Dryads' Mother Trees die, my kind will be lost from the world. The Cycle would end. Spirits would forever walk the world unseen.'

'But Dark Oak's Mother Tree is dead already,' said Tolucan. 'Has my quest not been fulfilled by another? Is he not already thrown down?'

All those years. I abandoned my sons - my boys.

'Oh no,' said Rowan, walking barefoot from under the oak towards him.

343

'Dark Oak may have become what I wrongly accused Morrick of being; a collaborator of Awgren, the Dark Lord that ripped our family apart.'

'Forgive me, ma'am, but I do not know you,' said Tolucan, swallowing hard and fighting back tears, watching as the little Naiad boy splashed against her leg and reached up for her hand.

'I am Rowan, appointed to represent humanity on the First Council. I was Morrick's wife before he became Dark Oak,' she said.

'Queen of theHumans,' said Nayr.

Tolucan's mouth fell open, but he remembered his manners, knelt and bowed his head to her. He saw that his hands were shaking.

'I don't understand why you believe Dark Oak is still alive,' he confessed. 'His Mother Tree looks dead to me. Surely I have quested for nothing?'

'I do not understand myself,' said Nayr, 'but the forest sensed Dark Oak's soul departing his Mother Tree. He did not die. It was not the same. By some craft, Dark Oak has severed his connection with his Mother Tree. He is no longer vulnerable to the forest.'

Tolucan watched as Nayr thrust out her arm, and it morphed into a long root as it grew, curling around the trunk of the Dark Oak's Mother Tree. Her wooden flesh bound to it, and she closed her imitation eyes as she poured her spirit within.

Dark Oak's Mother Tree resonated for a brief second and then it burst apart, shards of wood and bark flying in all directions. The Mother Tree was gone.

'I do not know how he has done this,' Nayr concluded, 'but perhaps our scouts will tell us more when they return.'

'Nevertheless,' said Tolucan, deciding in that moment, 'I have not completed my quest, if Dark Oak still lives. If he dwells now in Halwende, then to Halwende I will go.'

Tolucan remained on his knees before Rowan.

'If Queen Cathryn is dead,' he said, 'then King Annan is the rightful ruler of the Combined People, but he is under the sway of those who mean to harm him and steal The Isles from his line. I cannot serve him. If you will take me into your service, Queen Rowan, I will pledge myself to you.'

Rowan laughed and Seaborn clapped, his hands splashing together.

Tolucan looked up, surprised at the reaction.

'I feel like a little girl playing make-believe,' Rowan told him.

'And I, a boy with a wooden sword, and a head filled with dragons, I suppose,' he admitted as he stood. 'In fact, at the moment, I would be grateful for even a wooden sword.'

'Perhaps we can see you appropriately dressed and armed,' said Nayr, and the Queen of the Dryads set off towards the trees. 'Now follow me, and I will lead you to your new queen's abode. There will be much you can tell her.'

Rowan and Seaborn urged Tolucan on, but before he had gone a few steps, the boy Naiad took his hand, and he remembered his duty.

'I have two favours to ask,' he blurted.

Tolucan clasped his hands behind his back and took a deep breath.

'Can you send word to my friend?' he asked as Nayr turned to look at him.

He looked the Queen of the Dryads in the eyes.

'And can you find my sons?'

Chapter Thirty

The Wastes

Akiel, Sylphwarden, rode the wind, formless. She gusted across The Wastes in search of Dark Oak, one of many the First Council had deployed. Beneath her, she saw the entrance to Halwende. And movement around the tunnel. She knew, and the skies knew across the world.

'Inform the Oreads.'

She heard Mayri's command and obeyed, whipping vapour around her and diving down in the shape of a cloudhawk so that she could be seen.

Rondren of the Oreads was the closest. He burst from the earth as a boulder without marring the surface, then fell back underground as though the ground did not exist at all, like a whale breaching the surface before submerging beneath the waves again. Akiel predicted where he would next emerge, and she fluttered around his boulder as it shot skyward.

Rondren formed into a featureless human-shaped rock and landed on his feet. The land shuddered. Akiel retained her bird form, and spoke.

'There is movement around Halwende. It appears our suspicions were correct. Dark Oak may already have reached the Dark Lord's stronghold,' said Akiel, whispers on the wind.

'We must confirm it,' said Rondren, his words a rockfall. He plunged an amorphous hand into the ground.

'I have informed Wern. I will go in,' he said.

'I will slip through the gate and meet you within,' said Akiel. She shed her form.

'My lord,' said Ovi the Weaver. Dark Oak looked up from the tome he had been reading within Awgren's chambers beneath the fossilised Mother Tree.

'An Oread has come up through the ground within the menagerie. A Sylph is with him. They say they have been sent by the First Council, lord.'

Dark Oak smiled.

'They have come sooner than I expected,' he said, getting to his feet. 'Tell them I will meet them directly.'

Dark Oak strode to meet the intruders. His face was grim, still sculpted in imitation of Morrick's features, even down to the scar emblazoned on his cheek. But Dark Oak was no longer simply a Dryad, his wooden body designed to imitate such affectations as clothing or armour. He stood some seven feet tall, and he wore a breastplate of black steel, etched with tracings of blood-red filigree, marking out ever more complex patterns. The oak-lined steel bonded with his body. The long black ivy of his hair flowed back over his shoulders and trailed along the floor as he strode forward, the white light in his eyes shining through the gloom as the mist that hung above the floor of Awgren's chambers moved aside for him.

He climbed the stairs to the Mother Tree's island, and he crossed the river of souls by the stone bridge, faces appearing beneath the surface as he did so, iridescent hands reaching out for him.

He saw the Oread and the Sylph standing between enclosures, surrounded by both Devised and a few humans, all armed. More and more were making their way to see the spectacle from all over the cavern.

Dark Oak's stride was long, and each time his right foot thundered into the ground, the spear he carried, wrought of iron and ritual-forged, smashed down as well.

'Welcome to Halwende,' said Dark Oak, and the lamp-lit cavern was filled with the sound of his creaking, echoing voice. The Creatures of the Devising howled in response.

The Oread and the Sylph were not fazed, but the Sylph shifted form, gathering the mist about her, as she became a bird.

Beautiful, thought Dark Oak.

The Oread stood immobile, barely humanoid, with no face or discernible features. He was not concerned or intimidated, Dark Oak realised.

'I come at the behest of the First Council,' said Rondren.

Akiel flitted around Dark Oak's head like a hummingbird.

'Your Mother Tree is dead,' she whispered.

'And yet I am alive,' said Dark Oak, proclaiming it for all to hear.

'This is an ill place, Dark Oak,' said Akiel. 'Come away with us.'

'I will not abandon my cause,' said Dark Oak.

'You are no longer of the forest,' said Rondren.

'No,' said Dark Oak, lamenting it. It had not been an easy choice to sever his connection, but he had done it; drawn his soul from his Mother Tree and trapped it within his current form.

He held up his left hand and his arm grew suddenly into a lashing root.

'But I am still *for* the forest,' said Dark Oak, white eyes twinkling. He coiled the root around the Oread like a boa constrictor crushing his prey.

The Oread did not move, unaffected, but the Sylph drew off, circling overhead.

'The First Council will aid the humans,' said Rondren, sounding almost bored.

'Perhaps not,' said Dark Oak, and he raised his spear, ready to throw.

The gathered Devised and humans raised their weapons.

Rondren suddenly expanded into a huge boulder, bursting Dark Oak's root. It became a flailing stump, and the Dryad drew it back towards him, then reformed his hand.

Rondren shrunk back down to human size once more, this time making the effort to more accurately resemble the last man the Oread had been. The living statue walked towards Dark Oak.

'This is futile,' rumbled Rondren.

Dark Oak smiled.

The Dryad drew back his arm and threw the spear.

Akiel, a circling cloudhawk, saw the tip of Dark Oak's spear strike Rondren in the chest. She had expected it to bounce aside, but it embedded itself in the rock. Rondren reacted as she had seen no Oread react. He doubled over suddenly, losing all concentration, his form rippling and losing shape.

Akiel dropped her visible form and dashed towards the Oread as he let out a scream in the last seconds of his mouth's existence before it absorbed back into his face. He threw out what was left of his arms, and Akiel appeared in human avatar beside him as the Oread crashed down on to his back. The Oread lurched, solidified into a slab of rock, then crumbled to dust.

Akiel sprang to her feet and turned to face Dark Oak as the Dryad spoke.

'Send my regards to the Council. Tell them I will accept their surrender,' he said, a grin splitting his face. 'Unless you want to stay and see what else we have prepared for you?'

Akiel became formless, her consciousness dashing across the cavern, up stairs and through tunnels until she emerged into the daylight and blew like a hurricane out of The Wastes, calling all with her as she did so.

Ovi the Weaver emerged through the Devised, who howled and bayed, screamed and called out for their lord.

'Are you able to seal Halwende? They will be coming,' said Dark Oak.

'We will begin the ritual,' said Ovi, bowing his head.

'Good,' said Dark Oak, 'but let's not wait to be besieged.'

Dark Oak raised his voice so that it echoed all around Halwende.

'Prepare the Horde!'

All around the menagerie and beyond, those with words took up the call. Clanking and rattling started as the keepers unlocked the enclosures, and the newly Devised great beasts found their chains released. The whole cavern shook as they stood, and when they flapped their enormous wings, dust filled the air.

Beneath the cavern, the doors down to the world's fire remained sealed.

Dark Oak strode back towards his chamber. There were more weapons to test, and this one to duplicate in greater numbers.

He paused on the stone bridge to the Mother Tree island and, caressing the brand on his cheek - the traitor's mark - with his fingertips, he looked down at the swirling souls below. They reached for him and called out, begging for release.

The Lord of Halwende paid them no heed.

I hope you enjoyed Age of the Dryad. If you did, please leave me a review because it will encourage other people to try out my books! Would you like a FREE ebook? If you sign up to the Jacob Sannox Readers' Club newsletter, you will receive a free copy of The Ravenmaster's Revenge, the first book of my Arthurian fantasy series, The Return of King Arthur; a semi-finalist in the 2019 SPFBO competition. I will also keep you updated about new releases, giveaways and discounts. It will not cost you anything, you won't receive any spam, and you can unsubscribe at any time.

www.jacobsannox.com/fhome.html

King Arthur is back, but can he stop the Ravenmaster?

It is the autumn of 2019. Merlin's wayward apprentice has escaped from the Tower of London with his raven familiars. Legend foretells that the White Tower, then England, will fall.

Can King Arthur, a weary veteran of the English Civil War, Waterloo and the Somme, prevent the Ravenmaster from exacting his revenge?

Printed in Great Britain
by Amazon